Praise for *THE*
by Davi

"Rip-snorting, realistic action-adventure from a man who has been there. David Meadows is the real thing."

—Stephen Coonts, *New York Times* bestselling author of *Flight of the Intruder*

"An absorbing, compelling look at America's future place in the world. It's visionary and scary. Great battle scenes, believable heroes, plus villains you'll love to hate."

—Joe Buff, author of *Deep Sound Channel, Thunder in the Deep,* and *Crushed Depth*

"If you enjoy a well-told tale of action and adventure, you will love David Meadows's series *The Sixth Fleet*. Not only does the author know his subject but [his] fiction could readily become fact. These books should be read by every senator and congressman in our government so that the scenarios therein do not become history."

—John Tegler, host of the syndicated television show *Capital Conversation*

"Easily on a par with Tom Clancy, *The Sixth Fleet* provides an awesomely prescient picture of the U.S. Navy at war with terrorism and those who support it. It has the unmistakable ring of truth and accuracy, which only an insider can provide. In the aftermath of September 11, this is not just a good read, but an essential one."

—Milos Stankovic, author of *Trusted Mole*

"Although the U.S. had not been attacked when Meadows wrote this series, he was apparently only too well aware that some of this country's enemies would not rest until American blood was shed. Such foresight, in the aftermath of September 11, gives the books even more impact."

—*The Newnan (GA) Times Herald*

Berkley titles by David E. Meadows

THE SIXTH FLEET
THE SIXTH FLEET: SEAWOLF
THE SIXTH FLEET: TOMCAT
THE SIXTH FLEET: COBRA

JOINT TASK FORCE: LIBERIA
JOINT TASK FORCE: AMERICA

JOINT TASK FORCE
AMERICA

DAVID E. MEADOWS

BERKLEY BOOKS, NEW YORK

JOINT TASK FORCE: AMERICA

A Berkley Book / published by arrangement with the author

PRINTING HISTORY
Berkley edition / January 2004

Cover design by Rich Hasselberger.
Illustrations by Studio Liddell.
Interior text design by Kristin del Rosario.

For information address: The Berkley Publishing Group,
a division of Penguin Group (USA) Inc.,
375 Hudson Street, New York, New York 10014.

ISBN: 0-425-19482-5

Berkley Books are published by The Berkley Publishing Group,
a division of Penguin Group (USA) Inc.,
375 Hudson Street, New York, New York 10014.
BERKLEY and the "B" design
are trademarks belonging to Penguin Group (USA) Inc.

PRINTED IN THE UNITED STATES OF AMERICA

10 9 8 7 6 5 4 3 2 1

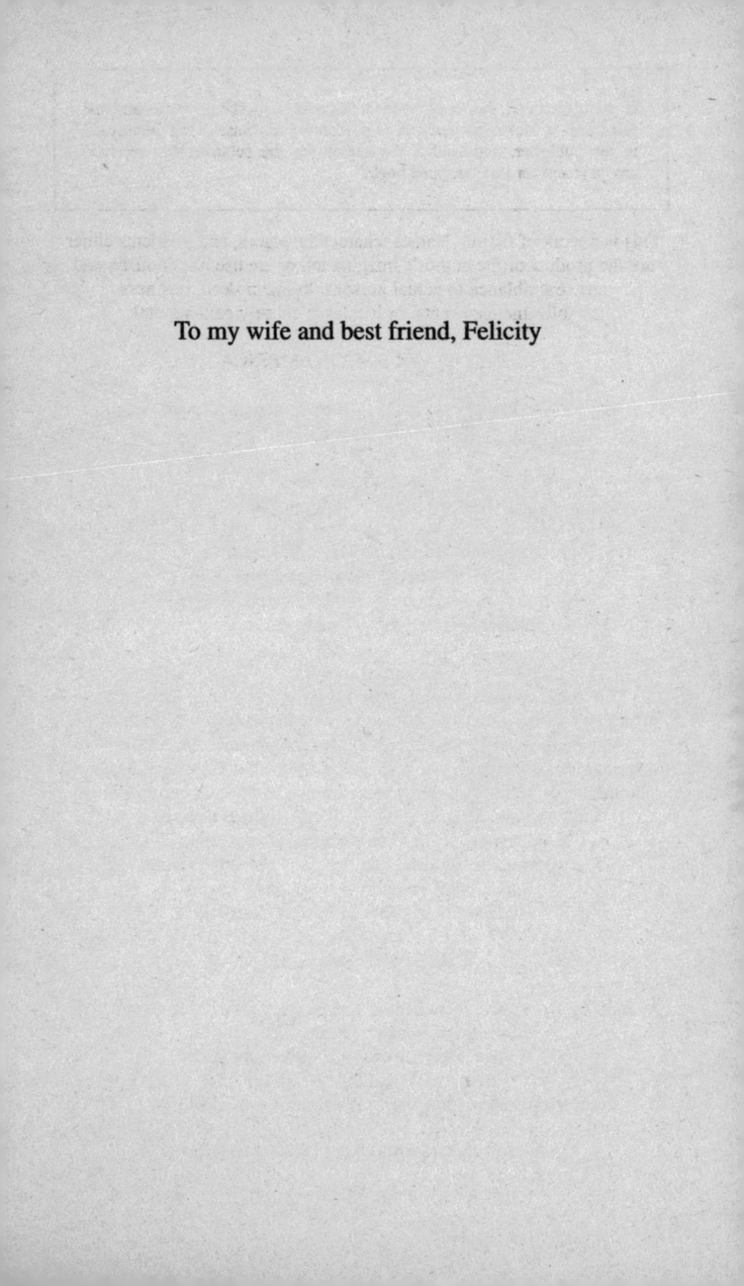

To my wife and best friend, Felicity

ACKNOWLEDGMENTS

It is impossible to thank everyone who provided technical advice and support for this and other novels. My thanks for those who visited www.sixthfleet.com and provided comments. I do read each e-mail personally, and my goal is to respond to each of them.

I have had so much encouragement that I know I'm going to miss some, so I both want to thank you and apologize up front if I inadvertently missed you. Many were kind enough to encourage, provide technical guidance, or many times just answer questions unique to their professional skills and qualifications: My mother, Wynella Meadows, Aunt Adele Burnham, Aunt Louise "Ease" Cole, Ms. Sharon Renike, Mr. Art Horn, LCOL David Nelson USMC, CDR Roger Herbert (who I served with in London), LCDR Nancy Mendonca, COL Bridgett Larew (Air Force nurse), CDR-ret Nancy Shank (a Navy nurse who insisted my book needed a Navy nurse in it), CDR Scott Fish (helicopter warrior), Mr. Ed Brumit, CPT Ray Zindell (HOOAH Armor), Douglas & Susan Rowe, Mike & Linda Boswell, Ms. Cheryl Sheppard, COL-ret Larry Huffman, Adam & Ann Marie Rowe, Ronnie & Charlene Hall, Tommy & Pat Ferrell, Mr. Bobby Burnham, Ms. Joan Cox, Ms. Helen Meadows, Ms. Shirley Borders, LTCOL Scott Herkert, Ms. Darlene Callahan, Ms. Betty Cort-Anderson, COL Marjorie Davis, Mr. Joe Rakosky, CAPT-ret Kathy DiMaggio, Rear Admiral Ken Deutsch, CAPT Todd Zecchin, the international member of the Combined Communications Electronics Board, my fellow J6'ers on the Joint Staff, and the great wealth of knowledge from members of the VQ alumni,

ICAF alumni, and the Naval Cryptologic Veterans Association. My thanks to all of you.

My thanks to Mr. Tom Colgan for his editorial support and to his able right-hand person, Ms. Samantha Mandor.

While I have named a few for their technical advice, rest assured that any and all technical errors or mistakes in this novel are strickly those of the author, who many times wander in his own world.

David E. Meadows

CHAPTER 1

MAY

TUCKER RALEIGH OPENED HIS EYES. HE NEVER SHOULD have jumped. A dry stick protruding from dank humus soil poked his cheek. Tucker rolled his head to the right, away from the stick, and waited several seconds for the daze to clear. On the other hand, maybe it was just the dark of night causing his vision to blur.

What was he doing amid the overgrown bushes and grasses? Above him, the edge of a balcony deflected light from inside the house, casting a shadow over where he lay. The wet spring smell of an afternoon shower rose from the moist ground. Wispy bits of fog created a six-inch-high quilt across the backyard.

"I'm telling ya I got him!" a voice shouted above him.

"He must have jumped."

"He didn't jump, Goddamn it! I shot him. He's in here somewhere."

The voices jumbled, but Tucker grabbed bits and pieces of the conversation. After about the third sentence he realized one of the accents wasn't American. The person was speaking English, but the accent wasn't British, Australian, or American. The sound of moving crates and boxes being shoved about obscured the voices for a moment. A long grinding scrape of a piece of furniture being dragged across the wood floor told him they were still searching inside the house.

Tucker moved his left hand cautiously to his head, feeling a wet stickiness—blood, seeping down from the top of his skull through his crew cut. He touched his cheek where the stick had been, but didn't feel any cut or blood there. His shoulder hurt. Must have been the jump. *It isn't the jump that kills you,* his jump instructor at Fort Benning had told him, *it's the sudden landing*. Tucker blinked his eyes several times, willing his way to full consciousness, past the pain and the spinning in his head. He wiped the blood away a couple of times when it threatened to cloud his vision.

This was his house—*his new house*. Well, nearly new.

Someone stuck his head over the balcony, scanning the darkness. The faint light from the living room cast the intruder's shadow across the overgrown backyard. But, why? It wasn't as if he knew anyone here. This was his first night in the house. Surely, they must have him confused with someone else. He shut his eyes for a moment, recalling the initial attempt to break in through the front door. The door had violently burst opened with the steel security chain abruptly stopping the door six inches later.

"I tell ya, he went over the balcony."

"Well, get down there and find him, lad. Don't let him get away. Son-of-a-bitch. . . . I've got to do everything, don't I?"

He detected venom in the voice. He had heard that accent before. Maybe Scottish?

"Keep ya voice down. Ya want the neighbors up and about?" the one with the accent asked, the r's rolling with a heavy brogue.

Tucker rolled onto his side. Never stay in one place long. Keep moving—*evade, make the enemy find you*—

keep them guessing. He had to shift his position—get away from here. Visions of the second Korean War flashed across his thoughts—*two weeks hiding in the hills, fighting his way back to his own lines.*

"Here, I found a flashlight, Sean." The voice was directly overhead on the balcony.

The balcony wouldn't hide him long, and if they came this far to kill him, they weren't going to let the job go undone just because he had disappeared. Eventually they would have to come down to search the yard. Dots of light flashed across his vision as Tucker stood up. Pain racked his left shoulder. Blood clouded his left eye. He reached up and wiped it away with the back of his right hand, leaving soil and dead bits of vegetation sticking to the side of his face. *Damn, at least the right half seems okay,* he thought. Tucker fell back against one of the four stanchions reinforcing the balcony and shut his eyes briefly, taking deep, quiet breaths. He definitely had that number-six Excedrin headache.

A beam of light shot out from above, sweeping the ground. It weaved outward from the balcony, back and forth across the overgrown backyard, toward the edge of a wood that separated the house from the Monocacy River. Urbana, Maryland, was supposed to be a quiet rural area. If this was how Frederick County welcomed its newcomers, he hated to think what his welcome party would have been like in Baltimore or Washington.

"We're going down there and find him."

"Not me. That's bullshit! We promised to bring you here and help you. But, by God, he's trained for this night shit. We ain't no more than hunters, and if you weren't . . ."

"Em," the one called Sean interrupted. "Casey, me lad, you're going to get your arse down there. We all are. If he gets away, the bloody raghead ain't going to be too happy is he? And, you won't be getting your money."

Were they talking about him? And who in the hell is the raghead? *Raghead—a derogatory term for Arabs.* It wasn't a term he used. He had been in combat against the

Jihadists, and regardless of how demonized they were, they were still motivated fighters. Even if he had had a desire to use the term, the U.S. military forbade it. The few times when he had heard a member of his team use any such derogatory terms such as this, Tucker had straightened the user out immediately.

"Yeah, so you say, Sean. But, money ain't gonna be much good if we ain't alive to spend it."

But they were right about one thing. This was his world. His head turned, taking in the playing field in front of him. He was trained for this—*what was the word? Yeah—night shit.* He had escaped and evaded hostile forces before—Afghanistan, Indonesia, Yemen. He'd just never expected to have to do it in the United States. Why should this be any different? *Why? Real simple. Because conducting an attack-and-evade mission needed a mind-set—you needed preparation.* He had never done a mission that hadn't been planned days in advance. *But you can't have it easy all the time, Tucker,* he told himself. He braced his right hand against the wall of the house and pushed himself upright. If he remained undetected until he reached the woods at the back, the pendulum would swing even more in his direction. The white T-shirt tugged his shoulder where blood matted it to the cement wall. A sharp pain whipped through him, sending a cascade of new stars racing around his night vision. He bit his lip and pulled away, simultaneously reaching up and touching his left shoulder. *Damn, he had taken a bullet!* He touched his head lightly, then looked at his hand. No wonder he had that headache. The grazing wound on his head was caused by either a bullet or when he'd fallen—*jumped*—over the banister. This made three times he'd been shot during his Navy career. He twisted and bit his lip, and a couple of contortions later managed to pull the shirt up and over his head. White showed too easily in the dark. The dark tan earned in Indonesia made it easier to blend with the shadows of the moonless night. With his right hand, he pressed the shirt against his stomach, holding it there as he wadded it up. Then he tossed the shirt behind a nearby bush.

Tucker opened and closed his left hand, making a tight fist each time. When he rotated his shoulder, the pain nearly caused him to pass out. Something was scraping against his shoulder blade. That something, he knew, was the bullet. He tried one more rotation, taking it slower this time, and felt it grate against the bone. The idea flicked through his thoughts that he would need a statement to get past metal detectors. Blood was thick on his hand, and he was still bleeding. How much blood does a person have in him? Tucker purposely slowed his breathing, his eyelids dropping until nearly closed. SEAL training taught more than killing. It taught how to grab pain, shove it into a closet within the mind, and lock the door. Ride over it. Survive—that was the key to winning. Once you've gone through Hell Week in Coronado, most combat looks amateurish. He locked the pain away, knowing even as he did it that the son-of-a-bitch would keep fighting to escape. The throbbing pounded, reminding him it was still there.

He shut his eyes briefly, as his memory of events before regaining consciousness under the balcony returned. He had been inside the house. When the door had crashed in, he had just set a fresh beer on the mantle above the fireplace. *He needed to have someone come in and clean the chimney.* Like most career military officers, the routine for the evening had already been mapped. He had unpacked the television, had promised himself he was going to soak a few suds—maybe even the whole six-pack—then lay on the couch with his leg over the back of it and watch a late movie before calling it a night. *Someone said they had soft porn on the cable channels after midnight. There's nothing like watching naked women and drinking beer to give a warrior a good night's sleep.*

He had turned as the door flew inward, mesmerized for a fraction of a second as the security chain stopped it from opening fully. The half face of a man had glared through the partially open door at him. He remembered thick red hair. The head disappeared and a hand holding a gun appeared, firing immediately. Tucker didn't recall being shot. The gun had jerked with small puffs of smoke coming from the barrel. No sound—*silencer.* What happened next was a vague memory. He recalled bouncing off the bricks of the fireplace before scrambling through the French windows and over the balcony. A civilian with no training would have taken refuge behind the furniture. A good fight needed space. The sound of wood splintering reached him as he disappeared over the railing. Then darkness had descended.

Okay, preliminary data review over. Tucker glanced up at the base of the balcony. Three sets of footsteps moved cautiously toward the stairs leading down and into the backyard. To his left, a string of scraggy bushes, planted by some long-ago occupant, gave him cover as he eased from the temporary shelter beneath the balcony. Almost squatting, Tucker inched along the bushes, gaining distance foot by foot from the balcony.

Light filtered from the opened glass doors on the balcony. He could barely make out silhouettes of the attackers. They were arguing, the heavy accent garbling any comprehension. The longer they argued and debated, the more space he put between them. He glanced in the direction of the Monocacy River. If he reached the thin line of trees and woods hiding the view of the river from the house, then the night would truly be his. He was good. And he knew it. You didn't go on the number of missions he had been on without one or two things happening; either you became better at your profession or they brought you home in a body bag. Tucker picked up the pace, using the moment to his advantage, his eyes adjusting to the moonless night. Light wisps of fog whirled around his ankles. Afternoon rain had soaked the sun-dried vegetation beneath his sneakers, softening the noise as he increased the distance from the house.

He had been lucky the security chain stopped them for a few seconds. Otherwise, he never would have made it onto and off the balcony. The mess of moving into his new home provided some distraction to the attackers. Stacks of moving boxes had, unknowingly, hidden his jump, causing the gunmen to search cautiously through the sparsely lit room, afraid he was hiding among the clutter. He must have been unconscious only a few seconds.

A low murmur reached his ears. He eased up between the bushes, between two branches, blending with the hedgerow. He didn't see them, but he heard the sound of shoes hurrying down the steps as the men left the house and entered the backyard. This Sean character must have won the argument. Tucker was glad he had put off cutting the grass and successfully fought the military urge to tidy up the unkempt condition of the yard. It was hard. The yard cried for his sense of order to do something with it. He hated disorder, but most in his line of work did. He slowly dropped lower, behind the bush, and crept left. Several steps later, Tucker stopped, crouching behind a rosebush. Thick thorns weaved in an undisciplined spread through the hedge growing alongside it.

His eyes narrowed. His peripheral vision was improving, giving him better acuity in the shadowy world of the night. The throbbing of the pain echoed in the background. He quickly drew away from it, knowing that if he allowed, the pain would sweep over him.

Initial fear gave way to professional training. His muscles tensed, contracting. Fear had also given way to anger. *Who in the hell were they to burst into his house?* He bit his lower lip. They have no idea who in the hell they're messing with. The mental image of a full auditorium cheering him on passed quickly through his thoughts. Tucker studied the terrain, searching for a better tactical position.

Movement caught his attention. The silhouettes of the attackers passed across the faint light spilling over the balcony, highlighting their line-abreast movement toward the tree line in back. When he'd first seen the house two months before, he had found pleasure in the haphazard way the dispossessed owners had planted various scrubs, flowers, and bushes. It offered him a chance to arrange the garden the way he wanted. Vacant for over a year, it had been repossessed by the VA four months ago. He'd purchased the house, knowing there would be work not normally associated with buying a new one. He'd just never assumed it would include getting shot.

The closest assailant was about forty feet away and slowly drawing nearer. The way the man's head kept going quickly back and forth gave Tucker the impression that this one was a little nervous—a little scared—and soon he would be a little dead. It was time to turn the tables.

"I tink you need to be careful," the man farther away said, the heavy brogue riding softly on the warm night air.

Irish. That was an Irish accent. What in the hell was an Irishman doing in the middle of agricultural Maryland at two in the morning? Shooting him. That's what in the hell he was doing. What a stupid question!

The assailant nearest Tucker turned his head and waved in acknowledgment, revealing a pistol in his hand. Tucker also saw in the faint light the fat outline of an extension on the barrel of the gun. Silencer. These were no "Bubba and Earl" small-time crooks. If they had been, they would have just rushed in, held him at gunpoint, and robbed him. For some unexplained reason, this bunch wanted him dead. Why? He had no idea. Maybe some irate husband, but he had always made it a point never to mess with married women—at least to the best of his knowledge. The military had tight *sex rules,* as he called them: never mess with married women; never mess with those you work with; and never mess with enlisted ones. Other than that, the rest were fair game as long as you were single and of legal age.

He would figure out later why they wished him dead—if any survived. The metamorphosis from being hunted to being the hunter took less than five minutes from the time Tucker regained consciousness. He had done the transformation before in a lot less time, but that had been in situations where he was expecting to roll with the blows of combat. Crouching, he sidestepped quickly, paralleling the row, narrowing the distance between him and the closest assailant, careful to make as little noise as possible. The pain slammed against the locked door in his brain, reminding him it was still there. Tucker took in the man's profile. Tall—only a little shorter than him. A paunch hung over the belt line. Probably not a professional, Tucker decided. Maybe this Sean was the only professional and the other two were locals recruited for the night. They wouldn't be expecting him—unarmed—to turn the tables. His eyes never left the silhouettes of the men, even as he focused on the one approaching his lair.

The pain in his shoulder rose briefly, fighting to escape its confinement. He pushed it down, but the brief interlude was excruciating. Prior wounds had taught him that he needed to stop the bleeding soon. All the mental commands in the world would not help if you bled to death. He could do little about it now. All he could do was hope that it stopped on its own, or that he finished them before the loss of blood finished him. The woods would give him a couple hundred feet of wild in which to maneuver, hide, or attack. Watching how the three operated, he realized two were little match for him outside the house. He gritted his teeth, his eyes narrowed, and he took brief pleasure in the feeling of vengeance that surfaced. Confidence was something he never lacked, and vengeance was something that had to be taken.

He wished he had a weapon. Damn, even a knife would be nice. His mouth tightened. His eyes alternated between trying to see where he was stepping through the thin blanket of fog and keeping track of his pursuers. Any weapon and he would make short work of these intruders. They were overconfident, making too much noise. He glanced over the heads of the three men, toward the next house. He was amazed the nearby neighbors' houses were still dark. They were less than a hundred yards from his. Neighbors he had never met. *After tonight,* he thought, *they may never want to meet me.*

The last bush in the row ended with about twenty feet of open space to the edge of the pine forest. He stumbled, twisting his ankle and falling to one knee, landing on the sharp edge of a rock, causing a grunt to escape. *Dumb!* He rolled away, unintentionally onto the wounded shoulder, drawing a short whimper before he clinched his mouth shut.

"Over here!" the man nearest him shouted.

"Shut up, ya fool. You want to have the coppers here?"

The sound of crashing feet accompanied the nearest assailant as the man ran toward him. Instead of jumping up and running toward the tree line, Tucker scrambled on all fours backward, putting distance from where he'd fallen. Across the yard, the other two approached more cautiously. He heard one of those two trying to catch the one hurrying toward Tucker. Who attacked him—the Three Stooges? Of course, what was he? One of the Marx brothers? *Stupid, stupid, stupid,* he thought. If this had been an exercise, the referee would have ruled him dead.

"Be careful, Ian," the one farther away warned.

The man's left foot stepped within a few inches of Tucker's right hand. Without thinking, he grabbed the ankle and jerked backward. The clumsy assailant cried out once as he fell. The two following stopped instead of hurrying forward. It both surprised and elated Tucker. It also confirmed that they were amateurs at this game.

"Ian?" the middle one called softly.

Navy SEALs were more than trained killers. They were also trained to conduct quick "look-and-see" reconnaissance missions, penetrating the enemy territory, identifying the targets, and returning without being seen. Covert operations was a Navy SEAL's forte. Most were capable of associating voices to individuals. This allowed them to map their targets in the day and recognize them in the night. Tucker had Ian, and that would be Casey calling. Which meant the remaining attacker, the one farthest from him, was the leader, Sean. *The Irishman!*

All of this flicked through his thoughts in the second it took for Tucker to let go of the man's ankle and leap forward onto the assailant's back. A deep whimper escaped the body beneath him. Tucker wrapped his right arm around the neck, blocking the air passage with the crook of his elbow, shutting off the man's attempt to shout, and to breathe. The man kicked out with his left leg, trying to dislodge Tucker. Tucker felt the sinewy muscles beneath the shirt. Whatever this man did in "real life" it involved labor.

On the other side of the bushes, the other two called to Ian again.

"Ian, you got him?" That was Casey.

Oh, yes! Ian's got me alright. Tucker tightened his hold, pulling the neck back.

"They're fighting, Casey. Go help him."

Fifty to sixty feet away. They weren't hurrying, which suited Tucker fine.

"Do I look like a fucking idiot? You go help him."

Even as he tightened the choke hold on the thrashing man beneath him, he knew he had to hurry before they worked up the courage to approach. He still had no weapon but his hands, unless he could find Ian's. This must be the first time these guys had worked together. From his experience, teams were like professional sports. You knew the capabilities and skills of your teammates—little verbal communication was necessary. He shoved the struggling man's head down, then quickly jerked it to the side. A small voice within his thoughts sarcastically asked, *Well, they shot you, didn't they?* He was rewarded with the sharp crack of the vertebrae that a moment before had joined the neck to the spinal cord. The pain from his shoulder erupted. It was out of the closet and running. The man went rigid for a second, and then his entire body trembled for several more before relaxing suddenly onto the ground. "Say, goodbye, Ian," Tucker whispered through the pain into the dead man's ear.

He rolled off. Taking deep breaths, Tucker brought the pain back under control, slamming the door shut again. Then he leaned forward and ran his right hand along the arms of the dead man, to the hands, searching for the pistol. Nothing. It must have fallen. The sound of running feet reached him. He pushed himself up, his left hand dragging across the pistol. *Thank God for small things.* He reached over and gripped the weapon in his right hand. Then, at a crouch, Tucker raced toward the tree line. *Once in there, they were his. One down, two to go. If they're having a potato famine in Ireland, there are going to be three less mouths to feed shortly.* All he needed was the right position.

He ran at a half-crouch, a "stop and go" pace to avoid drawing attention. Rapid movement attracted attention. Even knowing that, it took all his willpower and training to wait in the shadows and watch the silhouettes of the two searchers for the right moment to move. The two men had stopped near the edge of the hedgerow. They were facing away from him. He used the moment to close the tree line.

Nearly a minute after he had killed the first of the assailants, he melded into the pine trees. He glanced behind him. The silhouettes of the two remaining searchers showed them bent over, combing the area in front of them, looking for him or their friend or both. The outline of two pistols with the familiar fat-barrel of the silencer screwed onto the end could be easily discerned.

"Let's get out of here," said the one called Casey, turning back toward the house.

That was an American accent, Tucker realized. The words came in a quick, chopped accent, but it was American.

"No," the leader, Sean, answered, reaching out and jerking the man back by the arm. "We finish tis. Our lives don't mean anything . . ."

"An hour ago I would have agreed with you," the man replied, jerking his arm free. "You go do it. You're not married—Ian and I are."

He watched the argument, half hoping they wouldn't leave. He waited, squatting on his haunches behind a tree a few feet into the woods. The watery smell of the nearby river and fresh wet soil aroma rising from the pine-strewn forest floor filled the faint breeze. The buzz of mosquitoes circled his head.

His sense of the game had changed in the past few minutes. He wanted to take out the remaining two. He had been in Frederick County for five days—four of them at the Holiday Inn near the Francis Scott Key Mall. His one visit to the American Legion had resulted in two beers, one cigar, no conversation, and the discovery that food service closed early. The only people he had talked to who could say they may remember him were the ones at the reception desk at the Holiday Inn. Maybe a five-dollar tip to the young lady behind the bar at the Legion might cause her to recall who he was.

He sensed someone behind him. He turned slowly, reducing movement as he searched the surrounding shadows. His eyes swept the terrain for that telltale bit of gray or black out of context with the natural landscape—anything that didn't quite fit. This was his forte, and he knew he did it well. His head swiveled slowly, his eyes doing the moving, using his peripheral vision, the key for seeing in the night. All he needed was a small movement, a sound, and if another one were out here, he would have him located and assessed. But nothing moved.

He suspected it was Sean shoving the other man toward the forest. The two men inched closer. A small flashlight—one he had purchased earlier in the day from a locally owned hardware store in Frederick—swept the ground in front. It had been just outside the gate at Fort Detrick. The presence of the U.S. Army's biological complex at what had once been a World War I air base had played a large role in his decision to buy a house in the small suburb of Urbana. It gave him weekend access to the exchange, where he could cash a check, and the commissary, where he could buy groceries. Moreover, his one major vice was playing the horses, and Urbana had a nearby offtrack betting place that had a bar and a restaurant. What more could a man ask for?

He rose slightly off his haunches and shifted quietly to the right. His head buzzed and he felt faint. Tucker had to end this soon. He carefully took several steps to the left, away from where the men were about to enter the woods. He wanted a clear line of fire. Tucker lifted the pistol. Glancing down at the weapon, he hefted it a couple of times. It was a small pistol, probably a .38 caliber. Nothing fancy, but it would kill you. He leaned forward, bringing his head around the tree. The light from the balcony caught his attention, and he eased himself back behind the tree, letting the shadow of the pine hide him. He would have to be careful of the light. By now, their night vision was functioning at the same level as his. The other side of the coin of fighting in the night was knowing how to use that vision. Tucker was confident he could use the trees and slight undergrowth to mask his presence. If he was right and they were a bunch of first-time assassins—funny word to think of—then they were in for the shock of their lives. Whether they lived to tell was an unanswered question.

Ten yards farther, he stepped into a saucer-like depression hidden by loose pine needles. It nearly caused him to fall. He used his right hand to ease himself into the depression. In the dark, he completely disappeared from sight. He brought the pistol up in his right hand. He forced his left arm up, using the palm of the left hand to cup the right. Here he watched the two men enter the woods without them ever realizing they were walking into an ambush. That one must be Casey, Tucker figured, watching the man in the shadows whose head was twisting back and forth rapidly and whose gun was swinging from side to side.

The two men slowly opened the distance from each other. He knew the spread was unintentional. Little things continued to highlight their amateurism. Sure, they may have hunted their entire lives, but unlike him, their prey had probably been deer, wild boar, or turkey. His had been the two-legged kind. He was damn good at it, and he was no fucking turkey.

The soft sound of the sluggish Monocacy River intruded as the two men neared its bank.

"Quit that before you shoot me," the one named Sean said.

". . . got to be here someplace, or maybe he's gone back into the house while we've been here?" the nervous one complained softly.

"Oh, shut up. Don't be a coward. I told you I shot him. He's out here and he's wounded. He can't be far."

Behind the two, undiscovered, lay the body of Ian. They seemed less interested in what had happened to Ian, than they were in finding Tucker. Why was he so important that three men, at least one of them Irish, would try to kill him? *Robbery?* If he was going to rob someone and that someone escaped, he would be hightailing it for the nearest county line rather than trying to track him down on unfamiliar territory. Maybe they expected him to run or be so scared that he curled up in a fetal position, shut his eyes tight, and waited for them to find him. They were stupid. Of course, they had two weapons to his one, but it doesn't take a genius to pull a trigger. Plus, they couldn't know he was armed now. Then he recalled the comment the scared one said about him knowing how to operate in the night. No, they knew who he was, but why were they after him?

He took several deep breaths. Reaching around his waist, he ran his hand down the edge of his back. Around the waistline of his jeans, blood had soaked through to the point where the wetness slurped against his skin. He needed to wrap this up soon. Otherwise, he was going to lose consciousness because he was losing too much blood.

Tucker licked his lips. His head swam. He blinked several times to clear his vision, which seemed to swim in and out of focus. He shut his left eye and aimed over the top of the short barrel at the one called Sean. Sean led the two by a couple of steps. Tucker squeezed his finger slowly on the trigger, shifting the barrel slightly so it aligned itself with the front of the man. He pulled the trigger. The first shot hit the one called Sean in the stomach, causing him to arch forward. The second caught him in the chest. Tucker shifted the pistol to the second man. The one called Casey began firing wildly in the direction from where the two shots had come. Tucker fired. The first bullet missed the man, but the second caught him in the chest just as he turned to run, causing the man to collapse in mid step. The pistol fell from the man's hand, landing silently on the pine-carpeted forest floor. Tucker fired again. The third bullet caught the man in the head, causing it to jerk backward as he fell. The body hit the ground.

Tucker waited. The danger was past. The two were dead. If not, they would be soon. He looked toward the house. The balcony light shined outward, faintly outlining a peaceful backyard for anyone looking this way. He shut his eyes. He'd rest for a few moments and then force his way to the house and call for help. His breath came in rapid, short gasps. He'd be alright. He just needed a short breather to catch his breath and recapture enough strength to make it to the house and the telephone. Tucker faded into unconsciousness. He heard a slight moan from one of the two men he had shot, and then, as his consciousness evaporated, the sound of running footsteps approaching reached his ears. For a fraction of a second, a surge of panic nearly fought through the swirling fall into the darkness, but the loss of blood and the strength used to fight the killers were too much. Tucker passed out just as hands turned him over.

CHAPTER 2

AUGUST

THE GRINDING GEARS OF THE HEAVY TRUCK FORCED THE dockhands to shout instructions and questions. As it inched closer to where the tramp freighter was tied up to the cement pier, the Africans sidestepped gingerly out of its way, shielding their night vision from the glare of the yellow headlights. Several times, the brakes squealed—metal on metal—as the driver stopped. He would then tap on his horn a couple of times, whereupon Jihadist supervisors would shove Africans toward the truck, shouting at them to shift or move waiting boxes and loose gear out of its path. Then, with a smile, the thin reed of a driver would rev the straining engine up again, the gears grinding more metal from the thin teeth, and the truck would inch forward again.

Mixing with the smell of the unburned oil spewing dark thick exhaust from the truck was the fetid odor of human waste floating in the waters of this hidden African inlet. The pipe leading from the Ivory Coast port city of Abidjan worked its way through the jungle and rain forest of this West African country to pump unprocessed waste into the waters south of it. Tide and current carried most of the waste out to sea, but spin-off currents and high tide kept a large portion of the waste trapped inside this inlet of deep water. Floating on top of the languid water, the waste baked in the sun, soaked in salt water, and eventually drifted down to join the decades-old waste blanketing the inlet bottom. No fish lived in the inlet. They had either died or escaped years before.

The noise of the pier bothered Abu Alhaul. It bothered his bodyguards also. Standing in the shadows of the dilapidated warehouse, he watched the dockhands load the old freighter, occasionally glancing toward the truck working its way closer to the ship. Silently he wondered what they would do if the truck broke down before it reached the freighter. He reached up and stroked his dark beard, the thin white streak running along the right side hidden in the shadows of the darkness.

"I think we should return to the house," Abdo said, briefly touching Abu Alhaul on the arm. "You must eat something, my brother. You haven't eaten all day, and it isn't as if you have the weight I do to compensate." Abdo patted his huge stomach and chuckled softly. He licked his lips, his eyes darting to the dark African jungle that reached the edges of the inlet. "It isn't safe here."

"If it isn't safe here, Abdo, then it isn't safe at that hovel you call a house. It's night. The Ivorians will be sleeping off their drunkenness, and the French will be staggering from bar to bar. The earliest anyone would come to investigate the noise will be morning. By then, you and I will be far away, and the ship will have departed."

The grinding of the driver shifting gears drowned Abdo's reply. Abu Alhaul dismissed his brother with a wave and stepped away from the warehouse, directly into the faint light of the single bulb burning over double doors that lead into the empty building. Missing glass from windows on each side of the rusted doors told how African dockworkers passed idle time. One of the doors hung precariously from one huge rusty iron hinge, the bottom one missing, either broken off or stolen. Waist-high grass grew along both sides of the disabled door.

Abu Alhaul reached up and straightened his black headdress. African dockhands moved back and forth across the front of the truck, breaking up the yellow glow of the headlights. The workers, moving crates and boxes by hand, slid like a parting sea to allow the truck to creep closer to the freighter, never in danger of being run over unless they fell and refused to get up, able to wait the few minutes it would take the truck to run over them. Several patted the rusted fenders as they walked across its path to grab another box from the pier, lift it onto their broad shoulders, and with head down, walk toward the gangway leading onto the freighter.

"What if it breaks down?" Abdo asked. "We'd never be able to push the truck closer."

Abu Alhaul, whose Arabic name translated to "Father of Fear," replied, "No, we would have to shift the freighter backward."

"Not right now we couldn't. The truck needs to make another fifty meters. The water is too shallow to move the ship back. We would have to wait for high tide, and high tide"—he pulled the sleeve back on his robe and looked at his watch—"is three hours away."

"Three hours from now, Abdo, the freighter must be underway. It must be out of here and fifteen miles out to sea when the sun rises. That will take it over the horizon and out of sight."

The squeal of brakes reminded Abu Alhaul of the Egyptian teacher he and Abdo had had when they were growing up. A teacher who enjoyed trailing his fingernails down an old chalkboard, creating a chill-raising screech that caused his students to wiggle in agony as they covered their ears. He could still hear the old man's laughter. Abu Alhaul also recalled the glazed eyes in what remained of the old man's head after Abdo and he had smashed it in with bricks. It had taught him the value of terror. Of doing something so dramatic that those aware of it capitulated to his leadership. He had watched, mesmerized, as the fear in the eyes of the old man had faded into the gaze of death. Then he had slowly sawed his knife through the man's neck, realizing as the blood pumped from the arteries running along the sides of the neck that the man wasn't quite dead. When he held the head up for Abdo to see, there was no doubt the teacher was dead, but even so, Abu Alhaul had looked down at the stump of the neck to make sure the blood had quit pumping.

The teacher had been a Coptic Christian; one of many in Egypt, but with this death—Abu Alhaul's first—there was one less. In the life of a Jihadist, every death was important to remember and appreciate in the furtherance of teaching to the world obedience of Allah's will. He softly mumbled "Allah Akbar" a couple of times. Someday the world would bend to his will for his will, was Allah's will.

"It will make it," he said softly as he turned to watch the truck.

"Uh," Abdo grunted. "Let's hope Allah is beneath the bonnet of that truck."

Abu Alhaul glanced at his larger and younger brother. "Abdo, you blaspheme Allah's name?"

"Oh, I would never do that, my brother. You and he are close friends. Since you two are so close, I have decided that I'm here to serve you." He shrugged his shoulders nonchalantly and clasped his hands behind his back. "Allah just happens to be nearby."

Abu Alhaul leaned closer to his brother. "Abdo, you must learn to be more respectful. While I understand your sarcasm and how little the will of Allah means to you, others who follow me would not."

Abdo nodded and looked down. "They follow you; not me. I follow you, not Allah." He glanced over at his shorter brother. "Someday, my brother, you will need someone who will risk his life to save yours." Abdo pulled a white cloth from a side pocket and blew his nose. "Besides, where you go, I go. If you weren't here, I would not be." When Abu Alhaul failed to answer, Abdo lifted his headdress and ran the cloth through his thick black hair, the long strands falling over his ears and down the back of his neck. "You know, my brother. Right now, as we stand here fighting the heat and mosquitoes so big they could carry you away to feast on you later, the cafés and restaurants of Cairo are bustling with activity. The cool breeze of the Nile would be winding through the city streets, bringing a welcomed relief from the day's heat. We could be sitting, enjoying a small figan of coffee or tea, watching the tourists parade across—"

"In the new world, those tourists will stay in their own country, serving us," Abu Alhaul interrupted, his voice hard and firm.

Abdo nodded, waited a couple of seconds, and added, "Of course, they will, but right now they are promenading through the heart of Cairo, and with them they bring a light of enthusiasm; a light of humor; a light of life. And, the women bring a light of legs." He chuckled.

Abu Alhaul turned suddenly, slapped his brother, and snapped, "That is enough!"

Abdo's eyes moistened. He rubbed the growing red spot on his bare left cheek. Sometimes, even he failed to understand the man who had risen to replace Sheik Osama.

After the rebuke, the two men stood silent, watching the constant parade of Africans carrying the boxes up the narrow gangway, stepping down onto the deck, and then being directed various ways by the four Jihadists standing at the top. Like ants preparing a nest for the winter, the lines continued to move. Abu Alhaul couldn't understand the words the Africans were exchanging, but the laughter and gaiety told him of their expectation of good wages for this job. The Africans were used to smuggling, so the idea of loading a rust-bucket freighter in the middle of the night was not new to them.

One of Abu Alhaul's men held a clipboard, checking off an inventory list as the Africans paraded past him at the foot of the gangway. Two other Jihadists stood on the pier, each holding an AK-47. A short, squat man wearing a straw hat and dressed in a western suit moved among boxes stacked a few feet from the foot of the gangway. Periodically he would stop one of the Africans and make the man stack the box being carried with the others. Each time he did it, the man with the clipboard scowled and looked toward the warehouse.

Abu Alhaul knew the man was searching for him, but in the shadows of the building as long as he remained motionless, his silhouette blended into the shadows behind the unshaded light bulb that lit up the four men assigned to guard him.

Forty minutes later, the truck squealed to a halt, its flat bed parallel to the stern of the freighter. Two of the Jihadist supervisors pushed and cajoled the Africans onto the bed to untie a canvas tarp covering the contents. The rear tires were nearly flat from the weight of whatever was tied down on the bed.

Two Africans untied two lines running from the highest point of the tarp to the top of the cab of the truck. The line running from the bottom of the tarp to the edge of the bed untied easily, but the heavy weight beneath the tarp and the shifting of the truck had pulled the fourth line so tight that several of the dockworkers pushed and pulled and argued as they tried to untie it. Finally, tired of the wait, one of the Arab supervisors angrily pushed his way through the growing crowd gathering to provide advice to the Africans on the truck bed above them. The Arab pulled the light robe up between his knees, reached up, grabbed a handhold on a stanchion sticking out from the truck, and pulled himself up. He pushed the Africans aside, knocking one of them off the bed and into the arms of the small crowd below. Cocking his head back arrogantly, the thin reed of a man whipped out a long knife and in one smooth motion sliced through the hemp line.

"Pull it away!" he shouted, jumping down.

Abu Alhaul smiled. He had made the right decision to entrust this mission to Tamursheki. This worshipper was worth more here in the spread of Allah's word than wasting his time in some western university trying to become a doctor. Those with the greatest ambition are easily the quickest to change directions when success and glory are promised. Tamursheki was such a man, Abu Alhaul thought, as he watched him move back toward the end of the gangway and pick up his clipboard again. Every movement needs an educated cadre who can do the little things such as Tamursheki did. It was indeed unfortunate that even such a disciple as Tamursheki couldn't know everything about this mission. Such a disciple would be missed. In war, casualties happened, and sometimes those casualties had to be planned in battle. A master must be capable of sacrificing his own forces when it will help win the war.

The dockhands grabbed the sides of the dark tarp and pulled it, hand-over-hand, off the back of the truck, revealing the bottom half of a square container. The tarp caught on the forward edge of the huge thing beneath it. Grunting for a moment, the dockworkers jerked hard, ripping it free, cutting through the canvas like a knife. When the tarp cleared the truck bed, falling into a huge bundle beside the rear left wheels, a huge dark gray van sat exposed on the bed. Abu Alhaul's eyes narrowed as he searched along the front side of the van until finally he saw the faint outline of a small door.

Several Africans rolled the tarp flat, then took the ends of it, folding it up and over several times before throwing their bodies on top of it. A couple others hurriedly wound rope around the tarp, tied it off, and jumped out of the way of the two who had folded the tarp. The two grabbed the ends and carried it across the dock. Abu Alhaul watched with suspicion. Suspicion was a key to survival when you attempted to meld into the local populace and you knew others wanted to see your head on the end of a stake. The two Africans swung the tarp three times, letting it go on the third. The heavy tarp fell, landing about two inches from their feet, causing the two men to jump back involuntarily. How stupid they were, but just as he needed people like Tamursheki with some sense of intelligence, he also needed those who were stupid like these dockworkers who were already counting the money they thought to make tonight.

The two Africans laughed at themselves, with one pointing at the tarp and saying something in the local dialect. Abu Alhaul knew they intended to return later for it. Tarps such as this made excellent roofs for the thatch huts where many of them lived. It was too bad that none could return, but Allah demanded a lot in his service, and the life of a non-Muslim was as insignificant as a sheep. Without thinking about it, Abu Alhaul ground the ball of his right foot onto the pier. *As a sheep.*

The sound of heavy machinery filled the air, riding over the noise of the dockworkers and the grinding gears of the truck. A huge crane started creeping along the tracks running the length of the pier. Several minutes passed before it stopped, the arm with the heavy crane positioned over the bed of the truck. The strain of the machinery ceased as the crane stopped moving. The grinding noise from the gears of the truck had stopped, and the driver had turned the engine off.

"You, you, and you!" shouted the supervisor. "Get up here and help with this."

Three African dockhands leapt aboard the bed of the truck. One of them stopped long enough to run his hand along the flush edges of the small door leading inside the van.

Abu Alhaul saw the man, but considering the future of the dockhands, singling out the action would accomplish little other than to slow up an already slow evolution, so he kept his tongue. He wondered briefly who the man worked for? CIA? French? African nationalist?

Oh, yes, African nationalist, no doubt. This Mumar Kabir, who had at one time had been his number-one African leader, was building a rabble army north of Liberia and northwest of here. What did the African think they could accomplish? If it weren't for the Arabs helping the Africans, nothing would ever evolve in this dark continent.

Two of the Jihadists pulled themselves onto the top of the van. One motioned the crane operator to lower the hook, and when it was at head level, he placed the chains, handed to him by the other Jihadist, one at a time onto the huge iron hook. Then the two jumped down.

The people on the bed of the truck leaped down. The Africans shifted farther away from the truck as the crane took a strain on the weight. The screaming of the straining engine of the crane preceded the lifting of the van until it was several inches from the bed. Then the noise seemed to steady as the van rose higher.

The truck driver started the engine and eased the truck from beneath the heavy weight, knowing that if the crane lost purchase on the cargo, the drop would destroy his truck. Ownership of a commercial vehicle in the Ivory Coast was more important than protecting whatever it was they paid him to deliver. A television set. That was what he was going to buy with this money. All he wanted was the remainder of what was owed him and he was going to get the hell out of here; for whatever they were doing, he didn't want to know. The less known is better sometimes.

The flaking red hull of the freighter highlighted the dark van swaying minutely beside it. Abu Alhaul traced the slow pace of the van rising alongside the freighter. To his left, the Africans had resumed carrying the stuff from the pier onto the freighter. He looked at the top of the ladder and saw only two of his men. It meant one of the two missing would be at the stern of the ship, supervising the loading of the van. He was one of the Jihadist warriors. But where was the other one? Then he spotted him. The man in the western suit stepping off the bottom of the ladder had been hidden behind several large dockworkers as they worked their way up the narrow gangway. The man met Abu Alhaul's gaze and headed toward him. Abu Alhaul took a further step into the shadows. Ignoring the approaching man, he turned his attention to the van that had now reached a level above the safety lines along the edge of the deck.

The van wobbled about two feet above the height of the safety lines. Complaining gears matched with less strain on the engines, twisted the dangling cargo inch by inch across the edge of the deck. The engine pitch increased as the crane eased forward on its huge wheels, giving the arm better reach over the ship as the van inched forward. Beneath the van, a slight rise on the deck marked the helicopter landing pad. A yellow cross with a circle near the center of the 'X' highlighted the target for an approaching pilot.

As his engineer had explained to Abu Alhaul, this was the only place topside that had the reinforced deck to support the weight of the van. The crane started lowering the heavy van toward the deck several feet below it.

The sudden sound of snapping chains startled Abu Alhaul, causing him to cringe instinctively. Dockworkers dropped their loads as they ran. The chains spun through the buckles, smoke rising from the friction as the steel chain links whipped across the hook. The van tilted forward. The chain shot out, whipping across a supervisor standing to the right of the cargo. In the fraction of a second that the chain caught him, it snapped his spinal cord, bending the man's head backward to touch the heels of his feet even as it continued a deadly swath through the dust rising as the cargo unceremoniously crashed to the deck.

The stern of the freighter dropped nearly a foot in its draft before the water pushed it back up over two feet. The water of the inlet rushed between the ship and dock. The lines running from the bullocks to the ship groaned as they narrowed from the strain of the wave shoving the freighter away from the pier. The gangway fell, twisting to the side and tossing a couple of the Africans into the water between the ship and the dock. If any of the lines snapped, each would be like a razor whipping through the butter of human flesh. The deadly chain on the stern collapsed onto the deck, part of it still attached to the crane.

The mooring lines held, jerking the freighter back to the dock where it bounced off the line of old tires mounted in a line just below the edge of the dock, serving as bumper guards. A cry between the ship and the dock cut short. Abu Alhaul gave little thought to the two Africans flattened between the ship and the pier, their bodies already crushed and floating toward the bottom of the lifeless inlet. After all, they were just Africans.

Two of his men raced to the stern. Supervisors ashore screamed and berated the Africans until they emerged from hiding to hoist the loads they'd dropped and resumed the time-consuming work of loading the vessel. Abu Alhaul watched, emotionless. There was little that could be done, if it was Allah's will.

"I hope the seals are unbroken," Abdo said softly to his brother.

Abu Alhaul shrugged. "It matters little, if they are."

"I think you may be wrong, my brother. If they are broken then people—spies—could determine what is inside the van."

"The world will know soon enough what is inside it."

"But surprises are better received when unexpected."

"Abdo, you worry so much. You must trust Allah as I do."

"It's not Allah that bothers me, Abu; it is his followers—"

"—of which we are."

Not all of the Africans continued loading the freighters. Some cautiously approached the stern of the ship, trying to see what had happened on the ship. Two Jihadists unpacked detection gear and were quickly waving the long wands around the van, sweeping the corners and the seals, looking for signs that a break in the container had occurred.

Abu Alhaul seemed to be the only one calm as time continued to pass and it began to look as if they would fail to meet his timetable. He looked left at two of his guards. He nodded at the one with the long mustache and watched as the young man handed his AK-47 to his comrade. The man reached down and pulled a small package from a backpack leaning against a stack of wooden cargo pads. Glancing both ways, the man, crouching, ran to the truck. The driver had slid across the seat to the open door on the passenger side to watch the activity on the stern. The man slid onto his back and pulled himself under the truck. A few minutes later, he reemerged, looking toward his comrade, who had the automatic gun trained toward the truck. The comrade jerked his head, indicating the coast was clear. The man pulled himself completely out from under the truck, and with only a brief glance to assure himself the driver wasn't in the seat above him, he ran back to his friend. Breathing heavily, he took his AK-47. Then he looked at Abu Alhaul and, with a wide grin, nodded. When Abu Alhaul nodded in return, the man briefly touched his chin as a sign of respect and resumed his guard duties.

On board the freighter, the taller man handed his clipboard to a nearby Jihadist, and with the man wielding the wand, hoisted himself onto the roof of the van. He said something to the man with the detection gear. Taking the wand back, the younger man, bent at the waist, shuffled around the top of the dark van, sweeping the roof.

"Watch the edge, Tamursheki!" someone shouted.

Tamursheki never took his eyes off the man working the gear. He raised his hand motioning the comment aside.

Finished, the man stood, shrugged his shoulders, and said something to Tamursheki. Tamursheki looked over to where Abu Alhaul stood. He jumped from the top of the heavy cargo and grabbed a bullhorn from a nearby supervisor.

"Everything is okay, Alshiek!" Tamursheki shouted. "Amir has swept the . . . cargo." The man on top waved the detection wand in the air.

"Well, there wouldn't be, would there?" mumbled Abdo. When he saw the sharp look from Abu Alhaul, he offered, "After all, it's thick steel with lead shielding surrounding every square inch of the inside. Of course, if we had built it here instead of miles away, we wouldn't have had to transport it and this wouldn't have wasted as much time loading."

"The van is important."

A cough drew Abu Alhaul's attention. The man in the

western suit had been standing silently beside him throughout the incident. Abu Alhaul looked down at the man, his expression never changing. It was the Palestinian.

"Abu Alhaul," the short, stout man said, pushing the brim of a white fedora off his forehead. "My apologies for interrupting your thoughts, but I wanted to apprise you of where we stand."

"Continue, Doctor Ibrahim."

"Food and water is onboard. Captain Alrajool asked that I relay that to you. The medical supplies needed—*for the health of the martyrs*—are also on board."

Abu Alhaul reached out and touched the shorter, squared-bodied man on the shoulder, forcing himself not to jerk his hand away from touching the western garment. "Doctor, you're very important for the success of this mission. This is not a mission that will be accomplished in a week or two weeks, but it's one that will carry the jewels of obedience to the infidels. Those chosen to martyr themselves in this Holy cause must be *healthy* so they arrive at the right place at the right time. My friends in Somalia tell me you are the best, but then I have to ask myself, if you are the best then why do they send you. Could it be that maybe they have no further use for you? Can I count on their words of your ability to keep them clean and clear of focus?"

Dr. Ibrahim's eyes narrowed and he stopped himself before he said something that may cost him his life. Changing the subject, he pointed at the van. "Is this necessary, my leader? I thought I was the secret of the mission. Is this real? Is this something like a backup in the event I am unsuccessful?"

Abu Alhaul allowed himself a laugh. "Of course, it is necessary, Doctor. Every great plan has its details. Great plans are better carried out when the enemy realizes that he failed to watch the other hand of the magician. By then"—Abu Alhaul snapped his fingers—"the trick is over, the crowd is both surprised and perplexed in their amusement. You, my dear friend, are the magician. The van is the hand the Great Satan will watch."

The sound of the chains being secured to the van and rehooked to the crane drowned out the doctor's words, but Abu Alhaul nodded anyway. What did it matter in the scheme of obedience where the lesson was learned as long as those learning it recognized their decadence? But if America was as decadent and soft as Osama predicted, then why were they still fighting years later and still chasing the remnants of Al Qaeda around the world? He sighed.

The breeze changed slightly, blowing across the inlet, lifting the fetid smell higher into the air to whiff across the freighter, the pier, to flow across where Abu Alhaul stood.

"Whew!" said Abdo. "How do they stand living here? The smell, the dirt, the filth."

"They need to understand Allah's obedience before they can appreciate the depth of depravity in which they live."

"Depravity? I would call it more a lack of hygiene. I bet if you gave them a bar of soap each, half of them would think it was something to eat."

"And the other half?"

"Would *know* it was something to eat."

The crane strained as it lifted the van slightly. On board the ship, about twenty men shoved and twisted the van until the supervisor shouted for them to stand back. Then the crane lowered the van into the corrected position on the helicopter deck.

"I have several more crates to load with my medical supplies, then we'll be finished," Dr. Ibrahim added.

Abu Alhaul watched the van. If it was damaged or lost, the mission could be endangered. He nodded at Ibrahim. As long as the doctor did what he was supposed to do, they would succeed with a greater measure of success than having the van explode inside the American harbor.

"I talked with Captain Alrajool, Abu," Dr. Ibrahim continued, ignoring the inattention of the man in front of him. He wondered briefly what these Arabs saw in this man. "He is in engineering, checking the steam pressure. He says that as soon as the remainder of the supplies, including the zodiac rafts, are on board, and they finish securing the van, the ship would sail."

"Looks as if we have it loaded, my brother. I see that Tamursheki has taken charge again. You have a loyal servant in him."

"And, I don't in you, Abdo?"

Dr. Ibrahim sighed. "If there is nothing else, I'm going to return to the ship and make sure that the things I need to do my part have been properly loaded." He looked past Abu Alhaul to Abdo. If you wanted something done, never go to the number one person, always go to the number two. Then, things get done. "Abdo, would you relay to my bosses that everything is going according to the agreement and plan." He looked at Abu Alhaul, then back to Abdo. "That is, I trust everything is going according to your wishes?" He asked, peering over the top of his wire-rim glasses.

A few minutes later, the Palestinian was climbing back up the restored gangway to the ship.

"I am but Allah's servant," Abu Alhaul mumbled, just loud enough for Abdo to hear.

Abdo laughed.

"A servant such as you, Abdo."

"A servant, no. A loving brother who would sacrifice his life for his older, misguided brother, yes."

Abu Alhaul faced the freighter again. "You didn't always think I was misguided."

"I didn't always think I was going to have to follow you to places where humidity and heat create red patches to cover my body. Where fresh water is something unusual, but hot water is a normal occurrence. Where even the plants are dangerous. Where the snakes that are not poisonous can swallow you whole. No, my brother. Love is one thing, but being comfortable and happy would definitely improve my love for you."

Abu Alhaul shook his head. "You know, little brother, I fail to understand your attempts to distract me from my mission. If Allah wanted us to remain in Egypt, living off the sweat of others, and giving lip service to him, he would have shown me the way."

Abdo reached over and touched his brother on the shoulder. "Ramsi—"

Abu Alhaul jerked his shoulder out from under his brother's hand. "The name is Abu Alhaul. Ramsi is dead. He died years ago."

"Say what you will," Abdo said irritably. "You are Ramsi to me and will always be the younger brother who I carried from the house when it burned. You'll be the younger brother who I protected from bullies in our village. And who was it who pulled you away when you decided to die defiantly by standing in front of an American tank as it roared down the street? Ramsi, it was, and Ramsi it will always be." Abdo turned and walked away, heading toward the stern of the freighter. "What is wrong with a name of a Pharaoh?" Abdo muttered to himself.

On board the ship, Tamursheki jumped from atop the van to the deck. Shouting orders to the Africans and his fellow voyagers, the man watched closely as they quickly fell to the task of securing the heavy van to the ship. Both line and chain ran from the deck to the bolts on top of the van.

Abu Alhaul nodded, satisfied with Tamursheki. This Yemeni would need to maintain a strong hold on the martyrs accompanying him—taking the war to the country that had destroyed so much of the organization he had inherited.

AT THE BOTTOM OF THE GANGWAY, DR. IBRAHIM PULLED an African out of line and motioned him to put the two metal boxes he was carrying to the side. He reached up and pushed his white fedora back, revealing several sweat-soaked strands of hair plastered across the bald pate in a vain attempt to hide the baldness. He ran a handkerchief across his forehead, wondering how he came to be here. Was what Abu Alhaul said correct? Did the Iraqi underground want to get rid of him?

He squatted beside the two boxes, running his hands over the seals to see if they were intact. He licked his lower lip and felt a fresh wave of perspiration break out across his forehead. He wondered why. He had nothing to fear except those he was about to sail with. Satisfied the boxes were okay, he remained squatting, glancing back and forth along the pier, looking for what, he wasn't sure. Ibrahim pulled a dirty handkerchief from the back pocket of his white trousers and wiped the sweat from his brow. He never should have trusted Tamursheki to have them carried aboard. The Arab was as useless as the other fanatic martyrs signed up for this one-way trip. Of course, most, if any, didn't realize this was a one-way trip. Few knew it was, except for him and the Captain. All they had to do was deliver the van to operatives ashore. He had two options, he thought, reaching up and patting the papers in his right suit-coat pocket.

If it weren't for the money—and the knowledge that he wouldn't live long enough to make it to the exit of the port—he'd give this enterprise up. Plus, being a member of the Iraqi underground didn't mean being Arab. If they knew he was Jewish, he wouldn't live another second. He patted the keys jammed into his pants pocket. If anyone looked closely at his keys, they would discover a small Star of David hidden within one of the key-chain ornaments.

He patted the boxes as he stood. He needed the medicine in these boxes, otherwise he couldn't guarantee the degree of health that Abu Alhaul wanted for this bunch of human weapons. Without these containers, how could he fulfill his part of the bargain with this bunch of "let's die for Allah" fools?

Ibrahim had given strict instructions to this weasel Tamursheki to have these boxes carried directly to the medical facility on board the ship. Instead, if he hadn't seen them being carried by this African, they could have been stored anywhere on the ship, and it would have taken a long time to find them. Time was the critical element. If you managed the time right, then everything else fell into step. The loud voice of Tamursheki drew Ibrahim's attention to the stern. He gave a few seconds' thought to marching down there and shouting his anger at him. He sighed, reached down, grabbed the handles of the two boxes, and turned toward the gangway. This Tamursheki was mercurial. Ibrahim was unsure whether Tamursheki would leap down to the pier and cut his throat, ignore him, or offer a groveling apology if he marched down in righteous anger and shouted abuse at him. Ibrahim hadn't lived to be this age without being able to control his emotions.

Pushing his way into the line of Africans loading the ship, Dr. Ibrahim soon passed up the gangway and disappeared into the ship.

Abdo waddled back toward Abu Alhaul, his head down.

"It is loaded, Abu. We can go and watch the departure from the hillside."

Abu Alhaul shook his head. "Soon, my brother."

It took another thirty minutes to complete the loading of the old, rusting freighter. In that time, the man Abu Alhaul had chosen to lead this attack, Tamursheki, finished overseeing the anchoring of the heavy van to the stern. Abu Alhaul and Abdo watched from the shadows as Tamursheki mustered his fellow martyrs on the stern. They were unable to hear what the young twenty-five-year-old told the other young men, but Abu Alhaul knew it would be something about how they were working in Allah's name; that killing infidels increased Allah's might and joy; and, if he was there, he would remind them of the seventy virgins waiting for them in paradise.

"It's all Assassin, isn't it?" Abdo said

Abu Alhaul looked at him and smiled. "And where did that thought come from? Has some insight suddenly exploded within that fat brain of yours?" Abu Alhaul said, his voice betraying amusement.

Abdo grimaced. "Fat I may be, but I prefer to think of it as added padding to keep the bullets out of the vital spots."

"If fat can do that, Abdo, then you will be invincible. Now tell me what you mean by referring to Al Ahsan."

He pointed to the group of Jihadists gathered on the stern of the ship. "You know what I mean; you're doing it. What we do today is really a descendant movement of Al Ahsan."

"Al Ahsan was a great man."

Abdo chuckled. "He was a wise man who knew how to manipulate the emotions and the desires of young men."

The smile left Abu Alhaul's face. "Brother, you mock me."

Abdo shook his head. "I would never mock you. I admire and love you. You know that. No one loves you more than your own brother. And this fat may someday protect you from death."

Abu Alhaul turned away and continued his observation of the activity visible on the ship and the pier. Africans were crawling aboard the flatbed truck at the urging of their supervisors. A few were twitching their shoulders, loosening the tight muscles from the heavy carrying. The tone of the conversation, the friendly slaps and hits being exchanged, the joking banter of workmen finished for the day and happy at the thoughts of going home, made the scene almost surreal.

"During the Christian crusades of their eleventh century," Abdo recited softly, "there arose a great prophet in the land now known as Iran. And this prophet, known as Al Ahsan, gathered around him other mullahs of Allah and discussed how they could rid the Holy Lands of these defilers. And it was decided that to instill fear into their hearts would hasten their departure. And what weapon do we—people of the desert—have to throw against the infidels? And the only weapon they could find were the children. Al Ahsan, acting on the word of Allah, sent his followers into the barren cities of Persia and Iraq, and there they spread the word of Al Ahsan about an unbelievable paradise that awaited those who died in the name of their religion. A paradise oasis where those who died in Allah's name lived for eternity in a spacious home surrounded by fruit trees and flowing waters."

The engine died on the truck. The grinding sound of the starter caused Abu Alhaul to believe the truck had broken down, but then it caught. The driver revved up the engine. A backfire caused the Jihadists to crouch instinctively. A blast of dark, oily exhaust shot out from the tailpipe, and the wind blew it back across the Africans crowded into the bed, bringing forth shouts of displeasure.

"And when Al Ahsan and his followers believed they had found a willing disciple, they would drug him—"

"I prefer the version where he falls into a deep sleep."

"—and while he was asleep they would take him to a hidden place, so when he awoke, he found himself in a great mansion in the middle of nowhere surrounded by fruit trees and running waters. And, dashing through the house and among the garden were young girls—"

"Virgins."

"—virgins with whom the young man would have his way. And, after a few days—"

"Two days."

"—two days, they would dru—put him to sleep again and spirit him back to whence he came."

"That's better. We drug no one."

Abdo cocked his head at his brother, his eyebrows raised in disbelief. "No drug?"

"No drugs. Never, ever."

"Words and a willingness to believe; to echo words that mean nothing when you peel them back like an onion, but they bring tears to the eyes of those who bathe in them."

Abu Alhaul waved his hand impatiently. "Go ahead and finish, Abdo. I enjoy the story and it passes time."

The truck shifted into gear. The driver's head appeared out of the window, his left arm draped outside the door as he looked behind him. The engine noise rose in tempo as the driver pushed on the pedal and the gears ground as metal teeth tore against each other. The truck backed up, inching out of the narrow confines of the pier, past the stern of the ship toward an alley between the warehouses, where it could turn around.

"And, when the disciples awoke and told Al Ahsan and his closest followers what had happened, they convinced him that he had been blessed by Allah and shown what paradise would be like when he died."

The headlights of the truck played across the freighter as it backed into the alley. The familiar sound of grinding gears announced the shift from reverse to first.

"Convinced that he must die in the service of Allah, the leaders gave the young man a knife and whispered instructions on what he must do to re-enter the gates of paradise. Then, they patted him on the butt and laughed as they sent him off—"

"Abdo!" Abu Alhaul scolded.

"Okay, okay, okay," he said with a downward motion of his hand. "I will try to stay to the original story."

"That would be something I would like to hear."

Abu Alhaul nodded at the man who had crawled under the truck earlier. The man handed the AK-47 to the man beside him, reaching into the knapsack to pull out a remote control device, along with a couple of hand grenades. Glancing again at Abu Alhaul, who lowered his eyes in acknowledgment, the man ran down the pier toward the truck that had now reached the gate leading off the jungle pier and into the bush.

"And the young man would sneak into the camps of the Christian infidels and cut the throat of a single person sleeping among the others. Lying on his stomach, he would then saw the head off the body and place the head on the chest of the dead Christian before sneaking off into the night again."

At the gate, the taillights of the truck passed through the open chain-link fence. The man stopped, jumped behind a couple of large crates stacked on top of each other.

He leaned around the edge, pointed the remote control at the truck, and pressed the button.

"Eventually, he would be caught and killed."

The explosion split open the night darkness and rode over the sounds of the ship and the jungle. From beneath the warehouse, other members of Abu Alhaul's guard strolled toward the dead, dying, and wounded. The man who had blown up the truck pointed to the hillside outside the gate, pulled the pin on the grenade, and threw it over the fence. The explosion stopped some of the screaming. The men walked among the Africans. Those still alive they shot. Some near the fetid waters of the inlet they rolled into the bay.

"And the Christians called these silent killers of the night Assassins, which means followers of Al Ahsan. When they realized the nature of the killings and what those doing it believed, and to whom they swore undying loyalty, the Christians sought out Al Ahsan and destroyed his palace and him. And, to send a message to others who may follow, they killed his wives and his children so that his seed would not pass into posterity."

"That's the part of the story I don't care for."

Abdo nodded. "It is the part I don't like either, but a part that I do not worry about occurring in this day and age. The Americans would never do what is needed to stop those who willingly give their lives for their religion."

The shooting stopped. His bodyguards returned from their duties. No way could he allow the Africans to talk as soon as they reached home or one of those hovels converted to serve alcohol. It was in their best interests to have no witness left behind who could tell the Americans what was coming.

On the stern of the ship, the Jihadists clapped in appreciation to the executioners as they hoisted their weapons and spread out along the dock beside the ship.

"Single up all lines," came the shout from the bridge. Leaning out from the edge of the bridge wing, a thin dark man, wearing a dingy Greek Navy cap with dirty embroidered gold leaves on its brim, held a bullhorn to his lips. On board the ship, two men stood at each of the eight lines holding the ship to the pier. On the pier, the bodyguards lifted the top line off the bollards and dropped it. The seamen, hand over hand, rapidly pulled the lines aboard the ship.

The Captain rushed from one end of the long bridge wing to the other, watching his seamen build a stack of lines behind each portal where a mooring line threaded its way to the pier, until finally the end of each flew onto the deck and joined the neatly curled stacks.

Satisfied, he raised the bullhorn. "Cast off lines one, two, three, four, six!"

Four minutes later, the ship was tied to the pier only by the stern line. Abu Alhaul watched, but failed to understand why the Captain kept one line taut.

On board the ship, the Captain leaned into the bridge. "Helmsman, right full rudder, three revolutions ahead."

The helmsman swung the wheel to the right, watching it spin, hand over hand, the maneuver most mariner work required. He kept the wheel spinning until, "Right full rudder, Captain." He glanced at the annunciator. "Engine room shows ahead three revolutions."

The Captain ran to the front of the bridge wing and watched the bow as it slowly swung out, away from the pier. Then the ship inched forward. He glanced behind him at the remaining seventh line; it was slack as the stern swung in toward the pier. About six feet separated the ship from the pier. Raising the bullhorn, he shouted, "Take in seven!"

Ashore, the bodyguards shoved the huge line off the bollard. Aboard the ship, the seamen hurriedly pulled the line on board.

The Captain stuck his head into the bridge. "Ahead, twelve revolutions. Rudder amidships. Navigator, give me data."

"Recommend course two-eight-five, three knots."

"Helmsman, steer course two-eight-five, three knots."

* * *

ABU ALHAUL AND ABDO WATCHED THE SHIP UNTIL IT cleared the harbor entrance.

Abdo cleared his throat. "My brother, the Irish have asked again for their money."

Abu Alhaul shook his head. "We have given them over a hundred thousand British pounds and they failed their mission. What do they—"

"They think that they acted in good faith to extract your revenge from this American. The fact that they failed to do it is lost in their sense of mission."

Abu Alhaul stared at Abdo for a few seconds, then pointed toward the freighter. "That ship will take care of what they failed to do. I find it disgusting that we must work with infidels to do what we should do ourselves. They were your idea, Abdo—my brother—you take care of the Irish. I do not care to work with them again. Their battle with their British masters is theirs; not ours."

Abdo bit his lower lip, then replied. "Don't you think you are allowing personal vengeance to cloud our war of faith?"

Abu Alhaul remained silent, staring at the fading ship. Minutes passed with only the noise of the nearby jungle filling the air before Abu Alhaul finally turned and started walking away, remarking to Abdo, who joined him, "It's time to go. The French will be here soon. The explosion will have been reported."

With bodyguards leading the way, the group walked through the vacant warehouse to the SUVs on the other side. Thirty minutes later the pier and harbor were quiet.

Beneath the dock, the African pulled himself up until his head was just enough above the dock so he could see. He waited several minutes before crawling out and onto the dock. Another couple of minutes passed before he jumped up, and at a crouching run dived for cover behind a stack of rusting metal. Fifteen minutes he waited before he worked his way to the warehouse and followed in the direction Abu Alhaul had disappeared. At the far end of the warehouse, he squatted, running his hand along the tire marks on the ground. Then, apparently satisfied, he looked in the direction the SUVs had disappeared. He thought about going back to check on the other Africans, but to do so would leave signs of his presence. There had been a moment, when the ship was getting underway, when he'd thought the bow was going to jar the pilings where he had wedged himself. He rubbed his thighs. He was going to be one sore puppy tomorrow, but tonight he must report what he had seen. The lean African turned in the opposite direction from where Abu Alhaul and his group had disappeared. Moments later he turned off the road and onto a faint animal trail leading into the jungle.

CHAPTER 3

"TUCKER, COME IN!" REAR ADMIRAL DUNCAN JAMES said, a broad smile etched across his face. The muscular fifty-three-year-old head of Navy SEALs briskly walked around his Pentagon desk, firmly taking Tucker's hand and shaking it. "Here, have a seat and tell me how you're doing." Duncan pointed to one of the maroon leather chairs facing his desk.

"I'm doing fine, Admiral," Tucker replied, waiting a fraction of a second to sit, allowing Admiral James to sit first. Junior personnel never sit before the senior officer does. Neither do they sit first when civilian ladies are present.

The door opened and Yeoman Chief Gonzales briskly entered the room. Balanced between her hands was a small aluminum tray with a silver-plated coffeepot between two small cups and saucers.

"Thanks, Chief," Admiral James said as she set the tray down on the coffee table in front of the two men. James smiled. Tucker's eyes glanced for a moment at the nice well-rounded legs of the Chief. "Nice, eh?" he said to

Tucker, pointing at the coffee, and smiling at the slight embarrassment he caused the Commander.

"If you need anything else, sir, I'll be at my desk," she said, her voice a husky Chicano accent.

Without waiting for a reply, she turned sharply on her heels, closing the door quietly as she left the room. A faint odor of perfume whiffed behind her.

Admiral James waited a second for her to clear the outer door. "I'll get us some real mugs for this coffee, Tucker," he said, in a conspiratorial tone as if the two of them were breaking one of the Chief's rules of the house.

It made Tucker think of his two brothers and the night-time raids on Mom's cookie jar when they were lads. The Admiral rose quickly to cross the room to the cabinet where a host of official coffee mugs rested in a line. Mugs given to him from various commands and organizations over the course of his thirty-three years of service. "I've always thought that real men never drink coffee from a cup that causes your pinkie to stick out when you pick it up. I like a cup that fights back at you."

Tucker stood, waiting for the Admiral to return. "Some of the coffee I've had at sea would meet the Admiral's expectation."

"Sit down, Tucker," James said when he turned around. "It isn't as if we have a bunch of rank-conscious, tradition-loving, rear-echelon mother lovers here," he continued as he walked back, waving the officer down. James set the mugs on the coffee table.

Tucker reached for the pot, but Admiral James beat him. "Now tell me," he said as he poured, "how are you—*really?* Those wounds healed?"

Tucker took his cup and nodded. "Still a little tight, but thanks to you giving me the time off to get my physical strength and stamina back, along with that Navy Lieutenant Commander who says she's a physical therapist—but I think her real job is an interrogator for the CIA."

"So, you're ready to go back to the front lines?"

"I think I am ninety-eight percent ready to go, sir. Of

course, sir, if you listen to my physical therapist, I am about one step away from the grave."

Duncan laughed. "Yeah, I know who you're talking about. Nurse Bradley, right?"

"That's the one."

James shook his head, laughing. "She would have been at home during the Inquisition. When I came back from the North African campaign, from rescuing a bunch of American hostages"—he reached down and rubbed both knees—"these knees had given up the ghost. They went in, scraped some of the debris off them, then the doctors at Bethesda handed me over to her. They were as cheerful as sadists at a funeral. I know she may be your age, but she had no sympathy with an old man like me at fifty-two."

"She definitely believes in making you hurt."

"If it isn't hurting, she used to say, it isn't healing. I always told her that if hurting meant it was healing then I had two of the best knees in the military."

Tucker smiled. A memory flashed through his thoughts of the young, thin Navy nurse. They had become more than patient-doctor after about a month together.

"I am firmly convinced," James said, leaning forward and in a soft voice, "that the Air Force intentionally seeks out the best-looking women in America, and it's the Navy that puts them in uniform."

"She was definitely that," Tucker added. He recalled the forced march Samantha Bradley—*call me Sam*—took him on his second day out of surgery. Three miles up the Potomac and back—badgering him along the way about a lowly Navy nurse outpacing a hard, war-tempered Navy SEAL. It was only through tenacity and force of will that he had completed the walk. It was only through double doses of whatever the military was using for bad joints at the time that he had successfully forced himself out of bed the next morning.

Duncan chuckled. "I see from your face you agree with me. Sam Bradley forced me on a six-mile round-trip exercise my first week out of surgery, telling me how happy she was to know that a Navy nurse was able to outpace an old, has-been Navy SEAL." He paused. "I thought at the time, if I caught up with her, I'd throw her in the Potomac."

"The thought crossed my mind also, Admiral. I had a similar experience with her." Three weeks together and he had asked her out. Nice dinner, with wine, candles, and a horrible piano player with two left hands. He had been pleasantly surprised at her feminine side. Nothing pretentious, he dropped her off at her apartment in Crystal City; a quick buss on the cheek and the next morning she was twice as horrible. Next time, he had decided, more wine, less talk.

"How far you running now?"

"I jogged with a bunch of the Joint Staff J3 SEALs yesterday. We did a fifteen-mile run along the Potomac, across the Memorial Bridge, through Washington, D.C., toured all the monuments, ran through a nude 'no minks' demonstration, and returned over the Fourteenth Street Bridge."

"And, I suspect you felt wonderful," Duncan James remarked, thinking of his gone-to-hell knees and how they would feel if he did a fifteen-mile run.

"I felt like hell, sir. My lungs ached. My legs ached. I think even the hair on my head ached. But, when I finished, it was a great feeling. It was as if the exertion burned out the poison in my body. Not to mention that first beer tasted so damn good."

"I know what you mean, Tucker. The best reward for completing a hard physical workout is that first beer." He paused and then, with a sigh, continued. "Tucker, down to business. The reason I asked you here today is to personally provide you a debrief on the events at your home in Urbana, Maryland, three months ago—May. My contacts at Naval Security Group Command tell me you're asking questions and trying to determine why these three men attacked you." James leaned over and pulled a thick binder off his desk. He opened it, took a sheet of paper from it, and laid the binder on the coffee table.

Tucker recognized the sheet as a blue blazer. A one-page tickler of bullets that gave just enough information for an uninformed reader to comprehend what the subject was about; why it was important; and what courses of actions were being recommended.

Tucker set his coffee on the table and clasped his hands together. He did want to know what happened. He had spent nearly three weeks in Bethesda—one in intensive care—as they dug out the bullet and repaired the damage to his body. It had taken another six weeks of physical therapy to allow him to reach a point where he was able to return to the heavy physical regime demanded of a United States Navy SEAL. The vision of Sam broke into his thoughts as he recalled his first run after several platonic dates with her. They were standing on the paved trail that ran along the Potomac near the Pentagon North parking lot. The run was going to be a short one. Two miles up and two miles back. He finished stretching and turned to start, her alongside him to the left. Suddenly, she had leaned against him, pressing her small breasts against his arm.

"If you catch me," she whispered softly, "you can have me." Then, she had pushed him away, causing him to trip, while she took off at a dead-heat down the path. It had taken him several seconds to give chase, but he never caught her. It took a week to catch her. He smiled. She had been true to her word, and now he couldn't quit thinking of that lithe, smooth body—

Admiral James saw the smile and smiled himself. "You didn't think you could try to find out what was being kept from you without it being noticed, did you?"

Tucker quit smiling. What did the Admiral mean? "Sorry, Admiral, my mind wandered for a moment." His thoughts came back to that event in May. Every door he beat on since leaving Bethesda Naval Medical Facility had slammed shut in his face. Every question asked was met with feigned ignorance even as he knew they were lying.

"Yes, sir," he said, his voice slightly irate. "I want to know why I had an Irishman and a couple of dumb American buddies trying to kill me. And, Admiral, with all due respect, maybe someone can tell me why it seems that everyone but me knows why?"

"Don't blame you at all, Tucker. Let's start with the world in the twenty-first century . . ."

Tucker's eyes narrowed. He had heard so much about Rear Admiral Duncan James, and here the man was fixing to go off on some tangent to avoid telling him the truth.

"It's gone to shit in a handbasket. We fight an enemy who is stateless and ruthless. He crosses national borders as if they don't exist, and when we follow him to take out those nations who harbor terrorists and provide them sanctuary, we're the ones called terrorists. When we do find and shut down his financial backings, he moves on, depending on fake charities and business fronts to provide money to take anarchy, death, and destruction to those who refuse to believe as he does. Between you and me, nothing scares me more than a religious fanatic, regardless of what religion he or she belongs to. When you have no tolerance for how others believe and worship, then you're dangerous to everyone around you. They're the most dangerous of the terrorists because deep within their religion they believe that terrorism is an acceptable means to spread it."

Tucker listened even as he picked up the coffee and sipped. The words of Duncan James caused him to recall the story of a radio interview where the woman reporter proclaimed that if we hadn't taken God out of schools and turned our backs on Him in our lives, September 11th would never have happened. The radio show ended quickly when Admiral James pointed out that, one, it wasn't God that did the horrors of that day—it was his followers, and, two, the Taliban had prayer in every school and forced it on everyone's lives. Admiral James continued to talk about the importance of tolerance as Tucker feigned interest. He didn't care why they were killing and running amok. His job was to find and kill them. Tucker didn't see much reason to sit around philosophizing when the people he was fighting were shooting back at him. Tucker forced himself to pay attention.

When flag officers spoke, you at least kept your eyes from glazing over. Rumor had it the Chief of Naval Operations had *asked* Admiral James to avoid future interviews after several demonstrations broke out over his words. Someone had told Tucker that a mullah in Iran had declared open season on Admiral James. If so, Tucker could see why.

"Sorry about that," Admiral James said. "I tend to digress sometimes. That digressing keeps getting me in trouble. If it wasn't for some congressmen trying to insure that we in the military have some sort of freedom of speech, it'd be good odds I'd be gone by now. Let's get back to you and what happened in May. You recall a mission in Yemen two years ago?"

Tucker thought for a moment. There had been so many missions. It had to be one staged out of Djibouti. "Yes, sir," he finally replied. "I think I do. If I'm right, it would have been Operation Wipe-up. We followed a major campaign of Joint Task Force Promote Freedom. Promote Freedom was a massive hunt-and-kill operation against a reemerging Al Qaeda base in the Wild West hill country of Yemen. Lasted about three weeks. Everyone said it was a great success. Army Blackhawks dropped us to ground in the hills around a lawless tribal area of Northern Yemen. We waited a week after Promote Freedom had ceased and the bombing had stopped for those terrorists hiding to reemerge. Then we started a covert search-and-destroy against them. We had a two-prong effort with us Americans operating on the southern end of the operations zone and the British-Australian Special Forces working their way south from the northern edge of the zone. We engaged and destroyed numerous small groups of terrorists active in the area."

"I have read the operations report, Commander. You make it seem easier than what the reports show. Your group broke into teams, and our closest allies in the north broke into teams. At one time, we must have had twenty special-operations force teams running about the countryside killing and destroying. Essentially, when you finished, you had wiped out nearly all of the new Al Qaeda camps. The teams also stumbled on a couple of new training camps with young recruits eager to commit martyrdom to meet Allah, and the teams arranged those meetings for them. Nope, it was truthfully a great moment in special-operations history, which is one reason that as a commander you were awarded the Silver Star."

"Thank you, sir."

James nodded. "I can see the attack on you hasn't destroyed any brain cells. Another geopolitical reality of the twenty-first century is these nonstate terror elements converging with rogue nations and other nonaligned terror movements to form what I call associations of the moment. Al Qaeda tried to work with Hamas in 2002 when Operation Enduring Freedom freed Afghanistan. They were going to share funds and plan joint operations. Like most terrorist cells, they don't work well with two masters. Today—"

"Yes, sir," Tucker interrupted, "but what does this have to do with me?"

Duncan James paused a moment, then nodded. "Tucker, you're probably one of the best, if not the number-one terrorist killer we have on active duty. Wouldn't want to see that as a *Washington Post* headline. You work alone when required, with a squad when necessary, and have led major covert attacks deep into terrorist strongholds wherever they may be, whenever you've been ordered. As much as we try to keep the individual names of our Special Forces heroes a secret, our open society makes it damn right challenging. It's hard to balance secrecy against the rights of freedom of speech and press."

Admiral James's words caused Tucker to think of the news article in *Newsweek* magazine seven months before. The article had had a photograph of him, extolling Tucker as a secret warrior in the war against terrorism. It told of an unnamed source identifying him as the leader of the Special Forces teams in Operation Wipe-up.

"The attack against the compound where your reconnaissance team spotted this new character—the one called Abu Alhaul—wasn't that successful. He and his bodyguards had slipped away during the four hours it took for you and your squads to call in reinforcements. You blew the buildings in the compound, killed a lot of people—every one of the dead associated with this new Al Qaeda. Among those associates were the four wives and most of Abu Alhaul's children."

Tucker looked down. He remembered seeing the small bodies and the feeling of nausea sweeping over him. "Sir, I wasn't aware of the women and children."

"I know. And that was where the photograph that showed up in *Time* magazine was taken."

Tucker nodded. War is hell. The fog of war. Give peace a chance. No one can appreciate the dynamics of the moment when bullets are flying and time seems to stand still as the body count grows in the race to close combat. During those moments, things happen because of reaction and not because of predetermined intent. Many officers' careers have ended for doing what they were trained to do and achieving an outcome that didn't pass the "*Washington Post* test" as Admiral James alluded.

James took a drink of coffee and shrugged. "It isn't as if we plan on something like this happening, but when you run with terrorists, you must take your chances. What happened to his family is what will happen to others of his ilk who insist on trying to have a normal family life while planning destruction. If they want to protect their families, they would send them to where they would be out of the line of fire. They don't, because they don't care. In their own arrogance they believe—"

"It's just that—"

"—in their own invincibility." Admiral James paused for a moment, bit his lower lip, and then continued. "It happened, and with the exception of that lone photograph, no one ever associated a specific person with the mission." James leaned forward and poured more coffee in his mug.

"British MI-5 tells us this new Al Qaeda has a loose working relationship with the New IRA. This radical bunch of Irish terrorists need money, since we cut off most of their overt fund-raising here in the States. What didn't stop was some of our own citizens' fanatical loyalty to a homeland they've never known or visited. A fantasy Ireland constructed within their own minds."

"Yes, sir. I do remember one of the three had a heavy brogue. It took a few minutes during our backyard dance to identify it as Irish. That threw me. I could have understood if—"

Admiral James waved his hand at Tucker. "I know, I know. If it had been Arabic then you would have probably figured out what I think you already know." He tilted his head forward, raising his eyebrows at Tucker.

Tucker nodded, glancing down at the mug he held between his hands. "I take it this Abu Alhaul has a contract out on me."

Duncan James laughed. "You make it sound like an organized crime syndicate, but you're about right, Tucker. According to MI-5, the new Al Qaeda transferred two hundred thousand British pounds to a Swiss account. An account MI-5 is watching. Kind of surprised them, according to Admiral Seidman, Director of Defense Intelligence Agency. When they started backtracking the money trail, it led to Yemen, and from Yemen they followed it to this Abu Alhaul."

Tucker Raleigh leaned forward and put his cup on the coffee table. He crossed his legs. "Guess this means they'll be coming after me again."

James shrugged. "Who knows? But, if they do, I am sure the price will be more than two hundred thousand pounds. As for the other two individuals with the Irish hit man, you're right. They were Americans. Members of one of our home-grown Irish charities whose funds filtered into this radical branch of the IRA."

A knock on the door interrupted Admiral James and drew both their attention. The door opened, and Chief Gonzales stuck her head inside the room. Her dark-rim glasses slid down to the tip of her thin Roman nose. "Admiral, Admiral Holman is here."

James motioned to her. "Send him in."

"Yes, sir," she replied, then cleared her throat slightly. "Captain St. Cyr is here also."

James's eyes narrowed. "Give the good Captain a cup of coffee and ply him with doughnuts, Chief. I need a few more minutes with Commander Raleigh and Admiral Holman before we bring in the French Captain."

She nodded, pausing a moment before stepping outside.

She had barely disappeared before Admiral Dick Holman, Commander Amphibious Group Two, walked past her, pushing the door shut behind him.

Tucker stood as the two flag officers exchanged greetings. He took in the other two-star Rear Admiral who had joined them. Holman was a head shorter than James, with a growing paunch around the middle. When he turned slightly, Tucker saw the ribbon at the top of the six rows. Silver Star. He instinctively glanced down quickly at his own three rows, but then, he had only been in the Navy sixteen years. The top two on his were the Silver Star and Purple Heart, both awarded during Operation Wipe-up. The Purple Heart was one medal he would have preferred not to have earned.

"Dick, this is Tucker Raleigh—the SEAL I've told you about and the officer Admiral Seidman briefed yesterday."

"Tucker, it's a pleasure to meet you," Holman said, shaking the taller Navy SEAL's hand. Hope you have recovered."

"Yes, sir. I'm fine," Tucker said, as the thought of Sam Bradley flickered across his mind. It took him four runs before he passed her. He smiled as he recalled the expression on her face when he shot by her the first time without a word. It was priceless. She expected him to do something when he caught up; touch her; grab her; say something wily and ribald about winning the prize. Instead, he just raced by, without a word. She had picked up the pace and caught up with him, and even with obvious attempts to get him to refer to her taunt, he pretended not to understand.

"—is the reason he is here."

Tucker jumped slightly. "Sorry, sir. My mind wandered for a moment."

"Whatever it was, it must have been happy thoughts," Holman said as he walked around the back of the small tanned leather couch where Tucker sat. He reached down and patted the Navy SEAL on the shoulder as he passed. "Don't have many happy thoughts in the Pentagon."

"I think it's a Department of Defense regulation. Happy thoughts are to be tossed in the trunk of the car when you arrive. You pick them up when you leave," James added.

James cut his eyes at the young commander. "Dick Holman and I are old friends, in the event you can't tell, Tucker. Back to business. Admiral Holman is here because you're going to be spending a lot of time with him for the next couple to three weeks. Out in the next room is a French Navy Captain named Marc St. Cyr."

"I've had the pleasure of meeting this Captain St. Cyr," Admiral Holman said as he flopped down on the chair opposite Admiral James, who was sitting at the other end of the coffee table. "He was the aide-de-camp to Admiral Colbert, the French Admiral in charge of the French carrier battle group that I faced off Liberia." He pulled his handkerchief out and wiped his forehead. "Whew! I hate these Washington summers."

Holman reached forward and grabbed the silver-plated coffeepot. "Duncan, you got any real cups?"

"Impressions?"

"Well, Duncan, I would say St. Cyr is a professional Navy officer whose loyalty is to the person he is serving at the time. He speaks flawless English, and from the rough time he had between me and that *butt hole* Colbert, I would say he's politically astute. I spoke with him a few seconds before I came in here, so I guess the question I have is why in the hell is he here?"

Holman pulled one of the small coffee cups and a saucer toward him. The white Navy cups with their distinctive blue trace around the lip had been around for over a century. They held enough coffee to wet the palate, but—

"That's a good question, and one that deserves a good answer. Unfortunately, I don't have a good answer other than to say that it's politics."

Holman took a sip. "Then Marc St. Cyr is the right Frenchman for it."

Tucker wondered what the short, pudgy Admiral was talking about. If he met this Frenchman during the Liberian evacuation, then why did Tucker detect a sort of distaste from the Amphibious Group Two Admiral? From what he recalled, the French had sent their two nuclear-powered aircraft carriers off the coast of Liberia to help the United States evacuate their dual-citizen American-Liberian citizens. He even recalled how the two countries expounded on how close the cooperation was; so close, in fact, that Admiral Holman had placed his Joint Task Force under the French Admiral.

"Well, he's the one the French have sent. The British officer who will join Tucker will meet you in Norfolk. He's arriving late. Apparently staying in London for the Chelsea Flower Show," James continued.

"Hard to believe," Holman replied.

"Why?"

"The Chelsea Flower Show is held in spring, not August."

Holman recalled his first meeting with St. Cyr. They had arrived off Liberia about the same time the larger French carrier battle group showed up, acting like a blustery bully hell-bent on having him back down. St. Cyr had been the aide-de-camp of Admiral Colbert. Admiral Colbert had warned Holman that if he attempted to evacuate the American citizens who called themselves Liberians, the French would have to militarily oppose the operation. Seems the French government had decided Africa was their sphere of influence. If it hadn't been for those Unmanned Fighter Aerial Vehicles, he probably wouldn't have been able to sneak his Marines ashore under the eyes of Colbert. As it was, afterward, both governments decided it was best to show how they cooperated, once again proving to Holman and other senior Navy officers that the old adage of "out to sea is out of sight" was still true even in the information age.

"—the intelligence briefing."

"Sorry, Duncan. I missed that. What did you say?"

Admiral James's eyebrows bunched. "What is this? Is everyone asleep in this room but me?" He jumped up and looked in the mirror. "Or is it my voice? Have I reached the ripe age when utterances tend to induce sleep?"

Holman laughed. Tucker felt the blood rush to his face.

"Now, Duncan. You call a meeting for immediately after lunch in Washington, D.C., in the middle of a hundred-degree summer day, and you don't expect a man my age to fall asleep?"

"You're younger than me, Dick."

"And better-looking, too, but I try not to call meetings immediately after lunch."

"I said, we need to bring in St. Cyr, so Commander Raleigh can meet him, and then we need to walk down to Naval Intelligence for the Intelligence briefing." He pointed at Tucker. "Tucker, one thing you need to know. The failure of the New IRA to fulfill their contract means it's still out there. You're right to think they're going to come after you again. Whether they will send someone from Ireland, try to use a homegrown one here, or do it themselves isn't known. The FBI and CIA are both working to track down leads and see what they can discover."

"Thank you, Admiral. I also would like to thank you for having the Navy move me while I was in the hospital."

Duncan James raised his hand. "First, I understand it was easy to move you because most of your household goods were still packed and crated. And, second, it wasn't me that moved you but the Bureau of Naval Personnel in Millington, Tennessee. I didn't know it, but they have a shop down there that specifically deals with moving people who they believe are in physical danger. I think their primary customers are our married sailors who have a former spouse stalking them, or a sailor, officer, or dependent family living overseas who have unknowingly crossed a host country's criminal element. Seems to me they move a lot of people out of Naples, Italy."

"That's bull, Duncan. They never move anyone out of Naples. Everyone loves being there."

Tucker chuckled. "I recall a one-star admiral they moved out of Naples within two months of him arriving."

Duncan James grinned, pointed at Tucker, while looking at Holman. "Here is a prime example of an officer that BUPERS would have had to move out of Naples fast—probably same day."

"Why did they move this one-star, Tucker?" Admiral Holman asked as he patted his pocket a couple of times.

"I don't know for sure, sir. He was on the Joint Staff when I knew him."

"See. That's why he made flag, Dick. He knew better than to say such a thing while in Italy—and quit patting your pocket. I know you've got that ever-present cigar, and you're not allowed to smoke it here."

Holman brought his hand down and pointed his finger good-naturedly at Admiral James. "If you'd smoke one of these fine Havanas with me every now and again, Duncan, you might have been able to save some of that hair that's missing from your head now."

James rubbed the top of his head. "That baldness was from making fast turns under the sheets."

Holman nodded. "I've heard those fast turns were searching for your bifocals."

"Save the stogy." James glanced at his watch. "The Joint Staff Cigar Club is meeting in the center of the Pentagon around fifteen hundred. We'll sneak off and see what the gossip is in the Joint Staff, and you can impress them about how you get such a great smoke from a cheap cigar."

"I'll have you know these cigars cost . . ."

Tucker's mind wandered back to two days after he passed her. It was a Friday night, after a few drinks at this Irish bar in Pentagon City. She had grabbed his arm and insisted he come back to her place for coffee. He did, and stayed for breakfast. He recalled with a smile how the next morning the sheets wove over and under both of them, tangling their bodies between the linen. It was as if the bed had seen a massive fight and taken mystical actions to entrap them with the sheets. Moments later, when her eyes had opened, the sheets soon lost their entrapment. He grinned and surreptitiously glanced at the clock. While these two flags were pandering to some sort of Joint Staff cigar club, he would meet Sam.

"Commander, it's not good protocol to laugh when your superiors are duking it out."

Tucker's thoughts raced back to the room. "Sorry, Admiral. I don't know what I was thinking," he lied.

"He was probably imaging how a man with such bad knees and old age could rub his hair off making fast turns anywhere, much less under the sheets."

Admiral James held his hand up, palm out, and laughed. "This is fun, Dick. It's always good to have you come up," he said seriously as he stood. "Unfortunately, we only have a couple of hours before these two officers have to join you on the helicopter back to Little Creek Naval Base."

Two hours! Tucker's mind reeled. *Two hours!* He hoped they didn't mean today.

James reached over and flipped the intercom. "Chief, please ask Captain St. Cyr to join us."

First impressions are always lasting impressions, Tucker's father always told him. The Frenchman was immaculately dressed in his Navy whites with the familiar four stripes across his epaulets familiar to most every navy in the world. The face drew his attention. The French officer had his hard cover tucked under his left arm as he shook hands with Admiral James and Admiral Holman, his heels touching at a forty-five degree angle and him bowing slightly each time. The mustache—that was it. The dark mustache ran a thin line directly above the lip, with bare skin separating it between the upper lip and the nose. Shit! If he were going to have a mustache that tiny, it'd be just as easy to draw it on. Tucker had had his own experiments with a mustache years ago. The French officer had to spend time nightly to keep a mustache that thin peeked and marked.

He reached forward and shook the man's hand as Admiral James introduced them. Tucker was pleased to discover a firm grip. His father said you could always tell the caliber of a man by the firmness of his grip. *"Always give a firm grip—don't try to break the other guy's arm, but let him know you are glad to meet him. Don't give him one of these dishrag shakes that make you want to run to the bathroom and wash your hands. Christ! I hate men who shake like that."*

TUCKER GLANCED AT HIS WATCH AS THEY ENTERED THE Intelligence Briefing Room. Nearly an hour. The good news was the Navy had moved him to Crystal City across Interstate 395 from the Pentagon. The bad news was the Navy had moved him to Crystal City directly across Interstate 395 from the Pentagon. Seemed whenever anyone wanted to speak to him, he had to fight his way to the Pentagon, through increased security, diverted traffic, and humongous crowds of others trying the same thing. Then it took another hour to find where he was supposed to be in this five-sided wheel of national security.

"Admirals," the tall, thin Navy Intelligence officer greeted as he extended his hand. "I'm Captain Lawford, sirs. I will be the briefer today. The briefing room is down the passageway to your right, second door on the left." He glanced at his watch. "Sir, Admiral Marker will be here shortly."

"Quite all right, Captain," Admiral James said. "We're a little early."

The door opened behind them and in stepped a short brunette. Her brown eyes lit up as she saw James. "Duncan, good to see you."

"Grace Marker, late again, I see."

She shook his hand. "Seems to me you're early." She

turned to Dick Holman. "And, Dick Holman, what Christly twit convinced you to leave the sight of sea to travel inland to the Pentagon? Must be something really good."

"Or something really bad," Holman answered.

She turned to Tucker. "You must be Commander Raleigh," she said, shaking his hand with both of hers.

"Yes, ma'am, I am."

"Admiral James has told me you've fully recovered from your wounds and are ready to get back into the fight."

"I feel much better."

"You should. You couldn't have felt much worse."

Admiral Marker turned to Captain St. Cyr. Her smile broadened. "Captain St. Cyr, welcome to the Pentagon. I have established a traffic drop for you to exchange messages with DGSE, French Intelligence. You have several already there."

With a slight accent, he replied, "Thank you, Admiral. You are most kind." Shaking hands with her, he leaned forward, bowing slightly.

Admiral Marker jerked her hand back so fast she left the Frenchman's hand extended in the air. Tucker grinned. She must have thought the Frenchman was going to kiss her hand. That would have been a story Sam would have appreciated.

"That's good," she said, her cheeks turning red with a slight blush. She turned to Admirals James and Holman. Grins spread from ear to ear on their faces. She waved her hand at them. "Don't say a word, either of you."

"Captain Lawford, the briefing ready?"

Five minutes later, a Senior Chief Intelligence Specialist stood at the front of the room, flipping through the Microsoft PowerPoint slides as Admiral Marker and Captain Lawford took turns exchanging comments on them. During this time, an Intelligence Specialist had delivered a sealed legal-sized envelope to the French Captain, who had been going through the messages inside of it.

"This is where it gets murky," she said, nodding at the

French Navy officer. "And Captain St. Cyr may be able to help a little."

St. Cyr pushed the messages back into the envelope.

She motioned the Senior Chief to go to the next slide. "This is the chart of the small inlet where the unidentified ship departed four days ago. As you can see, it is south of Abidjan, Ivory Coast. French Intelligence arrived on the scene within twenty-four hours of the ship's departure. What they found were a lot of dead Africans and one barely alive. He passed a warning about loading a rusty steamship—at least that's what he called it—and that a bunch of Arabs sailed it out to sea after they loaded it. Captain St. Cyr, does French Intelligence know anything more than what they've shared so far?"

The Frenchman straightened in his seat, nodding at the three Admirals before addressing his comments to Admiral James. "Admiral, I have been reviewing the recent reports from DGSE. To summarize and add what little new has been recovered, we received words of an explosion near this inlet called Inlet del Rouge, which translates to Red Inlet. It is seldom used, we thought, because the waters are heavily polluted with human waste. Nothing lives in this small body of water except bacteria. The next day was what we would call a slow day in Africa, so the duty officer decided to send a patrol to the inlet to check the story of the Africans."

St. Cyr leaned forward, placing his elbows on the table and interlocking his fingers. "The entrance to this pier was open, and the smoldering shell of a truck was discovered. All around the truck, just inside the front gate, and along the sides of a nearby hill, were over fifty Africans—all but one was dead. The patrol thought at first that the truck had blown up on its own, killing the Africans. Africans sometimes overload transportation. What they discovered as they searched for survivors were some of the dead with single bullet holes to their heads. There would be no reason to put a bullet into the heads of people who are expected to die in an explosion, only to dispose of those who should survive one." His hands parted as he held up his index finger for a second. "One African was alive, but he died before an ambulance could get to him, but not before the patrol managed to interrogate him."

Tucker watched the movement of the French officer as he spoke. The motions revealed taught muscles; biceps stretched the openings of the short sleeves belying a first impression of a thin, lanky, Frenchman. As he watched, Tucker casually observed sinewy muscles creating faint ripples beneath the white uniform. This was no normal Admiral's aide-de-camp. What was his real job, he wondered?

"Based on what the man told before he died—about a huge square van so large a man could walk inside it—the patrol passed a code word to our military control center in Abidjan. Seems the van or container or whatever we call it suffered some damage, and the ones who had killed the Africans had waved a magic wand around it to check the damage. We dispatched a complete chemical-biological warfare team along with armed escorts to the inlet." He paused for a moment, slowly raised his hands from the table, leaving the elbows on it, and spread his fingers, palm outward, toward the listeners. "Just before sundown, one of the team decided to run a Geiger counter along the pier." He dropped his hands back on the table. "Nothing. Not a thing. He walked the pier, checked the few remaining boxes—of which nothing but rags were found—and still no detection. Unexplainable and against regulations, the sergeant forgot to turn off the Geiger counter when he had completed his check."

St. Cyr cocked his head to the side. "This is because the machine—how do you say it—eats up batteries, *n'est pas?*" Without waiting for an answer, he nodded again to Admiral James. "As he walked past the hulk of the truck, the machine clicked. Startled, the noncommissioned officer waved it around the area, and as he approached the bed of the truck, the needle went off the scale."

"What does that mean?" Admiral Holman asked.

"It means, Dick, that whatever they loaded from that

truck on board that ship is nuclear," Admiral Marker added.

"That is true," St. Cyr acknowledged. "The dead African said a heavy, dark van—probably black—was transported to the pier by the truck and loaded onto the ship. He did not say whether they loaded it into the hold or whether it was too big to fit. We think it could be tied topside on one of the weather decks. I would think the helicopter deck would be the better option. The other complication is that we do not know what type of ship it is. It could be a freighter; a collier; a cruise ship; a sailing vessel—though the size of the truck indicates it would be a large ship. A large enough ship to cross the ocean."

"You see where we're going with this, Commander Raleigh?" Admiral James asked.

Tucker shook his head. "Sorry, sir, I really don't."

"This ship that Captain St. Cyr has been telling us about is somewhere out there in the Atlantic Ocean. What we don't know is where it's going, and we don't know for sure that it has a nuclear weapon on board."

"Our analysis is very accurate," St. Cyr objected.

"Most likely it would be a dirty bomb," Admiral Marker interjected.

"That may be, Grace, but if that dirty bomb explodes in the Potomac, out there"—James pointed north—"near the Pentagon, it would contaminate everything within five to six miles."

"But Duncan, we don't know the size of it yet."

"Grace, prepare for the worst and you'll never be disappointed."

"We know it's loaded other supplies, but we're assuming it's the normal complement of food, water, and medicine for the voyage."

"Since we're unsure where the ship is headed, we have identified three possible destinations, using your concept of *worst case,* Duncan," Admiral Marker said, drawing out the last words. "We believe the ship is heading to the east coast or gulf coast of the United States. British Intelligence believes the ship may be heading toward Britain. The link between the Jihadists and the New IRA convinces them that since the New IRA did them a favor by going after you, Commander Raleigh, that the Jihadists owe a return favor. This theory complements the warnings to the British government that their unwavering support of America's war on terrorism would be punished someday, and this day has been identified." She nodded at St. Cyr. "The French, on the other hand, have ruled out Italy and any other country inside the Mediterranean Sea, because the choke points at Gibraltar and the Suez Canal are too guarded for a rogue vessel to successfully transit. Not to say one couldn't get through, but it would be very hard at this level of heightened security. Conversely, the French coast along the Atlantic and Channel are vulnerable."

"That is true, Admiral," Captain St. Cyr interrupted, holding up a message in his hand. "But, as of a few hours ago, DGSE believes the target will be Rotterdam."

"Rotterdam?" Tucker asked.

St. Cyr turned and looked Tucker directly in the eyes. "Yes, Rotterdam. Few people know that most of Europe's sea trade uses containers; ergo, container ships are the primary means by which commerce enters Europe. The superlarge container ships that travel the seas have only three seaports in Europe in which they can safely dock. Rotterdam, Netherlands; Algeciras, Spain; and, Livorno, Italy. Algeciras is on the Atlantic side of the Strait of Gibraltar, but we can safely seal it away because Gibraltar itself stands guard over this strategic city."

St. Cyr stopped and looked back at Admiral James, his eyes shifting as he talked between James and Holman. "Traffic into and near Rotterdam is thick. It would be quite impossible to inspect thoroughly every ship approaching this vital port. The Dutch Navy is aware and is increasing patrols. But if Rotterdam were shut down, then the economic fate of Europe would depend on how quickly another port could handle the merchant traffic or how quickly Rotterdam could return to service. Even a dirty bomb, as you call it, would effectively shut down the only city on this side of Europe to handle our imports and exports."

"And," Admiral Marker said, "*we* believe that this Abu Alhaul is more influenced by a desire for revenge than for tactical advantage. Therefore, the target will be an American port. And not a commercial port, but one of our military ports."

"Why?" Dick Holman asked.

"Propaganda. Imagine the mileage this Abu Alhaul will get out of exploding a dirty bomb in Norfolk, Little Creek, Jacksonville, or even Corpus Christi or Pascagoula, Mississippi."

"And there's New London, Newport, Rhode Island—"

"And Boston or Philadelphia," Tucker added.

Admiral Marker raised her eyebrows. "Why Boston?"

"USS *Constitution*. What better propaganda than destroying the oldest active-duty Navy ship in the world?"

Captain St. Cyr shook his head. "I disagree with you, my friend—a respectful disagreement." He turned back to Admirals James and Holman. "The Jihadists—"

"The what?" Admiral Marker asked.

"Jihadists," St. Cyr answered. "It is what we are calling those radical Islamists whose only call to their God is to die. Personally, I wish they *would* die, but they want to take a lot of people with them, as if their God would be overjoyed to see them arriving at the gates of heaven with a bunch of angry souls behind them."

"What do we call them, Grace?"

"You mean other than assholes?"

Everyone laughed. "No, we call them Jihadists, too. I just wanted to see how the French defined them versus our definition. Terms of reference are important for clarity."

"Same definition?"

"Close enough. The term Jihadists helps to differentiate the radical 'wanna die to be with Allah' bunch from the bulk of Moslems." She nodded at St. Cyr. "Go ahead, Captain."

"The Jihadists want to make a statement, but they must show they are able to take many with them. They do not differ between civilians or military. Age, gender, and religion mean nothing to them. If they could, they would line every non-Moslem up against the wall and put a bullet into each head with as little remorse as if they were grinding out the life of a cockroach." He ground his thumb on the top of the polished briefing table. "I believe their target will be either one of your Navy ports, one of the British Navy ports, or Rotterdam. My country's intelligence service believes the same, but places Rotterdam as number one."

Admiral Marker said, "We believe we can effectively seal the Yucatán Channel and monitor the traffic traveling in and out of the Gulf of Mexico. If our intelligence is correct, the target will either be Jacksonville, Florida, or the Norfolk/Little Creek areas of the Virginia Capes."

Admiral James leaned forward and drummed his fingers on the table. "Guess I don't understand why Washington has been ruled out. They have a proven track record of going after the same target until they have successfully eliminated or destroyed it."

She nodded in agreement. "I would agree, except this is a forewarned attack of immense magnitude. It's on the sea, and after Dick Holman sent their leader Abu Alhaul scrambling in Liberia, we think they will want to show their capability against the world's hyperpower. That means taking on our Navy."

James agreed, sighed, and looked at Tucker. "And this is where you come in, Commander." He pointed to Captain St. Cyr. "You will be working with Captain St. Cyr and this British officer, whoever he may be, to lead an American Special Forces team when and if this nuclear-armed vessel is detected."

Tucker leaned forward. "Yes, sir, Admiral—and, no offense to you Captain St. Cyr—but why are we integrating our teams?"

"Because our government, along with the French and the British, believe we need to reaffirm our support for each other in this reemerging global war on terrorism, and what better way than having warriors from our three nations working together to take out this rogue vessel?"

"Yes, sir, but—"

Duncan James held up his hand. "I know you're concerned about the work up and all that. I just sent my aide, Beau Pettigrew, to London to be our contribution to the British team, and Commander, Special Warfare Group Two, in Norfolk has dispatched a Navy SEAL from Little Creek, who is a Louisiana Cajun, to Paris to join that counterpart. We have three teams. One will be in Little Creek. Another will be in Portsmouth, England. And the French are working with the Netherlands to forward deploy the third team to one of their Navy bases near Rotterdam."

"And that is why you are coming back with me to Little Creek, Commander."

"Sir, I need a little time to pack my things," Tucker said, thinking about how he was going to tell Sam he was deploying.

Admiral James stood up. Everyone else stood also. "No bother, Tucker. While you were here, a couple of my staffers swung by your place and packed your sea bag. I apologize for doing it this way, but you can appreciate the precariousness of this situation and the importance of it being kept low-key until after we have defused the bomb or whatever it is."

Maybe he could call her?

"Plus, no telephone calls about this deployment. We will take care of your parents and will cancel any further medical appointments you have here. From now until we have found this ship and stopped it, covertness is the word. No telephone calls; no e-mails; nothing."

"Admiral Marker, are you going to tell him or should I?" Admiral James asked.

The head of Naval Intelligence inclined her head toward James. "He's your guy."

"Is there something I should know, Admiral?" Tucker asked.

James put both hands on the table, spreading his fingers so the palms were lifted. He took a deep breath. "This is where I tell you how your country needs you. How we know that your service to date has been outstanding and how you have been wounded in taking the battle to the enemy. Now that you are recovering, what you really should be doing is heading home. Take that second Purple Heart, wear it around—Where are you from? Georgia?" He lifted the edge of the folder in front of him, causing Tucker to glance at it. "Yes, Newnan. Take some time off with your parents and fully recover."

"Yes, sir. This does sound like the time to say that," Tucker replied. "I suspect there is something here I should know, Admiral?"

"Yes, there is, Commander Raleigh." James pushed back from the table. "We and the French have identified the one thing that could cause this terrorist leader to focus his plans on the United States."

Tucker raised his head. He was the reason.

"You're that reason. It is tenuous at best, but French Intelligence shows that if this Abu Alhaul discovers where you are, he may divert whatever plans are underway to take you out. In other words—"

"I'm bait," Tucker finished. He shivered slightly, unnoticed by the others around the table. An entire terror organization willing to—

"We think they're right in their assessment, even though they still place Rotterdam as their number-one priority. If this man is willing to spend hundreds of thousands of dollars to hire another terror organization for personal revenge, he would not hesitate to use his own."

"I understand, Admiral."

James shook his head. "I know we've subjected you to our frivolous banter this afternoon, but this is very serious. It's something that we've faced overseas; not here at home. This is where I ask you if you want to continue. If you decide to back out, no one will think the worse of you, Tucker. We'll ask BUPERS to move you again, and with a little tweaking, you'll disappear into the mass of the Navy; into the heartland of America to become anonymous until this passes."

He couldn't do that. For a fraction of a second, the idea appealed to him. "I can't do it, Admiral," he said, his voice harsh. No way anyone was going to chase him in his own country. He was no beardless ensign right out of college. He'd been in combat. He'd killed and been wounded. He'd chased and been chased. He'd also learned that the idea of the fight is always more frightening than the actual combat. If this Abu Alhaul wanted to come after him because he—Tucker Raleigh—had caused the death of the terrorist's family, then so be it. The asshole had better come well armed, because Tucker wasn't going to lay down and be executed like they'd done to so many others so many times.

James, along with the others, seemed taken aback. Then it quickly dawned on Tucker that they misunderstood his words.

Tucker's eyes widened and he held up both hands, palms out. "I mean I can't disappear and allow others to take my place. If we can stop whatever this man intends to do, and using me as bait brings him and his minions into the open, then I am prepared to do my duty."

Duncan James visibly relaxed. The two-star Admiral smiled. "Good, but I want you to know, Tucker, that you could be in Georgia by tomorrow and relaxing down there, hidden away from all this. While we are imposing strict operational security on this operation by restricting personal telephone calls and e-mail messages, Navy Intelligence is going to allow a slight slip in security—as if they never do—and ensure that word gets out as to you being located in Little Creek, Virginia. Then we'll watch and see if Abu Alhaul takes the bait. Of course, you can still take off to Georgia."

Tucker's grin caused his cheeks to rise slightly. "Sir, obviously you haven't been to Georgia in August," he said, bringing laughter to everyone but St. Cyr.

James pointed at Holman. "Admiral Holman is going to lead the at-sea search under the direction of Commander, U.S. Second Fleet. It means he'll be putting his amphibious ships out to sea along the east coast to hunt for this rogue vessel. Your job is to get the team ready and be prepared to act on little notice. Though Captain St. Cyr is senior, the fact that this is a U.S. action means you'll lead. The British will lead theirs and the French have control of the one protecting Rotterdam."

Admiral James walked over to Tucker and St. Cyr, shook both their hands. "A lot is riding on how we handle this. Tonight, the president will raise the alert code to red. That will bring lots of questions from the press that will have to be pared. Good luck, gentlemen. I leave you now with Admiral Holman."

Duncan James looked at Dick Holman. "Good luck, Dick."

Holman nodded. "Thanks, Duncan," he said, reaching out and shaking his friend's hand. "I'll need it." Holman unconsciously patted his left pocket.

Admiral James laughed. He looked at his watch. "Come on, let's head to ground zero and see if those shipmates from J6 are still there. You can smoke that damn thing before flying back. Otherwise, the way you keep patting that pocket, you're going to knock off what few medals you have or wear a hole in your shirt."

CHAPTER 4

"OK, BOSS," LIEUTENANT JUNIOR GRADE FORRESTER ANnounced as he leaned through the curtain leading to the cockpit of the Navy maritime reconnaissance P-3C aircraft. "We've a surface contact twenty-five miles ahead on a northeasterly course." The venerable P-3C maritime reconnaissance and antisubmarine aircraft was a four-engine turbo-prop.

Lieutenant Maureen "Gotta-be" Early shifted in her seat, tugging the seat belt to the right so she could look over her shoulder at the young man. "Alright, Win, tell the crew to strap in." When she faced forward again, she lifted one buttock for a moment and then the other. "This sitting is causing all the blood to settle in my butt," she remarked.

"Then, you must have a whole lotta—"

"Don't go there, Lieutenant," she interrupted good-naturedly.

"You know, Gotta-Be, all this up and down, flying around, buzzing holes in the sky may bother your butt, but it is upsetting my stomach," her copilot Scott Kelly said as he took another bite out of his tuna sandwich. A few bits of bread stuck to the side of his mouth. As he spoke, a piece of tuna fell onto his lap.

"Yeah, I see how much it's upsetting that cast-iron stomach."

"Yes, ma'am," Winfield Forrester acknowledged, his head disappearing back into the long fuselage of the four-engine propeller-driven plane. The curtain dropped back into place, separating the cooler cockpit from the heat of the multiple bays of electronics behind them.

Kelly held the sandwich away from his face, twisted it a couple of times, and through a mouthful of food, said, "You know, maybe keeping the stomach full of food helps keep it calm." He patted his stomach.

"Then you must have the calmest stomach in the squadron," Senior Chief Michael Leary said, leaning forward from the flight engineer seat located above, between, and behind the two pilots.

"That's why a young single bloke such as myself must forever keep watching his waistline and his health." He gave them both an exaggerated smile, revealing near-perfect teeth.

Maureen could learn to hate such perfection. She ran her tongue between the gums and teeth. Why should a man have those pearls after she spent her entire teenage years wearing braces?

"Hey! I heard that," Lieutenant Maureen Early said as she patted her own tummy. "Just because some can eat continuously and still lose weight doesn't necessarily mean you're normal."

"Well, the way you eat, Lieutenant Kelly, you'll soon have that waistline out where you can watch it better," Senior Chief Leary added.

"Funny, Senior Chief," Kelly drawled, as he dug into the brown paper bag lying on its side on the floor of the flight deck. He pulled out another sandwich. "Here, Maureen, have this one. It's anchovy with peanut butter," he lied, pushing his second tuna sandwich toward her.

She waved him away. "Gee, thanks. You want to see me throw up or something?"

"The something would be preferable, ma'am," the Senior Chief interjected. "We do have that new ensign back there," he continued, jerking his thumb over his shoulder. "Probably, if you offer it to her, she'd heave."

The voice of the Navigator over the intercom interrupted their banter. "All hands, set condition five. I say again, set condition five."

"Can we change the subject? The fine art of causing others to vomit isn't something that appeals to my well-tuned sense of decorum."

"Then you would surely hate playing jacks," the Senior Chief said.

"Jacks?"

"Or, worse, three jacks."

Kelly shook his head. "You don't want to know. Trust me. It isn't something sociably acceptable at most tea parties."

"I don't understand."

The Senior Chief laughed. "It's a Chief Petty Officer thing, ma'am." Jacks was an air-reconnaissance term for announcing when someone had passed or was passing gas. A rating of "three jacks" was an especially bad one, or a "good one," depending on your field of reference.

"Okay, if you two aren't going to tell me, then you both may go to that eternal place of damnation. Besides, whatever this three-jacks game is, if a man can do it, a woman can do it better."

"Ma'am, I have no doubt that women are probably better at three jacks than men," Senior Chief Leary replied, his face contorting as he fought back the laughter. "Many times I can recall losing to a female aircrewman in the middle of a flight."

Maureen nodded sharply. "I know I can beat you both. I played jacks when I was growing up—"

"Bet you were popular," Lieutenant Kelly said.

"—and if Chief Petty Officers can sit around playing three jacks, then I could probably play with the entire set of ten and beat your butt with one hand tied behind me."

Senior Chief Leary roared. "I can't help it! I can't help

it!" Tears rolled down his eyes. He pulled a handkerchief out of a knee pocket on his flight suit and began wiping his eyes. "Ma'am, I feel with the proper training, you could be a number-one jacks player. Here, Lieutenant Kelly, let her have your tuna sandwich."

Kelly spit part of his sandwich out, coughing to clear a half-swallowed mouthful. "I can't believe it," he stuttered, laughing through his choking.

Senior Chief Leary reached over and slapped the copilot's back. "Watch it there, Lieutenant. Choking has been known to cause an inadvertent three-jacks event."

"Okay, there's something here I don't understand, and chances are, when I do, I will be forced to wreak feminine vengeance upon you both."

Maureen tugged the green sleeves of her flight suit and glanced at her watch. "We'll give them a couple of minutes and then start our descent. Senior Chief, you and the eating machine keep a lookout for that contact. We'll loop down, fly around her a couple of times, and then return to altitude to continue our mission."

"Yes, ma'am, will do," Senior Chief Leary replied. He reached up, slipped a notch on the seat belt to give him more freedom to move; then he leaned forward, sliding the brown paper bag back out of reach of their copilot.

"Ah, Senior Chief, why in the hell did you do that?"

"Because, Mr. Kelly, at one hundred feet altitude, we need to keep both hands on the wheel. One of the first lessons my ol' pappy from Alabama taught me."

"Tell me, Senior Chief, if a man and woman get married in Alabama and move to Washington, D.C., are they still brother and sister?"

"Scott," Maureen said, "leave the Senior Chief alone before he reaches forward with one of those massive black arms and snaps your neck like a twig."

"Senior Chief, you wouldn't do that, would you?

"Sir, I have never disobeyed a direct order. Especially from someone who most likely can beat a Chief Petty Officer in a rousing game of jacks."

Lieutenant Junior Grade Forrester's head appeared between the curtains. "Condition five is set, ma'am."

"Win, have we notified home plate?"

"Yes, ma'am. Communications were rough since we are about fifteen hundred miles east of Roosevelt Roads, Puerto Rico. I also went ahead and relayed the contact through the USS *Spruance,* who is patrolling along the eastern end of the Caribbean Sea near the Lesser Antilles islands. Told her we were descending for a pass against a probable merchant contact that was a true course of zero-two-zero, speed twelve knots. They roger'ed up. We are to contact them once we regain altitude."

"We still have satellite contact?" Maureen Early asked.

"Yes, ma'am. The Cryptologic Technician Operator, or CTO, has contact, but once we descend to nearer sea level, the shaking and jerking of the aircraft will cause the antenna connection to be sporadic."

"You mean we'll lose contact until we ascend again."

Forrester shook his head. "Depends on the turbulence."

"I've heard that communicator mumbo jumbo before," Kelly interjected.

"*Spruance* says they've issued a weather alert. That storm west of us is turning toward our area. Home plate is weak, but I did get that they want us to turn toward home after this pass."

"That's great news. Only a ten-hour mission instead of a twelve-hour one where we drift back on fumes. Might actually have fuel in the tanks when we land this time," Kelly said.

"You got the contact report ready to go?" Lieutenant Early asked.

"Sure do. It's sitting on my screen. All I have to do is fill in the blanks, hit the transmit button, and the CTO will shoot the information to the satellite, where it will ricochet back to Navy Intelligence, where—"

"—it will be lost forever," Kelly said, taking a bite of his sandwich.

"Thanks, Win," Maureen said.

"Ain't technology wonderful?" the Senior Chief asked with a hint of sarcasm.

"Have we told Commander Joint Task Force America our intentions?"

"Yes, ma'am," Forrester replied. "I talked with their Operations after talking with home plate. The Task Force is off the coast of Norfolk, but we have better communications with them four thousand miles away than we do with Roosevelt Roads. They've given us contact number zero-five-six for this pass."

"We haven't identified fifty-six contacts this mission," Kelly interjected.

"No, sir. We haven't, but there were four other P-3Cs out here on this spread-fan search."

"And which, pray tell, part of the fan are we?"

"I would say we are the bottom part of it, Lieutenant. We're due east of the American Virgin Islands. The four P-3Cs north of us have already started their return to Roosevelt Roads."

"Lucky devils," the Senior Chief added.

The aircraft hit an air pocket, dropped several feet before its wings caught the air again. The Senior Chief reached out and caught Kelly's sack as it popped into the air in front of him. Forrester put his hand up, pushing down from the overhead.

"Wow, rough one," Kelly said.

"Okay, fellows," Early said. She glanced over her shoulders at Winfield Forrester. "Win, bring me a copy of the message you relayed to JTF America?"

"Sure, skipper. I can tell you what it said, though. It said we were descending to do an identification pass of an unidentified vessel—a vessel traveling on a northeasterly course of zero-one-zero, speed twelve knots. Also gave them the geographical coordinates of the contact along with our own position, course, speed, and altitude."

"That's good, Win, but I'd still like to see the report." She lifted up the metal-covered notebook wedged into a bulkhead pocket beside her chair. "I've found if I keep copies of what we send off the plane, then when I write our after-action report, I'll have all the data at my fingertips instead of having to chase down everyone on the flight to get the data together."

"Give him hell, Commander," Kelly said, referring to Early's title of mission commander. The copilot turned his head so the younger officer could see the exaggerated smile. He wiggled his eyebrows up and down several times. "No telling what he's been putting in those reports."

Winfield Forrester held up his right hand, and with his left hand wrapped around his index finger, he said, "You read code, Lieutenant."

"You two stop that," Early said. "Win, get me the message, okay?"

"Back in a jiff," he replied.

"Okay, team, let's go down for a look-see." Lieutenant Maureen Early reached forward and pulled the throttles back. The sound of the four engines reducing power vibrated through the aircraft. She pushed forward on the yoke, and the nose of the huge propeller-driven aircraft dipped as she headed toward sea level. It would take about five minutes for them to reach the low approach altitude. Then they would have to locate the vessel unless they gained visual contact on the way down. The way the cloud cover was thickening, Maureen knew there was a good chance they'd have to do a few circles to find it. Radar worked good on surface targets while flying at altitude, but the closer you flew to the sea surface, the more ground scatter affected the returns. But it sure beat boring holes in the sky.

Whiffs of dark clouds fluttered by the aircraft as they passed the ten- to twelve-thousand-foot ceiling where rain clouds formed and floated. Winfield Forrester's head reappeared between the curtains. He stuck his head inside the cockpit and handed a sheet of paper to Lieutenant Maureen Early. She took it, glancing back and forth between it and the front window as she watched the approaching ocean that filled her field of view. Passing the message to her left hand, she folded it with her fingers and pushed the message under the metal flap of the notebook.

"Passing nine thousand, skipper," Senior Chief Leary said to the mission commander.

"I've got a visual on the contact," Kelly said a few minutes later as they passed four thousand feet. "It's at our two o'clock."

Lieutenant Maureen Early eased the aircraft into a slight right turn, attempting to shift the target to their twelve o'clock position directly off their nose.

"Right there," Kelly said.

She straightened the wheel, steadying the aircraft in its descent.

"Still hazy, but looks like a one-two merchant," he said, using the Navy lookout description for a vessel possessing a raised deck at the bow and amidships followed by a flush deck to the stern.

"Look for some sort of huge black or gray van anchored to its stern deck," Early said.

Kelly lifted a set of binoculars from the small shelf to his right. He scanned the ship in the distance. After a minute, he lowered the binoculars and shook his head. "I can't see anything topside that matches that description. Could be they put it belowdecks. Maybe in one of those cargo holds. May be the clouds that are rolling in."

"Passing one thousand."

"Thanks, Senior Chief. Tell me cherubs, now." Most tactical aircraft reported their altitude in "angels" with each angel equaling one thousand feet. When an aircraft passed beneath the one-thousand-foot altitude, hundreds of feet were passed using the term "cherub." Reconnaissance and transport aircraft followed the commercial practice of reporting altitude above one thousand feet by referring to the first three digits of the altitude. They had passed through the cloud layer at altitude one-zero-zero—ten thousand feet.

"Yes, ma'am," he replied, rolling his eyes.

"Well, it's kind of hard for him to give it to you in thousands anymore."

"Lieutenant Kelly, let's be serious for a few minutes so we can make this pass, get the data we need for our report, and get back up where we can continue our dynamic discussions."

Kelly brushed his hands together, knocking off the crumbs, before grabbing the yoke tightly.

The aircraft banked right again, putting the contact onto the left side of the P-3C. "Let's bring the aircraft down to cherubs one before we fly by the contact."

"I doubt if we're going to surprise them," Senior Chief Leary said. "Unless they have no air-search radar."

"Why would they have air-search radar, Senior Chief? We've been flying all morning by these commercial ships. Commercial ships have little use for air-search radar. The first time they're going to know we're in the area is when we whip by their starboard side, wiggling our wings and displaying the huge American emblem on our port side."

For the next three minutes, conversation was limited to gauge checks as they eased down to one hundred feet. At one hundred feet, an air pocket, a sneeze, could send the aircraft into the drink, ruining everyone's day. The Senior Chief, in a low, steady voice, kept a running monologue of altitude as they continued their descent. When the P-3C reached a one-hundred-feet altitude, the two pilots, pulling back on the yoke together, leveled the Orion aircraft. Atmosphere is thicker closer to the ground. The sea-level atmosphere buffeted the P-3C as it fought its way through the clear air.

In the rear of the aircraft, the remaining, twenty-one crew members were buckled into seats, survival vests strapped tightly around chests and waists. A crash at this altitude meant a short, "tight butt cheeks" stay-afloat time.

Lieutenant Maureen Early pushed the internal-communications-system button on her control. "Listen up, troops, we're going to make an identification pass down the starboard side of the contact, cross her pointy end, and then come down the port side. Then, we'll decide whether we need to do another loop. If we do, we'll cut across her stern. Now, I know how much everyone loves to look out those small windows, but unless you need to be out of your seats, then stay in them until I set condition three."

"Dropping pass sixty feet, ma'am," Senior Chief said. "Ease up on the throttle and bring the nose up."

The specially modified P-3C slowed its descent. The strain of pulling out of the descent vibrated the aircraft. The rough weather moving into the vicinity added to the turbulence, jerking the aircraft violently for the few seconds it took to level out. A rough vibration settled on the aircraft as it bore through the thicker lower-atmosphere level. Early glanced out the small side window. The contact was stern on, about fifteen miles east. A spreading wake showed it heading on a northeasterly course. Probably toward the Mediterranean, or Portugal, or even the English Channel. It could be heading anywhere in that direction from this far away. Even with binoculars, the shaking and vibrating of the aircraft would stop her from focusing on it. She recalled the contact report LTJG Forrester had sent before they descended. The course of the ship had been accurately reported, she decided.

"Let's go," she said.

Maureen turned the yoke to the left, bringing the aircraft around and aligning it with the ship's starboard side. She estimated they were ten thousand yards; five miles from the contact. A few minutes later, the aircraft commenced a pass down the starboard side of the vessel. Besides the windows in the cockpit, three windows marked viewing portals along both sides of the aircraft. Along the port side the window directly behind the pilot was occupied by the CTO communicator who controlled the satellite communications between the aircraft and various intelligence agencies. Farther back, near an electronic warfare laboratory, a window allowed the mission evaluator and communications evaluator a viewing portal they could use, if they bent over and braced themselves against the bulkhead. Then, in the tail section of the aircraft, was the last of the windows located beside a small table where the crew ate their packed lunches. The main hatch had a small porthole window in it, but it was useless for surveillance. This main hatch separated the windows along the port side of the P-3C and the "feeding area," as the crew called the small kitchen. This hatch was where they entered and departed the aircraft. It was also where they would bail out or ditch the plane, if necessary. No one ever expected to bail out or ditch, but at the beginning of every flight, they executed the drills for each event. If you had to leave an aircraft before it landed, then your training had to kick in, ride through the shock and fear of the event, to help the aircrewmen survive. You couldn't trust your brain to figure it out in the short time available, so you trained and trained and trained, and hoped you never had to use it. A successful flight was one where you left the aircraft the same way you entered it. Alternatively, as Senior Chief Leary was fond of saying, *"A successful career is where the number of takeoffs equals the number of landings."*

Early pushed the intercom button. "You got the data you need, Win?"

"Doing fine, ma'am."

"I didn't ask how you were, Win! I asked if you had the information you needed to update the contact report."

A moment of silence passed. "It's a one-two hulled freighter, Lieutenant. Rusting red sides with even rustier white superstructure amidships." A one-two hull was a commercial vessel with a forward structure on the bow rising notably above the main deck. The superstructure near the center of the hull, usually where the bridge and living accommodations existed, counted as the second structure rising above the main deck. If the hull design had been identified as a one-three, then it would have rising structures at the bow and stern with nothing amidships.

"That's really nice, Lieutenant Junior Grade—*never to become Lieutenant at this rate*—Forrester. How about the important data?"

Lieutenant Early turned to her copilot. "Let's take us across her bow."

"There is something on the stern, Lieutenant. Could be that van we're looking for? It's covered with a tarp. We might be able to get a view beneath the covering, if you can bring us down another notch or two."

"Notch or two?" Kelly mouthed.

Senior Chief Leary rolled his eyes. "What would my mama say?" he asked to no one in particular.

"Okay, Win," Early replied over the internal communication system. "We're going to cross the pointy end of the ship; you get the name of this bucket of bolts so we have something for those pulling our strings from shore."

"We've got the name, but there seems to be some disagreement back here. The white letters on the stern identify her as the *Rinko Steel*. We looked her up on Lloyds' and it identifies the *Rinko Steel* as a Liberian-registered dry-cargo ship with a traveling crane. *Rinko Steel* is also a one-three hull construction. This *Rinko Steel* is a one-two hull with no visible crane structure.

"Sounds like a *bingo* to me," she replied.

"Bingo? We heading back?" Kelly asked. Bingo was the aviation term for an aircraft with just enough fuel to head back home or to an alternate airfield.

"Not that bingo," she replied, looking at him and seeing the mischievous smile.

"It could be, ma'am, but Master Chief Fremont seems to think it could be just another vessel with the same name. Plus, he did the scan analysis of the stern and saw no indications of a name change."

Changing the name of a boat by painting over its original or sand blasting it off was a common practice for pirates and drug smugglers who wanted to hide the true identity of a ship—a ship for which the authorities may be on the lookout.

"So, we think if we can get a sneak-peep under the tarp we can see if it has this gray or black van we're looking for."

Lieutenant Early turned to her copilot and flight engineer. "Let's go down the port side, so our crew can make their minds up."

She turned the yoke to the left, pushing her feet against

the pedals. The sharp sound of the hydraulics answering her motions was followed by a dip of the left wing. Early pushed forward on the yoke, taking the aircraft lower. She hoped this provided those cryppies in the back what they wanted. "Cryppies" was a slang term used by fellow Navy officers to refer to any of the small number of cryptologic officers and technicians who made up the Naval Security Group, a small nondescript command with a legacy of covert operations. If something bad was happening, or if the Navy wanted to know what the enemy was thinking, it was the skilled, silent teams of cryptologic warriors they sent forward. On board the P-3C, their keen analytical skills combined with technology made them a formidable asset on the front lines of surveillance.

Lieutenant Early turned and peered at the front of the merchant vessel less than two hundred yards from the aircraft. Several sailors on the bow of the ship wearing white sleeveless T-shirts waved. On the rusting white bridge of the vessel a couple of men, one wearing what she thought of as a captain's hat, trained binoculars on them. She half-raised her hand to wave back, but thought better of it.

Turning the yoke to the right, she leveled the aircraft for about thirty seconds and then put it into another left-hand turn to take them along the port side of the merchant.

"Damn! I've got a third *Rinko Steel* here. Naval Intelligence database lists *Rinko Steel* as a Greek-owned ship under Panamanian register," said Lieutenant Junior Grade Forrester over the ICS. "But, she's flying the Liberian flag."

"Sounds to me as if she got up on a bad day," Lieutenant Kelly broadcast back.

"Sounds to me as if she *ain't* what she is dressed up to be," Forrester replied.

"I've met some women like that in Naples," Senior Chief Leary volunteered.

"Okay, Win," Lieutenant Early said. "Take those photographs and let's get that contact message off the plane."

"We'll have to ascend to re-establish radio communications. This storm is kicking the butt out of our comms."

"Just think," Kelly added. "Here we are flying several hundred thousands of parts screwed together for our safety, built by the lowest bidder—"

The P-3C hit a small air pocket, dropping about twenty feet, sending the loose items around the cockpit off the shelves and onto the flight deck.

"Holy *shit!* With loose things such as that—could cause systems not to function properly when needed. I'm sure somewhere at Naval Air Systems Command there's a program manager who can explain why this is expected."

"When we gain altitude, we can transmit them. Meanwhile, ma'am, I have the communicators storing the contact reports into their 'waiting-to-be-sent' files for release."

"At least our search-and-rescue frequencies work," Senior Chief Leary said, replying to Kelly's observation.

"That's because they're commercial and not government issued."

"Okay, gents," Early said, "less bad-mouthing our fellow aviators in Washington and more attention to the controls and readings. We're at seventy-five feet, Senior Chief, so there's not much room for error. Keep an eye on our gauges."

Out the side of her window, the bridge of the ship passed directly to her left. Two men standing on the bridge wing watched the aircraft through binoculars. One of them stepped into the bridge. Within seconds, the object of interest on the stern of the ship replaced the bridge. A gray-black canvas tarp tied down by eight lines stretched tight over the object hid it from view.

"What do you think it is?" Kelly asked, leaning over so he could see out of the port window also.

Early shook her head. "Don't know. Could be anything." She pressed the TALK button on the ICS. "Win, you got enough data so we can gain some altitude and get off this jerky roller coaster ride?"

A gust of wind must have blown across the deck, for the edge of the tarp facing the aircraft raised slightly.

"Wheels!" shouted Kelly. "Whatever is beneath it has wheels. Look! They're untying the covering," he announced, pointing across Early.

She leaned back away from his arm. "How about grabbing the yoke and helping me fly this thing instead of acting like a kid on a sightseeing trip."

She peered out the window, having to look over her left shoulder as the aircraft continued its bow-to-stern passage along the port side of the merchant. Several sailors on the *Rinko Steel* worked furiously on the lines holding the tarp. Suddenly, the tarp flew off, giving Early a glimpse of black. She was too far past the stern forward to get a good view.

"We got it!" Win shouted through the ICS. "Ma'am, can you turn right and make another pass along the port side?"

In front of the cockpit, the wake of the ship showed the vessel turning to starboard. She shrugged. What was it going to do? Put on full throttle and outrun the P-3C? Even though the huge reconnaissance aircraft was slow by aviation standards, it was still faster than any ship.

"Let's put her into a right turn, Scott, and make another pass down her port side."

"Ma'am, this low altitude is eating up flight time," Senior Chief Leary announced.

"That's great news," added Kelly. "Means we can bingo to Roosevelt Roads sooner than we thought."

"Only a few more minutes, Senior Chief, and we'll go up a few hundred feet. Besides, we need to re-establish radio contact with *Spruance* and Joint Task Force America so we can update the contact report."

The aircraft leveled off and approached the turning merchant vessel from the rear. The wake revealed that the Captain had put the ship into a hard right-hand turn. Whatever the ship had, they didn't want the aircraft to know.

The ICS inside her helmet crackled for a second before LTJG Forrester's voice replaced it. "Lieutenant Early, Win here. We got the updated contact report off. *Spruance* rogers up receipt, but we lost contact before JTF America responded."

"Good work, Win."

"We're working a third update to tell them what's under the canvas."

As the nose of the P-3C reached level with the stern of the ship, a dark car slid over the railing and hit the sea. Early and the other two in the cockpit watched it sink. As it turned on its end, heading downward, she was able to see the tan interior of the automobile. Looked like leather to her. A sea of bubbles rose around it as it disappeared beneath the surface.

"Now, why in the hell would anyone throw away a perfectly good Mercedes?" Kelly asked, staring at the spot in the ocean where the car had sank. The churning of the merchant's propellers tore up the sea behind the commercial ship as its stern crossed over the bubbles where the car had disappeared.

"Looks as if we've caught us a car smuggler," Forrester said over the ICS.

"Car smuggler?"

"Yes, Ma'am. Ever wonder what happens to all those stolen cars in America? Well, they're shipped out of the country where they were stolen and resold overseas in some third-world country where documentation can be rubber-stamped with a slip of a dollar or two. My-oh-my, the Coast Guard is going to love this one."

"Okay, Win. Sounds like a nice interlude to an otherwise boring flight. You got enough so I can climb?"

"I do on this one, but the lab operator has a Marconi radar bearing two-seven-zero relative from our position. If we have it at this altitude, then the contact can't be more than twenty or twenty-five west of us. If we go up, we could lose the contact. The passive contact on the surface-search radar is weak, but surface-search radars bend to the earth's surface. If we go up, the lab operator may lose contact."

"Win, quit beating around the bush. What do you want?"

"Can we stay at this altitude and approach the contact? This way, we can maintain electronic contact and it'll guide up right onto the commercial vessel using the Marconi. Plus, it means we can probably sneak up on the son-of-a-bitch."

"Two things, Win," Maureen Early replied over the ICS. "One, yes we will maintain this altitude—"

"Ma'am," the Senior Chief said, his hand over the mike so it didn't carry into the ICS. "That is gonna eat up more of our flight time."

She nodded to the Senior Chief's comment and finished her sentence, "—and, two, watch your language. You want to be a bad influence on the young men and women who look up to you?" She smiled, exchanging winks with her copilot.

"Ah, Lieutenant, most of these men and women are older than me. Besides, it was the Senior Chief who taught me that phrase."

Early and Kelly glanced back at Senior Chief Leary, who placed his palm on his chest, fingers spread, and mouthed the French word, *Moi,* while shaking his head.

"Alright, you two," Early said, "let's bring it around left and steady up on—"

"Win," she said into the ICS. "Relative bearing is alright for visual lookouts, but what about a true course so we can turn this little piece of America?"

A few seconds passed and the Navigator's voice joined the ICS. "Pilot, navigator; recommend course two-five-zero to target."

Kelly pushed his mike down from in front of his lips. "Does Stan ever quit working?" he asked.

"Stan's the man," Early added, shaking her head. She turned the yoke, pushed the pedals down, turning the huge aircraft left. "I think he was born with a work defect. Put him in a room by himself with a sheet of paper and a pencil, and in twenty-four hours he will have developed a watch schedule. Come to think of it, I don't think I have ever seen him in the Officers' Club for Friday-afternoon Captain's Call."

She eased the yoke back, steadying the aircraft on course two-five-zero. The altimeter read one hundred feet, so sometime in the past thirty minutes they had ascended twenty-five feet. The shaking was still present, but seemed less intense. The turn west put the wind at their tail, and speed increased a few knots without her giving it additional throttle.

Fifteen minutes passed with the cockpit crew checking and double-checking the gauges. Early even had time to quiz her copilot on proper procedures for ditching one of these flying rocks. Every routine flight required the pilot in charge to conduct crew training, plus, as the senior pilot, she was also responsible for the professional development of her flight crew. Though she did wonder just what a Lieutenant could teach the Senior Chief that the old man didn't already know as a flight engineer. A quick erotic thought flashed through her mind, making her blush. "No way," she said.

"No way what?" Kelly asked.

She grinned. "That's for me to know and you to find out."

"Don't you hate it when she has these silent arguments that she settles this way?"

The Senior Chief leaned between the two pilots and pointed left about ten degrees off their heading. "I've got distant smoke," he said.

Early and Kelly looked. After several seconds, a faint but discernible white smoke rising from a funnel or funnels broke the horizon.

The Senior Chief used to be a Boatswain Mate before changing his rating to aviation technician. There weren't many AT's who were flight engineers, and he knew it. Of course, there weren't many sailors who recalled or knew how to report visual lookouts at sea. Distant smoke always was the first indicator of a ship in your vicinity. The horizon was approximately fifteen nautical miles from a surface position. It was a little higher at one hundred feet altitude. Distant smoke was a ship-lookout term to report a contact just over the horizon. The next to appear were masts, and when you saw them from sea level, you knew the two of you had fifteen nautical miles of separation. Then came the funnels and superstructure, followed shortly by the complete distant view. Another critical thing he'd learned as a young seaman during his deck plate life aboard the Destroyer *Stribling* DD-64 was that when you saw a contact growing bigger and it remained on a contact bearing, then you were going to collide with it. "Constant bearing, decreasing range," or "CBDR," was the term to describe this relative phenomenon.

Early turned the aircraft slightly, bringing the nose to bear on the visual contact. "Win, we've a visual on the merchant contact." She looked at the compass on the flight console. "We're steady on course two-four-zero."

"I hold us on two-four-two, ma'am," Forrester added.

"Thanks, make that two-four-two."

"I bet he folds his underwear after he washes them," Kelly offered.

"And why wouldn't he?" Early asked, perplexed at the comment. Her eyes remained fixed on the contact on the horizon. Visual contact at this range was tenuous. If she broke eye contact for more than a second, she could lose it for several minutes.

"He's single!" Kelly said as if that explained everything.

Twenty minutes later, the complete ship was visible.

"Win, this is Maureen; we'll do the same as before. Make a starboard pass, turn across its bow, and then pass down along its port side. You pass this contact to *Spruance* for further transmission?"

"Nope. We got that one transmission off, then lost contact. We'll keep trying, but we haven't had radio contact since we issued that contact update on the car smuggler. But I have everything on a file. Once we regain communications, we'll transmit the second update telling them it's a car smuggler, then we can sit back and watch the Coasties go eat them some crooks."

* * *

TAMURSHEKI PUSHED DR. IBRAHIM, CAUSING HIM TO stumble against the table. "Everyone is ready for when we reach America," he snarled. "Abu Alhaul insisted that you make sure we are healthy for the land of heretics. I have men leaning over the rails, throwing their food into the ocean. They are dying instead, and when they come here for help, you give them some trash about motion, old man. If they are sick now, they will be sick later."

Dr. Ibrahim pushed himself upright off the table where he had caught himself. He straightened his bifocals. He shook himself as if straightening his clothes, and with tight lips, the square-bodied Palestinian leaned forward, his face only inches from the lean, angry Tamursheki. "Let's get one thing straight, young man. I'm the doctor." He poked himself in the chest to emphasize his words. "I'm the only one on this death trap who knows what has to be done."

Tamursheki turned his head and spit in disgust. "And I am the one who is in charge." He turned, walked across the small wardroom compartment, and flopped down on a tattered sofa that was bracketed to a spotted bulkhead where paint from long ago had flaked off. "I am going to send them down again. You give them medicine or a shot or whatever to make them feel better."

Captain Aswad Abu Alrajool leaned back in his chair and laughed. "You are both fools," he said, looking at Ibrahim. When he turned his gaze toward Tamursheki, the laughter stopped. "But I'm sure you both believe very strongly in what you do," he said, licking lips that moments ago were moist with humor.

"I would be careful, Captain," Tamursheki said, his voice threatening.

"Yeah," Ibrahim added, looking at the Jihadist leader. "I would be careful, too, Captain, for this man—this youngster who is still wet behind the ears—may decide you don't know your job either."

Tamursheki leaned forward and put both hands on his knees. "As Allah wills, so shall I do."

Ibrahim laughed. "You don't scare me, Tamursheki.

You need me, and even when you have finished your mission, I am the only one who can ensure the *other* is completed." Ibrahim walked around the end of the table, behind the Captain, to the other side, putting the table between him and the fanatic. If Allah, God, or Yahweh, or whatever anyone calls their God, really existed, he wouldn't allow assholes like Tamursheki to be a member of his flock."

"We will reach the coast of America within the next few days."

Captain Alrajool shrugged. "That is true, but we don't know our final destination yet. Abu Alhaul told me to expect final instructions when we near the coast."

"Blessed be his name," said the Jihadist.

Ibrahim angrily shoved papers and charts across the table, some falling onto the carpeted deck. "And that is why, my angry friend, I cannot complete my medical duties. How do I know when to check the medical health of your men when your leader hasn't even told you the destination of this weapon? There will be shots to give to protect you from the diseases of America. Do you want your men or even you to catch AIDS? You've seen what it has done to Africa."

"There is no cure for this disease," Tamursheki said arrogantly.

"Abu Alhaul believes I can help protect you from this disease and anything else that may stop you from completing your mission, which is . . . ?"

Tamursheki's eyes narrowed for a moment before his face relaxed. He leaned forward, placing both hands flat on the table, leaning across toward Ibrahim. "We are to activate the device on the ship and then work our way to various American cities to await other missions. That is why you are along. We may be there years before we are called to do our duty."

"Glad you know what you're supposed to do," Captain Alrajool said. "What I need is a port where I can transfer this van. You want to activate it! I want to get it off my ship before it blows. Just remember that Abu Alhaul wants a seventy-two-hour setting on it. Less than that, and my beloved freighter could be dust."

Thinking of the large ticking van strapped to the stern deck, Tamursheki nodded. "It matters little where the destination is. What matters is that we martyrs are in good health and prepared to cross into paradise."

Captain Alrajool grinned. "You want paradise, then you have to go to Cocoa Beach, Florida. I went there once to see the rockets lift off from Cape Canaveral. My friend and I visited many of the dance places to discover that the women—no, young girls—dance completely nude. Without any clothes. They would change your dollars into single dollar bills—"

"That is enough, Captain," Tamursheki warned. "Your words are obscene to the word of Allah."

Ibrahim turned to the forward-most porthole in the compartment, leaned against the opening, and muttered, "That's really great. Bars in Cocoa Beach, Florida, are an obscenity to a prophet who married a five-year old girl." He turned back around, his finger pointing at the Jihadist. He started to say something, stopped, shook his head, and sighed. Where do they find these young men and women who want nothing more than to grow into young adulthood so they can rush off to kill themselves in some sort of macabre religious fever? Seventy virgins? Who do they think are going to get the seventy virgins? Martyrs or Marines?

"Something bothering you, Doctor?"

He ran his tongue across his upper lip, his thoughts on a bottle of whiskey, third drawer down, in his desk in the clinic, hidden under a bunch of papers. With this bunch, he wasn't so much worried they'd drink than they'd destroy it.

"I said, Doctor," Tamursheki said firmly. "Is there something bothering you?"

Ibrahim shook his head.

"Good. Then what do we do?"

"You asking me?"

"Of course, Doctor. You're the one who must see to

the welfare of my warriors. Regardless of where Abu Alhaul orders us to go, the men must be in the very best of health to accomplish their mission. Today, most are shaving their body hair."

"That's a thought I can do without," the Captain added.

"They are preparing themselves for the final battle."

Ibrahim pulled out a chair, swung it around, and straddled it. His chin level with the back top, he leaned forward. "What I will do is start the shots today. It will take a few days for the medicine to work."

"What does this medicine do?" Tamursheki asked.

"Didn't Abu Alhaul tell you?"

Tamursheki shook his head. "No, he said that you would ensure we were in the best of health to take the battle to those who have offended Allah. He said the days at sea would take its toll on his warriors, and that is why you are here. But, in the ten days we have been at sea, you have yet to see one of my men."

Ibrahim shook his head. "Not true. I have been seeing Fakhiri nearly every day."

"Now, there's a man with a stomach for the sea," Captain Alrajool added sarcastically. "He has seen more of the side of the ship than anyone else on board."

"He hasn't been the only one, as our dear friend Said Tamursheki has pointed out. The truth is, he is the only one who has come to see me." Ibrahim looked over his glasses at Tamursheki. "Instead of telling me how I have failed to take care of your martyrs, tell them to come see me when they're feeling bad. For Fakhiri, I gave him pills to control the nausea. He's getting where he can keep some soup down."

"Maybe you're right, Doctor," Tamursheki admitted. "He was rotund and cheerful in the ways of the Koran when we started. Today, he looks as if he hasn't eaten in months. He is growing gaunt and irritable."

"He is growing thinner, which is a good thing for a man his age. If you can't keep the fat off now while young, imagine how it will be when you reach my age and discover that you and your fat have grown quite fond of each other. He will get over it when we reach our destination and he puts his feet back on solid earth."

Tamursheki disappeared below the edge of the table, kneeling on the discolored carpet to pick up the papers Ibrahim had brushed onto the deck. "We must go over the plan again."

Both men groaned.

"I think we know it by heart by now," Alrajool objected.

"Let's do it another time."

Tamursheki pulled a bulging folder to him and untied the black cord keeping the opening closed. He pulled out a bunch of tickets. "I will send Fakhiri with the first group. His heaving and vomiting is causing concern with the others. They believe it is a sign of failure—a sign of weakness. Give him the medicine to protect us in America."

Alrajool laughed. "It's a sign of weakness—a weak stomach for the rocking and rolling, up and down, sideways to sideways, that a ship at sea endures minute by minute, hour by hour, continuously through the day; through the voyage. Even tied to a pier tides reach out to keep the movement going, as if to remind those who go to sea that the seas are the masters of the world. Complicating this normal rhythm at sea is the fact that a weather warning has been issued for this part of the Atlantic. Right now, we are running in front of a tropical storm that will give birth to a hurricane."

Tamursheki ignored the Captain's comment as he shuffled through the papers. Ibrahim recognized the bundle as the various airline, train, and bus tickets purchased in Mobile, Alabama, by one of Abu Alhaul's operatives. Federal Express had delivered the tickets to Tamursheki, and he had brought them to the ship. He figured since the tickets were to various destinations within the United States, once the men were ashore they would split up and head to wherever their ticket took them. He was glad that he had the highest honor for this job. Once the last martyr departed the ship, Tamursheki would set the timer on the device. He would ride with the ship into the harbor, and while they offloaded the device, he would disappear into the vast wilderness of America with his ticket.

"There," Tamursheki said, holding aloft four tickets. "Badr will lead the first group ashore and to the nearest city, where they will disperse to their assigned cities and locations. Fakhiri will go with him. His departure will relieve some of the tension from the others. Hisham, who has relatives in Chicago and has prayed to Allah to be in the first group; and, Jabir, the cook who has been told to take a job with one of America's fast-food places so he can be in place when the order to martyr himself comes."

Ibrahim stood up, glancing over at Captain Alrajool. "You need to find out where our final destination is going to be. Once this fool and the others are off the ship, then we have our own job to do, and that doesn't include killing ourselves for some—"

He saw Tamursheki's head whip around and realized he might be pushing the envelope. "—thing we haven't been told to do." He stared at Tamursheki, who with an unwavering stare narrowed his eyes at Ibrahim. For that fraction of a moment, Ibrahim saw the fate this man desired for him. For Tamursheki, the fanatic, death was an honor to share with others. Ibrahim had little doubt the man would consider killing him before the terrorist left the ship. He nearly grinned when he thought to himself that this lean, angry religious nutter had to receive the same medicine as the others. Abu Alhaul wouldn't be happy if Tamursheki did anything to him while the ship remained in transit. Come to think of it, Ibrahim wouldn't be happy either.

The door to the compartment burst open. Qasim, the huge Iraqi Shiite bodyguard and enforcer, blocked the doorway. "My friend," Qasim said, his deep bass voice filling the wardroom. He held the door open with one massive hand on the doorknob while the other held down the edges of his beard. "There is an aircraft approaching."

"Quick, get the men out of sight and off the deck!"

"Yes, Said. I have already ordered it done."

Tamursheki pushed against Qasim's chest. The Shiite stepped back into the passageway, opening just enough space in the hatchway for Tamursheki to run out.

"Come on!" Tamursheki shouted at Qasim as he sped toward the ladder at the end of the passageway.

Qasim followed. Captain Alrajool was only a few steps behind them. Tamursheki took the ladder two rungs at a time, heading up to the bridge. Alrajool's anxiety grew as Qasim blocked the ladder with his slower pace. The hatch leading to the bridge swung shut behind Tamursheki as Qasim reached the top.

Captain Alrajool pushed past the huge Shiite to rush to the starboard bridge wing just as the gigantic P-3C reconnaissance aircraft filled his vision. Tamursheki stood to his right, watching the American aircraft pass down the side of the ship. From the cockpit, he saw the pilot's head turned toward him. The sun visor on the helmet was down, blocking the pilot's face. Tamursheki's eyes traveled along the white fuselage to the two small windows near the exit door located about ten feet from the edge of the wing. The flash of a camera from the forward window drew his attention. Filling it was what appeared to be a giant lens.

He shut his eyes and lowered his head. *They've found us.* So much planning. He turned to Qasim, who stood just inside the door to the bridge wing. "Run! Get the missile!" he shouted, motioning frantically at the man.

The aircraft passed the bow of the ship and continued on its current course. *It must turn around,* Tamursheki prayed. *It must turn around.*

"Come to course zero-zero-zero!" Captain Alrajool said, poking his head inside the bridge. "Keep your speed twelve knots."

As if hearing Tamursheki's command, two Jihadists emerged out of the starboard side of the forecastle, onto the deck immediately below the bridge wing. He shouted, "Get up here! Now!"

The two men scrambled up the outside ladder leading

to the signal bridge above the bridge wing. Ahead of the ship, the P-3C turned left, crossing the bow of the merchant vessel five miles ahead of it. The American aircraft steadied upon a return course that would carry it down the port side. By the time the two men reached the signal bridge, the American aircraft was approaching the ship on the port side, off its bow.

Tamursheki ran from the starboard bridge wing to the port bridge wing, pushing a crewman, who was standing in the hatchway watching the approaching aircraft, out of the way. He stopped his forward rush with both hands grabbing the top link of the safety chain running along the port walkway. The roar of the four turbo engines flew across the ship, riding the wind blowing from that direction. He shouted instructions to the two warriors above him, and then realized they couldn't hear him. He climbed the ladder leading up to the open signal bridge and ran to where they squatted beneath a canvas awning.

"What are you doing?" he screamed.

"We are waiting for your orders!"

"I told you, *shoot it down!*"

They looked at each other curiously, turned their eyes up at Tamursheki, and nodded. He reached down and grabbed the nearest man to him—Boulas, the Yemeni camel herder. Why did incompetents surround him? Why did he have to make every decision? Did it take even a man with a little bit of schooling to make a decision to shoot down the infidel?

Qasim appeared at the top of the ladder. "It is turning again, Ya Affendi."

Tamursheki, still holding Boulas by the top of the white aba, turned and looked at Qasim.

Qasim made a circling motion with his right index finger. "It is coming back. Coming back down the right side," he explained in his deep voice.

Tamursheki pushed Boulas. "Quick. You and Dabir, get over there!" He pushed the man toward the starboard side of the signal bridge, forcing him from beneath the small canvas erected to protect the signal bridge from the hot sun.

Boulas grabbed Dabir, and the two men ran to the safety lines along the edge of the signal bridge. Tamursheki was directly behind them. He looked aft and saw the nose of the aircraft growing in size as the American aircraft approached for another pass. Near him, Dabir knelt on one knee. A mast jutting out from the deck masked him from the eyes of the pilots. Tamursheki reached out and pulled Boulas back slightly, positioning the Jihadist behind the mast.

"Ready?

Boulas looked at Dabir who nodded. "Yes, we are ready. God willing."

"Shoot it down when you have a clear shot."

They nodded. He noticed both were grinning. It is nice to enjoy one's work.

Qasim bumped into him as the big man joined them on the signal bridge. Tamursheki turned and shoved him away. Stupid giant!

The ship turned slightly to port as Captain Alrajool changed direction again. *What is he thinking?* Tamursheki thought. It wasn't as if they were going to lose the aircraft. It was there. Eventually other American aircraft would rush to join it. He may be unable to stop the others, but he would take at least one American aircraft with them.

Dabir stood and stepped closer to the deck edge of the signal bridge, turning so he could aim the missile launcher at the aircraft.

The engines of the aircraft suddenly increased in power, and as Tamursheki watched, it turned right, away from the ship, its tilt so sharp that it appeared to be standing on its wing. *They've seen the missile.*

The blast of the missile singed the right side of his face as it blasted out of its canister. A white contrail twisted behind the missile as it headed toward the aircraft. The aircraft righted itself. It was heading down, closer to the sea. The missile looked as if it was going to fly past the tail before it sharply corrected its flight path toward the aircraft. It must have locked on one of the right engines because it tried to fly through the tail of the aircraft toward it. A huge explosion rocked across the ship.

Boulas and Dabir started a round of "Allah Akbar" cheers. Dabir dropped the useless canister. The two men hugged and kissed each other on the cheeks before turning back to watch the wounded aircraft fight to stay in the sky. A huge gaping hole was visible beneath the tail of the aircraft.

A dark plume of smoke trailed from the hole, along with boxes and debris from inside the fuselage of the aircraft. A couple of bodies tumbled into the sea. The P-3C pulled left, bringing itself parallel with the course of the freighter. "Shoot it again," he ordered.

The two men looked at him. "Affendi, that is the only one we have."

"We have more," he said.

"Yes, but they're below. By the time we get them, the aircraft will either have crashed or flown away."

Everything; he must think of everything. Incompetent—the lot of them.

The aircraft was losing altitude. It could not be more than fifty feet from an ocean where increasing winds whipped the waves higher. It wouldn't recover, he told himself. It was too low. Suddenly, flames shot out of the hole, engulfing the tail section of the aircraft. The engine noise began to sputter and cough.

Five miles ahead of the merchant vessel, the engines quit. They watched, mesmerized as the aircraft slammed onto the surface of the ocean and bounced back into the air. The tail dropped next, dragging for a few seconds before pulling the fuselage into the water. The cockpit was the last portion of the aircraft to hit the ocean surface. Spray rose around the aircraft, blocking the view for several seconds. When it cleared, the aircraft rocked on top, sinking. Smoke curled around the tail section.

Tamursheki ran across the signal bridge, down the ladder, to the bridge. "Quick, head toward the aircraft," he ordered Captain Alrajool.

The Captain's bushy eyebrows bunched. "Why would I want to do that? They are soldiers. They will have guns and they will endanger my ship."

"They are not soldiers. They are pilots. And pilots won't have anything more than pistols." He stepped onto the starboard bridge wing, looking forward at the P-3C, assuring himself the aircraft was still afloat. A bright orange package tumbled out of the escape hatch over the left wing, quickly blossoming into a huge life raft. People scurried out of the hatch, sliding down the wing into the water near the life raft. Tamursheki saw the bow of the ship shift as it lined up with the aircraft. Those who had crawled into the life raft were helping others into it.

A blast of wind caught him in the face as the ship changed direction, causing him to shut his eyes. He thought he saw another life raft on the other side, but the waves blocked his view when he opened his eyes again. He grabbed a pair of nearby binoculars but couldn't see a second life raft, although with the seas rolling up onto themselves and breaking, a raft on the other side of the slowly sinking aircraft could be hidden. He tossed the binoculars back onto the nearby shelf, drawing an objection from the Captain about not breaking his glasses. They will make good hostages when the Americans show up.

"I'm not sure if we want to do this," Alrajool said, stepping out onto the bridge wing with Tamursheki.

"Did you hear me ask what you thought? No, you didn't. Your job is to do what I tell you to do. Not make suggestions, recommendations, or decisions. I will tell you what to do, when to do it, and most times how to do it," he said, never realizing that his minutes-before thought of being surrounded with independent thinkers who could make the right decisions conflicted with his actions. Arrogance is a vice always clouded with illusions. "Do you understand?"

"Yes, I understand," Alrajool answered with a sigh. He would be glad when this bunch was ashore. His bigger challenge was dumping the weapon on the stern into the waters off shore. He stepped back into the bridge and ordered another slight course change to correct for the actions of the wind against the freighter. The life raft ahead was being pushed away from the aircraft. On this course and at this speed, when they reached the crash area, the ship would be between the aircraft and the raft, putting the raft on the lee side of the ship.

Tamursheki nodded in agreement as he saw the bow of the merchant vessel line up with the orange life raft. It would take a few minutes to get there. He rushed into the bridge just as Qasim stepped inside from the port bridge wing. "Qasim, tell the men to get their weapons. We're going to have some Americans for entertainment."

"Yes, Affendi," he said respectfully. Qasim opened the interior door leading down the ladder to the main deck.

"Qasim, tell them they're not to kill them. I want them alive. If you have to kill one to make an example, make sure it is one of the leaders, but not the senior leader. Okay?"

"I understand," he said. The big man turned and hurried down the ladder.

Captain Alrajool listened stoically to the exchange, wondering how any of them would be able to tell who was the leader and who wasn't. Tamursheki's age exceeded the man's experience. He steeled himself for the carnage he knew these disciplines of Abu Alhaul were about to commit. Though he heard Tamursheki indicate they were going to bring them on board, he doubted the Americans would come willingly. He looked around the graying horizon as clouds continued to grow overhead and wondered how soon it would be before American aircraft filled the skies. Alrajool watched Tamursheki out of the corner of his eye as the terrorist leader ran from the starboard bridge wing to the port side of the bridge. The bridge wing on the port side was through a hatch that opened onto an open walkway running below the signal bridge. Alrajool ran his hand across his forehead. He should have brought his entire crew instead of the ten men he had with him. If he had his crew, he might overpower the Jihadists, kill them, dump their bodies in the sea, and flee south. Take refuge along the West African coast until they changed the appearance of the ship again. He glanced to the right as the aircraft approached off the bow of the ship and watched dispassionately as the nose disappeared beneath the ocean. For a brief moment, he thought he saw another life raft ride the top of a wave about a mile away, but then it disappeared. The shouts of the Jihadists and the sound of gunfire caused him to forget it. Tamursheki stuck his head back inside the bridge, and at the terrorist leader's command, Alrajool ordered all to stop.

The helmsman reached over and shut the hatch.

Tamursheki had no way of knowing that the aircraft had failed to report the presence of the terrorist merchant vessel and that the last message from the reconnaissance aircraft to Joint Task Force America was the report of the contact heading northeast toward Europe or the Mediterranean. Tamursheki looked down at the compass in front of the helmsman. Two-nine-zero.

The ship rocked as the waves coming from the west crashed against the side of the hull. He ordered a couple of revolutions on the shaft to keep the bow on course.

CHAPTER 5

"TUCKER, CAPTAIN ST. CYR, COME IN," REAR ADMIRAL Holman said, motioning the two men into the room. "Wing Commander Tibbles-Seagraves, you, too."

The three warriors represented the Special Forces of their respective countries. Tucker Raleigh had the sleeves of his camouflage uniform rolled up. The dark oak leaves of a Navy Commander pinned on his collars seemed out of place with the gold-plated parachute wings over his left pocket. The name RALEIGH was embroidered over the buttoned right pocket. Silver oak leaves identified the rank of Commander, but on combat utilities, the oak leaves were embroidered in black.

Marc St. Cyr, French Navy Commandos Marine—the term used for the French equivalent of the U.S. Navy SEALs—a head shorter than Tucker, followed directly behind the Navy Commander. St. Cyr's blue shoulder boards conflicted with the darker green camouflage uniform he wore. Where Tucker's utilities were clean and pressed, the Frenchman had permanent sharp creases along the front and back of the trouser legs. The sharp creases pulled tight from where the trouser legs had been wrapped toward the inside of the leg, then trapped by the sides of tightly tied combat boots. The spit shine of the black combat boots gleamed from the overhead florescent light. The creases on both the front and back of the trousers stopped a couple of inches north of the crotch. Two creases on the shirt rode upward directly above where the creases on the trousers faded into the waistline and continued onward to the shoulder, where they disappeared under the shoulder boards of five gold stripes. When St. Cyr turned slightly, the creases reappeared on the back of the shirt to complement the military preciseness of the creases on the back of the trousers. Three sharp creases ran down the back of the shirt.

"Thank you, sir," St. Cyr said with a nod. He held his dark beret in his left hand. A set of parachute wings decorated the spot over his left breast pocket.

Tucker and St. Cyr moved aside to allow their British counterpart to join them. Wing Commander Tibbles-Seagraves had been waiting for them at Commander, Special Warfare Group Two, in Little Creek, Virginia, when the two men had returned with Rear Admiral Holman. The short, squat Brit with his aristocratic accent had been participating in a field exercise with SEAL Team Six, the highly secret SEAL Team the U.S. government kept hidden away at a secret location for hostage rescue.

Tucker had been surprised to discover a Royal Air Force officer as the third member of their allied Special Forces group. He wondered briefly if his counterparts in France and England had had the same shock when a Navy SEAL had appeared as the U.S. member of this strange coalition. Politics were wonderful. One moment we're ready to go to war with another nation, and the next we treat each other as if we are long-lost siblings suddenly returning home. He glanced at Marc St. Cyr to discover the man looking back. France! Here was a country that had a love-hate relationship with the United States. One moment they could be the loyalest ally, and then you go to sleep to wake up the next morning to discover them tossing rat poison in your breakfast. Going to war with

France was like fishing with your mother-in-law. When they're not complaining and pointing out your faults, they're taking credit.

Tibbles-Seagraves saluted the Admiral as he emerged from behind the taller Tucker and St. Cyr who stood in front of him. His dark blue Special Air Service uniform—the famed SAS—deeply contrasted with the two sets of cammies to his left. "Good afternoon, Admiral," he said, raising his right hand in an open-palm salute. The man's eyebrows rose as he spoke, rising on an otherwise expressionless face. Slight jowls below each cheek twitched as his lips moved. The slight pouches beneath the Englishman's eyes made Tucker think of what his mother always said about them being an indication of heart disease. An old wives' tale, but one he had heard from others during his life and long after she had passed away. The image of the British bulldog came to mind as he assessed this new arrival.

"How was your experience with SEAL Team Six, Wing Commander?" Holman asked.

Tibbles-Seagraves answered, going over the challenges and the professional satisfaction of working with America's best. The SAS officer spoke with a nasal tone common to the higher classes of British society. It made Tucker think of a superior addressing a subordinate, instead of a Wing Commander addressing an Admiral. *How in the hell did the British manage to do that so well?* he thought.

"Thanks, Jonathan," Holman said, turning back to his taller Chief of Staff, Captain Leonard Upmann.

Tucker caught a slight wince from the British officer. He glanced away as he smiled. First-name basis wasn't in the British military manual.

"Leo, why don't you bring these gentlemen up to speed on events?"

"Yes, sir," the African-American Navy Captain said. He turned his gaze toward the three men standing at parade rest in front of him.

"Why don't you relax?" Holman said, motioning at the

three men. "You gentlemen, relax. This isn't an inspection," he said, interrupting his Chief of Staff. "Sorry, Leo, continue."

"Of course, sir," the man answered, bobbing his head slightly.

Tucker had read the Chief of Staff's biography before they had checked on board the Commander, Amphibious Group Two flagship, the USS *Boxer*. It never hurt to always do a little intelligence gathering when you were going into unknown territory, even when that territory was your own Navy. Bald on top with a light gray perimeter of military-trimmed hair. The deep bass voice rode easily through the compartment. Tucker had learned that the Captain had been Admiral Holman's Chief of Staff for nearly two years, which meant the man was up for orders. The last year was always the lame-duck year in any tour. He glanced at Holman, wondering what level of confidence the Admiral had for a man who had made headlines becoming one of the first active-duty officers to accept a Liberian passport as a sign of dual citizenship. It was legal. Congress had passed it on par with the laws authorizing American Jews dual citizenship in Israel. Tucker had mixed feelings about the idea of an American military person having dual citizenship, but he reconciled his feelings within the apathy familiar to military members who recognize an issue is outside of their control or authority.

"As you three probably know, one of our reconnaissance airplanes staging out of Roosevelt Roads, Puerto Rico, made contact earlier today with a merchant ship. It descended to make a visual identification pass and it hasn't been heard from since. That was six hours ago. About an hour ago"—he glanced down at a sheet of paper in his hand—"a commercial airliner landed in Johannesburg and reported picking up a distress signal around the same time Recce Flight 62 disappeared. By then, we already had a search-and-rescue operation launched on the fact that they only had fuel for two hours when they disappeared."

Upmann moved to the small table in the center of the

Admiral's stateroom, put spread fingers on top of a chart, and twisted it so it faced him. "Come here," he said, motioning the three men forward. Admiral Holman moved to the top of the table, looking at the chart from the top.

"Right around here is where we figure the aircraft went down. Center of this area is where we commenced our search effort."

"Thank you, Captain Upmann," St. Cyr said when the Chief of Staff paused to take a breath. "But, what does this have to do with our mission? We are here for the possibility of the terrorists moving a weapon of mass destruction into the area." Each "r" trilled off the Frenchman's tongue like a bubbling brook.

Tucker noticed Admiral Holman's eyes narrow as he stared at the Frenchman. Something had happened between the two men during Holman's Joint Task Force Liberia, where the Commander, U.S. Amphibious Group Two, had had to avoid French resistance to an American noncombat evacuation operation. But it hadn't been noncombat. The Admiral had had to fight his way to the trapped Americans and rescue them. Today, those same Americans now governed the country with democratic elections scheduled sometime early the next year.

"Hold on, my fine French friend," Upmann said, holding his hand up, palm out.

Tucker caught a slight flash of anger cross the Frenchman's face, quickly hidden behind a forced smile and the nod he gave Captain Upmann. Looking back at Upmann, he saw no recognition that the Chief of Staff understood—or, if he did, cared—the slight he'd given the French teammate. But he also recalled the sense of humor the French had when they would laugh at someone for their faux pas. Where had it been? Oh, yes, Marseilles, 2006, during a port call. He and a fellow male friend had been reconnoitering the dockside bars, soaking in the French social life along the waterfront. He had turned to his friend when they stepped into one of the rougher establishments and said, "Shut the door." The establishment had gone quiet when they entered. When he said, "Shut the door," they had erupted into laughter, ordering them drinks and singing drunken sailor songs until the wee hours, asking numerous times for them to say, "Shut the door." Shut-the-door became more slurred as the night wore on.

It was only later, near the end of the night—or had it been the beginning of the day—Tucker had discovered that "shut the door" sounded like the French *je t'adore,* meaning "I love you." The French sailors had found it amusing for American sailors to keep saying 'I love you' to each other.

". . . the contact reported before we lost contact with them."

Tucker felt foolish. He should be paying attention instead of recalling liberty ports and fun times ashore.

"What do you think, Commander?" Upmann asked Tucker.

He didn't know what he thought. Like a mouse in a trap. "I'm not sure what you mean, Captain?"

"I mean if the contact reported was last on a northeasterly course . . ."

"It means the rogue ship is heading toward England, Europe, or will attempt to go through the Strait of Gibraltar," Tibbles-Seagraves offered, avoiding eye contact with Tucker.

Marc St. Cyr shook his head, his dark hair remaining immaculately in place. "No, I disagree," he said in a rising curt voice. "I do not think they will go through the Strait of Gibraltar."

"Why?" Admiral Holman asked.

"Because, Le Admiral, if they're going to go into the Mediterranean, there are easier and better hidden ways to get there than sail from western Africa through the Strait of Gibraltar. They could have sailed from Libya or Algeria. They could have trucked it across the continent via Turkey and Greece. No, I do not think they will go to the Mediterranean. What I think is that they are heading toward Rotterdam."

"You may be right," Wing Commander Tibbles-Seagraves said. "But I would have to quantify the destination as Rotterdam. While Rotterdam is a damn fine choice to disrupt the European economy, sailing up the Thames and blowing up this superbomb in the middle of London would be along the lines of this terrorist organization. It would not only be an attack on both an economic mainstay of the global economy but against the Western world."

"France is not the Western world?"

"It could be one of many choices," Admiral Holman said. He looked at the aggrieved St. Cyr. "The good thing is France, Great Britain, and America are in agreement that the rogue ship is heading toward Europe and away from America. That means we're shifting from the original operational plan of dispersing our fleet along the East Coast to defend the homeland to one of defending our European allies."

"That means we're going to pursue them?" Tucker asked.

"Yes, in a way, Commander. We're going to pursue them, but you aren't, which is the real reason you're up here."

Admiral Holman moved away from the table and over to the green couch braced against the forward bulkhead. He sat on the edge of an arm of the couch and casually crossed his legs. Tucker expected the Admiral to slide off onto the deck at any second. "You three with the other members of your allied Special Forces are going to be off-loaded. We are sending you back ashore to Little Creek," Admiral Holman said. "Between the ship heading northeast and the approaching storm, our shores should be safe long enough to hop across the Atlantic and take out this latest threat."

"But, sir, if you run into this ship . . ."

"Commander Raleigh, if we do, then the French- or British-led teams will be responsible for taking it out. You're going to be detached to Special Boat Unit Twenty under Commodore West. That's in the event we're wrong and/or the rogue ship survives being sunk by the storm and is detected off the East Coast."

Wing Commander Tibbles-Seagraves covered his mouth with his fist and coughed, drawing their attention. "Sir, with all due respect, having three teams will increase the flexibility of the operations, and, even *if I do say so myself*—if they run into more opposition than they can handle, we would be a welcomed asset; I am sure you agree, sir."

"You're correct, Wing Commander. Having three teams would be best, but the agreement between Washington, London, and Paris is we divide this operation into three distinct lines of authority. Right now, Paris will assume command until it is sure the rogue vessel is not headed toward France or the European mainland. . . ."

Eyes shifted toward Captain St. Cyr, whose head tilted up slightly, chin stiffened, as if slowly coming to attention; the man's eyes focused on Admiral Holman.

"In the event the vessel's ultimate target is Great Britain, command will shift to Northwood, north of London, for their prosecution."

St. Cyr's chin lowered as everyone looked at Wing Commander Tibbles-Seagraves, who nodded sharply, never breaking his concentration on Admiral Holman.

"Sir?" Tucker Raleigh asked, raising his hand.

Holman held up his hand. "We can't take a chance they may change course and head toward the United States from a different direction. That being said, our agreement also says we will keep our teams within their own areas of responsibilities. The USS *Boxer* has two other SEAL teams on board that can be thrown into the fray if they need them. Plus we have Cobra attack helicopters that can blow the hell out of the ship if it looks as if the Special Forces team can't capture it."

The three Special Forces men exchanged looks.

"I guess, sir, if we know where it is then why don't we just launch some F-18 Hornets and blow it out of the water?"

"Because, Commander Raleigh, we need to know just

what that weapon is they loaded on this freighter. What does it do? Is it nuclear, as the French suspect? We think so. Both we and the British agree with their assessment. Do you know what this does to the war on terrorism if those spreading anarchy and death around the globe have nuclear weapons?" Holman held up one finger. "They only have to have one. They're like mines. You only have to throw one into the water to make the entire fleet start mine-hunting just to make sure there's only one. No, we can't take a chance on the ship reaching land, but at the same time, we need to know what the weapon is. Therefore, we will attempt to capture it at sea."

"Yes, sir. Then that makes it even more important we be involved in this operation."

Holman nodded, glancing at Captain Upmann for a moment before turning to face Tucker.

"You know, Tucker, if it was up to me, I would; but you, Captain St. Cyr, and Wing Commander Tibbles-Seagraves have to return to Little Creek." Holman sighed and held up his hand. "Gentlemen, that is the end of the argument. I know how you feel. I'd feel the same way if someone told me to turn around and head back to port when I know the enemy is ahead of me."

"Aye aye, sir," Tucker acknowledged.

Holman reached over and pulled a chart of the eastern United States toward him. The outline of the coast identified various navigational landmarks while small black figures dotted the waters, identifying the rolling depths.

"Come closer, gentlemen," Holman said.

Upmann reached over and pulled another chart in front of the Admiral. This one encompassed the Caribbean Sea and part of the central Atlantic. "Thanks, Leo."

"We are here," Holman said, placing his finger on the waters southeast of Virginia Beach, "on the farther end of the Virginia Capes operating area, VACAPES, as Surface Warriors like Captain Upmann call it, about one hundred nautical miles off shore, along with twelve other amphibious ships spread out in a line along this one-hundred-mile line." He leaned back and put his hands on his hips, reaching up for a moment to pat his left shirt pocket. "Each ship is separated by thirty miles as we patrol our sector. Nothing can get through that can't be visually seen for nearly seven hundred miles in the area that Amphibious Group Two has been assigned to patrol. Now, I'm going to regroup my command, under the orders of Commander Second Fleet, and head east. That means the Coast Guard will replace us, only they will be operating at about twenty to thirty miles off the coast and only have six ships they can deploy."

"Will this be leaving our coast uncovered, sir?" Tucker asked.

Holman shook his head. "It will reduce the coverage because the other ships of Second Fleet are returning to port, not only because Intelligence believes the rogue vessel is headed toward Europe but because of the approaching storm. If this ship should change course, we expect they're going to run smack dab into the U.S. Navy steaming right at them."

Tucker watched as the creases along the Admiral's forehead deepened. Holman looked up from the charts at Tucker. "Commander, you may have a point. The one thing I have learned over the years is to always expect the unexpected and you'll never be disappointed."

"We have our carrier the *Charles de Gaulle* coming out of the Mediterranean," St. Cyr volunteered. "It has its full complement on board."

"That you do, Captain," Holman answered. He reached over, shuffled the papers on the table, found what he was looking for, and held up a message. "This is the operational plan for bottling up those assholes. My good friend, and yours, Captain St. Cyr, Admiral Colbert has operational command from the middle of the Atlantic east to Europe and every spot of water starting one hundred miles south of England. Wing Commander Tibbles-Seagraves, your country has the OPCON of our three fleets north of those boundaries." He tossed the message back onto the charts blanketing the table. "The Royal Navy's new nuclear aircraft carrier, the HMS *Churchill*, has broken off sea trials in the north sea and is leading its battle group toward the English Channel. The British report their carrier battle group will be through the Channel and in position at the edge of their area of responsibility by late tomorrow night."

A brief knock on the stateroom door drew their attention. The operations officer, Captain Buford Green, entered. Buford's heavy Southern accent belied the Rhodes scholar brain behind it. Many first-timers in meetings with Captain Green came to regret their miscalculations after a session with this Georgia bulldog.

"Buford, glad you could make it," Upmann said.

"Admiral, sorry for my lateness," he said, drawling out the last word. "But we have an update on the search for Reconnaissance Flight 62."

Everyone turned toward the Commander, Amphibious Group Two, operations officer. "The four P-3 Charlies operating north of Recce Flight 62 landed safely at Roosevelt Roads, Puerto Rico. After refueling, they took off in a fan search toward the area where Recce Flight 62 last reported their position." He looked down at his shoes. "So far, Admiral, no joy. They have been ordered to return. Sun sets in about an hour down there, plus wind speed is picking up and rain is increasing in intensity. Our weather-guessers say the storm will either hit Puerto Rico or skirt by it to the north. Either way, they have put themselves in a position where they are right."

"Is there any way to keep them out there, Buford, for a short time after sunset? You can see lights on the water for miles in the dark."

Captain Green unfolded a slip of paper he had been holding. "I'll check and see, sir. I think they want to ensure they don't lose a second aircraft so soon after Recce Flight 62. A couple of other things, Admiral. Commander, Second Fleet, continues to be Joint Task Force America, but because the Atlantic Fleet is being ordered further out to sea to pursue this rogue vessel further east, they have taken the coastal operations away from us, sir."

"So, we are no longer running the Atlantic coast operations?"

Green shook his head. "No, sir. The Joint Chiefs of Staff have shifted responsibility to Northern Command for the defense of the coast. I suspect the Navy four-star at Northern Command will have the pleasure of working with the Coast Guard."

Holman nodded. "I can understand the shift of responsibilities. It'll be hard for us to execute two operations at the same time, and Northern Command is officially tasked with Homeland Defense. So, tell me, Buford, what is the search-and-rescue plan for tomorrow?"

"That's the second shoe, Admiral. Second Fleet has asked Admiral Pfeiffer at Roosevelt Roads to assume SAR responsibilities."

Holman nodded. "Good decision. Makes sense," he said, glancing down at the charts. "Would have been nice if I had had a chance to comment, but one thing we learned from September eleventh; you can't fight a war by committee. Someone has to make decisions, make them fast, and hope they're close enough to be right. As I always say—"

" 'Give me an eighty percent solution and I'll go to war with that,' " Captain Upmann finished.

"Leo, remind me to transfer you when I return," Holman said good-naturedly.

"So, what other good things do you have to tell me, Buford?" Holman asked.

Green opened the brown folder and handed the Admiral a sheet of paper.

Tucker recognized the paper as that used by the intelligence and meteorology departments. Downloaded satellite images were photocopied on this slick imaging paper, and when the machine printed it out, it left the unused side of the sheet with a shiny, slick gleam as if a fine coat of oil had been brushed across it.

Holman looked at the image on the paper. Tucker caught a movement out of the corner of his eye. St. Cyr moved forward toward the coffeepot sitting on a table across the room. Tucker looked over at Tibbles-Seagraves. The British SAS operative's eyes had narrowed, focused on his French counterpart. The spread of the SAS man's feet was not lost on Tucker. Did Tibbles-Seagraves really believe the French Special Forces partner was dangerous? The posture of the shorter Brit told Tucker the man was ready to make a move if something happened. Of course, the French had a long history of being the English foe. It should concern him, but no one would try something here—aboard a U.S. Navy amphibious aircraft carrier.

He turned his head in time to catch St. Cyr peering over the Admiral's shoulder. Intelligence collection! He should have known. The French were notorious about their intelligence collecting even against supposed allies. They had a different slant on it in comparison to the Americans and English, whose intelligence and military ties were so close that many times it was transparent to where the intelligence information originated or whose military forces you were working with.

Holman handed the paper back to Green. "And what does this mean, Buford? Maybe we should have our weather-guessers up here?"

"Yes, sir, Admiral. They're scheduled to brief you following this meeting. What it means is a tropical depression in the middle of the Atlantic has shifted course to a more northwesterly heading. And unless we want to go through the bulk of the storm, we're going to have to change our course to a more northerly heading for a couple of days."

Holman looked up and saw St. Cyr pouring coffee. His head twisted around to look at Tucker and the British SAS trooper. Tucker saw the expression turn to amusement as the Admiral looked back at St. Cyr. "Coffee good, Captain St. Cyr?"

The Frenchman took a sip. "It will do, Admiral."

"Good." He turned to Tucker. "Tucker, you three prepare for transfer. One of the Mark V's will be closing our position within the next couple of hours. You should have a nice ride in these developing seas on the Special Operations Craft. Captain Green will take care of arranging a helo with the Air Boss to take you across to the small boy."

The ship rolled slightly to starboard and then righted itself. "Buford, looks as if the storm has already reached us." For a ship the size of the USS *Boxer* to be affected by the seas, the waves had to be higher than normal or picking up strength.

"Just the fringe of it, Admiral. It'll pick up in the next twenty-four hours, and if we still have the pleasure of being around this area in the next three days, we'll get to see what an eye of a tropical storm, just shy of a full hurricane, looks like."

"Captain St. Cyr, Wing Commander Tibbles-Seagraves, and Commander Raleigh, it has been a pleasure to serve with you," Holman said, dismissing them. "I think you're going to have a rough ride back to Little Creek in that eighty-two-foot patrol craft. Hope none of you are prone to sea sickness."

After shaking the Admiral's hand, the three Special Forces men left the compartment. Minutes later they were in the stateroom where the ship's executive officer had assigned them bunks. Normally, a person of Captain St. Cyr's rank would have had a one-man stateroom, but unknown to the three men, Admiral Holman had dropped a hint that for security reasons it would be nice if the three shared the same six-by-eight-foot room. The French were known to march to their own interests, and Holman's experience off Liberia did little to resolve his intense distrust.

THE BOATSWAIN MATE FIRST CLASS MANNING THE helm of the Mark V Special Operations Craft took a hand off one of the long sticks controlling the waterjets, reached up, and pushed in the controls to the wipers. The spray of the rough seas slammed against the windows, shattering into millions of droplets to rain back down with the next spray. The sprays arrived in such quick succession that it seemed as if a fire hose was aimed at the windows, diffusing one moment and blocking the sailor's vision the next.

"Watch your course, Jenson!" the young Lieutenant standing to the helmsman's right said, his right hand above his head holding tight to a handhold like those in subway cars.

Without taking his eyes from the window, the Boatswain Mate replied, "I'm sure, skipper, we be going west."

"What course?"

"West, sir."

"West? What course west?"

"Don't know, 'xactly. Right now, I just wanna keep us heading west, sir."

The Lieutenant waved his left hand at the window. "Make it so, Jenson."

Tucker shook his head and pulled back into the small area behind the bridge. St. Cyr had his eyes shut, pretending to sleep. Wing Commander Tibbles-Seagraves's eyelids widened with each crashing wave, reminding Tucker of a deer caught in the headlights. Obviously, this British SAS had not been around the Royal Navy's Special Operations boats. But to the older man's credit, he hadn't been seasick.

Tucker Raleigh leaned back and glanced out of the small window behind him. Clouds were closing fast from the east, and they still had another twenty-five to thirty nautical miles to travel to reach the safety of the Virginia coast. The amphibious battle group under Admiral Holman had disappeared nearly an hour before, the faint wake showing their change of course before the growing ocean turbulence erased the watery trail of the ships.

Tucker forced himself up, grabbing the line strung from the front of the compartment where they waited to the rear near the hatch leading to the outside. He leaned down and stared at the ocean behind them. The Mark V was a fantastic craft. Two 2285-horsepower engines propelled the craft, using two specially configured waterjets. The Mark V could approach land so close that many times SEAL teams practically stepped ashore. The challenge for the small crafts, which operated in pairs, was to leave the shelter of shore and tackle the wild side of the ocean. Something they were doing now. Normally they'd be hitting forty to fifty knots across a normal sea state of two. He pressed his face to the small glass panel in the door and looked both right and left. A wave hit the side of the craft, causing him to nearly lose his balance. Probably a sea state five, he guessed. But, no way he was going to voice that opinion. The young Lieutenant up front with the Boatswain Mate was a Surface Warfare type. If he said sea state five and was right, they'd agree with him and exchange glances as if asking each other, *why is he telling us something we already know?* If he was wrong, they'd exchange the same glance as if telling each other, *See! Navy SEALs! Don't know a damn thing about sailing a ship.* That was true, but he knew lots about single-handedly sinking them.

He made his way back to the row of cushioned seats built along the side of the craft. The Mark V had a permanent crew of five and could carry sixteen passengers. They had more than enough room for the two SEAL teams that had been assigned to him and his two allied friends. However, Green told him, the Admiral was keeping the SEALs on board. Just because he couldn't use the three of them because of politics didn't mean they couldn't use the remainder of the team. So now the three of them rode the rough seas back to Little Creek to twiddle their fingers, make noises of allied cooperation, and when this crisis was over, tell each other how much they had enjoyed working with each other.

The craft tilted to port. Tucker twisted in the middle of the roll and allowed the momentum to seat him beside St. Cyr. He bumped the man, causing the Frenchman's eyes to open for a moment before they started to fade shut again.

"Sorry," Tucker shouted over the noise of the engines and the seas.

St. Cyr shrugged, his eyes opening. He leaned toward Tucker and nodded across the small compartment at Tibbles-Seagraves. "I think our English friend is finding the ride a little too exciting for his taste."

"I think it's a little too exciting for mine."

St. Cyr grinned. "I know what you mean. Most of my time in boats of this size has not been in the middle of an ocean inching toward shore." He nodded toward the bridge area. "Do you think they can increase their speed?"

Tucker looked toward the bridge for a moment, heard the Boatswain Mate shout something that sounded like "west," and then turned back to St. Cyr. "I think they're having to keep it at this speed because of the sea state."

"Bien sur," St. Cyr said, leaning back against the thin bulkhead and shutting his eyes. "I would do the same thing, I think. Just I would do it faster."

"We should be through this within the next three to four hours."

The Frenchman nodded without opening his eyes. "I believe you. I just hope this small craft holds together, because I hate to swim to shore from this far out."

"It would be a long swim."

"I'm more concerned how it will cause my skin to wrinkle," St. Cyr replied, winking. "Then how will your American women be able to truly appreciate a well-groomed French warrior, if I look like a prune?"

Tucker laughed. He glanced at Tibbles-Seagraves, who forced a faint smile in reply. He doubted the Englishman wanted to take a chance on talking. "Air Force," he said without thinking.

"*Oui.* And British, too."

CHAPTER 6

CAPTAIN ABU ALRAJOOL LEANED AGAINST THE FORward bulkhead of the small bridge. Taking the washcloth from the ledge beneath the windows, he reached up and wiped away the fog from the window. The shielded forward light on the bow did little to cut through the night. Its primary purpose was to warn other ships of the freighter's presence. He grasped the line running overhead as the ship rolled to starboard. The inclinometer read fifteen degrees. *Not bad that time*, he thought. The rain beat down on the large windows across the top half of the forward bulkhead. Eight wipers beat out of sync, fighting a losing battle to clear the torrent of water coming from the sky and the sea, pounding the ship.

"This is terrible," Tamursheki said from the darkness near the hatch leading off the bridge. "Maybe we should head in a different direction?"

Alrajool laughed. "This is nothing, my friend." He tossed the washcloth on the ledge, turned around, and brushed his hands against each other. "I have been through worse and so has this ship that you keep calling a tramp." He pointed toward the hatch leading to the starboard bridge wing. "What makes you nervous is that the clouds have blocked out any light a normal clear night would gain from the stars and the moon. Mix that with a slight sea . . ." He turned to the helmsman. "Ramos, what would you say the sea state is? Four? Five?"

The dark-skinned Filipino, one of the remnants of Abu Suwayf, licked his lips. His eyebrows scrunched as if he was thinking. After nearly a half-minute, he said, "I think, sea state six, boss."

"Tell our leader, here, why you think it is sea state six, Ramos."

Nearly a minute passed before the small, thin Filipino former-terrorist answered. He lifted his hand and pointed to the anemometer. "First, true wind is thirty-seven knots, coming from our stern. Second, the waves breaking across our bow, which is twenty-five feet above the water. Third, slight roles—ten to fifteen degrees; and the pitch, she is acceptable."

"Pitch?"

"Pitch is when the bow and the stern move up and down but not at the same time. If we reach the point where the whole ship is moving up and down, we call that a heave, and if you've a weak stomach, you'll discover another reason it's called heave."

"I don't understand a word that you say, old man," Tamursheki said defensively. "Your job is to drive the ship and get us to our destination. I have met you sailors before. Always talking in a strange language, as if the language of the streets is not good enough for those on the sea."

"For a man about to die, you possess a strong sense of arrogance."

"Do not toy with me."

Alrajool shrugged, walked over to the radar repeater on the port side of the ship, presenting his back to the terrorist leader.

Tamursheki watched the ship's captain bend over and put his face against the rubber face guard that surrounded and masked the radar video repeater. He had no experience with the sea, having grown up in the deserts of Arabia. His sea had been the shifting sands of the desert, and his ship had been the camel in his youth. The bow of the ship rose, a fresh wave of rain hit against the bridge windows. The sudden intensity of the water caught and held Tamursheki's attention. He wiggled his fingers slightly, letting blood flow through them. He hadn't realized how tightly he had been holding the metal bar protruding from the starboard bulkhead. He should go below. But he had been below, and the rocking and rolling of the ship made him nervous, which was why he had come to the bridge.

The hatch behind Tamursheki opened and another one of Alrajool's sailors entered. It amazed him to watch these men walk the decks without holding on to anything as the ship tossed and rolled from side to side. He had bounced off the bulkheads just walking from the galley to the bridge. The sailor turned, his legs bent slightly to compensate for the ship's movement, and pushed the locking bar down on the watertight hatch.

Alrajool looked up from the radar repeater. "Nothing out here but us and land smear to our southwest. Navigator, where do you have us?"

The Navigator, a slight man of Asian descent sitting on a metal stool behind Alrajool, reached over and flipped on a red light mounted directly over the table in front of him. He reached up and pressed a button to activate the Global Positioning Satellite System. "Ummmmm," the man mumbled.

"I need more than a guttural noise, Hung."

"I am taking a fix now, Captain," he said, using a compass to make a light pencil mark on the chart. "I have us . . . right here." He tapped the chart with the penciled end of the compass.

Alrajool turned around to the chart table. "Hung, we have to talk about your navigation terms. 'Right here'? What kind of talk is that?"

The man shrugged, picked up his tiny Turkish coffee cup, and tossed the thick, hot mixture down his throat. "Right here," he said again, his voice neither hostile nor pleasant. The Navigator revealed no emotion. It told Tamursheki the man cared neither whether he pleased Alrajool or made him angry. He had met men such as him everywhere he had fought. Men who had reached a point where even survival meant little to them. They surfed along the surface of fate, willing to follow whatever paths others chose.

"Where are we?" he asked.

Alrajool looked toward the dark silhouette of Tamursheki. "We are north of the American Virgin Islands; about two hundred miles." The captain turned to the sailor who was standing quietly beside the radar repeater. He held out his hand. "What do you have, Latif?"

The man handed Alrajool a sheet of paper.

Tamursheki caught the motion of the Captain's head as the old man looked up from the paper toward him. If he or any of his men knew how to drive this ship, he would throw the old man over the side to let the sharks feast on him. During daylight, of course, because he wanted to see the fear on the old man's face.

Alrajool reached forward and patted the sailor on the shoulder. Tamursheki strained to hear what the Captain whispered to the young man. He reached out to stop the sailor as he passed, but Alrajool spoke, distracting Tamursheki's attention for that fraction of a second needed for the sailor to disappear through the hatch.

"Here," Alrajool said, approaching Tamursheki. "You have your destination. Seems your boss, Abu Alhaul, has his own ideas of where we should go."

Tamursheki reached forward and jerked the paper from Alrajool.

"God grant me peace from children who never grow up," Alrajool muttered.

Tamursheki held tight to the bulkhead rung, afraid the erratic movement of the ship would toss him to the deck if he let go.

"There's no light here. Why don't you move to forward, where there are some red lights and you can read it," Alrajool offered acidly.

Tamursheki knew the man wanted to see him fall. This man, whose neck he could easily break, was trying to humiliate him in front of the seamen. He could do this. If this old man could do it, he could. Tamursheki eased his grip for a fraction of a second. The ship abruptly rolled to port, as if knowing the precise moment Tamursheki released his hold. He fell into the bulkhead, his hand eagerly grabbing the bulkhead rung again. He tightened his grip, ignoring the smile barely visible in the shadows across the Captain's face. The day would come when he wouldn't need this man, nor his crew. When that day arrived, he would make sure the man knew who put the bullet into his head, or knew who the man was who sawed the knife slowly across and through his neck as if working through a tough side of beef. He would enjoy the death of this man, even if Abu Alhaul trusted him to carry the word of Allah, but who Tamursheki knew lusted only after the American dollar. His lips curled. He handed the paper back. "You've read it. You tell me where we are to go."

He saw the shrug of the shoulders. Alrajool turned away from Tamursheki, moving near a red light mounted over the Captain's chair on the starboard side of the bridge. The Captain had little respect for him. This he knew. Alrajool turned so he faced Tamursheki, the red light directly on the paper in front of him. A flash of lightning lit the bridge, revealing a grin stretched from one side of Alrajool's face to the other. The Captain's eyes burned into his, but Tamursheki refused to look away. To look away would be to lose face to this man who would never know the pleasures of paradise.

These men of the sea thought themselves above those who had never crossed it. They thought themselves above the Allah of all men.

"You're right. I have read it, but you have the orders to execute. I can only tell you where we are going, and I can tell you how we are going to get there. But you must be assured that how and where I take you is where you are supposed to go." He handed the paper back to Tamursheki. "I'm not going to tell you what it says only to have you later say you never read the message. What do you take me for? A fool? I have dealt with others of your ilk and I know the games played to keep the advantage."

He jerked the message away. "Don't play with me, old man. It matters little to me if you die now or . . ." He stopped abruptly, but the words were already said.

"Or, what? Later? Don't try it, Tamursheki. I have more than the ear of Abu Alhaul. Here," he said, handing Tamursheki a red-shaded flashlight. "Even you can't read in the dark, my friend."

Tamursheki took the flashlight and pushed his arm through the metal handhold, using the crook of his elbow to hold him against the bulkhead. With the flashlight rigged for the night, Tamursheki read the short paragraph in English. When he looked up, Alrajool reached over and took the flashlight.

"I hate to lose these," Alrajool sneered, waving the flashlight at Tamursheki.

"He says we aren't going to Savannah nor New Orleans. We are going to . . ."

"I know. I didn't understand why either of those two were more important, would yield more damage, but"—Alrajool shrugged—"my orders are to drop off some of you along the way, and once at the destination, disembark the cargo. I'm sure you look forward to becoming a martyr, and the more I get to know you, young man, the more I, too, look forward to providing the opportunity for you to achieve your just rewards."

Tamursheki shifted, freeing his elbow and grasping the handhold again. The bow of the ship rose and fell. A wave broke across the bow, sending water breaking over the main deck and splattering against the bridge windows. "We will have teams to let off along the coast."

Alrajool nodded. "That's true, and I'll get you within range. After that, it is up to you. But I will only promise to disembark a team if we can do it without much danger to my ship." He turned and worked his way to the bank of windows along the front of the bridge. His knees bent, adjusting to the tilt of the ship as it pitched and rolled with the sea. A gust of wind whipped along the sides of the ship, drawing a long shrill as it hit the slight divides between the hatches and the outer skin of the ship. The weather was behind them. Its wind pushed against the stern of the freighter, driving it ahead of the slow-moving storm. "I won't jeopardize the ship any more than I have to, Tamursheki. There are other missions and only so many ships available."

The ship steadied for a moment. Tamursheki released his hold and fell more than walked toward the hatch leading off the bridge. A minute later, he was through the hatch and using his hands along the bulkhead to balance. He stumbled aft and down, seeking a place where the movements of the ship lessened.

Alrajool watched the terrorist from the open hatch for a few moments before shutting the watertight door and pulling the handle down to seal it. Several flashes of lightning lit up turbulent seas around the freighter. He looked around at the crewmembers on the bridge, who exchanged glances with each other. Then one laughed. Soon all of them were holding their stomachs, laughing at the "terrible" terrorist who could barely stand from his fear of the sea.

TWO DECKS BELOW, TAMURSHEKI OPENED THE DOOR leading to Dr. Ibrahim's clinic. Most of his men were there. Some sat cross-legged on the deck. Two lay on top of thin cotton blankets thrown on the deck, an arm across their eyes. The compartment smelled of vomit and tobacco. Four stood together at the far end of the large compartment that made up this makeshift clinic, talking and smoking.

Two stainless-steel medical tables were bolted to the deck in the center of the compartment. Jabir lay on one of the tables. The huge giant Qasim moaned softly from the other. Between the two tables lay Fakhiri, curled in a fetal position, spittle running from between his lips onto a towel stained yellow from vomit.

Ibrahim looked up as Tamursheki entered. "I see you found us," he said.

Tamursheki ignored the comment as he took mental muster of those here. The movement of the ship was less belowdecks. Of course, on the other hand, they were below the waterline. . . . He quickly changed thoughts. To drown before he sacrificed himself for Allah would be a great crime.

"I said, *I see you have found us*."

Tamursheki's eyes narrowed, his thick eyebrows bunching into an angry V. "Yes, I have been on the bridge with the Captain."

Tamursheki watched as the doctor lifted a hypodermic needle from the aluminum supply table beside the patients. Ibrahim pulled a small bottle from the metal chests, pushed the needle into it before lifting it to eye level to watch the liquid flow into it. He glanced over at Tamursheki. "You want one of these?" he asked, nodding toward the hypodermic needle.

"They stop the nausea," volunteered Hisam. He rubbed his ample stomach. "I am beginning to feel better already. Maybe some food . . ." His face turned gray. He grabbed a towel and heaved several strings of yellow bile into it.

"Give it a little time, my friend," Dr. Ibrahim said. He removed the full hypodermic and set the vial back into the gray metal container from where he had taken it.

Ibrahim looked from Hisam, who slowly slid down the bulkhead to squat with his back against it, to a cabinet on his right.

"I was throwing up and believed that my time to go to paradise was tonight," Hisam said weakly.

"It is amazing what this stuff will do with the proper administration," Dr. Ibrahim added with a wide grin.

"What do you mean?"

"Well, I was going to give this tomorrow, but the men were complaining of nausea, so I have given them the miracle drug purchased by Abu Alhaul and provided by my company."

"How long will it last?"

"Long enough. I can't say it will stop the nausea, but it will eventually take their minds off the rolling and tossing of the ship. What matters is they will be able to do their jobs when we arrive."

He plunged the hypodermic into Qasim's arm. Tamursheki saw the biceps contract as the needle traveled over an inch before the base of the hypodermic stopped it. A groan escaped. Ibrahim pulled the needle out and patted the huge man on the shoulder. "There, there, my gentle giant. That should do you. Just lay there and let the shot take effect," Ibrahim said with a chuckle. "Nausea will no longer be your worry in a few days," he said quietly to himself.

Ibrahim laid the needle on the cabinet shelf. "You're next, Tamursheki. Roll up that sleeve," he said, pointing at the leader of the terrorists.

Tamursheki saw the men staring at him. They wanted to see if he was going to take the shot. He straightened. The ship slowly rolled a few degrees to port, stayed there for a few moments, and then returned level for a couple of seconds before the opposite roll began. He waddled across the moving deck to where Dr. Ibrahim had prepared a needle. His lower pushed against his upper lip, and he stared with narrow eyes at the Palestinian as he rolled his sleeve up.

"Now you, Doctor?"

Ibrahim shrugged and turned his back to the terrorist leader, hiding the sweat that broke out on his forehead. "Don't need it. I have spent so much time at sea that I've grown used to how the ocean sometimes displays its displeasure at those who sail upon it."

"Maybe we should give this medicine to our guests?"

Ibrahim looked up, his mind alert. Did Tamursheki know what was in the shots he had just given? Something had alerted the terrorist leader, or else Abu Alhaul had entrusted the information to him.

Ibrahim lifted the cover to the metal container. "I have enough to take care of their nausea as well."

Qasim pushed himself up to a sitting position on the table. "Doctor, I feel better already. What is that stuff?"

"It is a placebo for nausea."

The men mumbled in appreciation, none of them knowing what placebo meant but all able to tell by the name that it was something medical.

"Well, this placebo is very good. I am hungry again," Qasim added, rubbing his stomach.

"When are you not hungry?" Ibrahim offered, his voice tense.

"Has everyone received their shots?"

"Yes. You were the last. And you were the one most deserving."

"Get your stuff together. We will go see our guests and take care of their nausea." Tamursheki looked at Qasim. "Are you well enough to visit our guests?"

Qasim pushed himself off the table and stood up straight. He weaved for a moment, the deck tilting forward as the ship rode down a wave. He grinned, balancing himself with both hands on the table behind him.

"You four, come with us."

"You should shave the back of those hands, Qasim," Dr. Ibrahim remarked as he picked up the chest. He started after Tamursheki, stopped suddenly, and put the medicine chest down. "Wait a minute," he said.

The leader of the Jihadists stopped halfway through the hatch. The ship rolled to starboard. He jumped back as the door slammed shut. A moment of hesitation and he would have had his fingers broken—possibly cut off. He hated these mercenaries Abu Alhaul had hired. Had they become so small that they couldn't find the skills needed within their own organization?

"What is it?" he demanded, his voice curt and harsh.

Dr. Ibrahim grabbed a couple of aerosol cans and held them up, just as the roll of the ship changed directions. "Take these and toss them into the compartment. It'll render them unconscious and easier for me to examine them and, if you so decide, give them a shot for their nausea like you have for your men."

"Let them suffer," said Qasim. "They are heretics. Worse yet, Americans. Let me slit their throats like the sheep they are."

Tamursheki shook his head. "You will get your chance, Qasim. We will take the videos we need when I am convinced that we have no use for them."

Qasim pulled his dagger and drew the back of it across his neck. "What use could we have for them?"

"I would use them as hostages," Tamursheki said. "I would kill them one at a time if the Americans should discover us. No, we must care for them as we would our own," he said, feeling no remorse in lying to a follower. Lies were okay in the eyes of Allah as long it furthered his word. "I may even allow the leaders of these Americans to live." He looked at Ibrahim. "So they may carry the fruits of our fight for us."

"I don't understand."

Tamursheki grinned. He reached up and slapped Qasim on his broad chest. "It is not for you to understand, my friend. It is for you to obey as Abu Alhaul has directed."

LIEUTENANT MAUREEN EARLY BRACED HER BACK against the aft bulkhead of the compartment. She shifted her legs farther apart to help keep her body steady, bending her knees so she could push against the vessel's movement. She had already fallen twice, and getting back up with your hands tied behind you was nearly impossible. She had had to wait until the ship rocked to the other side and then shift her body with it to roll upright. It was like doing a sideways sit-up.

"Must be some storm," Senior Chief Leary said, his deep voice carrying through the shadows of the compartment. "How is he?"

"Hard to say," Lieutenant Scott Kelly replied. "If we had more light than what's getting through that small porthole on the hatch, we might be able to tell something."

"His breathing seems fine," Early offered, looking down at the body lying on the deck between her and Kelly.

The ship creaked as it started another roll. The deck tilted to starboard for several degrees, rested a moment, and then rolled to port.

"Win!" Early called. She moved her foot left and pushed Forrester's leg. No response. The young mission evaluator had been unconscious since their captors had hit him upside the head the day before. The faint light shined on the caked blood that matted his hair all along the right side of the man's head.

"Where do you think they have the others?" Scott asked.

"I think they're in one of these compartments on this deck," the Senior Chief said. "At least some got away."

"Let's hope they did. I didn't see the life raft deploy on the other side of the aircraft."

"Yes, ma'am, but the aircraft stayed afloat longer than I thought it would. If they got out, maybe they stayed close until we were taken and then deployed it."

"I doubt it," Kelly said. "They would have deployed it as soon as they hit the water just as we did. If they got away, it will have been luck, seas, and Neptune looking over them."

"I would think they would have seen it from the height of the deck."

"I thought they were going to shoot us when they came alongside."

The ship creaked and rolled to starboard again. This time it took a few seconds longer to right itself. The lights flickered in the passageway outside the darkened compartment.

"I think that was what they intended," Kelly said. "I think it was only at the last moment that they threw the rope ladder down and ordered us to climb aboard."

"What do you think they want?" Early asked.

"Probably film us as they cut our throats," Senior Chief

Leary said. "I knew I should have gotten a haircut before we took off."

"Just what I need. More worry," Early replied.

"How many did we have in the life raft? How many of us do they have?"

"Ten—maybe a few more, I didn't get an accurate count before we were captured."

Senior Chief Leary sat across the compartment from them. She could see his flight boots flat on the deck in the faint path of light coming through the porthole. His legs splayed out on the deck like hers, he, too, was trying to maintain balance.

"Maureen, if I haven't told you, that was a text-book ditching you did yesterday," Kelly offered.

"Was it yesterday? Seems a lot longer."

"Any landing you walk away from is a good landing," Leary said, repeating an aviation mantra.

"In this case, we swam."

"I think you're right. They were going to shoot us. I wish I knew what changed their minds. I don't think it's, as the Senior Chief offered, to film our throats being cut, though terrorists in the Middle East, Asia, and Africa have been doing that. No, they have something else in mind."

"It can't be any worse than the thought Senior Chief Leary has provided, Maureen. Do you think we got the word out before we ditched?"

"No, sir," Senior Chief answered. "Not a snowball's chance in hell. We had no communications. The last message, according to Mr. Forrester, was the one giving the contact information on the ship heading north—the car smuggler. Unless someone picked up our distress signal, there's no way they'll know where we are. Lieutenant Jenkins would have been on the other life raft, and he is the one who would know."

"Even if they did get it, I don't see them being able to launch a search-and-rescue until this storm lets up."

"Well, where we ditched may not have any storm activity. It's been over twenty-four hours. At least that's what I'm estimating," Kelly said.

"We gotta get out of here," Senior Chief Leary said.

"How? Our hands are tied. The door is probably locked, and we've seen them looking in every so often. And, if we do get loose, what are we going to do? Jump overboard?" Maureen Early asked, bunching her shoulders.

"Ma'am, whatever we do, we need to do it soon. Whatever they plan won't be associated with us living. We already have our legs free."

"Yeah, and our hands tied behind us with those plastic thingamajiggies I've seen riot police use," Kelly said, pausing for moment before he added, "And, I lost feeling in mine a few hours ago."

Maureen shifted her legs. At least the compartment was warm. The dampness between her legs caused her skin to itch. She licked her dry lips. Water would be nice, she thought. She recalled her Marine Corps Drill Instructor during Officer Candidate School in Pensacola saying something about never going into battle with a full bladder or bowel. At the time, she thought the comment was crass and gross and meant only to embarrass the women in the company.

Today, she understood the relevance of it. When the body is in danger, not only does adrenalin rocket through it to bring the senses to full bore, the body either rids itself of unnecessary waste or it seals off the sphincter to further business. The bladder, on the other hand, has no such sealing mechanism. It just lets go. Another thing Early had learned in the past twenty-four hours was that life-threatening events caused the body to use up moisture as adrenalin spun up reaction time. The others hadn't had anything to drink either.

The smell of urine whiffed about them. The Jihadists had separated them from the enlisted aircrew. They had tied the hands of everyone with plastic handcuffs and shoved them into separate compartments. No food or water. No sanitation facilities. To the captives, they were no more than sheep, waiting for sacrifice.

"You're right, Scott. Between the three of us that was a perfect ditch."

"Yeah, you got that right, Lieutenant," Senior Chief said, a hint of amusement behind the reply.

The ditching had been perfect, she told herself, allowing her head to drop onto her chest. So tired. Sleep had been in dribs and drabs of seconds complicated by the pain in the shoulders, arms, and hands and, as the storm picked up in intensity, the increasing tempo of rolls and dips of the ship.

She had kept the wheels up. Never took her focus away from the control panel or the approaching sea but recalled hearing release of CO_2 on the number-one engine where the missile had hit. The flight engineer would have done that without asking. She was blessed to have Senior Chief Leary as her flight engineer. A good flight engineer was worth his or her weight in gold.

Moments such as this are truly moments of truth. How her flight crew performed determined whether they lived and whether they would be rescued. Even then, that "Old Man up above" had to be involved.

The Navigator, Stan 'the man' Jenkins, would have hit the prerecorded distress signal while slapping his hand down on the button that would have inserted their position based on readings from four of the twenty-four Global Positioning Satellites. GPS maintain stationary orbits around the world. If a commercial or military aircraft or ship is within signal range, an onboard emergency receiver activates. Those emergency receivers give a relative heading to the transmitter, and military receivers would have printed out the coordinates. She could only hope that everyone had been doing their jobs as the ocean surface hurried to greet them. Otherwise, Recce Flight 62 would become just more grist on the History Channel mill for disappearances in the Bermuda Triangle, even though they were at least one hundred miles from it. But far be it to let accuracy cloud a good story.

Something blocked the faint light coming into the compartment. A face peered through the porthole. This happened every few minutes. She wondered what they could see looking into the dark compartment. They could barely see each other, and they had their night vision. When they looked through the small window into the compartment there was no way they could see what their captives were doing. The face disappeared, and the faint trail of light appeared once again along the center of the compartment.

"Whoa, there," Senior Chief Leary said as the compartment dipped and then rose again. "I think we hit a big wave with that one."

The creak of the watertight latch drew their attention.

"Looks as if our hosts are returning."

"Hope they brought food and water."

"I wouldn't count on it."

The hatch opened about six inches—wide enough for a hand to reach in and toss a long can into the center of the compartment. It rolled into the faint light. A cloud of spray spewed from the nozzle, carrying a fine vapor into the air.

"Grenade!" Kelly shouted, rolling to the right.

"It's not a grenade. Hold your breath and shut your eyes!" Early shouted, knowing it was futile. They would have to breath sometime, and when they did, whatever was filling the compartment would fill their lungs.

Minutes later the three of them collapsed on the deck.

CHAPTER 7

TUCKER LEANED AGAINST THE DOOR, FIGHTING THE WIND trying to blow it open. The wind sent a keen whistle whipping around the edges of the heavy wood door. Rain blew almost horizontally, shooting through the opening, soaking him and the black plastic sheet someone had thrown on the floor at the entrance to keep others from slipping on the wet tile. St. Cyr dashed through the door, stopping a couple of feet inside, the rain beating against the Frenchman's back. Nonchalantly, St. Cyr pulled his wet beret off, shook his head, sending water everywhere as it flew off his thick stock of black hair. He squeezed the beret, water dripping on the floor, and then tossed the head cover onto a nearby coffee table to the left.

Tucker peered around the door, the wind and rain causing him to squint through closed eyes. Up steps, leading to two piers below, came the stocky outline of the Special Air Service Wing Commander, head tucked down with his chin against his chest. Tucker jumped back, holding the door against the wind, leaving it opened only wide enough so a person could slip through.

Tibbles-Seagraves shouted his thanks as he more dove

into the room than walked. Tucker pushed the door shut. Tibbles-Seagraves casually removed his rain slicker, picked up the Frenchman's cap, and hung them on the coatrack to the side.

"I say, chaps! Is this the Virginia weather for lovers I've heard so much about?" Tibbles-Seagraves asked, running a small linen handkerchief over and through the sparse strands matted across the top of his head.

"Seen worse," Tucker replied, struggling out of his raincoat.

The Chief Petty Officer standing behind the desk that doubled as the quarterdeck walked around the counter. "Morning, Commander," he said, reaching out to St. Cyr and taking his rain slick from him. "I'll put this over here with the others, sir." The Chief turned to a young sailor who was leaning against the counter near the opened green logbook, reading a comic book. "Thompson, put that shit away and go grab the swab again. Get this water off the deck."

"Aye aye, Chief," the young man said, hurrying over to the closet and removing a huge mop with a handle too big for the sailor to get his hands around.

"And when you finish with that, Thompson, get your ass upstairs and see how the coffee situation is."

"Yes, Chief," the young man grunted as he pulled the metal tub along the floor toward the front of the building.

"Chief, where is the meeting?" Tucker Raleigh asked.

"Most of them are already up there with the Commodore, sir. I would say it's more of a free-for-all than a meeting—what with this weather and all."

The Chief glanced at the sailor swabbing the deck and pointed to a puddle on the other side of the door. Without missing a beat, the young man spun the mop, the cotton strands spreading out like a fan, and dropped it where the Chief pointed.

"You have a friend here, too, Commander Raleigh. A Navy nurse who came in with the response team from Bethesda a couple of days ago. She's in the wardroom."

The Chief smiled as he walked away, chuckling as he shook his head.

"Ummmmm; must be nice, Tucker. Does each officer in your Navy have his own nurse?" St. Cyr asked, raising his eyebrows in amusement. "Of course, in France, they would bring a picnic basket"—he brought the tips of fingers to his lips and kissed them—"With a nice bottle of wine."

"Of course," Tucker said, convincingly. "Why else would we choose such a dangerous job if we couldn't get decent medical support?"

"In England, we have the National Health Service . . ."

"And I am sure some of the finest-looking nurses," St. Cyr said.

"It really depends."

The sound of approaching heels down the hallway to the right of the quarterdeck stopped the banter.

Lieutenant Commander Samantha Bradley appeared, a smile breaking across her face. She stopped at the end of the hallway and stared at Tucker. He was surprised to see she wasn't in uniform. Sam was wearing the revealing white blouse he had complimented with a risqué comment after a tryst in a park near the Pentagon. The fear of someone catching them had added to the moment. A pair of dark pants ended a few inches above black pumps. The overcast of the storm had forced the quarterdeck to turn on its fluorescent lights, inadvertently creating a makeshift stage for her appearance from the darker doorway. The light gave her dark hair a reddish sheen that Tucker had never noticed. It also played through the see-through blouse, revealing a low-cut bra, pushing pert breasts together, creating a small but eye-catching cleavage that enticingly appeared and disappeared between the two opened buttons on her blouse as she walked.

"Are you going to speak, Commander?" Sam asked, coming to a stop at the edge of the quarterdeck. A huge grin spread across her lips, along with a slight shade of red creeping up her neck.

He had lost himself in watching her approach. Tucker

stuttered a few times before taking a couple of steps forward to embrace the woman he had left abruptly a few days before in Washington. "What are you doing here?"

"What am I doing here?" she said, leaning back in his arms to look him in the eye. "Why, Commander Raleigh, I am your physical therapist, aren't I?" she asked, teasingly.

"I give up. We have nurses in the French military, but we would never give our junior officers a physical therapist," St. Cyr said.

Tucker reluctantly released his embrace of Sam, his left hand trailing down her left arm as he turned to face the two men. When his hand reached her hand, she took it.

St. Cyr and Tibbles-Seagraves stood side-by-side, broad smiles across their faces. Remnants of rain continuing to trail down their cheeks, dropping onto their cammies. Tibbles-Seagraves cleared his throat.

"Sorry," Tucker apologized. "Sam, this is Wing Commander Tibbles-Seagraves of the Royal Air Force, and this fine gentleman with the bushy mustache is Captain Marc St. Cyr of the French Navy."

Sam shook hands and smiled at St. Cyr. "I would say, Captain, that someone has removed most of the bush from your mustache."

The Frenchman smiled and nodded slightly. "I think your boyfriend makes fun of it." He reached up and ran his finger along his thin mustache. "I prefer to think it is the right statement without being too gaudy. I would hate for someone to think I was British." He nodded toward Tibbles-Seagraves, who reached up and twisted the end of his long handlebar mustache.

"I say," Tibbles-Seagraves retorted. "We, too, would hate for someone to make that mistake." He reached forward and shook Sam's hand.

Tucker smiled. Sam covered her mouth; a mischievous twinkle in her eyes met his. It was good to see her, but it would have been better if she had at least let him know she was coming down. Even though the focus of the search for the terrorist ship had shifted to the European theater, they were still on alert. Granted, sitting in the Bachelor Officers' Quarters, drinking beer, arguing whether to watch American or European football, and periodically commenting on the wind and rain slamming against the windows wasn't really what the general public would think of as military men on alert. These past three days had been boring. Today, they had been ordered to move their gear to the alert headquarters of Commodore West's near the Special Boat Unit Twenty piers. He hadn't decided whether to argue about moving here or not. He failed to see any reason for them to rough it here when they could stay in the Bachelor Officers' Quarters, where there was at least television.

"Penny for your thoughts?"

"I was wondering why you are here," he lied.

She released his hand. "Hope you're not disappointed."

"I am looking forward to seeing how you manage to disengage your foot from your mouth with this one, my American friend," Tibbles-Seagraves offered.

The telephone on the quarterdeck rang, saving him.

"They're here, sir. I'll tell them." The Chief hung up.

"Commander, the Commodore is in the control tower topside. He says y'all should come on up and join him."

"Sam, I have to go."

"Not to worry, I'm going with you," she said. She took his arm and pulled him aside. "Sorry, gentlemen, I need to give some professional instruction to my patient."

The other two men started up the stairs.

She kissed him on the cheek. He reached forward to take her in his arms, but she gently pushed them away. "You know, you're cute when you're lost for words. Bethesda needed a volunteer to augment the ready-response cell here on the waterfront, and the DiLorenzo Clinic at the Pentagon let me take it. I didn't know you were down here until I arrived at Portsmouth Medical Center and saw that Navy medicine had transferred your digital records to SpecWarGru Two. It was that little tidbit of information that told me why you hadn't returned my telephone calls."

"I wanted to—"

She laughed. "Sure, you did."

"No, honestly, I wanted to, but was ordered to board a helicopter with Admiral Holman—"

She laughed.

"No, it's true," he protested.

"Of course, it is," she said with amusement in her voice. "I have to admit, it's the best line I've heard so far." She waited a moment, and when he didn't say anything, she added, "Go ahead. I'm listening."

"Well, when I got down here, Admiral Holman hustled us aboard his flagship, the USS *Boxer,* and we set sail. We only returned to port three days ago."

"Telephones don't work?"

"Wait a minute. I tried to call. I even left messages."

She reached forward and touched him on the arm. He eased her into an embrace. "I did call, you know," he said.

"I know. I got your messages when I checked my answering machine yesterday. I tracked you down to the BOQ late last night and they told me you had moved out. It didn't take long to track you down. After all, you did say you missed me."

He lifted her chin and kissed her—a kiss that lingered, warmed, and drew his body closer to hers.

A series of loud coughs caused them to break apart. The Chief Petty Officer at the quarterdeck stared at them. Near the door, the young seaman was scrubbing the deck, back and forth the swab went, as fast as the young man could move it.

"Sir, ma'am; if you don't mind," the Chief said, jerking his thumb at the seaman. "Young Thompson isn't used to how officers greet each other, and I think the Commodore is waiting for you. He's not the patient type."

They broke apart, neither speaking to the Chief as they headed down the hallway toward the stairs.

"It's not as if this is a top-secret Special Forces mission, is it?" She stuck her arm through the crook of Tucker's elbows.

Tucker let out a deep breath. The building vibrated to a long roll of thunder. Behind them, a torrent of rain rattled the windows. He squeezed her hand. Everything was right with the world. He had worried his disappearance had sealed the fate of their budding relationship. Then again, others would say this relationship was moving too fast—doomed to failure and all that bullshit. Deep inside of him was the professional bachelor's mixed fear about rushing head-on into something where he may wake up one day to discover himself walking glassy-eyed down an aisle in the church with all the exits locked. Tucker ran his free hand along the mahogany railing of the stairs as they climbed toward the control room of the old 1950s tower.

The tower had been used to control seaplanes during World War II. It lay at the edge of a sea ramp where decades ago amphibian aircraft had rolled into and out of the manmade canal that lead to the sea. What had once been a tarmac for the vintage aircraft was now a parking lot for the sailors. He glanced at Sam, watching how her hair bounced softly off her shoulder. How like a curtain it hid her eyes and with each movement revealed a glimpse of her nose; a flash of smooth cheek; and always the dampness of full lips, leading the assault on his senses. He hated to admit he was glad the rogue freighter was somewhere in the East Atlantic. He was going enjoy this deployment.

TUCKER, ST. CYR, AND TIBBLES-SEAGRAVES STOOD slightly behind the Commodore, who had quickly dismissed any concerns with having a Navy nurse accompanying the men. He was a surface warfare officer assigned as the Commodore Special Boat Unit Twenty. Commodore Tony West stood about five-foot-five and had come up through the ranks as a mustang. A former Chief Petty Officer, he was fond of telling people that he had been a horrible Chief. When they had decided to clean up the ranks back in the nineties, they'd commissioned him as an ensign, figuring it didn't take much technical know-how to be an officer. He had had a good career. Not one that was going to catapult him into flag ranks. When you reached your fifties and you were a mustang to boot, the establishment still sat there like an anchor on top of the ladder. The ever-present "they" wanted those who wore the stars to have sufficient time left in their careers to make full Admiral—*four stars*. Fifty-plus-old captains just don't meet this unwritten age criteria.

But no one ever heard West complain about it. Most envied him. In the last three tours of duty, a small cadre of loyal officers and enlisted had followed him from his command in Rota to his duty in the Pentagon, and now to his twilight tour at Special Boat Unit Twenty in Little Creek, Virginia. You could say what you wanted about the old man, but you couldn't say it in front of this group.

"Commander," Commodore West said, the slight tremor in voice revealing his age. "Hope all of you are having a great vacation here in the land of love, as Virginia likes to be called."

St. Cyr nodded graciously at Tucker and mouthed the words "land of love," drawing a smile from him.

As much as Tucker hated to admit it, he was beginning to like the Frenchman, though as a whole Americans would just as soon see them stay in France. The old European country had taken a mantle upon its shoulders to be the balancing power of America's superpower, believing active diplomacy was an effective weapon to fight an overwhelming military strength. Even Evian water had suffered an economic setback since the debacle of 2003 when France led a coalition opposing American hegemony to dismantle rogue regimes. A few years later, when radical terrorists had hit Paris with a combined biological and chemical attack in the subway, the source had been traced to the former Iraq—the "Arsenal of Terrorism."

Commodore West had a deep voice, but he spoke fast, running his words together, and unless you listened closely, Tucker was discovering, you missed most of what the seasoned veteran said. His attention wandered in and out, as the Commodore addressed the weather and the Special Boats tied up at the base of the tower.

Tucker wondered briefly whether if he stayed for thirty-plus years in the Navy he would become prematurely gray and going bald on top like old-timers such as West. He patted his stomach. Would he get the leadership paunch that came with it? Must be stress. Of course, could be the liberty. Liberty before the notorious Tailhook Convention in the early 1990s was something that could shorten your life. The same sort of liberty after that Tailhook Convention would shorten your career.

"This has been some storm, Commodore," Tucker replied.

Commodore West laid his binoculars on the table in the center of the small control tower. "That's what I just said, Commander. Weren't you listening?" He took a step away, the binoculars falling off the ledge to dangle from the strap still wrapped around his wrist. West calmly unwrapped them and put them back in their storage area. "Don't know why I even bother with these things. Especially with weather like it is today. Can't even see the channel out there, and it's only two miles away."

West reached over and pulled a chart over. "I know this is boring for you three, being snake-eaters and everything. If I was as young as you and in your line of work, I'd want to be somewhere painful rather than twiddling one finger in your mouth and the other up your—" He looked at Sam and stopped. "Well, you know. Different subject, gentlemen and lady. First, let me say, the Admiral briefed me on the rationale for combining operations with our British and French allies." He nodded sharply, and then looked up at St. Cyr and Tibbles-Seagraves. "Can't say we have seen much cooperative spirit with our French allies this century, so this makes what I hope is a pleasant change, especially after the confrontation off Liberia last year."

St. Cyr raised his finger. "Ah, Commodore, with all due respect, sir," he said. The Commodore and he were the same rank, even if West was older than his father. He wagged his finger at the Navy Captain. "There was no confrontation. We had an unfortunate misunderstanding during a combined exercise. I am sure Admiral Holman would agree with that statement."

West's lower lip arched upward, covering his upper lip. His eyes narrowed. "Of course, Captain," he said sharply. "One thing we understand thoroughly in my United States Navy is that our government is never wrong regardless of which administration is in office. Luckily for us, the misunderstanding failed to stop our evacuation of American citizens. But, then, with allies such as France, we were doomed to success in the first place."

Tucker saw a faint red color his French counterpart's neck. One thing about the French—they were a nationalistic bunch that demanded respect.

"Of course, Commodore. I am sure it is as you say," St. Cyr responded tartly. "I meant no offense."

"Offense!" Commodore West guffawed. Then, in barely a whisper, he added, "That's a word I doubt you know."

This was headed downhill fast, a direction Tucker would prefer to avoid. If this continued, the Commodore would probably start working his way back in history to other instances of French and American differences, such as the Iraqi War.

"Sir, when can we expect the weather to clear, and have you heard anything from the operations around Europe?"

The old Captain sighed, rubbing the slight stubble from his early-morning shave. "Touché, Commander. You'll go far in this Navy." He turned to a slim Commander who had the countenance of a long-distance jogger, thought Tucker, until he noticed the half-opened pack of cigarettes half-hidden under the newspaper near the Commander. The officer pushed himself off the forward bulkhead.

"Yes, sir, Commodore."

"John, tell them what you told me earlier."

The man moved out of the gray shadows caused by the morning overcast to the lighted area near the table. "First," he said, in a high, tenor-like voice, "the tropical storm is wavering between remaining a tropical storm and being reclassified as a hurricane." He pulled the chart away from in front of Commodore West, flipped it around so it was right side up for Tucker and the others. He placed his finger on an area north of Bermuda and about five hundred nautical miles off the east coast of North Carolina. "The storm has slowed here. It's being hit by a high front to the north and an equally low front from the south and east. It's created a weather anomaly that has slowed the storm's movement while keeping its energy from growing. Moreover, it's keeping it from losing any of its energy, as these fronts have one giving the storm more moisture and the other maintaining the wind momentum for it. Within the next twenty-four to thirty-six hours, one of those fronts is going to give way to the other. Until that happens, the storm is going to keep its slow movement on the same heading. Which front gives way and how it moves will determine the course, speed, and whether we inherit a hurricane or not."

"Could it blow itself out?" Sam asked from the rear.

"No, ma'am," the Commander replied.

"I'm a ma'am, but I'm also an active-duty Navy nurse—Lieutenant Commander," she said, making sure the meteorologist knew she was junior to him in rank.

The meteorologist nodded. "No, it won't blow itself out immediately. What'll happen is it will react like a blast of water trapped in a garden hose when you first open the nozzle. It'll shoot out of the entrapment, taking everything in its path with it. I talked with the National Weather Service earlier this morning, and while it's still classified as a tropical storm, they're preparing to call it a hurricane if the wind picks up speed, when it catapults out of this frontal vise."

"I guess I don't have to ask which direction it's headed?" Tucker asked.

"Right now it's moving at five knots on a northwesterly course."

"Northwest. Means it's headed this direction?"

"Yeap," the Commodore acknowledged. "Means it is headed this direction. Also means that we're going to batten down everything we can in the event it should decide to come ashore here in the Tidewater area."

"The Commodore is correct," the Commander agreed. "If the storm heads directly for us, it'll most likely be the most powerful hurricane to hit Virginia since Isabel. It's only five hundred miles away and traveling at five knots. Every ten hours it chops the distance by fifty miles." The officer paused for a moment, shaking his head. "Lots of unknowns here. How much is the slow movement of the storm influencing the balancing act of the high and low fronts? How much speed will it pick up when the balancing act ends? And will the balancing between the high and low fronts dissipate slowly or"—he clapped his hands together—"disappear all at once? If it's slow, then it may not reach hurricane force, but if those two fronts move apart suddenly, then I agree with the National Weather Service's worse-case analysis that the winds could quickly go from eighty miles an hour to one hundred sixty miles an hour. And with only five hundred miles between it and the East Coast, there's insufficient distance to give the winds time to lose strength before they slam ashore somewhere along our middle Atlantic coast."

Tibbles-Seagraves leaned forward. "So, the storm may hit here?"

The Commander shook his head. "Could," he said, shrugging his shoulders. "But not necessarily. We won't have a good idea where it's heading until those fronts move. If the high-pressure front to the north shifts west and the low front to the south moves northward, then the storm could close our coast as it curves out to sea toward the North Atlantic. As I've said, when it comes out of the high-low pressure vise, the final direction will be determined by which pressure system shifts east first." He pointed toward the open sea, visible about a quarter mile away, whitecaps whipping across the high waves being blown into the Hampton Roads complex of harbors, piers, and shipyards. "If it does, it will come directly across this body of water, hitting land here, blowing this building to hell and gone."

Tucker looked to where the meteorologist pointed.

Tibbles-Seagraves's eyes bulged.

"Here?" Tucker asked.

"John, stop teasing," Commodore West said. "It'll head toward Virginia as its land-crossing point. That being said, it doesn't matter whether it shoots out of the frontal vise, as John calls it, and heads north or east; some of it will hit the Tidewater area. Right, John?"

The meteorologist nodded several times, grinning. "Yes, sir."

Commodore West, Tucker, and Sam laughed.

"A joke?"

Tibbles-Seagraves reached up and shook the Frenchman on the shoulder. "You wouldn't understand, my friend. It is a bit of humor that only we who speak the international language of English could understand."

"And, French isn't an international language?" St. Cyr protested.

"For surrendering," Commodore West muttered unheard beneath his breath.

"Commodore, what about the search-and-rescue mission for Recce Mission 62?" Tucker asked.

West put his hands on his hips and shook his head. "Sorry. Everything is grounded along the East Coast and out of Roosevelt Roads for at least the next couple of days. I hate to say it, but if they survived the crash—and we are assuming they crashed—then they will need a lot of luck and God's grace to survive this." He turned to one of several televisions mounted above the front windows of the control tower and pushed the ON button. A satellite picture appeared. "This is the Atlantic. Look at this! About the only clear area for this storm are the farther areas of the Eastern Atlantic. Torrential rains are pounding the Caribbean Islands, south of it. If you watched television last night, you've seen the floods." He turned back to the men. "As for the crew of Recce Flight 62, I don't see much hope for them. The only thing we can hope is that Admiral Holman and his international partners across the ocean catch the terrorists."

"You think they were shot down by those on the ship?" St. Cyr asked.

West shrugged. "Who knows? They report no engine problems; had made over fifty ups-and-downs identifying merchant vessels, and the one vessel they identify heading in a different direction than the others is the last one they report. If they had crashed near it and it was a friendly, we'd've known by now. No, whatever happened, that vessel had to have seen it or been the cause of it, which means whatever is on that vessel and whoever is manning it doesn't want us to find it."

Movement to his right caught Tucker's attention as he was listening to the Commodore. Sam had moved to the ever-present coffee pot and poured herself a cup. The Chief from the quarterdeck below walked into the tower.

"Commodore, we're ordering Domino's Pizza. Would you like us to order some for you and the others?"

"Chief, you think they're working?" West asked, and then continued before the Chief could respond. "If you call them and if we should be so lucky, order enough for all of us. I think we're going to be here through the night."

Tucker walked over to the port windows, tuning out the Commodore and Chief working out the pizza order. Looking down at the two small piers where the Mark V Special Operations Crafts were tied up, he watched, mesmerized, as the six crafts pitched and rolled with the rough seas being forced through the narrow waterway entrance to where Special Boat Unit Twenty called home. As he watched, a couple of sailors on board one of them jumped onto the pier and, with movements born of experience, loosened the lines running between the boats and the wooden piers. "Looks as if those boats are going have a rough night," he said to no one in particular.

The others joined him.

"Just hope the sailors on board have strong stomachs," West offered. "Can't really take them off and can't have them sortie out to sea like the big boys are doing and the small boys plan."

Tucker looked at the Commodore. "The fleet is setting sail?"

West nodded. "Best thing they can do. It's far easier for carriers, cruisers, even destroyers, frigates, and most of Admiral Holman's amphibious ships to ride out the storm at sea than be tied up where severe winds and tides can slam them against the piers and shores. I recall a storm in Jacksonville once—years ago, probably while you were in high school—that put a frigate on the beach. The Commander of Atlantic Fleet was not amused."

Sam walked up with a tray bearing several cups of coffee. "Here, gentleman, and don't get the wrong idea. I don't do windows." She sat the tray on the table in the center of the tower. "As the lead medical person on this team, I made a fresh pot after doing a visual analysis of the older pot of coffee and determining it was growing new and unidentified bacteria, possibly as a fallout of evolution since the coffee had been there so long."

The coffee did taste good. Tucker thought about asking the Commodore if this meant securing from the terrorist alert and allowing the three of them to return to their respective bases. He grinned slightly at the thought of how Tibbles-Seagraves had looked when the British airman had heard about the possibility of the storm crossing right up that narrow channel. Come to think, it took the Commodore's comment to make him realize the thin Commander was making a joke. Neither the man's voice nor facial expressions betrayed this sense of humor.

Commodore West held the steaming cup of coffee between both his hands. "Let me tell you why I asked for you here," he lifted the cup and took a sip. "I wanted to give you background about the weather because it does impact you. I have asked Washington for permission to return you home." He nodded toward the Royal Air Force Wing Commander. "I think our Royal Air Force counterpart would prefer to be inland when the storm does break free, and since the focus of the search for this rogue merchant vessel is on their side of the Atlantic, both he and Captain St. Cyr may be of use to their own countries."

"Are you sure you should be the one making this decision?" Captain St. Cyr asked in a nonconfrontational manner. "My orders were to remain here until the chase is completed. I would be disobeying orders if I departed based entirely on only the American decision, sir."

West set his cup down on the table. "Right you are, Captain, which is why I have asked Washington to work out the details. Heaven forbid that America would even presume to decide something for France."

"I think my country would acquiesce to the American decision," Tibbles-Seagraves said. "We have too close of a trusting relationship not to work together."

Tucker saw a flash of anger in St. Cyr's eyes. You would think after all these centuries the animosity between England and France would have died out, but it remained. Two old empires and cousins still fighting on the international playing field, but with words and diplomacy as their weapons. The twenty-first century had added America to the game with France.

"Bottom line, gentlemen, is that until Washington, London, and Paris tell us otherwise, you three are the international Special Forces effort to stop that rogue merchant vessel in the event it sails this way."

"Our teams?" Tucker asked.

"No teams, Commander. Your teams, as you know, remained with Admiral Holman. The SEALs I have assigned specifically for Special Forces work I've sent home." He held his hand when he saw Tucker open his mouth. "I know what you're going to say, Commander. But I discussed this with Commander, Special Warfare Group Two, and between the two of us decided their families needed them while we play out this game of Russian roulette with the storm. Plus, everything we are seeing from the intelligence community, including the CIA and DIA, all agree the rogue vessel is on the other side of the Atlantic heading toward the Mediterranean or, as the French believe, toward Rotterdam. Wherever it is, it isn't here."

"I have found that most intelligence becomes politically tainted as it rises through the levels of government," St. Cyr offered. "What if the ship isn't heading east?" he asked, his voice rising. "What if it's sailing to here? How are we going to take it down, as our countries would prefer, if we have no teams? Have no one but ourselves?"

West turned, his lips clinched, and walked to the window. Down below, the Mark V Special Operations Crafts bounced on the turbulent water. "Then, Captain, you will just have to use one of my boats. No aircraft are flying—couldn't if they wanted to. They aren't going to be able to fly for at least another two days, and if that storms does what we think, then you can count on that being a week," West said, his words crisp and sharp. "And don't expect more help from larger ships, because starting at about"—he looked at his watch—"In two hours—seventeen hundred our time—the fleet is going to start sortieing, heading out to sea to ride the storm out. The only ships remaining in port are those who can't get underway for various reasons or because their mission design such as our SpecOps craft limit their survivability in heavy seas."

"So should we return to our quarters?" Tibbles-Seagraves interrupted Captain West's rising voice.

"Wing Commander, you may return to your quarters, or you can stay here with me through the night. I have bunks on the first deck. But you can't leave until I get orders authorizing it."

"Maybe we should go back to the BOQ?" Sam asked, looking at Tucker.

His eyebrows rose as thoughts of how to improve the passage of time flickered through his mind.

The Chief came back up the stairs from below, balancing a couple of pizzas on his arms. "Here you are, Commodore," he said, sitting the boxes down on the table." He turned to the Tucker. "Commander, your bags, along with Commander Seagraves's and Captain St. Cyr's, have arrived downstairs. I've put them in the bunk room."

Tucker and the others looked at the Commodore, who was taking a bite from a slice of pizza. "Of course," West said through bites, "you'll have to carry your own bags back."

Two hours later, they watched the first of the aircraft carriers sail past the entrance to Special Boat Unit Twenty harbor. Close behind it sailed an assortment of cruisers, destroyers, and several frigates. The remaining bulk of the United States Navy Second Fleet was underway, making its way through heavy seas, heading to the open ocean where they had the freedom to maneuver to avoid the worst the storm could offer.

Darker clouds sailed in as the ships sailed out, darkening the skies and casting a heavy gray pale across the landscape, accompanying the last two aircraft carriers as they sailed past. It was an impressive parade of American Navy power for the six people who stood in an old World War II seaplane tower; their own special review platform. Few words were spoken as they watched the warships, amphibious ships, and auxiliary ships sail out to the sea, fighting against the wind that sought to blow them into shallow waters along the coast. South, along the coast of Florida, another ship worked its way north, unaware that the United States Navy had vacated its major hub on the East Coast.

CHAPTER 8

THE DARKNESS RECEDED SLOWLY AS EARLY BEGAN TO regain consciousness. A kaleidoscope of faces, knives, guns, and a roaring bull chased nightmares across jumbled thoughts. There was pain ahead, and it grew as she struggled upward. The last thing she recalled was seeing the tall man with the mustache draw back. It was as if slow motion had taken over as she watched the first fist arc toward her face. After the first couple of blows, she had passed out. She rolled her head to the side, expecting to feel the hard deck of the ship against it, but instead discovered a softness that made her think of a pillow.

Maureen Early opened her right eye slowly, feeling her eyelids fighting against dried moisture gluing them together. Her left eye, swollen, didn't want to open, and with her hands tied behind, there was little she could do. Her legs, toes pointed outward, lay splayed in front of her with two untied boots resting in the faint passageway light filtering through the small porthole in the door. She stared silently, watching the toes of the boots sticking straight up and realized they weren't moving. She wiggled her toes and felt relief when they touched the top of the steel toes of the flight boots. She still had feeling in her feet. She scrunched her head into the softness beneath it. The ship didn't seem to be rolling as much as it had been yesterday.

"Lieutenant, you awake, ma'am?" Senior Chief Leary asked from behind her.

She looked up with her right eye. He was leaning over her from behind, looking down, his eyes searching her face. "Yeah," she said, the word forced through cracked lips and a dry mouth. "You look like shit, Senior Chief," she mumbled.

"Don't try to talk yet, Lieutenant. You took a few punches, but I liked the way you avoided the rest by passing out."

"Don't be funny. It hurts too much. Water?" she asked weakly. She forced her left eye open against the strand of mucus that had dried across it. The vision was blurred.

"Mr. Kelly, can you do it?" Leary asked.

Early shut her eyes and did a mental assessment of her body. Her arms hurt. Four, maybe five now, days they had been tied behind her back. She wiggled her fingers; still had feeling. Her stomach hurt when she breathed, and her face felt as if someone had taken a hammer and beaten her with it.

"Did they—?" Her voice trailed off.

Senior Chief Leary shook his head. "No, they didn't."

"My face hurts," she said. Early raised her head, opening her eyes. The vision in the left one was a little clearer. Her copilot Scott Kelly was knee-walking across the metal deck toward some bowls near the door.

"What's going on?" she asked, her voice trailing off.

"They finally decided we needed more than a cup of water a day. You've been out of it for the past twenty-four hours, Lieutenant, but from what we can tell, there's nothing broken."

"You sound different, Senior Chief," she said. She took a deep breath and started coughing.

"On the other hand, you could have a cracked rib."

Across the compartment, Scott bent over, dipping his

face in the bowl and sucking up a mouthful of water. He turned and knee-walked over to where the Senior Chief and Early sat.

"Lean up, Lieutenant," Senior Chief Leary said, raising his knee to force her head up. "Now this is going to be shaky, but Lieutenant Kelly is going to put his lips near yours. You have to open them, so he can give you the water he's carrying in his mouth."

She blinked several times, loosing the yellow strands of mucus from her left eye. She opened her mouth and shut her eyes. A moment passed and the wet, satisfying taste of water filled her mouth. She swallowed. The short flood quit and she opened her eyes. Scott Kelly looked down at her. "You all right?" he asked.

"I'm stiff and my face hurts when I talk. Can you squirt some of that in my eyes?"

"Think you can move?"

"Push me up, Senior Chief," Early said. She pulled forward, doing a sit-up. Bright spots swam across her vision, and her body swayed to the right, where she fell against Leary, who had shifted his body so he was behind her.

"Take it easy, Lieutenant," he said. "You've been horizontal for a day. Let your body adjust to the new position."

She opened her eyes. Scott had worked his way back to the water, filled his mouth again, and was returning.

"Open your mouth again," Leary said.

She kept her eyes opened. Kelly squirted a little water onto each eye, then spit what little remained into Gotta-Be's mouth. A few seconds later, she had swallowed the water. "Thanks." She blinked her eyes rapidly, the water stinging slightly. Her vision cleared.

"Much better than doing the Senior Chief," Scott said, smiling, revealing a long open gap where white teeth had once been.

Her eyebrows bunched. "What happened?" she asked.

"It looks worse than it is," Scott replied, his tongue

visible as he ran it over the stumps of missing teeth. "You should have seen the other guy."

She drew another deep breath. Her ribs on the right side hurt. She rolled her upper left shoulder, sending a dull pain across the top of her chest—as if something was sticking into her from beneath the skin. The pain from the shoulder was manageable. Early pulled herself all the way up to a sitting position, moving off the Senior Chief. She blinked several times and then turned to face him without falling over or passing out.

She looked his face over, saw the swollen sides of the cheeks. "Open your mouth, Senior Chief."

He grinned, revealing a spilt lip caked in blood. "Nothing like a good beating to get the blood flowing . . . if you know what I mean."

She couldn't tell if any teeth were missing in the faint light of the compartment.

"Where is Win?" she asked, looking to where the young Operations Mission Evaluator had lain yesterday.

"They carried him out hours ago. There was a man with them, wearing a white smock, who told us in broken English that he was a doctor and wanted to see if there was anything he could do for Win."

The three remained silent for a moment, knowing that whatever they were going to do to the young OPEVAL would not be pleasant. What happened to them told the true story of what would happen to the unconscious Lieutenant Junior Grade.

"We can only pray the man told the truth," she said softly.

"Yes, ma'am. That'll do a hell of a lot of good," Senior Chief Leary mumbled. "The only time I've seen prayer solve a problem is when you solve it yourself. Then you can say something like 'Thank God.' "

"Huh?"

"We gotta get out of this," Leary continued. "They ain't keeping us alive because of some misguided charity. They got something planned for us. And whatever it is, it ain't gonna be good, and it ain't gonna be pleasant."

Maureen Early, using her hips to move, wiggled back, alongside the Senior Chief, until her back reached the cool bulkhead. She raised first one hip, then the other, letting the blood circulate in her buttocks, the familiar tingling sensation grew in her buttocks and legs as feelings returned.

"Damn, Ma'am. I hope you ain't . . ."

"Butt's asleep, Senior Chief. That's all." She took a deep breath. "You're right, Senior Chief. We have to escape."

"How?" Lieutenant Scott Kelly asked. "It isn't as if we could do anything. Our hands are tied. They feed us once a day and barely give us enough water to keep us from becoming dehydrated."

"Regardless, Scott. The Senior Chief's right," Early said, tenderly running her tongue along her lips. At least the dryness from her voice was gone. "Just don't know what we can do." She looked at the Senior Chief. They may be officers, but this tall, muscular Senior Chief had ten more years of Navy service than both her and Scott together. A smidgeon of doubt bubbled from beneath a brief moment of confidence that maybe the Senior Chief had a way for them to escape. Then, recalling the man's Naval history, she realized there was no way he could have experienced anything such as this. She doubted if anyone had and lived to tell about it. Damn! For the first time, she truly realized they were going to die. The dryness returned. They didn't teach anything about escape and evasion while imprisoned on a ship when she went through Survival, Escape, Resistance, and Evasion—SERE, they called it—training. SERE training for flight crews was targeted toward being shot down over land and avoiding or escaping capture from the same. No one taught them what to do when they were shot down at sea and captured by an enemy ship.

"I ain't sure myself, but I know we have two chances. One when they bring the food and water every night. Of course, if they decide to keep us alive, eventually they're going to have to wash us down—fire hose or something.

So far, that ain't happened, and we can't wait around thinking it is."

This would be one part of their captivity she had no intention of sharing with anyone when they returned to civilization—how she'd sat in her own urine with two men while a prisoner. At least, so far, it had only been urine, though they knew Win Forrester had lost his bowel control soon after they were thrown into this compartment. She suspected the Senior Chief had also, but it wasn't something that civilized people discussed. It was just something that happened when you were cast into a brutal situation that left no choice. She had feared when she first woke that they had molested her. Sure, the Senior Chief said they hadn't, but the three of them were unconscious for a period, and who knew what happened during that time. She shut her eyes, trying to feel "down there" to see if she could tell if anything had happened. It didn't feel like it to her, and she had some confidence that she would have known if she had been raped, but the only way she would know would be when she was rescued—if she was rescued. They could always change their minds if they hadn't done anything to her. Then, just as suddenly, the fear passed. They never would have taken the time to redress her if they had. Being soaked in one's waste is a great defense against rape.

"We have to figure out how to get our hands untied."

"The only way I figure we can do it is to cut through these plastic ties."

"Even if we had something to cut through them, and even if we managed to get free, our hands are going to be useless until we get some circulation back in them."

"Lieutenant Scott, I would rather slap them to death with dead hands than sit here and wait for them to put a bullet between my eyes."

"So, how do we free our hands?" Scott asked, nodding in agreement.

The Senior Chief looked at Early. "You're looking at me. What can I do?" she asked, confused.

"Ma'am, you're the only one of us with a full set of teeth."

"I think I've heard that line before. I believe it was in South Carolina, or maybe West Virginia. It didn't work then either."

The continuous engine noise with them for the past four days, with its low monotonous vibration in the background, increased in tempo for several seconds, then the vibration intensified as the ship started to reverse.

"What's happening?" Kelly asked, a tinge of fear in the question.

"Whatever it is, it can't be good," the Senior Chief offered.

Suddenly the engine noise quit. A few seconds elapsed, and then the ship began rolling slightly from side to side as the wave motion of the Atlantic Ocean pushed against the starboard side before rolling under the aged freighter.

"Looks as if we've stopped," Early said. She forced her right eye open, feeling the thick moisture that had been holding it together give. The water earlier spit in her mouth by Kelly had provided some relief. Shuffling around the deck, even with her hands tied, had restored circulation to her body. Her face hurt. It hurt like hell. She moved her jaw back and forth several times, sending slight pain waves down the right side of her face when she shifted her jaw to the left. How did that joke go? *Doc, my arm hurts when I do this. Then, don't do that.*

"That jaw hurting you?"

She glanced at Kelly, who was sitting cross-legged in the middle of the compartment in the small beam of light from the passageway outside. She nodded. "No . . . well, a little. But, I don't think anything's broken, just swollen and sore."

"If it's broken, you'd know."

She turned to Leary. "Okay, Senior Chief, let's say I manage to use my God-given talent with teeth and get us loose. What then? As soon as they see we're loose, they're going to tie us up tighter or kill us."

"Ma'am, they're going to kill us anyway. Why they're

keeping us alive is the question, and the more I think about it, the more I'm damn sure it ain't from any sense of human compassion. They've got some sort of plan for us, and whatever it is, it ain't gonna be pretty."

"THERE YOU ARE, TAMURSHEKI," CAPTAIN ALRAJOOL SAID, pointing west. "That's called Florida—"

"The land of the infidel," Tamursheki muttered softly as if offering a prayer.

"You can call it that, but those infidels seem to be kicking your butts all across the globe. We're about ten miles south of the American city of Jacksonville. The Americans have their second largest Navy base along the East Coast there."

Tamursheki glared at the freighter's Captain. "You make me angry, Alrajool. I would even suspect that you lack conviction of our righteousness. They have their aircraft carriers there?"

Alrajool shrugged. "Who knows where the American aircraft carriers are. I know that some are home-ported there, along with an airfield that has many of their maritime patrol aircraft. What really worries me is that if they are looking for us and those aircraft over there"—he pointed toward the northeast—"don't find us, the Air Force has reconnaissance aircraft stationed further inland. They'll find us."

"How do you know all this?"

"I only have this ship, my friend, and the job. Our boss Abu Alhaul sends me into places where they would just as soon sink this ship as to board it and take me alive. It makes little difference to these people. What was done to them years ago has never been forgotten, and in their own unforgiving and unflinching way, they intend to kill and subjugate every person who may be a threat to their *heathen way of life*."

"I didn't know this about Jacksonville."

"Oh! And, I should be surprised?" Alrajool laughed, pushing away from the metal railing running alongside the port walkway leading to the bridge. "You have work to do. So do I. Let's not confuse a business deal with religious fever. My job is to deliver you, your men, and this van on the stern of my ship. Along the way, I am to drop off one group of Islamic martyrs for the glory of Allah and the tidy sum of two hundred thousand American dollars. We are here at the first part of the job—drop off your first group. Then, we'll continue on to Norfolk, Virginia, where I will off-load you along with the remainder of your men, and the van. Afterward—and that will be soon afterward—I will put back out to sea and be hundreds of miles away when whatever is in the van explodes. Then I wait for Abu Alhaul's next assignment." Alrajool smiled, delighted with the anger blazing in Tamursheki's eyes. *Stupid little shits,* he thought. Young and impressionable. Able to believe their one little death could change anything. "He pays well. You know you are not the first transaction I have had with your organization. Considering there aren't many ship owners who would take the risk of transporting you, you should be happy I am here." Alrajool pushed his black captain's cap up off his forehead. The gold embroidering on the brim had dirty smudges from many years of his hands touching it. He would be glad when this bunch of fanatics was off his ship. It's hard to trust those who eagerly seek death. Give him those who want to live forever anytime. He had carried weapons, arms, ammunitions, and even once sailed to Bulgaria to pick up plastic explosives for Abu Alhaul. This wasn't his first time transporting terrorists, but it sure was going to be his last.

Tamursheki started to reply, then decided against it. He knew this was a one-way voyage. He touched his shirt pocket where the message Abu Alhaul had sent announcing their final destination had been neatly folded and tucked. He grinned. No one else would have ever figured out the varying convolutions his master devised to sow terror into the homeland of the infidel. Only he had been honored with the true plan; a true plan that would probably mean the death of everyone on board, but he was prepared to sacrifice himself for Allah and the future of Islam. Only Abu Alhaul truly spoke for the prophet. His eyes narrowed. Dr. Ibrahim also knew the true weapon on board and it angered Tamursheki that he needed information from the Palestinian. For the nearly ten days they had been at sea, Tamursheki had refused to share his relevant information, and he had refused to concede to Ibrahim that the doctor had the same knowledge. Even though he knew the doctor would have to know. Maybe he should kill the man before he left the ship for his own mission. He glanced at Alrajool. And why not take the good Captain and his crew with them into paradise? They could argue the particulars of his actions while with Allah.

"I don't think I have seen you so quiet, my friend," Alrajool said, trying to pull from behind those evil eyes the thoughts that seemed to capture hourly the man beside him.

The ship rolled to port a few degrees before righting itself. Alrajool stuck his head through the hatch into the bridge. "Helmsman, rudder twenty degrees starboard," he ordered.

Even with no engines on line and the shaft locked, the movement of the current here, along with the waves, shoved the ship toward the shore. Shifting the rudder was the only means Alrajool had to keep the ship pointed into the waves without re-engaging the engines and putting minimum revolutions on the shaft to maintain station. He had already used nearly half his fuel, and he would take any chance to conserve.

"Okay, Tamursheki. If you're going to get your group off my ship, you better start doing it now. We're five miles from the coast. By the time they work their way ashore, it'll be dark. That is, if your desert sailors know anything about rowing."

Tamursheki agreed and headed aft. "Tell them they need to work those oars front to back, if they want to reach the beach. We haven't lost that storm, and if it turns around and catches them, then they won't have to worry about paddling ashore. They'll just have to worry how long they can tread water."

A port hatch opened on the deck below the causeway, just as the ship rolled to port again. Dr. Ibrahim stepped outside on the main deck, holding his hat on his head so the wind wouldn't blow it away. The heavy hatch swung shut, slamming against the hatchway a couple of times. The outside handle turned as some unseen person inside the ship locked the hatch down.

Ibrahim saw the two men above him. He took his hat off and shoved it inside his coat before grabbing both of the handrails for balance. Navigating the rolls of the ship, Ibrahim climbed to where the two stood.

A wave crashed against the starboard side of the freighter, causing the port roll already underway to increase a degree or two.

"How long are we going to be here?" Ibrahim shouted above the groans of the freighter.

Alrajool nodded at Tamursheki. "As long as it takes this fine Jihadist to get his group into the water and headed to shore."

Ibrahim looked at the leader of the terrorist group. "They going to be able to make it?" he asked incredulously. "Look at the waves."

"Allah is with them. They will make it," Tamursheki answered.

"If you two will excuse me, I am going inside to the bridge," Alrajool said, jerking his thumb toward the forward hatch a few feet away.

When Captain Alrajool had closed the watertight hatch behind him, Tamursheki turned to Dr. Ibrahim. "How long will they have?" he asked in a commanding voice.

Ibrahim put his right hand, palm spread against his chest. "I can only say they should be good for another four days. They're right where we want them now."

"What happens if their boat is overturned and they should drown?"

Ibrahim bit his lower lip for a moment. "That is a good question and deserves a good answer, of which I have none. If the bodies wash ashore, there is a good chance the trap will be sprung as tightly as if they were alive, but the key to the plan that your boss hired me to do is that they be able to travel across the country to wherever they have been ordered to go. If they reach their destination via the ways they are told to go, and if they aren't caught or interfered with, then you should have your answer within twenty-five days."

Tamursheki turned away without replying and hurried down the ladder to the main deck. He soon disappeared toward the stern, where his men were busy inflating a Zodiac raft. Zodiac rafts were used for pleasure throughout the world, and many times as life rafts for pleasure boats. Along with its pleasure applications, it was also the choice for terrorists and Special Forces for covert insertion and recovery along hostile coastline. It's low profile to the sea and the ease by which the inflatable rubber craft could be stored added to its covert attraction.

Soon Tamursheki would have his time with both of these men. They sneered at him as if he was trash instead of the leader of Allah's troops. They were little different from the infidels against which the Holy Jihad fought. Alrajool balanced his faithfulness between money and religion, and there was little doubt in his mind which of the two the man preferred. Ibrahim was the same. The man was for the money Abu Alhaul had given him to bring the drugs and administer it to his team. He reached up and touched the flesh beneath his upper left arm. The sting of the shots from two days ago still reacted to the touch. The burning sensation as the contents of the hypodermic flowed from the needle into his body was a reminder of what he carried. His life was but a drop into the plan for a world dominated by the one true faith.

Tamursheki moved to the right to walk between the next ladder and the bulkhead of the first deck. No reason to take a chance of being tossed overboard by going on the far side of the walkway. The sound of voices reached his ears as he reached the end of the forecastle of the freighter. The noise of the wind wove around him, and tiny bits of ocean spray peppered his face, causing him to squint in an effort to keep the stinging salt from his eyes.

The Zodiac raft was inflated. It was a large model capable of carrying seven people. The small engine laying on the deck would power the craft most of the way to shore, but the four men chosen to take it would have to paddle the remainder of the distance. Tamursheki smiled. Alrajool had hidden the small portable engines that came with the three Zodiac rafts, thinking he wouldn't know about them. Qasim had discovered them while rambling through the aft storerooms. It was a secret he kept to himself. Information was power no matter how small it was. To keep it to oneself gave one power over others.

The four chosen martyrs were making the rounds of their fellow warriors, receiving hugs, best wishes, and promises to carry word of their martyrdom back to their families. In his mind, he saw each family reverently receiving the word and announcing to others their pride in a family member who had given his life to spread the word of Allah. It would never have dawned on Tamursheki that a family would be heartbroken or sad over what these men were about to do. To him, martyrdom was the ultimate reward for fighting in the name of Allah, and to fight for Abu Alhaul was the same. Every religious war needed its chaste generals to mark out the strategy to rid the world of the infidels and install the one true religion along with its fair Sharia—religious laws. Every family would invite others to share their pride, and in his thoughts, he wished for a fleeting moment that he could be in the hills of Yemen to see his own family celebrate his martyrdom. He knew for once in his father's life the old man would straighten with pride at the son he had cast out. For Tamursheki, it was completely alien to believe that his father would want him alive when he could achieve such fame or that his father who had once disowned him would continue to deny Tamursheki the honor he sought.

"Tamursheki!" Qasim shouted as he neared.

Everyone turned and in unison began shouting "Allah Akbar!" at the tops of their lungs. One of the men reached out and grabbed another, who had tittered backward into the lifeline surrounding the aft deck.

Tamursheki held his hands up, a broad grin. His face felt naked without a beard, but to go into America, to seek martyrdom, meant ridding oneself of hair. He would shave the mustache when they reached Norfolk. His heart burst with pride. These comrades had elected to die with him, though none of them knew they were to die. They believed as the Captain did that when they reached their final destination, they would pull alongside a dock and unload the miracle weapon tied down on the stern deck near them. Then, when the ship had safely sailed away to support other missions of their cause, they would explode the weapon. *Oh, glorious day,* he heard someone say. The life of a Jihadist belonged to those such as him who carried the word of God within them.

The shouts died, and the men gathered around as he stopped near the side of the raft. A couple of men held the tethers on the front of the raft, which was pointed east into the wind. The four men destined to go ashore stood on the other side of the Zodiac raft from Tamursheki. They had long ago replaced their desert abas for the rough dress of the country into which they were about to descend.

"Is everyone ready?" he shouted above the thunder, the wind, and the rain.

"We were waiting for you," Qasim replied, his voice just loud enough to be heard.

Tamursheki rubbed his cheek a couple of times as he faced the four men. There was Badr, short with a nose that had been broken so many times it lay permanently to the left. He was the leader of the group until they broke up ashore. The man wore a long-sleeve light-blue shirt that Tamursheki recognized as the type worn by laborers in Europe. The blue jeans lacked a belt, but Tamursheki doubted anyone would point at Badr once he got ashore, or accuse him of being a terrorist because he had no belt.

Tamursheki walked around the Zodiac raft to where the four men stood in a line. "Badr," he said, reaching out and putting his hand on the shorter man's shoulder. "You are the leader of this group of Holy warriors as you head toward the camp of the infidels. Do you know what you are to do?"

The man nodded sharply once. "Yes, Amir. We will row ashore and work our way north to the city of Jacksonville." He patted his shirt pocket. "I have a Greyhound 'See America' ticket that will allow me to go anywhere in America for thirty days. I can get off the bus when and where I want to; and I can get back on the bus when I want to."

"And, your orders?"

"I am to go to Atlanta. I will wander the streets and visit a place called Grady Hospital. Then I will return to the bus and go west, through Dallas, to San Antonio, and when I reach San Diego, I will stop my travels. I am to visit coffee shops and even the bars where American sailors enjoy."

"And, the weapons you are taking with you ashore? You know you cannot travel across Satan's land with these guns," Tamursheki said, reaching out and patting the dark AK-47 Badr gripped across his waist.

"They're only if we are caught before we can disperse. Once we leave the beach, we will toss them away; preferably into water."

"You will do well, Badr. Make sure the others leave before you depart Jacksonville."

Tamursheki turned to Hisham, the American-born Saudi Arabian who still had relatives in Chicago. The man had shaved off his beard only a few days ago, and the whiteness beneath the beard contrasted sharply with the darker tan of the face. The other three had shaved their body hair before the ship ever sailed. He reached out, and as he had done with Badr, he touched Hisham's shoulder. "And, you, our American friend," Tamursheki said loud enough for everyone to hear. It caused everyone to laugh, for it was a big joke to all of them, including Hisham, that because of where he was born he was considered American, though his father had taken him back to Saudi Arabia when he was only four.

"This American is ready," Hisham said, his Arab accent barely detectable. "And yes, I know my job. I will stay in Jacksonville for several days before taking a bus to Pensacola. At Pensacola, an e-ticket will be waiting for me to fly to Chicago. In Chicago, I will stay with relatives who are expecting me. They believe I am coming to America to go to college. While in Chicago, I will be out and mix with people every day. And I will wait for the word for whatever mission I am called upon to do."

"You are very brave, Hisham."

"Thank you, Amir, but the bravery is with those who take the weapon"—He reached behind him and patted the dark gray side of the van —"Into the heart of our enemy's homeland and explode it. I will be watching the news and the papers for word of your success. Do you know where you will go with the weapon?"

Tamursheki thought for a few moments and then decided against confirming their destination. There were no secrets aboard a ship, he had discovered. The radio operator would have shared the message from Abu Alhaul with the cook, who would have shared it with the deckhand, who would have shared it with one of the Jihadists, who would tell the others. But what if any of these four were captured before the next two days passed? Maybe Hisham was the only one who didn't know. Then again, what if Hisham was CIA. Tamursheki, like Abu Alhaul and the other Jihadists, believed the CIA was everywhere, and it only took an innocent questions such as Hisham's to convince them that he was a member of the dreaded CIA with its covert warriors and assassins.

"I think you know, Hisham, as everyone here probably knows. I don't want to say it, for if you are captured, the enemy uses vile drugs and torture to cause its captives to speak against their friends. I only ask this: if you should be captured, keep the secret for two days. If you can keep it for two days, it will be too late for them to do anything."

Hisham nodded as Tamursheki moved to the third man of the group. Jabir, the cook, who had grown tired of butchering, cooking, and washing. The Yemeni who would leave behind two wives and more children than he could keep track of. He was the oldest of the four. Tamursheki looked around at the others who were watching him and the four. Every now and again, someone would work their way behind the four warriors and pat them on the back as if touching these first martyrs of their voyage would bring good luck to them. As if touching transferred part of them to these four on their mission.

Jabir straightened, exposing his thin neck to Tamursheki. Tamursheki looked up at the slightly taller man. "Jabir, we will carry your sacrifice to your family," he said, touching him briefly on the shoulder. "You have given so much in this war against the infidels. No one can ask for more than what you are about to give. Are you truly prepared for this mission?" he asked, for he had always wondered why the man came with them. Were his wives so horrible the martyr preferred death than a life with them? Or was the lure of eternal life something a man who did woman's work sought, to prove himself a man?

"Yes, Amir, I am prepared to give my life, to be an eternal example to my family and to my sons, who will walk through our village with their heads high, extolling the martyrdom of their father. They will be in high esteem, and their future will be assured." Jabir reached up and ran his hands along a series of small bumps along the edge of his right ear.

"And, your job?" Tamursheki watched the hand push at the bumps. Wait, he thought, until they mature before you burst them.

Jabir tugged the waist pack around front and patted it. "I have a train ticket from . . ." He stuttered, trying to think of the name of the city. ". . . Florida," he finally said. "North to Washington, D.C., then to Baltimore, and finally New York City. In New York, God willing, I will find a job as a cook." The word cook was whispered as if he were ashamed of his profession.

Tamursheki patted him on the shoulder again. "You will do well, my friend, and we will tell of your martyrdom when it comes to future warriors who even now are learning the ways of jihad."

The fourth man was the one who had shot down the aircraft. Tamursheki gave the same encouragement to him and listened as he talked about hitchhiking across Florida to Miami and from Miami onward. Fakhiri was to fly to Seattle before working his way to San Francisco. Only the center part of the States was missing from this group's sojourns, but there were others in the group who would head to Oklahoma, Kansas, Michigan, and other states in the center of America. *Oh, to be able to live long enough to see the panic and terror he was bringing!* Tamursheki noticed small bumps across the man's lips. When he touched him, his skin was hot. Already it was starting. He hoped that Ibrahim had estimated correctly.

Thirty minutes passed while Qasim led the others in launching the Zodiac raft over the side where the lee of the ship produced a small windbreak from the east winds. Two men held a tether line at the front of the raft while two others held a similar line at the rear, holding the raft against the side of the ship. The men crawled over the side, down the rope ladder, and into the lurching raft. Then it was a quick flick of the wrists below to free the lines, and the zodiac raft quickly turned away from the freighter. The noise of the small engine was lost in the noise of the sea, the wind, the storm, and the men who stood waving and cheering. The raft was soon lost amidst the valleys of the waves, to reappear for a moment on the crest of a new series of waves. Tamursheki whispered a prayer for the men to reach shore. Even great plans such as this depended many times on luck.

Minutes after Alrajool, who had been watching from the bridge, sighted the raft away from the ship, the engines were engaged and the familiar vibration through the ship returned.

Tamursheki stayed on the stern with a few of the others, catching glimpses of the raft until it became a speck on the ocean, hard to see in the fading light. The freighter turned out to sea, away from the coast, and continued its unhindered trek toward Norfolk, Virginia.

East of the freighter, the high-pressure ridge holding the storm near stationary slipped to the east. The low-pressure front moved slightly northwest, and like a small opening of a closed hose with built-up water pressure, the tropical storm picked up speed. A speed slightly below the threshold required for changing its designation to hurricane. Its movement across ground increased to twenty-five knots. Satellite photos quickly relayed the danger to the National Weather Service at Sterling, Virginia. The situation was debated for several hours at NWS whether to err on the side of caution and recommend evacuating areas along the coasts of Maryland, Chesapeake Bay, New Jersey, and Delaware, or take a chance its wind speed would stay the same until the pressure ridges pushed the storm northward and away. In the end, they gave residents both options; stay or leave.

In Norfolk and Little Creek areas the exodus of Navy warships continued, while at the Oceana Air Station, the F-14 and F-18 squadrons flew their aircraft inland away from the storm, joining other Navy aircraft such as the venerable C-130 and the P-3C maritime reconnaissance aircraft at Air Force bases in Ohio and Kentucky. Nothing gave Navy pilots more pleasure than occupying Air Force officers' clubs. Naval Air always pissed off its sibling Air Force rivals in air power, and what better place for Naval Air to do this than in an Air Force club. Jealousy was a great fruit best eaten away from home.

CHAPTER 9

TUCKER RALEIGH BRACED HIS SHOULDER AGAINST THE door and pushed it shut. Wind whipped around the edges of the door, spraying rain into the alcove of the quarterdeck. He pushed the door shut, the wind rattling the facings when he stepped away. Tucker stepped away from the door, expecting it to blast open from the outside elements pressing against it. Like a fierce beast growling, running back and forth along the length of the building, the noise of the storm rose and fell to the tempo of the rain. The door beat cadence to the storm's rhythm.

"Whew!" Tibbles-Seagraves said, removing his beret and twisting it in both hands to remove the water. "I say—next time, we must insist the driver drop us nearer the door." He unbuttoned his rain slick and held the sides apart to shake them. Water quickly pooled beneath him.

"Commander, great to see you again, sir."

Tucker turned. Standing in the doorframe was the lieutenant who commanded the Mark V Special Operations Craft that had brought them from the battle group three days before. The lanky officer was buttoning his rain slick and tucking his gloves beneath the sleeves of the bright orange garment. Behind him stood Lieutenant Commander Samantha Bradley, Navy Nurse Corps, in a short-sleeve khaki uniform, her gold oak leaves reflecting in the fluorescent light on her collars. She winked at him and pursed her lips.

"Skipper," Tucker acknowledged to the young officer, his eyes coming off Sam to the officer. Regardless of rank, a commanding officer earned by virtue of the job the honorary titles "Captain" and "skipper." Even Master Chief Petty Officers given command of harbor tugs were referred to as 'Captain,' much to their dismay.

"Lieutenant MacOlson, sir," the skipper said, touching his chest. "Pete T. MacOlson—P.T. Last time together we didn't get much of an opportunity to meet." He looked around the quarterdeck area, pulled out his ball cap, and tucked a heavy stock of red hair beneath it. "And, it doesn't look like we'll have much time this time either."

Tucker shook hands with P.T. Rain dripped from the three men onto the tile floor. The First Class Petty Officer manning the nearby quarterdeck leaned forward across the counter, his eyes rolled upward for a moment, and then the acting Officer of the Deck mumbled something to the young seaman who was serving as the duty runner. "Hey, SLOJ," the First Class said to the Seaman, motioning toward the area near the door. "Grab the swab again." SLOJ was slang for what the Navy called those assigned to Shitty Little Odd Jobs.

"Looks as if you've just come in yourself, Lieutenant . . ." Tucker slowed for a moment as he realized he had forgotten the man's name after just having been introduced.

"Pete, sir. Peter T. MacOlson. Most call me P.T. Wouldn't say I've just come in. Would say, unfortunately, that I'm heading back out." He bowed slightly. "I have the honor of being the duty vessel for the upcoming weekend. Rather than try to trade places tomorrow morning when the storm is supposed to reach the Tidewater area, the Commodore decided in his infinite, aged wisdom to make the trade Friday while the weather is halfway decent."

"If this is decent," Tibbles-Seagraves said softly, "then I will never ever say a bad thing about British weather again. Did I ever tell you that London only averages an inch of snow a year?"

The helmsman who had steered the small eighty-two-foot craft through the heaving waves a couple of days before walked into the room, dressed similarly to his skipper with the exception of the headgear. Seeing the officers, the broad-shouldered sailor stopped a few feet behind MacOlson.

MacOlson turned to the First Class Boatswain Mate. "Boats, you ready? Think we had enough of the good times?"

"I'm as ready as I can be, sir," he replied, scowling, his voice a husky bass. The Petty Officer reached up and pulled his black watch cap down tighter, part of it covering half his ears.

Sam worked her way around the two wet men to where Tucker and Tibbles-Seagraves stood. "You're wet," she said quietly.

"Well, sir, it was a pleasure to see you again," P.T. said with a grin. He looked around the room. "Where is the other Special Forces type that came with you? French, wasn't he?"

"He's here someplace. The Commodore moved us here to the Crisis Control Center since the weather seems bent on turning worse. Seems we are the duty SEAL team in the event we are needed."

Tucker started taking off his rain slick. Sam reached behind him and took it from him, hanging it on a coat rack that someone on the quarterdeck had strategically placed on a sheet of plastic matting.

MacOlson laughed. "Crisis Control Center? That's a good one, sir, though he's right. It is getting worse, but only for a day, I'm told, then the storm's center is supposed to curve northward and away from us." He jerked his thumb toward the stairs leading to the tower above.

"Commander, Second Fleet, has ordered the bulk of the SEAL teams to protect some of the critical nodes around the area, and I understand from reading the message traffic that two additional teams were flown out late last night to the UK to support Joint Task Force America." MacOlson grinned. "That's another good one, isn't it? Joint Task Force America is nearer Europe than us." He moved toward the door. "Let's hope we aren't needed. Boats, myself, and the other members of our crew are going to berth aboard the boats tonight. They're not really designed for living quarters, but we have to keep an eye not only on our ship but the other craft also. Plus, in the unlikely event that we lose cabin pressure and they need a SEAL team, then it will be my sailors who bulk you out."

"They're SEALs?"

"Next best thing, Commander Raleigh. They're Explosive Ordnance Disposal qualified. EODs. Most have had snake-eater training unlike us surface-warfare types whose primary job is to bomb the shore, land the troops, then stand off over the horizon and drink coffee."

Most SEALs, at one time or other, qualified as EODs. EODs were underwater experts who prepared beaches for amphibious landings prior to the Marines showing up. They would sneak close to shore and remove any explosives found, as well as blowing up obstacles designed to stop landing craft. Their physical qualifications were similar to Navy SEALs, and like SEALs, EOD personnel had to be qualified marksmen with a range of weapons.

Tucker nodded. He doubted anything SEAL-like was going to happen with this weather. "Don't the other boats have anyone on board?"

The young Lieutenant's smile widened. "Sure they do. One person as a general rule. Our job is work them as part of our security team and keep the boats safe through this storm. We'll be doing more Boatswain Mate work than security work, which makes Boats here very happy, doesn't it?"

"Yes, sir," the Petty Officer replied morosely.

"Isn't going to be easy, what with the winds playing

havoc with the tides. Good thing the weather isn't bad yet."

"This isn't bad?"

MacOlson looked at the Royal Air Force officer. "No, sir. I've seen worse." He turned to Jenson. "Come on, Boats, let's get out there in this fine Navy weather and check the lines."

"Then this shouldn't be too bad tonight for you, Lieutenant," Tibbles-Seagraves volunteered.

MacOlson laughed and glanced at the Boatswain Mate standing slightly behind the Royal Air Force Wing Commander. Tucker saw the sailor roll his eyes.

As MacOlson tugged the sleeves of the rain slick down, unwrapping the Velcro edges and rewrapping them so they caught the top of the work gloves, he replied, "Unfortunately, sir, we'll be lucky to get an hour's sleep, but what sleep is to a Surface Warfare officer is but a nap to our opposites." He looked at his watch. "High tide around midnight, and with this tropical storm whipping up wind gusts between fifty to sixty miles per hour, it'll push the water level up. The water will back up in the channel, and then when it has nowhere else to go, it'll flow back out to sea, lowering the level." Finished with his sleeves, the young officer jerked his thumb over his shoulder toward the two piers where the six Mark V's were tied up. "And, as the water level changes and the wind intensity—oh! can't forget the wind direction—changes, then the lay of the boats change. I suspect that Boats here"—he pointed to the sailor behind Tibbles-Seagraves—"and the other men will spend their time taking in and resetting lines most of the night to keep the boats from getting damaged by the storm." He moved to the large window in front of the building. "That's what they're doing now," he said, pointing down at the two piers beneath the old watchtower. "Then, there's the fenders—"

"Fenders?"

"Yes, sir, Wing Commander. Fenders can be anything from old tires, costing a few dollars, to the more acceptable pneumatic fender made of rubber, about four feet long and three feet in diameter, designed for Navy use and carried in the Naval Supply System. They only cost several hundred dollars to the American taxpayer but take several weeks to arrive. The thing about fenders is whatever you throw over the side of the boat to keep it from bouncing off other boats and the piers is a fender. The one thing we hate to see act as a fender is a sailor, and unfortunately, that does happen every now and again." He motioned the RAF Wing Commander to the window of the compartment. "Look there," he said, pointing down to the piers.

Tucker grinned. Here was an officer who loved his job, and even though the Boatswain Mate's screwed-up face gave the impression of someone dreading the night ahead, he could also tell the sailor had respect for this young Lieutenant. Being liked was nice; being respected was better.

"See how those boats are bopping up and down, and the waves rolling in from the sea are breaking across their hulls? Look how the wind hits their small topsails as if the boats themselves were designed to catch it." MacOlson removed his ball cap, shook his head, and then jammed his hair back under it. "Yeap, wouldn't last long in this weather outside of the channel."

Tucker and Sam moved to the window to watch. Outside, the six boats rocked and rolled to nature's hand, their fenders banging against each other. Periodically, a huge wave would break over the side of the two boats tied at the far end of the piers. A couple of sailors worked the lines on those two boats, pulling the line through a capstan as their efforts secured the crafts closer to the fenders along the pier. Then, with quick movements, they figured eight the line around the T-shaped cleats on the deck. On the pier, a sailor watched as the working party moved to the next line and lifted the eye of the topmost line from the bollard. On board the small crafts, two sailors untied the line moments before the eye of the line was once again pulled over the bollard. Then the same scene as with the last line occurred.

"See that working party? That man standing there is Petty Officer Jacobs. Petty Officer Jacobs is the leading Boatswain Mate on the number-two boat nearer the shoreline. His job is to check every one of those lines, and then when he's satisfied that every one of them is secure and properly tightened, he starts over. On top of all of that, sir, he is responsible for the safety of his men and women. The line is synthetic fiber, which has horrible knot-holding capability. Means you have to keep inspecting it to make sure it doesn't come away. Unfortunately, not every ship can have the more expensive manila line." MacOlson looked around at the faces watching him. "Sorry. I seem to have gotten carried away with Surface Warfare talk. With this weather, that is what the majority of our job is going to be through the night and through most of Saturday—a little marlinspike seamanship, of which Boats, here, is an expert."

Tucker felt Sam ease against his side. He folded his arms across his chest as he watched the nautical scene in front of him, afraid she was going to reach out and take his hand in hers. The Commodore had already had a little private chat with him the day before. If he knew about last night, he'd come unglued. The seasoned veteran was old Navy, where public display of affection was frowned upon within the military services. PDA was doubly hazardous to a bachelor's health. Of course, if it was private, under a well-hedged row of bushes with all this rain—*that would be something different, and no doubt his Sam would be game for it.*

"What are you smiling about?" Sam asked softly, smiling up at Tucker.

He shook his head. "Nothing in particular. Mind just wandered for a bit, thinking about hedge rows and bad weather." He winked.

She elbowed him slightly. "Can't fool me, Commander. Every five-point-six seconds, they say, it passes through a man's mind."

He grinned, blushed slightly, but kept his arms folded, "Don't know what you're talking about. There's no football game tonight."

Lieutenant MacOlson was off again. This time, how boats could be lashed up and how the organization of Spec Boat Unit Twenty worked.

Tucker found the scene fascinating. He tuned out the Surface Warfare officer's words as he watched the sailors on the double piers below the hill of the old tower. Along the two piers jutting out from the concrete wharf were sets of bollards. The squat cylindrical black metal structures, anchored to the piers with thick, heavy steel bolts, had lines running from them to the T-shaped polished-metal cleats on the deck edges of the boats.

"So what happens if the line breaks?" Tibbles-Seagraves asked.

"If he keeps asking questions, we'll be here forever," Sam whispered.

"Sometimes people die. That's why we have that small piece of line running between two points on each line. It's hard to see here, but we call that the 'tattletale.' When the tattletale is stretched tight, then you run the risk of the line breaking from the tension on it. When a line breaks, it whips out"—he raised his left arm and brought it around in a large semicircle from right to left—"and around like a razor, cutting through anything and everyone in its path. Right, Boats?"

"Yes, sir. Remember last year?"

"Yes. Last year one of the cruisers at Norfolk Navy base had a line part, and it cost a chief petty officer both his legs. The line cut through him like a knife through butter."

"I'm going to be sick," Sam said.

"How can you be sick? You're a nurse," Tucker whispered.

"They relieved the commanding officer," Jenson added softly.

The rain rode across the landscape like cascading waves of theater curtains, rising and falling to the wind, the noise whipping around the buildings, trees, and vessels like some earthly applause to its performance. Most times the slight angle of the rain hitting the sailors barely changed. They kept their heads down, their gloved hands playing the lines like musicians, lifting the eye of one line up and over the bollard, while on the boat another couple of sailors untied the figure eight, pulling it tighter, while others, standing in tandem, worked together weaving the lines around the bollards. Tucker could see the lips of the Boatswain Mate in charge moving, the noise of the storm drowning the words. As the mariner spoke and pointed, three sailors on the pier hopped and shuffled in choreography as old as when sailors first went to sea. They expertly and quickly adjusted the mooring lines of the six dark boats, moving from one to the other as a team. Each boat had six lines across. The bow and stern lines ran directly from their cleat on the ship to the pier, while the other four lines made a pair of X's as they connected to the pier. The X type of mooring played the movement of the tide and current against itself, helping to keep the boat steady. Even Tucker knew that, and he was a Navy SEAL.

Every few minutes, a strong gust danced through the tableau, rippling the edges of the rain curtain, raising the water parallel with the earth. When that happened, the rain hit the sailors squarely in the face or the backs of their heads, chins involuntarily tightened against heaving chests, as they fought the elements to protect the boats. The boats were all that were in the minds of the sailors out there. Everything else was secondary, shoved to another part of their minds. Even the rain and wind pelting them were elements the working party fought to ignore. They focused on the job, getting it done, and having a quick break before starting over again; for storms never played the same act twice. The winds and seas forever evolved in a storm, as if eagerly seeking an opening to wreak havoc on those who would challenge it.

"With synthetic lines, when they're wet you can see when the tension on them increases. First it squeezes the water out, and then, when they are nearing breaking point, actual vapor rises all along the length of it caused by the heat generated when the tension actually vaporizes the moisture."

The gusts sneaked under the pulled-down soaked watch caps of the sailors and blew water from the slicks. Vaguely, Tucker heard MacOlson correct something Tibbles-Seagraves said and then explain again what the sailors were doing. Bet ol' Tibbles-Seagraves wished he had never asked the Surface Warfare officer "What was going on?" Tucker grinned at the thought.

"Five-point-six seconds."

With the exception of the sleek, low-profile warships rolling alongside the piers, the scene could have been from the age of sailing vessels. Securing a ship alongside a dock or a pier was more than wrapping a line around a cleat and a bollard and hasting off home for a meal, a beer, and a quick romp in the sack before Monday night football started. It was an art—an art only learned by hands-on experience. Storms were the final exams that separated those who had truly mastered their art and those with still much to learn. If they lived.

Lieutenant MacOlson explained what it meant when each line was "doubled up," and immediately went into details of how a ship "singled-up" all lines in preparation to get underway. Tucker glanced at Tibbles-Seagraves. The man politely nodded at Lieutenant MacOlson. The Royal Air Force officer's eyes were beginning to glaze over.

Tucker laughed, catching the attention of Tibbles-Seagraves who smiled in return. In that fraction of a second, it was apparent to Tucker that MacOlson had long ago lost Tibbles-Seagraves, who had drowned in the mariner chatter and was only politely listening to something he failed to understand and minutes ago had lost interest in.

The room was growing warmer. Tucker shifted his survival knife farther back on his belt so it wouldn't jut into his stomach when he sat down. He lifted his foot and rested it on the vent beneath the window, bent down, and retied the boot, making sure the pants leg was tucked tightly into the green socks. He liked the camouflage uniform. Even without the rain slick, they had certain chemically treated fabrics that made the outfit water-repellant.

Finished, Tucker looked back out the window as a strong gust ripped open a sailor's rain slick, causing the mariner to drop his grip on the forward line of the boat at the end of the pier. The second sailor who was supposed to be grasping the line also was running over to another work party.

"Oh, shit!" P.T. shouted. "Boats!"

The bow of the boat edged away from the pier.

The Boatswain Mate in charge dove for the flapping line, missing it. Two sailors farther up hurriedly tossed the eye of the line they had over the bollard and ran toward the boat. The wind pushed the bow of the boat away from the pier. The other five lines held, but as Tucker watched, the number two and three lines began to smoke as water vapor rose.

The bowline flopped back across the pier. The nearest sailor grabbed it and quickly wrapped it around his wrist, while shouting at the Boatswain Mate supervisor. The Boatswain Mate began to shout, waving his arms frantically as he ran toward the sailor. The Petty Officer's watch cap blew off, tumbling over and over as it rose above the row of boats behind him and then disappeared into the wind, heading farther inland. The Boatswain Mate slipped on the wet pier. Even from this distance, Tucker saw the fear and horror in the Petty Officer's face. His mouth contorted in what appeared to Tucker to be shouts. The Petty Officer's hands stretched toward the young sailor even as he scrambled on all fours toward the sailor, who now stood, his head turning side to side as if trying to figure out what was wrong. The supervisor's face glowed red as he screamed at the man, his feet slipping as he fought to regain his footing.

The door to the quarterdeck flew open as P.T. and the Boatswain Mate dashed out of the building.

On the pier, two other sailors reached the Boatswain

Mate. One grabbed him under the arms as he passed, pulling him upright. The other, the rankings of a Second Class stenciled in black on the right sleeve of his rain slick, hopped over the two sailors in a headlong dash toward the sailor with the bow line. The smile of the sailor who had thought he had saved the line faded into fear as the boat pulled him toward the edge of the pier.

Tucker gasped, "Oh, no! Come on!" He watched the sailor futilely fight to unwrap the line from his wrist, his feet slipping on the pier as he attempted to dig in against the pull of the boat as it eased away from the pier. The number-two line parted, whipping out, passing harmlessly over the Boatswain Mate in charge and the sailor helping him up. The two of them dove for the pier, throwing their hands over their heads. The other sailors ran up the pier away from the whipping mooring line. The snapped mooring line reached its limit to the left and immediately whipped back to the right, riding safely over the two sailors lying on the pier and barely missing the struggling sailor as the bow line pulled him toward the edge. The line whipped around, and a gust of wind changed its trajectory enough that it caught on the number-five line, wrapping itself around and around it.

Tucker and Tibbles-Seagraves ran down the stairs leading to the wharf, taking them two at a time. Behind him, he heard Sam shout, but her words were lost in the mayhem.

Tucker looked up into the rain as he stumbled on the last two slippery concrete steps. The sailor was gone. The other three sailors were running toward the end of the pier, looking over the side between the pier and the Mark V boat. He knew if the wind twisted slightly and pushed the boat back toward the landing, it might crush the sailor between it and the pier. There was no space beneath the piers where someone could take refuge, and with the heavy mooring line wrapped around the young man's wrist, most likely the sailor would be unable to swim to the surface.

The Boatswain Mate in charge grabbed the two sailors

and sent them scurrying aboard the drifting Mark V. They had to reset the lines. Right now, only four lines held the craft to the pier.

By the time MacOlson, the senior Boatswain Mate, Jenson, and Tucker hit the end of the pier and started sprinting toward the scene, several other sailors had fenders from nearby boats and were doubling them up between the loose craft and the pier, trying to keep the bow from crashing back against it.

Tucker glanced around Tibbles-Seagraves who was directly behind, surprised and glad to see Sam following. If they rescued this sailor, her services would be needed.

The supervising Boatswain Mate pushed his shoes off with his feet and ran toward the edge of the pier.

"No, Jacobs!" MacOlson shouted. "Don't do it."

The man looked back at them. It was hard to tell from the rain whether those were tears running down his cheeks, but the man's face was scrunched in a look of terror.

A cry rode across the wind, reaching their ears.

"Jenson, get that boat secured!" MacOlson shouted as he ran toward the end of the pier. He touched Jacobs on his shoulder. "Come on!" Along the piers were wooden pillars that ran several feet above the pier through the concrete and deep into the waters beneath. Hanging on each of them were life rings. MacOlson grabbed one. Tucker Raleigh reached MacOlson as the Lieutenant stopped at the end of the pier. At the bottom of a wave about ten feet out, the head of the young sailor appeared, his free left hand waved wildly as he fought to keep his head above water. He screamed once and then quickly was jerked beneath the surface.

MacOlson drew back and slung the life ring. It sailed into the wind for a fraction of a second before the storm grabbed it and took it end over end past the spot in the water where the man had disappeared.

Tucker dove from the end of the pier into the water, the scream of "No" from Sam Bradley ringing in his ears before the water engulfed him. This was home to a Navy

SEAL, but cammies weren't the uniform of choice for diving. He dove deeper, trying to dive through the current pushing him away from the direction in which he had seen the young sailor disappear. Tucker struggled east in the exit direction of the small channel the boats used. Visibility was limited. The motion of the water steered up the sediment on the bottom. Lights came on above, filtering into the water. Without warning, a line bopped up from beneath and whipped across his face, bringing pain with it and causing Tucker to involuntarily crunch his eyes tight.

He felt the line near his hand and grabbed it. He opened his eyes and started pulling on the line. The effort moved him along it. A hand appeared, flapping at the wrist in the water. The line was wrapped around it. Tucker reached down to his ankle for his knife. His fingers searched for several seconds before he recalled strapping it to his waist earlier. He pulled his survival knife out and with a couple of quick slices cut the sailor free. The man's face was back there somewhere in the murky water. Tucker's lungs ached.

Tucker pulled the man to him, flipped him around, and wrapped the sailor's neck in the crook of his arm. Tucker swam toward the surface, kicking his boots as fast as possible, aware of the water filling them, weighing them down and threatening to drag both of them down. He released a few bubbles of air. Then, just as suddenly, Tucker was above the water, gasping for breath even as he pulled the sailor over, freeing the man's face from the water. Several life rings bopped around him. He grabbed one, looped his free arm through it, and then turned, lifting the sailor's face further out of the water. A wave washed over them, disrupting his paddling and causing his boots to drag downward. The edge of the life ring pulled down for a second, then Tucker felt the tension on the life ring as those on the pier pulled him in.

He reached forward and pulled the sailor's face to his. He opened the young man's lips. In that brief moment, Tucker took in the freckles and glazed eyes. The eyes were always the first thing to go in death. One moment they sparkled and shined with vitality, and the next, a fine dull gray clouded over them like someone closing a door on a party. The sailor couldn't be more than nineteen or twenty, he thought. He pushed the drowned man's lips apart and began a makeshift CPR, forcing air into water-filled lungs. Tucker quit trying to stay afloat, depending on the movement of the life ring to do the job. He had to keep up this happenstance CPR until the man was ashore where proper medical attention could be administered. Where Sam waited. She could save him.

His head bounced lightly against the ladder at the end of the pier. Hands reached from above, grabbing and hastily pulling the drowned sailor onto the pier. Tibbles-Seagraves's face appeared above Tucker's. The SAS's hand reached down and gripped Tucker's wrist. "I say, my friend, time for you now."

With Tibbles-Seagraves holding his left wrist, pulling upward, Tucker climbed back onto the pier. Water spilled from his boots as he stood atop the cement pier, the wind whipping around him. Ahead of him, Sam knelt beside the man. One of her knees positioned between the man's legs with the other to the victim's left, she pushed with both hands on the sailor's diaphragm; down and up; forcing air in and out of the lungs. The wind drowned out her counts. Riding the winds came the faint sound of an ambulance approaching. Tucker sat down on the pier, looking up at the tower. Down the steps came the Commodore in his soaked khakis, the rain giving them a dark, dirty color. Behind the mustang Captain walked the French Special Forces officer Captain Marc St. Cyr, his head moving from side to side as if he was a spectator of some morose event to be assessed and weighed.

Sam rolled the young sailor onto his side. From the drowned man's mouth, water rushed out, followed by a cough. Sam shifted her knees to one side of the man, quickly rolled him onto his back. She put her head against his chest for a moment, mouthed the word *damn,* and recommenced CPR.

Across from Tucker, staring helplessly, Lieutenant MacOlson stood on the deck of the boat. On the pier, Jenson and another sailor dropped a new line around the bollard, singling it up until they could get a second out and around it. Tucker watched as the Surface Warfare officer took his eyes off Sam and her ministrations.

"Boats!" the lithe skipper shouted. "I want two more lines across the Mark V's berthed at the end of the piers. The hell with six lines, I want eight. And, if we have anyone else who is so new they don't know to never wrap a line around themselves, then put them with someone who has the experience to train them."

Jenson gave a half-hearted salute to show he heard.

Against the dark sky, the rotating lights of the ambulance joined the cascading noise of the storm. The siren picked up in intensity for several seconds before it stopped. Tucker looked toward the tower. A minute later, two corpsmen with a stretcher and a female doctor scrambled over the rise, slipping on the grass for a moment before they reached the concrete dock.

A movement to his left caught his attention. The Commodore put his hand out and leaned down to where Tucker sat. "You okay, Commander Raleigh?"

Tucker reached up and took the man's hand, surprised at the firm grip. The slight buldge around the Commodore's waist belied the strength in the man's arms. Tucker allowed himself to be helped up.

"That was a brave thing you did."

Tucker nodded, not in the least thinking it was brave. It was just something that needed doing, and he was trained and confident enough to know that he could do it.

He looked over to where his girlfriend—*was that what he thought of her? His girlfriend?*—Sam shifted the man's head, shoving it back to align the mouth and neck into as near a straight line as possible. Sometime during the CPR, she had shifted her knees and was now leaning back on her haunches. The young sailor he had rescued was heaving. Meant he was breathing again. The boy would live, he figured. Sam tilted the sailor's head to the side. Vomit spewed from the unconscious sailor into the rainwater being shoved by the wind across the pier.

The two corpsmen pushed through the sailors, shouting several times, "Make a hole," as they maneuvered the stretcher beside the victim. Sam pushed herself up to talk with the doctor. The woman nodded several times as a corpsman strapped the man to the stretcher. The other took a portable oxygen bottle, put a mask around the sailor's mouth, and laid the bottle in the crook of the man's arms. The doctor motioned them to go, and the three took off back up the hill. Tucker winced as the corpsman holding the rear of the stretcher slipped on the wet grass, falling to one knee for a moment before regaining his footing. In that fraction of a moment, Tucker had a vision of the poor sailor rolling back down the hill.

He looked over his shoulder. Sam was standing several feet away, watching the ambulance crew carry her patient away. He walked over and touched her on the shoulder. Her hair was matted across her head, over her ears, and down her neck, splayed along her shoulders. "Good job, Sam."

She pulled him to her and held him close. He nearly pushed her away, thinking of the Commodore behind them, but then his hands reached around her and he pulled her close as she rested her head on his chest. She said something. He pushed her away slightly so he could look down into her face. "Sorry, I didn't hear you."

"I said, I thought I had lost you."

This was the time he would usually make a smart comeback, but words escaped him. He wrapped his arms around her, pulling her head back against his chest. They stood in the rain as the sailors returned to their business. He glanced up, his eyes meeting those of the unsmiling Commodore, who stood halfway up the steps leading back to the tower. St. Cyr and Tibbles-Seagraves waited at the end of the pier, watching. Well, so much for public displays of affection, but in crises a little PDA could be comforting. Even her wet hair smelled nice.

* * *

"DID YOU SEE THE LOOK ON THOSE TWO FACES?"

The other deputy laughed. "Yeah, you'd think after all these years word would get around that this ain't the place to park and neck. It ain't as if we didn't use it ourselves."

Josiah Henry opened the door to the sheriff's cruiser, laid his arm across the top of it, and placed his boot on the bottom of the door frame. "Have to admit it beats hauling drunks out of Maude's at this time of night."

The radio beeped, followed by a quick radio announcement, and several seconds of static as the transmission finished. One thing about Janet, she never let those on patrol go to sleep. She stayed on that radio even when there was nothing to share. She had a hell of a voice. Rumor had it she worked part time for one of those 1-900 numbers. Damn good thing she had a voice, because she outweighed him, and he was two hundred fifty pounds. Being six foot two and lifting weights every day, along with jogging, kept those pounds firm.

"I think, Josiah, if we had waited another few minutes, it might have been more than a little heavy kissing we broke up," Harry Johnson chuckled, pulling a crumbled pack of cigarettes from his shirt pocket. "Now, that would have caused both of those kids to give up sex." He shook out one, used his fingers to straighten it, and then lit up before leaning against the hood of the Ford Crown Victoria.

"Man, you ought to do yourself a favor and toss those coffin nails away. Ain't no good coming from polluting your lungs with that shit."

The sounds of heavy surf rode the stiff breeze coming off the Atlantic. The overcast from the storm northeast of Florida hid what little light the moon and stars could have provided.

"Look, Josiah, do I say anything about your vice?"

"What vice, man? I ain't got no vice."

"You don't call getting up at six every morning to go running a vice?"

"Man, that ain't a vice. That's called keeping healthy."

"Did you know more people died jogging last year than smoking?"

Josiah's brow wrinkled for a moment before the big man laughed. "Man, you're lying. Where in the hell did you get a fact like that?"

"It's a well-known fact. It was all in the newspapers. Even Rush Limbaugh commented on the enorm . . . enoman . . . Ah, he was just as surprised as you."

"Well, I don't believe you. I enjoy the morning run, and I intend to keep doing it."

"I call it habit. I may smoke, but you have become one of those health do-gooders who spend all their time trying to convert those of us fighting for our rights."

Josiah shifted his foot off the door panel, shut the door, and walked to the top of the dunes. He put his hands on his hips, staring at the small paved parking area used in the early mornings by dedicated beach combers. Many a time he had spent a few hours in darkness parked there, but that had been many years ago when he had been in his teens and before it was paved. He met his first wife, Gloria, there. Well, not exactly. He met her in high school, but he really *met* her there. That *meet* resulted in marriage at the early age of nineteen and being a father six months after the wedding. If he didn't do anything else, he probably saved a few young men from the same fate, though he doubted any would recognize how much they owed him.

He looked back at Harry. "Don't see anyone else down there."

Harry looked at his watch, reading the glowing hands. "It's getting on about eleven, Josiah. There'll be a fresh wave between twelve and one." Even in the dark, Josiah saw his friend and partner flick the finished cigarette. The glow of the butt flying through the air traced the path over the slight dune in front of them, disappearing from view before hitting the white sand on the other side.

"One of these days, you gonna start a fire, my friend."

"Well, not tonight. Not with this on-again off-again

rain we've been having for four days. Besides, what's going to burn here? The sand? You're just giving me a rough time."

"If getting you to quit smoking is giving you a rough time, then so be it."

Harry walked up to the crest of the dune where Josiah stood. A break in the clouds exposed the moon, lighting up the darkness below them. For a half mile each way, white sand shined in the reflected moonlight. Heavy waves crashed ashore, rolling up the low beach before losing their momentum and pulling back out to sea. A line of washed-ashore seaweed wove along the beach where high tide had deposited it. A light mist fell as they stood there silently, watching nature paint a tableau with choppy seas, rolling mist, and white beaches. Josiah reached up, lifted his dark deputy sheriff's hat, and ran the back of his hand across his forehead, clearing away the water.

Harry craned his neck forward, staring out to sea.

"I think we should go and do a drive around the county. Maybe stop at Maude's and see who's injured tonight. I think if we keep standing here, we're going to be one pair of soaked puppies."

"Josiah," Harry said, reaching out and tugging his friend's sleeve. "You see that?" He pointed to the right, out to sea.

"See what?"

"Look where I'm pointing, about a hundred yards off shore. Looks to me like a boat."

"What would a boat be doing out on a night like this?"

Harry shook his head. "I don't know, but it sure looks like something floating out there."

Josiah moved forward a few steps, raising his hand to shield his eyes from the rain. "Get me my binoculars." Behind him, he heard his partner open the door to the cruiser.

"Here," Harry said, returning with the binoculars.

Josiah lifted the binoculars, twisted the knobs to improve the focus, and scanned the edge of the water, working his way out to sea in the direction that Harry had pointed. Wouldn't be the first time they'd stumbled on refugees trying to enter the United States illegally. The bad thing about it was the two of them would have to go down there and round them up before they scattered in fifty-eleven different directions and disappeared into the vast expanse of America. The good news was the CIS would take them off their hands. The bad news was you never knew when the CIS would show up to do it. Sometimes they were there within an hour. Other times, they got to house and feed them in the county jail for a couple of days—without compensation for the expense, as the sheriff was fond of pointing out.

Josiah shifted the binoculars right to left and then back again, continuing to inch his way out to sea. He saw nothing. Then, suddenly, a dark shape rode over the crest of a wave, catching his attention as it broke the monotonous bounce of the sea. He jerked the glasses on the spot, which was nearer the beach, twisted the knobs to regain focus on the dark area, and as it became visible, a flash of lightning on the horizon lit up the area. Josiah had seen enough.

"Looks as if we got us a boatload of refugees, Harry."

"Damn! Why don't we just call the CIS and have them come down and take care of this?"

Josiah laughed. "Man, you know the CIS are home in their warm beds with their cute blondes, cuddled up in a cocoon of air-conditioning while us country boys are out here communing with nature."

The rain increased in intensity, coming down heavy now.

"This pisses me off. Why couldn't the refugees come earlier, when it wasn't raining?"

"Get on the horn and tell Janet what we got here."

"You want me to tell her to call the CIS and let them take it from here?"

"Give it up, Harry." Unseen in the dark, Josiah shook his head and sighed. "Naw, bro, I'm like you and would surely love to give this to them, but we gotta see who they are first. I only got a glimpse, and it may not even be a boat. What I saw was too dark to be a boat." He paused a moment. "Maybe it's capsized and that was the hull. I mean I didn't see anyone, but I didn't get a clear view before that flash of lightning near destroyed my night vision."

"Don't tell me."

"Yeah, we gotta go down. You got those plastic thingies?"

"Yeah, I got those *plastic thingies*. And I even have two sets of handcuffs if we need them."

Josiah gingerly stepped over the lip of the dune, planting his foot in the wet sand on the other side. With a hand raised to keep his balance, the Florida deputy started down the dune toward the beach. A moment later, Harry was beside him. "Don't use the handcuffs if you can avoid it, Harry. Last time we used handcuffs, those old boys at the Bureau of Citizen and Immigration Services didn't return them, and the Sheriff wanted me to pay for them." Josiah stumbled, falling to a knee before he recovered himself. The rain was coming down fast, limiting their visibility. He was soaked now. It was bad enough they were going to have to round up a bunch of illegals, but to have to do it in this weather even pissed his stoic self off. "Damn."

"See! I told you. If they'd come earlier or waited until our shift was over, I might be better inclined toward them."

"Harry, you're so full of bullshit your eyes are brown. Aren't you the one still flying the Confederate Flag on the back of your pickup?"

"That's heritage, man. Ain't got nothing to do with racism, regardless of what you think. If it did, you'd think I'd be working with you?"

The wind blew off the sea inland, hiding their voices as they talked. It never dawned on the two to silently approach the drifting boat, edged toward the beach by the wind and incoming tide. They had done this many times and knew the refugees would be tired and dispirited when they hit the shore. Even though Josiah knew Janet would have already sent other cars their way, the two of them could handle any group of refugees small enough to fit into the small object he had seen.

The two men reached the edge of the beach where the slant of the sand dunes stopped and the slight decline of the beach to the sea started. Off to their right, the black shape rode a wave onto the beach. It was one of those rubber crafts. Didn't look like one of those wooden boats the Haitians always used.

The sound of someone talking reached their ears. Josiah reached out, touched Harry, and the two deputies drew their revolvers. They hadn't run into illegals who were willing to fight or kill like they'd heard about, but there was no reason to take chances. This high up along the Florida east coast, most likely they were Haitians—rich Haitians if they could afford one of those rubber boats—and most likely they were Haitians who had tried to land at another time and been caught. Usually they got up this high along the Florida coast on their second or third attempt to land in America. Josiah moved along the edge of the beach, using the perimeter of dune plants to shade his approach, blending with the dune behind; whereas if he skipped across the white sands, even in the darkness the movement would have been detected.

Two men were pulling the rubber craft farther inland. Another two lay in the bottom of the raft. Probably sea sick, Josiah guessed. He saw the small engine mounted on the rear of the rubber craft. If those four rode this thing ashore then they had to have been dropped off shore by a bigger ship. Another tidbit to pass to Janet, who would notify the Coast Guard up in Jacksonville.

Josiah crouched, watching the two men and listening to them grunt as they pulled the raft away from the clutching suction of waves rolling back out to sea. The conversation was clear, but he couldn't understand a word of it. Josiah had heard enough Spanish and Haitian Creole to recognize it when he heard it, but this language didn't sound like either of those. He shook his head, concentrating on the two men talking, trying to figure out what nationality they were.

Harry startled him, reaching out to touch Josiah on the shoulder. "Man, I thought you stayed back there to cover me. Scared the living shit out of me," he whispered, the wind carrying their words up the dunes and away from the ears of the two men leaning against the sides of the rubber craft.

"What in the hell are they speaking?"

"I don't know," he whispered back.

The two men stood and tossed the lines back into the raft. The two deputies watched, knowing they had the edge on the refugees, but Josiah liked to wait long enough to assess a situation before he barged into something. Even at Maude's, he'd watch two men bashing each other's heads in with their fists for a while before separating them. Better to have them too tired to fight back when he did step in. That philosophy had done him well during his fifteen years of law enforcement and three sheriffs.

The two men lifted the other two out of the raft and half carried, half walked them to the edge of the beach about forty yards from Josiah and Harry. A flash of lightning lit up the sky for a moment, causing Josiah to cringe, expecting one of the refugees to spot them and shout a warning to the others.

"They gonna see us."

"Well, they going to see us anyway eventually."

The two men returned to the raft and pulled two weapons out of the back.

"Shit! These ain't yore normal run-of-the-mill illegals."

The slight sound of Harry slipping off his safety reached Josiah's ears. Using his thumb, he flicked off his own. Those were automatics, and here he and Harry were stuck with a couple of light .38s. This wasn't going to be a pretty sight!

"Harry, stay here and cover me. I'm gonna move closer to the two laying down. When I arrest them, you shout out at the two with weapons to drop their guns."

"Oh, man . . . oh, man, I don't like that idea," Harry said, Josiah detecting a tremble in the voice.

"I don't either." He glanced around them and saw a small rise near the edge of the dune. "Get behind that in case they start shooting."

"I've got a better idea. I'll go arrest those two who look dead and you stay here and arrest those two with the automatic rifles."

Josiah couldn't see the incredulous look on his partner's face, but he could imagine it.

"Well, we gotta do something before they discover us."

"Why don't we sneak back to the car and wait for reinforcements?"

Josiah shook his head. "Naw, man. I'm just as nervous as you. We're gonna arrest them."

"You gonna arrest them? Jesus, Josiah. They got guns bigger than ours."

"Yeah, well, our balls are bigger."

"Right now, mine don't feel bigger. I think I see another car up there at lover's lane. Why don't we go check that out and call in reinforcements while we're doing that?"

"Those ain't Haitians out there, Harry. You know and I know what they are. If we don't do something, they gonna be spread all over America before we can stop them."

"Yeah, and if we do, we could be spread all over this beach. That's a *real* gun the tall one near the boat is holding."

Josiah rose off his haunches and creeped to the right, closing the distance with the illegals. They were either terrorists or drug runners, and his money was on terrorists. Druggies would at least have some dope on them, and it's the dope they would have hauled out of that boat first. Human life was inexpensive when it came to transporting drugs. But whatever or whoever they were mattered little right now. What mattered was they were in his county and his responsibility. What had the old sheriff who'd retired twenty years before told him? "Shoot first and clean your pistol later."

There was more the man had said between his quick breaths on the oxygen bottle, such as "Lie, lie, lie, because, boy, it don't matter what you did and how right you were to do it, they still gonna come after you because deep inside, right here"—the old man had weakly punched his chest—"We Americans don't really trust the government. We may trust our sheriffs, but we don't really trust those who wear civilian clothes."

Josiah glanced back at Harry. He could barely make out his partner's head and shoulders visible above the slight rise. He wished he had brought his walkie-talkie with him. One reason they seldom carried them was that Janet had a habit of broadcasting at the most inopportune times. If he had it, he might be able to reach Janet, and if he could reach her, she could hurry the backup along. Maybe Harry was right. He stopped. Maybe they should retreat to the cruiser, wait for backup, and then take on these four. If they did that, they ran the risk the four would disappear before backup arrived. Plus, the element of surprise they had now would be gone.

He crouched, leaned forward on one knee, and held the pistol—which felt awfully small—with both hands. He licked his dry lips. Damn, it wasn't as if this was something they did every day in Summer Haven, Florida.

"Put your hands up! You're under arrest!" Harry shouted.

"Damn, Harry!" Josiah muttered softly. "I'm going to kill you, if they don't."

The two men near the raft stopped, stood straight, searching in the direction from where Harry's shout had originated. Then suddenly the two shouted something in a language Josiah didn't recognize and began firing wildly with their automatic rifles. One of them charged in Harry's direction. The other followed.

Josiah knees felt like rubber. He moved the pistol to the left, aiming for the one in front, the barrel tracking the running figure a few inches in front. He pulled the trigger. The crack of the gunshot echoed off the sand dune behind him. The man tumbled forward, his arms outstretched, sending the automatic rifle spinning into the air. It was only then that Josiah realized he had been repeatedly shouting *"Shit!"* at the top of his voice.

The second man stopped firing and dove toward the beach. One shot came from Harry's direction. The bullet hit the man as he fell, causing him to throw his hands up. The weapon sailed out of the man's hands and landed half in the surf. The man Josiah had shot lay motionless on the sand. The two men dragged to the edge of the beach never moved.

Josiah, crouching, ran to the right, his gun in his left hand, digging with his right hand in his back pocket for the plastic strips used for makeshift handcuffs. They had the familiar metal cuffs, but the jingle they made when they were trying to roust sex-starved teenagers from lovers' lane spoiled the fun of the moment when they tapped on the open window of a parked car. He kept his eyes on the two wounded men outstretched between the boat and where Harry crouched. Josiah glanced out to sea, expecting to see white running lights of the ship that had dropped these four, but fog, rain, and darkness obscured anything farther out than about a hundred feet from the ocean edge. Josiah dropped to his knees. He was about ten feet to the side of the two men dragged from the boat. Another flash of lightning lit up the beach, and when the following thunder dissipated, Josiah heard moans coming from the two men. One of them lifted a hand and threw it across his face. Josiah nodded. He'd be sick as a dog too if he had ridden through that rough water to shore. The man lifted his head and turned it in Josiah's direction.

He could hear the heaving as the man vomited.

Seems these four had plans that did not involve staying on the beach long. He glanced back toward the top of the dune. What if someone was supposed to meet them here? Shit! He and Harry were going to be caught between two groups if that happened. Seeing no one coming over the top of the dunes, he turned his attention back to the two men. The rain slowed for moment, and as if in tempo with several heavy gusts, it came back with renewed intensity. The strong gusts off the sea drowned out the noise of the two in front of him. It took a few seconds for his night vision to readjust. In that flash of lightning, he hadn't seen a weapon with the two men, but that didn't mean they didn't have one.

Josiah glanced back toward where Harry should have been, but in the darkness he couldn't see his partner. Harry may be the cautious type and may even have been right in wanting them to retreat back up the dune and call for reinforcements. Damn it! No doubt about it, his partner had been right. Josiah wished he had listened to the younger man this time. He took a deep breath. A brief perverse thought of his wife looking down on his bullet-ridden body passed through his mind.

He stood, spread his legs, and gripped the pistol with both hands. One of the men sat up, his head turning back and forth, no doubt searching for his other two comrades. He aimed his pistol at the man. The other remained motionless, too ill to offer resistance. Well, if the gunplay didn't tell them they were here, it was time for him to let them know.

"Stop where you are! Raise your hands!"

He heard the sound of running feet from behind him. That'd be Harry. He stepped out and held up his hand, failing to realize that Harry couldn't see the sign to stop in the dark.

"Stop, Harry!" Josiah shouted.

A ripple of bullets tore up the beach as they worked their way in the direction of his partner. The man who had managed to sit up was shooting. The bullets raced out to sea, never coming near Harry. Josiah ran several steps to the right, kicked the gun, knocking it out of the man's hand and onto the beach several feet away. Harry ran up beside him and pointed his gun past Josiah at the man, who began vomiting.

Josiah reached out with his shoe and turned the man's face to the side so he wouldn't drown in his own vomit.

"Sick assholes, aren't they?"

Josiah nodded. "I can't imagine anyone trying to sail ashore in this mess. I'm surprised they made it."

"Kind of glad they did," Harry said, his body practically dancing as the flood of adrenalin eased. "Man oh man, did we do well or not?" He waved his pistol in the air. "Did you see that, Josiah? One shot. That's all I fired was one shot. And, you—you only fired one shot. Four of these assholes—who are they, anyway?—and we took out an armed gang with automatic rifles, grenades, and—"

"What grenades? There ain't no grenades." Josiah reached up and with the back of his hand wiped the rain from his forehead. "Let's get cuffs on these buggers, and then you hightail it back up the dune and tell Janet to notify our CIS friends to get their butts down here right now. Tonight! If we're going to get soaked wrapping up this little episode, I want as many people as possible wet with me."

"You got it, boss," Harry said, pulling out a few of the plastic handcuffs from his back pocket.

Josiah realized he'd dropped his somewhere, but he stood at the feet of the two men, his gun trained on them, keeping an eye on the one he figured was dead—*you could never tell when they were faking.*

A wail from behind him nearly caused him to shoot. He turned quickly, corkscrewing downward to a crouching position. One of the men he and Harry had shot wasn't dead. They should have checked those two. Josiah noticed that the weapons of the men were nowhere to be seen, and he rightly assumed that Harry had detoured by them to throw the weapons out of their reach. He had also assumed, wrongly, that Harry had checked them to see if they were alive.

He ran toward the second man. The one Harry had shot. The wounded man was moaning facedown in his own blood and vomit. He was alive, but Josiah wasn't sure where Harry's bullet had hit him. From the amount of movement and the complaining noises the man was making, it wasn't life threatening.

Josiah rolled the wounded man over, holstered his pistol, and pinned the man's hands behind him. He might be wounded, but he wasn't sure how badly. Josiah detoured a few feet around the man; out of range of any high jinks the asshole might try, and ran toward the other one, whom he had shot. He put two fingers on the man's neck, moving it around searching for a pulse, unable to find one. "Dead," he said to himself, whipping out one of Harry's plastic handcuffs. He wasn't the county mortician. Let them confirm it. Josiah quickly tied the hands of the dead man behind the body.

"I called Janet!" Harry shouted from down the beach where he was running toward Josiah.

A few seconds later, Harry stood over Josiah. "They'll be here any moment," Harry said through deep breaths. "Man oh man, I can't believe you made me run all the way to the car. Here," he said, holding a walkie-talkie out for Josiah. "I ain't going back up that dune for some time."

This time several flashes of lightning crisscrossed overhead. They walked back to where the other two men lay. One had his hands tied behind his back, but the other's hands were crossed over his chest.

Josiah reached down, keeping his gun pulled back slightly in the event the man was faking and tried to grab it. He tugged the man onto his back. He didn't want any more to die before higher authorities got here. Already, he was going to be spending the rest of the night doing paperwork on this. The more dead bodies, the more paperwork.

He pulled the second man over, glanced at the wounded one in the middle of the beach. The man had somehow turned onto his side. At least that one wasn't going to suffocate, though he was going to have a lot of sand in his mouth.

He looked down at the two men breathing heavily at his feet.

"Here," Harry said, handing him a flashlight. "I brought both of ours. Figured we might need them."

Josiah turned the flashlight on and shined it on the two men at their feet. Their faces were covered in small blisters. The second one looked worse than the first, with blisters so large Josiah was sure the man couldn't open his eyes. If these men were sea sick, that wasn't the only thing bothering them. He walked over to the wounded man and shined the flashlight on the man's face. This one was also covered in blisters.

Whatever was wrong with these men, Josiah just hoped it didn't mean more work. Bad enough he was going to have to call Harriet and tell her he'd be late. Bad enough he was going to have to listen to her twenty questions and convince her that he had little choice. Bad enough he was going to have to listen to CIS question everything he told them. He stuck his shoe under the body of the dead man and pushed it over.

He shined his flashlight on the dead man's face and wondered what had happened to cause the sea of blisters that covered the faces of these four men. They were like bumps, and for a fleeting moment, they made him think of acne gone so bad it was forcing the man's eyes shut. He flicked off the flashlight. Josiah hoped whatever these men brought ashore with them wasn't contagious. If it was contagious and he brought it home, he'd really catch hell from Harriet.

CHAPTER 10

LIEUTENANT EARLY LIFTED HER HEAD, SHIFTING HER JAW back and forth. Her vision had returned, though her left eye remained swollen. She twisted her head back and forth, trying to ease the muscle tightness of her neck. Early pulled herself to a sitting position from behind Senior Chief Leary. Senior Chief Leary leaned back against the bulkhead.

"Senior Chief, it's not working."

"We've only been at it a few minutes, ma'am. Besides, it's all we got."

"I'd say more like a couple of hours."

"Let me see," Lieutenant Scott Kelly said. He knee-walked across the small space between them, deliberately fell across the Senior Chief's legs, and pulled himself around so he was between them.

"Gotta-Be, you can't see shit. Your eyes are too swollen. You can't see and the Senior Chief doesn't have eyes in the back of his head."

"I've heard that punch line, Scott," she replied, her voice slightly slurred. She tightened and released several times the muscles in her jaw, then moved the jaw back and forth a few times. "I tried to get a grip with my teeth on the plastic strip, but the thing is so tight on your wrists, Senior Chief. Then, when I do manage to get a bite on it, it slips out as soon as I bite down hard or attempt to saw through it with my teeth. I just can't get a good grip."

"Lean up, Senior Chief," Kelly said, nudging Leary's hard shoulder with his head.

Leary leaned forward so the copilot could look. "Yeap, you're right, Gotta-Be," he said. "Your teeth have nipped the Senior Chief's wrist, but the plastic is still intact."

"Lieutenant," Senior Chief Leary said, turning his head so he could look at Kelly. "How about yours? Are they as tight as mine?"

Kelly sat back up, tried to smile, and quickly stopped. "Ouch," he said. "That hurt. Senior Chief, I can't tell you if mine are looser or tighter. I lost feeling in my hands days ago, but if we stay here another couple of days, I'll be free because my hands will fall off; so either way, I won't be much use."

"Come here, Scott, and let me look," Early said.

The young Lieutenant leaned forward.

"Turn around."

Kelly pulled himself onto his knees and shifted his body so his back was to Early. "What do you see?"

"Wait a minute. I haven't even gotten myself where I can see. Turn a little bit to the left, so the light from the porthole falls across your hands."

A moment later, he felt a tug on his restraints. "What are you doing?" he asked, looking over his shoulder and trying to see what she was doing.

Early leaned back. "You got a small link that's kinked in the plastic. I think I can get a better bite on yours than I did on the Senior Chief's."

"We should have checked before we started on me," Senior Chief Leary said.

"Yeah, but we're tired."

"That may be, ma'am, but we can't afford to let that cloud—"

She interrupted. "When they pulled the tongue through

the lock, they didn't pull the plastic handcuffs as tight as they could."

"I still have no feeling in my hand."

"Wiggle your fingers."

Early and the Senior Chief watched as Kelly's fingers wiggled. "Well, they still work, and the Senior Chief's didn't. At least you'll still have your sex life if we get these cuffs off."

"I don't want to be a killjoy or anything, but even if we free one set of hands, how am I going to free you two? It isn't as if hands are going to be better than teeth on these things."

"That's easy, Lieutenant," Senior Chief Leary said. "What do we got laced to our boots?"

The three looked at their flight boots. Each had a metal dog tag with their name, service number, blood type, and religion embossed on it. The shoelace ran through a hole in the end of it.

"They aren't the sharpest thing around."

"They're better than nothing, and if you get free then you can use the edge around the hole on it to cut through these things."

"Ouch! What are you doing?"

"She's working on your plastic, sir. Just sit there and let our Commander do her thing. You'll have a great story to tell when we get back to the squadron."

For the next few hours, Early nibbled on the plastic between mouthfuls of water. They stopped for a couple of hours when their captors arrived with the evening meal. It was hard to tell what time it was. Their watches had been taken the day they had been captured, and the meals the silent captors provided were always the same light soup with bread thrown on the deck.

Early was about to quit. Her jaws and neck hurt. Her teeth hurt, too, and the warm iron-like taste of blood told her she had ripped her gums doing this. She was tired. Two more tries and then she was going to hang it up for the night and get some sleep. Maybe tomorrow she would be more successful.

Early leaned forward and bit into the plastic. Getting a grip on it between her front teeth, she shook her head back and forth, hoping the movement simulated a sawing motion. Suddenly, part of the plastic gave way, a strip of it ripping her lip as it sprung apart. The pain brought tears to her eyes.

"I felt that," Kelly said. "I felt something give."

Early leaned back, breathing heavy and trying to stop the bleeding with her tongue. the Senior Chief Leary wiggled forward on his hips and leaned toward Kelly's hands for a better look.

"Shit, man. There's only a thin strip of plastic holding those things together. Try to pull them apart."

"I don't know—"

"Lieutenant, try to pull them apart," the older man said, a slight trace of urgency in his voice.

Kelly pulled.

"Come on, Lieutenant! You gotta put some strength about it. If you ain't gonna try, then it ain't gonna break."

Early leaned against the bulkhead. Her strength was gone. She had spent hours with the Senior Chief and at least the same amount of time with Kelly. This had better work. Scott had his head down, and she could see from the movement of his shoulders that he was trying to break free. She also saw when he stopped.

"It's not working," he said.

"Here," Senior Chief said, sliding forward. "Push your hands out behind you as far as you can. I'm going to slide forward and put my feet between your arms. Then, you're gonna pull while I push your arms apart with my legs."

Kelly raised his arms as high as he could.

"Lean forward, Lieutenant. That'll take those arms a little higher."

He did as the Senior Chief ordered.

"Now straighten up, Lieutenant."

Kelly raised himself. The space between his arms slid over the Senior Chief's boots with his tied hands stopping near the top of Leary's ankles.

"This is gonna hurt, Lieutenant, because I'm gonna use

my legs to push your hands apart. At the same time, you've gotta pull your hands apart. Together we might be able to break the plastic."

Early opened her mouth to say something about the possibility of this effort dislocating Kelly's shoulders, but realized they had no choice.

"It can't hurt any worse than it already does, Senior Chief."

"Think of it as visit to the dentist, Scott," Early offered through deep breaths. "Pain for a few seconds and then it's over."

"A few seconds! What dentist you been going to?"

"On the count of three, we push and pull," Leary said. "One, two, three . . ."

Grunts from both men filled the compartment, overriding the low monotonous vibration of the ship's engine. Early held her breath and mentally crossed her fingers. This had to work. This was their only chance. She glanced at the small window in the hatch. If someone happened along now, there was no way the two men could separate, and this single opportunity to escape would be gone. They knew their captors would kill them rather than be bothered with them trying to escape.

A sharp twang caused Early to jump. Kelly was falling forward. Both hands of the copilot came around to break his fall, but they didn't make it past his shoulders. They flapped uselessly by his side. Kelly continued forward, his cheek bouncing once off the metal deck. He was free. She glanced toward the small porthole, expecting to see a face. But no one was there. The faint light continued to shine into the compartment. Kelly pulled himself up with his legs and stomach muscles. The copilot used his shoulders to flop his arms, one at a time, into his lap. He moaned, "Christ! This hurts."

"It's the blood returning, Lieutenant. Give it a few minutes and keep trying to move those fingers. It'll hasten the—"

"My left hand," Kelly muttered, staring down at his twitching hands.

The man's right hand was free of the plastic handcuff. The remnants of that half hung from the remaining portion still pulled tightly around the man's left wrist.

"You're free."

Kelly looked down at his left wrist. "I think we pulled it tighter when we broke it."

"No time for that, Lieutenant," the Senior Chief said. "Untie my flight boot and take my dog tag off the shoe lace."

Kelly moved forward. "Damn," he said softly, scrunching his eyes shut. "Damn! That hurts!" He waved his right hand back and forth, forcing his hand into a loose fist. He reached over and squeezed his left hand a couple of times, then looked up at Early and the Senior Chief. "They're not working," he said in a high voice.

"Keep squeezing your hands, Scott. They've been tied up for a few days. Give the blood a chance to circulate and you'll be okay in a few minutes."

"Meanwhile, Lieutenant," the Senior Chief said. "Start getting that dog tag off my flight boot before someone comes along."

Kelly shook his head. "With what, Senior Chief? These fingers? I can only wiggle them."

Early leaned over, grabbed the end of a shoelace with her teeth and pulled it. The knot came loose easily.

"Thanks, boss, but I was thinking of Lieutenant Kelly untying it."

Kelly reached over and, with fingers returning to life, pulled the laces through the holes until the dog tag fell away, the sound of metal hitting metal as it bounced off the compartment deck. "I didn't even feel that."

"I've been meaning for about a month to take a file and shave off the sharp edges from where maintenance had bored that hole for me. Just never got around to it, and it seemed the only time I remembered to do it was when tying my boots and the damn thing would prick me."

Kelly squeezed his hand together in a tight fist. "I think I've got some feeling."

They looked at the copilot's right hand. Even in the

low light, the hand had a pinkish color to it. The left hand had turned blue. Freeing Kelly had pulled the cuff on the left hand too tight, cutting off circulation completely. Early knew they had to free that hand quickly before the lack of blood permanently damaged it, if it wasn't already permanently damaged after four days of these damn things.

It took two tries before Kelly was able to pick up the dog tag. He ran his fingers over the hole where the shoelace had been threaded. "Yeah, it's sharp," he said, holding the dog tag between his finger and thumb while he briefly sucked the cut on the knuckle of the finger.

"Lieutenant, you gotta get that other half off your left wrist ASAP!" the Senior Chief said urgently, keeping his voice low. "If you don't, you ain't gonna have a left hand."

"And if I don't free you, my left hand will be the least of our worries."

"Scott, take a moment and cut your left hand free. You'll work better with two hands."

He opened his mouth as if to protest and then shut it as if he knew he would lose an argument with Early. A minute later, the sharp edges on the dog tag cut through the remaining cuff, freeing the left hand.

"Get the Senior Chief next, Scott."

Kelly crawled forward on his knees, dragging his still-useless left hand, but already Early could see the blue being replaced by a pink tint as blood flowed back into the limb. The Senior Chief turned so his hands faced the copilot. Several minutes later Leary was free, rubbing his wrists as Kelly worked on Early. She watched as Leary rubbed his hands together, muttering to himself as he worked to get the blood flowing freely through them.

"Ouch," she said when the sharp edge of the dog tag nicked her wrist.

"Sorry."

"They're coming back," Leary said, holding up his hands and making loose fists with them. "Yeah, they're coming back." He looked at the hatch. "Now, assholes, let's see how you like these hands untied."

Early's hands fell apart at the same moment a face in the porthole obscured the light from the compartment. The three captives stopped what they were doing, staring at the face as its eyes squinted. Then the face disappeared.

"He may be opening the door," Early suggested.

"No, ma'am. I don't think they can see in here when they look. Ain't enough light. I think they just look because someone told them to. They're so dumb that they don't know what they're supposed to be looking for." Senior Chief Leary leaned back against the bulkhead and, using his feet, forced himself upright.

Early watched as the senior chief's hands fought to close into a fist. The pain must have been excruciating, for his wrists had been tied a lot tighter than hers. The tingling of blood rushing through her hands tickled at first and then as feeling returned it brought with it pain across her shoulders, down her arms, and in her hands. She blinked away the tears from the pain. "Damn," she said in a low voice.

"It ain't pleasant," Leary offered as he rubbed his hands together. "You two, stop looking at your hands and rub them together. Squeeze them into fists. It ain't gonna be pleasant, but the alternate is less so."

Early followed the Senior Chief's direction, even though as her hands rubbed against each other, it was as if they were touching someone else's. She could see them entwined but could barely feel them. Minutes later, the pain seemed to ease. For a brief moment, several tears flowed down her cheeks, not from the pain but from realizing they at least had a chance. A poor one, but if you're going to die, then any chance is a good one. Their captors were planning to kill them. To believe otherwise was to overlook past events. If they were going to die then at least they could go down fighting. She recalled her father telling her after September 11th that deep within each American burned that spark of bravery that, once stirred, rose and burned with patriotic fever. The war on terrorism, now in its twelfth year, had revealed one startling difference between the United States and countries such as Britain and Israel in the fight against terrorism. Other countries took out individuals; America took out whole countries.

"Eventually they are going to bring us more water and food. When they do, that's when we do it."

"Do it?" Kelly asked, looking at the Senior Chief.

"Yes sir. Here is what I suggest . . ."

TUCKER WALKED SOFTLY UP THE STAIRS LEADING TO THE observation room at the top of the tower. He had been unable to sleep, and after tossing and turning for most of the night, he had finally reached over, pushed the clock alarm off, and rolled out of bed, knocking over the neatly aligned combat boots. This new pair he would have to break in. The other pair was sitting near a radiator drying out. Three-thirty.

A dark compartment greeted him at the top of the stairs. He didn't know why he expected the tower to be manned. The green glow of a radarscope drew his attention. During the daylight hours, a rubber eyepiece shielded the scope, but at night, the green glow helped light the darkened compartment. Rain drummed against the windows with rising and falling intensity. When it slackened for a second or two, Tucker could see the faint lights of the distant shore that made up Hampton Roads.

Tucker set down the cup of hot coffee. A gray color when he'd put in the instant creamer told him the coffee had been there for quite a while. The First Class manning the quarterdeck had mumbled apologies but hadn't offered to make any fresh. And Tucker hadn't felt up to doing it himself.

He crossed to the set of windows overlooking the piers beneath. Bright harbor lights lit the double piers running at a ninety-degree angle to the dock. As he watched, MacOlson emerged from the shadows near the end of the first pier and with his leading Boatswain Mate walked along it, checking the lines. Both men had a hand across their hats, holding them against the wind.

He had been gratified to hear that the young sailor he had rescued was going to live. The man had drunk a lot of harbor water—and from what he'd heard, that alone should have been enough to kill him. If it hadn't been for his quick action and Sam's emergency medical attention, the young man would be in a plastic bag somewhere waiting for the chaplains to knock on his parents' door somewhere back in middle America. For that he was very thankful.

Tucker took a sip of the old coffee, grimacing at the heavy tannin taste caused by the after-perc drippings through old coffee grounds. He made a note to himself to tell the watch to remove the grounds after the coffee was made and then, just as quickly, told himself that it wouldn't be appreciated by the enlisted troops who had to make it. Sometimes leadership meant leaving well-enough alone. Nothing was ever perfect. Not even Sam.

It had surprised him to discover the two of them in each other's arms after the ambulance departed with the sailor. Was this moving too fast? She was attractive. He enjoyed her company and looked forward to the times they were together. She must feel the same way, otherwise why would she travel all the way down from Washington in weather such as this? Of course, she said it was because she was detached to Portsmouth Naval Hospital as part of Bethesda's ready-response team, but did he really believe that? It raised another question—if he doubted her telling him the truth, then why was he so happy when they were together? The life of a Navy SEAL wasn't a safe, honeymoon-making life.

He let out a very audible sigh.

"It's nights like these that really make me glad to have made the Navy my life," said someone from the other side of the tower, startling Tucker.

He looked to where the voice came from as a captain's chair twirled on its single stanchion, revealing Commodore West.

"Sorry, Commodore, I didn't know you were up here."

West crawled down from his chair and made his way over to where Tucker stood. His head came up to Tucker's shoulder. Tucker had the height on West, but the Commodore had the width.

"Sometimes you can do your best thinking up here. I sent John home to check on his family. Me? I'm a widower and this is my home," he said, waving his hand around the compartment. "This, the small building I call headquarters about a mile from here, and those sailors down there who man those six boats."

Tucker picked up his coffee.

"Anyone who'd drink quarterdeck coffee at this time of the night is a brave man, Commander Raleigh."

"It is terrible, but it's the only drink in town."

West nodded. "Sometimes the only drink in town isn't worth the effort. Now, why are you really up here, Commander?"

"Couldn't sleep, sir. Thought I'd come up and see what was going on."

West took a couple of steps to the table that occupied the center of the tower. "Not too much so far. The storm has slowed its approach from twenty-five knots to fifteen and started the slow curve northward away from us. Winds are still fluctuating between sixty-five and seventy knots. Hasn't crossed that magical seventy-two knots for any length of time to where the National Weather Service could change its designation to a hurricane."

Tucker joined the Commodore at the table. "Any news from Admiral Holman, sir?"

West shook his head. "Last intelligence report we got showed no contact. Joint Task Force America has turned back to the East Coast. Joint Chiefs of Staff are concerned that we may have acted in haste in deploying the fleet toward Europe based on a less than fully evaluated report by the missing Recce Flight 62." Commodore West chuckled. "Admiral Holman is going to have to sail through this tropical storm on his way back. Don't envy him one bit." West glanced up for a moment at Tucker before returning his gaze to the chart taped down to the old metal table. He tapped the chart a couple of times with his finger. "They're having slightly less of a problem with the weather on his side of the Atlantic than we are here. According to another message I read, we, the British, French, Portuguese, and, I think, the Spanish also will be able to launch our maritime patrol aircraft tomorrow. With luck they will regain contact with the freighter that Recce Flight sixty-two reported before it disappeared."

"How is the rescue operation going for the P-3, Commodore?"

The shorter officer cinched his teeth for a moment as he shook his head. "It isn't. We haven't been able to put aircraft out for the past forty-eight hours. With the storm turning away, my fine friend at Roosevelt Roads, Puerto Rico—Admiral Sagan—intends to recommence searching at daybreak." He looked at his watch. "Which should be right about now for Puerto Rico."

"I hope they made it."

"We always hope they made it, whenever a plane crashes, even when we're standing on the deck of a carrier and see the aircraft disappear beneath the bow. You always hope they survive even when you know there is little to no hope. It's hard to accept mortality, especially your own. I think I was in my mid-forties when . . ."

Tucker nodded. The forlorn voice of the Commodore told more than his words. The man was speaking from experience; what experience, Tucker wondered. No one completes a full career in the military without encountering death at least once. Tucker could tell the older mustang officer would do more than what was expected if it meant saving sailors. There is a phenomenon in the Navy where you transition from being a member of the Navy to becoming part of it. No one could really tell you how long you had to serve in the Navy for that subtle transition to occur, or even how to recognize it, but standing here beside him was one of those who considered the Navy his. Tucker didn't. For him, he worked for the Navy—a Navy he truly enjoyed. The Commodore mentioned Sam, disrupting Tucker's thoughts, bringing awareness back to the senior officer who stood beside him.

"Sorry, sir. What was that?"

"I said, I know this is personal and we've discussed it. The crew would have to be blind not to see that you and Lieutenant Commander Bradley have a very serious relationship." Commodore West waved his hand, motioning Tucker to silence. "But for good order and discipline, I would appreciate if you two could dash some cold water on those raging hormones and act like officers when you're around each other."

Tucker didn't reply right away. He didn't know what to say.

"I'm telling you this off the record, Commander Raleigh, because you're both attached to my command right now. It's a small command. You and her keep this hanky-panky going on between these government walls, I'm going to be forced to take action. I would just as soon avoid emotional shit like that. Get my drift, Commander?" West smiled for a brief second.

"Yes, sir. We do have a close relationship, Commodore, and we both know what we can and can't do within these government walls," Tucker replied, miffed at the Commodore addressing him as if he was some school kid. Who in the hell was this man to be asking him about his personal relationship? Then, just as suddenly, Tucker calmed as he realized that West had already answered the question. West was Navy. Through and through, the old mustang was Navy. Anyone or anything that messed with West's Navy or even hinted at a degree of disgrace on it would be forever the man's enemy. Tucker wouldn't be surprised if the Commodore pulled his sword and tried to run through anyone besmirching the Navy. He couldn't help but smile.

"Glad you understand, Commander."

"Sir, I better understand your position than mine."

Commodore West, holding the message board under this arm, walked to the window overlooking the pier. "You see those men out there, Commander? Every day we ask more and more of them. We tax their energy, emotional well-being, and right to a family life. In return for this punishment and the right to live just above the poverty line, we give them the honor of serving their country. As long as we call ourselves Navy officers, we must never forget that they are the reason we lead, for without them, we would cease to be the most powerful Navy this world has ever seen."

Tucker nodded silently. The man was right. Every now and again, you needed a dose of patriotism and reality to steer you back on course and remind you of the reason you do what you do. He took another drink of the bitter coffee.

"Now, back to you, young man. It's obvious you and this young lady are either in love or falling in love or—pardon my words, Commander Tucker, I don't mean to be out of line—found the greatest sex you two have ever found."

Tucker nearly spit the coffee out, forced himself to swallow it instead, with about half going down the wrong way. Tucker started coughing, spilling coffee as he put the cup down. He bent over, trying to clear the liquid from his windpipe. The Commodore hit him a couple of times on the back.

"Never knew I could surprise a Navy SEAL like that."

"Sorry, sir, wasn't expecting the question."

"That's okay, son. Wasn't expecting to get an answer. Just being a nosey old codger now—a dirty one at that. Seems like only yesterday I was meeting my wife the same way, except it wasn't on active duty. She was a reserve officer who came to visit a friend of hers. We were introduced, I was smitten, and two years later, we were married." Commodore West leaned forward against the bulkhead, straining to see the piers beneath the tower. Then he leaned back. "I truly believe we're put here on earth as a test by some Supreme Being with a misguided sense of humor. Every challenge we encounter is part of that test, including marriage. Rennie and I had a great thirty years. I still miss her."

"Yes, sir. Lieutenant Commander Bradley and I have only known each other about four months. I was wounded—"

"I know, Commander. I read the report when they sent you down here. You're the one reason we thought this Abu Alhaul would try for Norfolk. Naval Intelligence believed this new terrorist leader would forego irrational terrorist acts for the rational opportunity of revenge. You."

"Yes, sir. I have always enjoyed being bait."

"Looks as if this time you weren't."

The radio crackled from the front of the tower, followed by a broadcast. "Hampton Roads Maritime, this is Freighter *Maru Tania*. We are ten miles from mouth of channel. Should we try to enter as scheduled?"

"*Maru Tania,* Hampton Roads; Request you remain out to sea for time being. Change to weather channel and get latest update. Weather is expected to deteriorate in next twelve to twenty-four hours. Try again this afternoon if you see the winds and seas decrease. Right now, we intend to reopen the port tomorrow morning."

"Roger, out."

"Bridge to bridge," Commodore West said, nodding at the radio. "We keep it tuned to channel sixteen. It lets us keep track of the ships going in and out, plus it's the primary warning system for the Department of Homeland Security in the event we need to seal the East Coast."

"Ever had to do that?"

"You mean seal the East Coast?" The Commodore asked and then continued without waiting for an answer. "This has been the first time we tried it, and one of the lessons we've learned is that Mother Nature doesn't always cooperate. Of course, you could say Mother Nature closed the East Coast ports for us."

Commodore West glanced at the clock over the forward bulkhead of the tower. "Zero five hundred, Commander. We've been here an hour shooting the bull, and while you haven't asked for my advice, I want you to know that failure to ask has never stopped me from giving it." He reached up and touched him on the shoulder. "Take your time."

"Take my time?"

He removed his hand and looked down at the piers before glancing up at the clouds. "Another overcast day. You know, life can be like that if we make the wrong decision—a series of overcast days." He turned and walked by Tucker. "Got to go down and tell the watch to put on some fresh coffee. Five-thirty is when I have my first cup before my oatmeal at six followed by man's greatest friend to the prostate—aspirin." He turned as he reached the staircase leading down. "Commander, go get some sleep, and remember, if and when you ever get married, always use those most important words to a wife's ear."

"You mean, 'I love you?' " Tucker asked with a chuckle.

"No, I mean, 'yes, dear.' 'I love you' is important, and they'll expect it, but 'yes, dear' can make married life a lot more peaceful." With that, the old mustang disappeared down the stairs.

More calls from merchant vessels trying to enter and leave Hampton Roads grew on the bridge-to-bridge radio as the maritime day emerged into rough weather in historic Tidewater, Virginia.

"WHAT IS THIS?" SCREAMED TAMURSHEKI.

He drew back and slapped Ibrahim again. The blow caused the doctor to take a couple of steps back. Qasim, the huge Shiite from Iraq, stuck his foot out, tripping Ibrahim and causing the doctor to fall onto the deck of the wardroom.

Tamursheki reached down and grabbed the collars of Ibrahim's smock.

"Look around your little hospital here," he said, his voice angry and low. "Why are my men laying about the place, moaning; and what are these things popping up on their bodies? And, on my body?" He threw the smaller man across the compartment. Ibrahim hit against one of the two medical tables, sending medical instruments flying off the table and onto the floor. The sound of the metal instruments bouncing off the metal decks punctuated Ibrahim's cry of pain. The doctor raised his hand, blood welling from a sliced palm where a scalpel had cut him.

"Oh, don't worry about that little nick, *Doctor Ibrahim*. You should worry about the one along your neck if you don't get these men well before we reach our target today," Tamursheki threatened, his voice trembling.

Tamursheki jerked Ibrahim up, holding him by the collars of the smock. He shoved the doctor toward Qasim, who grabbed the doctor by the arms, holding them trapped against Ibrahim's body. The gigantic arms of the Jihadist giant held Ibrahim as if the doctor was trapped in an iron vise.

"Look at this!" Tamursheki said, pointing to his face. Small pustules, some barely visible and some the size of small peas. A couple of spots above Tamursheki's right eye were the size of the man's thumbnail. "And I feel a fever aching to bring me down." He looked behind him and flopped down in a nearby chair, running his hand lightly over his head. "Already half my men are here, laying in their own shit and urine, unable to move. You promised Abu Alhaul to keep us healthy so we could take our cargo to the enemy. Instead, everyone is sick." He pointed at Qasim. "With the exception of Qasim. I should kill you like I did the Americans." He placed his finger at his neck and drew it slowly across from left to right. "Slice you through the neck slowly so you feel the blade sink into your throat and clog your airways. Therefore, you can experience the thrill of seeing your life flow from your neck across your chest and onto the floor. You—" He stopped, his head dropping and his breath coming in quick draughts.

"What would you have me do, Said Tamursheki?" Ibrahim asked, running his tongue across bleeding lips, his mouth achingly dry. He tried to shake himself free of the strong hands holding him. "Let me go!" The hands tightened on his arms.

"What is this?" Tamursheki demanded. He pointed at Dr. Ibrahim. "You were suppose to keep us healthy. The shots you gave were suppose to protect us from what we carry on the back of the ship, but instead you have betrayed us—"

"I have not betrayed you! You knew what the shots were. If anyone betrayed you, it was Abu Alhaul!" Ibrahim looked up, narrowing his eyes at Qasim, whose grip loosened. "Let me go!" The grip returned.

Tamursheki jerked his knife out from where he had it shoved into his belt. "You dare to talk about Allah's right arm. Abu Alhaul takes his guidance from Allah and is above worldly things."

"Then you're as dumb as you look, Tamursheki."

Tamursheki placed the edge of the knife along the left side of Ibrahim's neck. Ibrahim forced his head backward until it touched Qasim's chest. His eyes wide as he tried to look down at the knife.

"Oh, Qasim, my apologies, my friend, but the blood of this infidel is going to soil your new clothes."

"I look forward to bathing in his blood."

Ibrahim whimpered. Tamursheki knew that the true weapon was him and the other martyrs. There was no nuclear weapon within the large van. At least, he didn't think there was. Maybe if Abu Alhaul had betrayed his warriors, the terrorist leader had also betrayed Ibrahim and Alrajool. "Don't," he begged. "Let me explain. Abu Alhaul had bigger plans for you and your men, Tamursheki. So big that he only wanted you to know it once we reached our destination."

The pressure of the knife eased slightly. Tamursheki laughed. "I know. I know those shots you gave us had nothing to do with being sick at sea. I also know that the disease you injected into us wasn't suppose to erupt now! It was meant for the infidels."

Ibrahim shook his arms again, trying to free himself. Tamursheki pulled the knife away from Ibrahim's neck, looked up at Qasim, and nodded. The giant released him. Ibrahim rubbed his arms as he walked away from the two men.

"So talk, Doctor. Maybe you know something I don't. Tell me what this plan is that you would know and the loyal followers of Abu Alhaul would not."

Ibrahim positioned himself at the end of one of the tables on which one of the terrorists lay moaning. He glanced down at the man, reached out, and patted him slightly on the shoulders.

"Speak!"

Ibrahim nodded. "We're nearly at our destination. There are things that you're going to need to do even though I know that you are sick—"

"I am sick because of you."

"Oh, yes. That is very true," Ibrahim said, his voice failing to betray the amusement he found in the statement. "You're sick because Abu Alhaul wanted you sick. He wanted you to leave the ship and go throughout America, spreading the germs that I have given you."

Tamursheki pointed to the men lying around the medical compartment. "Then, I was right. But, now I can't do this mission that Abu Alhaul intended. Look at them, they are dying, and they're dying on board the ship instead of in the middle of America."

Ibrahim moved slightly, easing around the edge of the table until it separated him from Tamursheki and Qasim and put the door leading out of the compartment about twenty feet behind him.

"Abu Alhaul knew the Americans would fixate on the black van tied to the stern of the ship. While they focused on the black van, thinking it a weapon, my job was to infect each of you with smallpox. It was his planning that determined how and where within this large country each of you would travel."

The hand holding the knife lay alongside Tamursheki's right leg. "If that was so, Ibrahim, then you have torn asunder his plan because we are already sick."

"Yes, it seems that the smallpox virus was more virulent than I expected." He pointed to Qasim. "He seems to be the only one unaffected. That's probably because of his size and weight. If he was as small in body as you, Tamursheki, Qasim would already be among the others suffering here."

"We will still do what we must. We have the papers to sail into the harbor where we are to be met at the pier by those who would remove the van." Tamursheki reached in his pocket. "And I have the key to activate the weapon while it is still on the ship. We would become martyrs of Islam."

Ibrahim leaned forward, putting both hands on the table. He glanced for a moment at the man laying on it, looking at his face, a mass of pustules covering every square inch of exposed skin. The eyes shut and mouth pulsing like a fish gasping for water. Unseen, but deep within the man's lungs, the same sores were growing, collapsing the vital fibers that forced oxygen into the blood. With a clinical thought, Ibrahim knew the man would die within the next few hours, if he lived that long.

He looked up at Tamursheki. "You really believe that, don't you? You really believe that you"—Ibrahim waved his hand at the others in the compartment—"and those who follow you are more than pawns in a gigantic game of revenge by Abu Alhaul? Get real! You're just dumb wanna-be warriors suckered to do his bidding. At least I know what my chances are, and if by a slim chance I do survive this mission, I know what my rewards are." He pushed himself off the table as he spoke, inching nearer the door.

"There is no one who is going to meet you. The van will sail with the ship, unless Abu Alhaul has surprised me and planted explosives in it. Then the ship will sink and the real weapons aboard this ship—*you*—will disappear into America." He jabbed his finger at Tamursheki. "You are the weapon. You and everyone around here. The others wandering around the ship, guarding and feeding the prisoners, trying to keep dry from the storm around us, or even back on the stern worshipping the black kabala strapped down on the deck, waiting for some revelation that will never come."

Tamursheki jerked the AK-47 off a nearby counter, flipped the safety off, and aimed it at Ibrahim. "You lie! Abu Alhaul told me himself that we would be heroes. If Allah sees fit we should live, we will be future leaders of the conquest of Africa. You lie!" He brought the weapon up and aimed it at Ibrahim.

Ibrahim licked his lips. His mouth was dry. The man was mad enough to kill him and any of the others in the compartment the bullets happened to hit. He held his hand up. "Wait! Killing me will not stop what is happening. I'm your only hope." His voice trembled. He needed to learn when to shut up.

Tamursheki looked up, his eyes glistened. He lowered the automatic rifle so it pointed directly at Ibrahim. "What can you do?"

Ibrahim walked briskly to the refrigerator and opened the door. He pulled out a large flat metal tray that took up most of the second shelf. Numerous small glass vials filled most of the holes in the tray. They rattled against the sides as Ibrahim moved the tray from the shelf to a nearby counter. "See these," he said. "If I give you a shot of this, it will slow down the disease and give you time to do your mission," he lied, running his hands over the vials of the smallpox germ. If anything it would further infect those already infected.

Tamursheki raised the AK-47. "I want it slowed, Doctor. Or I want it stopped. If you can't slow it, then stop it. Stop it until we are at our various destinations where we can reinfect ourselves."

Ibrahim met Tamursheki's hard brown eyes directly and, without breaking contact, lied. "Then, I would have to give you two of them."

He flew backward across the compartment, pulling the tray full of the smallpox virus off the counter. Ibrahim heard the sound of the gun firing before he bounced off the medical table behind him. Pain—unbearable pain—swept over his body. Red rivulets flowed from his chest.

Between his legs lay something that looked like a human intestine, and his last thought as he died was the question as to whose it was.

Tamursheki looked at Qasim. "Why did you kill him?" he screamed at the giant. "He could have stopped this illness until—"

Qasim shrugged. "We must go forward. We can't stop what has happened, my leader. This man is a heretic, and to trust a heretic is to endanger our mission. I killed him for our souls."

THE DOOR TO THE COMPARTMENT OPENED. A SINGLE CAPtor stuck his head in the door, and once assured the three Americans were in their usual place with their hands tied behind their backs, he stepped inside. Like always, the large black man was squatting on his haunches and the thin white man was braced against the forward bulkhead opposite the woman. He nodded to someone out of sight and stepped over the transom into the gray shadows of the makeshift prison.

In a loud voice, he said something in Arabic. Early and the others had no idea what the man said, but they recognized that it was the same words each time he brought their bowls of food and water. The way the man's nose wrinkled in disgust told them that whatever he said wasn't something nice.

Usually, he backed out of the room, sealed the hatch, and watched through the small glass porthole. If they moved too soon to eat or drink, more faces would join their keeper. Even though they couldn't hear what was said, they knew those watching were ridiculing, enjoying the spectacle of Americans shoving their faces into bowls for food and water. The three ignored the insects crawling in the food and swimming in the water. Early figured the terrorists spent more time hunting for the cockroaches they threw into the bowls than they did preparing it. She hated to think what else these men could have done to the mixture, because when she did, it made her want to vomit.

This time, a second man entered the compartment. He seemed to stagger over the raised transom at the foot of the hatch. He was carrying an AK-47. An involuntary shiver raced down Early's backbone. This wasn't the first time their captors had entered with weapons, but it was the first time that only one entered. Usually there were two or three.

The man in front squatted as he sat the bowls down, staring directly at Early. Kelly farted. A long, loud one, drawing the attention of both men. The Senior Chief was a blur. In one motion, he was erect and moving toward the armed man. The man near the bowls jumped up as the Senior Chief moved past him and hit Leary on the side, diverting him slightly.

Kelly leaped on the man with the AK-47, hitting him on the chin with his fist. The man collapsed on the deck. Kelly caught the gun before it hit the deck. Senior Chief Leary brought the back of his fist down on the first man's neck. A sharp crack filled the compartment, then it became silent.

The three of them looked at each other. Kelly and Leary smiled. Early forced herself up. "Don't laugh," she said. She smiled slightly, and the pain of her lips spreading stopped her. "We're not out of here yet."

Senior Chief Leary reached over and took the weapon from Lieutenant Kelly. "Sir, you know how to fire one of these?"

Kelly shook his head. "No, do you?"

"Of course," Leary said. "I'm a Senior Chief, ain't I?" He turned the AK-47 automatic rifle around and around, running his hand over it. After several seconds of this, he looked up and asked, "Anyone know where the safety is on this thing?"

Kelly reached over and pushed the safety forward. "There, Senior Chief."

"Did that turn it on or off?"

Kelly shrugged. "Not sure. If you try to shoot it and nothing happens, then push it the other way."

Leary moved to the door and stuck his head into the

passageway. "Okay, coast is clear." He motioned them to follow.

Outside, the bright lights of the passageway caused the three to squint as their eyes adjusted to the glare after seven days of captivity.

"They've got to be near us," she whispered.

"You take that side and I'll take this one," Leary said.

"No, Senior Chief," Early corrected. "You have the weapon. You watch, and Lieutenant Kelly and I will search the compartments."

Each hatch had a small porthole like the hatch leading to the compartment where they had been held captive. Three compartments later, Early looked through the small porthole and saw several pairs of flight boots in the slight light.

"Here!" she whispered urgently. "I've found them." She tried the lever locking the door and was pleased to discover that while it had been secured, their captors had been so confident that no one would escape that they had neglected to do more than wedge the lever down. She wiggled the triangular piece of wood, attempting to dislodge it. Kelly reached around her, grabbed the lever, and joined in the effort. A few seconds later, the wood came free, bouncing off the deck. The two of them swung the lever up and over, hearing the rubber gaskets around the edge of the watertight door break suction. Then, the door opened.

"Hurry up," Senior Chief said. "I'll stay out here."

The two of them stepped into the room. No one said anything.

"Hey!" Early said. When no one replied, she grappled along the bulkhead until her fingers hit the light switch. Light flooded the room.

Along the bulkheads, the other crewmembers of the P-3C sat with dull glazed eyes staring forever forward, their hands still tied behind their backs. Blood soaked the fronts of their flight suits from deep cuts across their throats.

"They're dead," Kelly said, his voice trembling.

Early hurried toward the nearest crewmember and put

two fingers against the neck. “Check each one of them,” she said, her voice trembling. What creature could do this? And why hadn’t they done it to them?

Ten minutes they spent going from one crewmember to the other. Tears trailed down Early’s cheeks. The shadow of the Senior Chief blocking the hatchway flew over her a couple of times while she and Kelly moved from one to the next, hoping to find one of them alive. These were her crewmembers. Sailors—friends who were her responsibility and they lay dead, and there was nothing she could have done. She imagined the scene of their deaths. Dozens of terrorists scrambling into the compartment, cutting the throats of the crewmembers as some begged and others cursed.

Early and Kelly stepped back into the passageway. Kelly leaned his head against the far bulkhead and threw up. Senior Chief Leary glanced at him before returning his attention to watching the ends of the passageway.

Early took several deep breaths. “We’re it.” *What do we do now?* she asked herself. They were free, but where in the hell were they? Do they try to find a life raft or something, ease overboard, and hope no one spots their escape? The ship took a quick roll to starboard, throwing Kelly off the bulkhead and into the Senior Chief, who had spread his legs to keep his balance. The big man grabbed the Lieutenant by the arm and leaned him against the bulkhead.

“Thanks, Senior Chief,” Kelly said, his voice weak.

The ship rolled back to port.

“What now?” Kelly asked Early.

“I think—”

“I think you’re right, ma’am. We take the ship away from these assholes. We make our way to the bridge, call for help, and kill anybody we meet on the way. Then—” The Senior Chief stopped abruptly as the sound of gunfire caused the three of them to throw themselves against the bulkhead. Senior Chief swung the AK-47 one way and then the other. When no one appeared and no further gunfire occurred, they moved away from the bulkhead.

"What was that?"

"I think it was one of these," Senior Chief said, patting the AK-47. "I just hope they're using it against each other."

"Okay, Senior Chief. Sounds like a plan," Early said, slapping the huge man on the back. "Let's take the bridge."

"You know—" Senior Chief Leary started.

"I know—we know," Early interrupted. The three of them looked at each other. They were outnumbered and outgunned. Their fellow crewmembers were dead and most likely, today, in the next few minutes, the three of them were going to die. They reached forward, placing their hands over each others'. Early took a deep breath. "Let's take as many of them with us as we can."

Leary reached over and threw the handle on the watertight hatch, sealing the compartment where their dead comrades lay.

The ship continued to roll with the storm outside. They probably could have slipped over the side, but then they would have died at the hands of the sea, and those carrying destruction to America would continue on their way, unopposed. When you know you're going to die, taking your enemy with you is a patriotic duty.

Senior Chief Leary led the way, cradling the AK-47 in his hands. Early was surprised, but glad, to see how nimbly the large man moved. She had always associated Leary somehow as slow, plodding, but sure of himself. She was seeing him in a different light. How far could they go before they ran into the terrorists?

They needed more weapons than the single AK-47. Kelly had a little martial arts training—or so he liked to boast—but even he outweighed her by another seventy or eighty pounds. A hundred-forty-pound female pilot drawing back and punching someone the size of the Senior Chief would be more a nuisance than a danger. Yeap, of the three, she really did need a gun—preferably a big one.

This was a damned-if-you-do, damned-if-you-don't situation.

They needed more weapons, but to get more weapons they had to run into more terrorists, and the more terrorists they ran into the more chances they had of getting themselves killed. She mentally crossed her fingers as they moved down the passageway, ignoring closed hatches, stopping at every intersection only long enough for the Senior Chief to peer around the corner. They maintained their forward movement. It seemed a long trip to the bridge; a bridge they had no idea where to locate. Frame numbers painted in black on a yellow rectangular block told everyone on a Navy warship exactly where they were inside the ship. It identified the frame number and within the numeric code lay information for the sailor to determine which deck he or she was on as well as on which side of the ship they stood. From what little she recalled of their capture, she was sure they had been interned somewhere on the port side, aft section of the freighter. The bridges of most ships are located amidships or slightly forward, where the Captain can watch the ship as it cuts through the waters. On some of the larger tankers, she recalled the bridge was all the way aft, but so many decks above the main deck that the Captain could still see the bow. The bridge on this freighter would be high in the amidships forecastle, probably the topmost deck.

So the three followed the motion of the vessel, working their way forward. Eventually they arrived at what looked to be the final intersection. Directly across was a brown metal door. Likely it marked a logical rather than a physical separation of the passageway. Once through it, it should either continue forward or reveal a ladder leading up or down.

Senior Chief Leary leaned around the corner, exposing his face only enough so he could see. He motioned to Early and Kelly indicating the passageways to the sides were clear.

The brown door opened, startling them. The man coming through the door was as shocked as they were, tripping over the transom and falling onto the deck. Senior Chief Leary kicked at the man, his flight boot glancing off the thigh of the fallen terrorist. A second man stopped halfway out of the door. Leary brought the butt of his gun around and hit the man in the chin. Teeth flew from the mouth as the man collapsed in a heap.

The one on the deck scrambled down the passageway a couple of body lengths and turned, struggling to free his AK-47 from around his neck where the effort had pulled it tight. The Senior Chief ran down the passageway and slammed the heel of his right boot into the man's groin, drawing a long moan from the terrorist's lips. The man's hands reached down to his crotch, forgetting about the weapon.

"Get the gun, Kelly," Early urged, keeping her voice low. She pushed her copilot, who was blocking the passageway in front of her, toward the man lying halfway through the door. "Get it, quick!"

Kelly moved. Early squeezed past him and hurried toward the Senior Chief, seeing him raise the weapon above his head and bring it down on the man's head several times.

"Senior Chief—" she said.

He reached down and jerked the gun from the terrorist's neck, forcibly freeing the strap. He handed it to Early. "Here, Lieutenant," he said, looking back over her shoulder where Kelly stood with his own weapon.

"We should hide the bodies," the Senior Chief said.

Early shook her head. "We don't have time, Senior Chief. If they don't know we're free yet, they will soon. We need to get to the bridge and to the radio."

Kelly walked up. "Two down and probably only a couple hundred to go." "Then that leaves only a hundred ninety-six, if your estimates are right, Lieutenant," Leary added as he reached forward and flipped the safety off on Early's AK-47. "Seems a little lopsided if that's all they have."

"Let's roll," Early said.

"Right quote for the right time," Kelly added as Early pushed the door open and led as they continued on the way she hoped would lead to the bridge.

* * *

THE DOOR TO THE MEDICAL CLINIC OPENED AND CAPTAIN Alrajool stepped into the room, holding the door open with his right hand. He looked at the dead Dr. Ibrahim, around the room at the six or seven people moaning, a couple laying in their own urine, and then at Tamursheki. The leader of this band of terrorists met the ship Captain's eyes with a hard, angry stare as he handed Qasim's weapon back to him.

"Why'd you kill him?" Alrajool asked, looking at Tamursheki.

"Because he has killed us."

Alrajool shrugged and nodded his head once to the left. "Doesn't matter, Amir," he said, acknowledging Tamursheki with an honorary title familiar to the Bedouin tribes. "We're entering the channel to Hampton Roads."

The ship rolled steeply to starboard before righting itself. Everyone standing reached out and grabbed hold of something to keep from falling. That is, everyone but the Captain, who bent his knees and adjusted to the roll of the ship—a common skill learned by mariners after years at sea. Alrajool smiled slightly at the wide eyes of the landlubbers who were falling all over the place. He wondered briefly how long they would last in a real hurricane.

After they righted, Captain Alrajool continued. "This is going to get worse before it gets better. We have to travel along the eastern shore for several miles in the channel, where there is nothing to our starboard side to deflect the winds or seas. That means the shallower the water—"

"That is your job. I don't need to be impressed with your knowledge of the water. It is information that will be useless to me after I get ashore."

"Did Doctor Ibrahim per chance leave the name of the person we are supposed to contact to help remove the cargo?" Alrajool asked. He pushed the door away, only to have it swing back against him. He didn't want to come all the way into the clinic. The open door at least gave him an immediate exit if the mercurial Tamursheki decided that he didn't need him either.

Alrajool glanced down at his feet, saw the shattered vials, and took a deep breath. He held his breath as he stepped back into the passageway. "I'm going to the bridge. I would recommend you start preparing for your departure. As much as this weather is making our trip rough and complicated, on the positive note, it keeps the American Navy and Coast Guard ashore. We are nearly to the entrance of the channel leading into the port of Hampton Roads. With luck, they will think we are a normal merchant ship running from the storm, trying to make harbor before it fully hits. You can't be on board when we dock. You have to gather those men, even if they are sick, and leave the ship." He pulled his cellular telephone from his pocket and hit the telephone listing buttons until the right number appeared. "I am calling our contact, and we will off-load the cargo as soon as conditions permit. We can't have you on board when we reach the pier. American customs is too strict these days." The telephone refused to connect. Alrajool knew it wouldn't, but he kept the phone wedged against his ear. "We can convince the Americans of our cargo, but we can't convince them that a ship this size needs eighteen young men such as yourselves to handle the cargo."

He pulled a folded piece of paper from his pocket. "I know that only you and three others are to remain in Norfolk. The rest of your team is to split up and disappear across America until they are contacted again." He closed the telephone and slipped it into his shirt pocket. "I will try from the bridge."

"And how are they going to disappear across America?" Tamursheki shouted. "Look at them. Whatever the dead doctor did has rendered them useless."

Alrajool handed the paper to Tamursheki and shrugged. "I can't help what he did. They have to go with you or you must tie weights to them and toss them overboard. If they are found on this ship, then Abu Alhaul will have lost not only a ship that he depends upon, but also the mission, with which you have been entrusted, will be a failure. Your failure will live with your family's name. It will be kaput. Either you will die in a blaze of gunfire without ever leaving this ship or you will join the hundreds that America still holds in Cuba. You will talk. They all do. The Americans are not fools. They know what makes a hostage side with their captors as we do, and eventually—maybe not today, tomorrow, or even in the next week, month, or year, but eventually—you'll talk."

Tamursheki's eyes blazed with anger. "I would never betray Abu Alhaul or Allah. I am a disciple of both."

"Yeah, yeah, yeah," Alrajool said. "As I am, also. Here," he said, leaning into the compartment to hand the folded paper to Tamursheki. "This is the telephone number you're to call once you are ashore."

Tamursheki nodded.

"Get your people together. There are a couple of large Zodiac rafts in the stern compartment near the van. Unlike the one we used in Florida, these are camouflaged. That way, when you abandon them on shore, people will think the American military lost them. By the time they figure otherwise, we'll have the van off-loaded, inside a lorry, which they call a tractor-trailer here, and ready for you to head to your destination."

"I don't like this," Tamursheki said.

The ship took another roll. This time to the left, farther to port than previous rolls. Everyone grabbed something to hold onto. One of the sick men on the medical table fell off, hit the deck with a thud, never saying a word.

"Look, Amir," Alrajool said, his voice cajoling. "I have to get to the bridge. The weather is going to play havoc with this ship this close to shore, and the last thing we want is to run aground while we still have the weapon on board."

"I will get the men together," Tamursheki said. He looked around the compartment. The lights faded for a second before returning to brightness. "I will get them back there somehow."

"Don't forget the prisoners," Alrajool said, knowing that as soon as Tamursheki and his fanatics were off the ship he would send his sailors down to verify the prisoners were gone. "You need to dump the dead overboard and—what are your plans for the three still living?"

Tamursheki's eyes narrowed. "Ibrahim gave them shots. I had plans for setting them adrift and having the Americans find them. It was an opportunity to have the infidels participate in our mission, but the weather kept us from doing it and now we are already here." He reached up and ran his hand along the bumps covering his face.

"Then you need to throw them overboard. Tie something to their feet first so they don't float ashore while we are still in port."

Tamursheki nodded. "I will think about it."

"Don't waste a lot of time thinking. You don't have much of it. It'll take about two hours to make the transit to the mouth of the harbor channel and another four until we are inside Norfolk Harbor. In two hours, you have to depart the ship." He paused as he watched Tamursheki stare at him. He knew the terrorist was trying to assess if they could do all that Alrajool asked in two hours. Even he had doubts the young man was capable of doing it. He looked at the sick and dying men. Some stood, leaning against the bulkhead, one was on the floor where he had rolled off the table. Three sat in the chairs around the small medical facility, vomit surrounding two of the chairs. He was glad he had demanded and received the vaccinations for himself and his crew. They would have been useless for future missions if they died with the martyrs. How stupid, he thought. Who can believe the rhetoric espoused that when you die you go to some sort of heaven? On the other hand, his off-shore bank accounts were growing, and that was heaven enough for him.

Alrajool nodded. "Good luck, my friend. We won't see each other again."

Tamursheki stared for several seconds at the Captain. The look of anger returned. "Then return to the bridge,

Alrajool!" he spewed, his voice full of venom.

Alrajool needed little encouragement. He nodded once, reached out, and pulled the hatch shut. He stood for several seconds looking at the closed hatch. This was the critical part of the mission. They had to leave the ship in the next two hours. Once before he had had a martyr group on board. It was a mission near Crete, and they had decided that blowing the ship up in the middle of Chania Harbor was a better mission than the one assigned. Tamursheki was a smarter man than the one who had led that mission, plus the terrorist leader had nearly ten more men with him, even if about half were sick. He touched the set of master keys in his pocket. He reached out and placed his hand on the main part of the hatch, shook his head, and headed toward the bridge. He would lock the hatch to the bridge, even though locking it would only slow them down a couple of minutes. He had to be prepared. Tamursheki would either move aft to execute his mission or the mercurial man would come hunting for him. You never knew with fanatics what they would do to fulfill their beliefs, and it mattered little if those fanatics were Moslem or Christians; Jews or politicians. The ironic thing about fanatics, Alrajool had discovered, was they regarded everyone who believed differently as the enemy and a danger to their way of life. He pulled himself up the ladder to the inside passageway leading to the bridge. Even having no strong beliefs except one for tolerance was unacceptable to a fanatic. You either believed as they did, or you died.

An able-bodied sailor waited at the top of the ladder for Tamursheki. No, get inside the harbor; do what he was paid to do—*and quite well, too*—then sortie out to sea before the Americans realized why they were here. He had done this several times in American ports. This one should be no different—if Tamursheki left the ship as planned. With luck, once he was back out to sea, his company might even have a return cargo for him to pick up somewhere in this hemisphere. What he did know was the safest place on this earth for the next few months was going to be out at sea hauling legal cargo.

"DID YOU HEAR THAT?" KELLY ASKED IN A WHISPER. HIS eyes widened. He looked both ways.

The three crouched slightly at the base of a ladder leading up to the next deck. Early doubted there were many more ladders they could go up before they hit the open deck. She recalled that this merchant ship—a freighter—had the superstructure amidships with a raised bow and stern. They had to be somewhere in this superstructure, and if they were, then the bridge should be forward on the top deck.

"Sounded like glass breaking," Senior Chief added.

The ship heaved upward as a heavy wave rode under its hull, moving the entire vessel up for a moment before dropping it back into the valley of the wave. They grabbed the rails of the ladder as the storm shoved the bow of the ship to starboard, its stern traveling right.

"Felt like a yaw to me."

"A what?" Senior Chief Leary asked

"A yaw," Kelly said, his head moving, searching the passageway in the event that someone appeared. Lifting his arm, he wiggled it back and forth a couple of times. "You know, where the bow moves in one direction and the stern in another."

"Lieutenant, you've been spending too much time with the Surface Navy," Senior Chief said. "I would call it a turn."

"Yes, but it's a turn without the Captain wanting it to turn."

"I find it entertaining that we're standing here discussing nautical shit when we need to keep moving," Early said. "Can we continue this conversation on the bridge?"

Senior Chief Leary turned and raced up the ladder with one hand holding the railing while the other pointed the AK-47 toward the top of the ladder. A few steps farther from the top of the ladder a closed door waited for them.

The ship tilted to starboard. Kelly lost his balance for a moment, stepping back one rung before he regained it.

"Be careful. Don't need you to break something now," Early said, reaching out and touching Kelly on the buttocks to steady him.

"Got it," he said softly, taking two steps at once to catch back up with Leary.

This was going too smoothly, Early thought. So far, only one encounter, not counting the two men at their compartment. Where was everyone? Somewhere ahead—or behind—somewhere around them, there were more terrorists. She bumped into Kelly's butt at the top of the ladder. The Senior Chief had stopped. The big man leaned around the edge of the ladder, checking the passageway running cross-purposes to the one they traveled. Early waited, turning sideways and leaning against the railing, facing down in the event someone appeared behind them. Somewhere on the deck they were leaving had been the sound of glass breaking, but the punishment the ship was taking from the storm could have caused loose gear to fall. Be just their luck to make the bridge about the time the storm capsized the ship. Then they'd be on the bottom again, having to work their way up.

"Come on," the Senior Chief said softly.

Kelly reached back without looking and touched her on the shoulder. Early turned and swiftly followed the two men, wondering how many terrorist were they facing. There had been quite a few, it seemed to her, on the ship's deck, pointing guns at them. It's hard to count when you're scared and wallowing in a life raft, looking at gun barrels pointing down at you. She recalled of the capture how the lee side of the freighter had sheltered the life raft from the wind as terrorists ordered them up the rope ladder one at a time onto the freighter. After that, everything had been a blur as they were roughed and shoved below-decks, divided into two groups, and locked in compartments. Her breathing increased at the thought of the dead crewmembers. Someone was going to pay for that. She tightened her grip on the AK-47. She had never fired a gun except for a shotgun at the Rota Naval Base skeet range, and here she was toting an automatic weapon. Was the safety on when pushed forward, or off?

If she was going to die on this ship far from everyone she had ever known or loved, she was going to take as many of these assholes with her as she could. Two down, but how many to go?

"Maybe they're sea sick," Kelly said.

"Who?" she asked.

"The fine managers of our accommodations. I seem to remember—"

"Eighteen, I counted when we came on board," Senior Chief offered, opening the door and stepping into a short passageway. Flakes of brown paint decorated the deck where the force of the storm had knocked them loose from the bulkheads and overhead. Ahead, a watertight hatch blocked their way. "Eighteen, and they all had pieces like this one." He held up the AK-47 for a moment.

"And we only know where four of them are," Early said.

"We gonna run into them soon. Ain't no way we can keep moving on this ship without running into them eventually."

"Scott may have something. If they aren't used to the sea, then maybe this weather is playing havoc with their stomachs."

"It isn't too good with mine," Kelly said.

"And pigs fly," the Senior Chief muttered, motioning them to stop. They had reached the hatch. The sound of the sea came from the other side. The lever on the hatch was shoved all the way down, locking it from the elements on the other side.

"I think we have reached the end of the yellow brick road," Kelly said.

"I think we have reached the end of the superstructure," Senior Chief said. "We may have come too far up."

Early pushed her way to the front. "If we have, we aren't going to come out on the main deck. We've gone up two or three decks since we left the compartment. We only went down one set of ladders when they captured us." She pointed to the hatch and then wishfully said, "Either this is going to lead us to the bridge or we're going to find ourselves staring at the stern of the ship."

"Either way, I think we're going to find ourselves outside the skin of the ship," Kelly offered.

Senior Chief Leary reached forward and pulled the lever up, unlocking the watertight door. "Then we best be doing what we needs be doing, as my father used to say."

The wind grabbed the hatch, ripping it open, nearly jerking the Senior Chief out. He let go. It slammed against the bulkhead, the noise lost in the screams of the storm. Rain and spray blew into the passageway, quickly soaking them. The Senior Chief brought his left arm up across his eyes. Kelly ducked slightly, using Leary as a shield. Early caught the full force of the spray as it whipped around the two men, taking her breath away for moment. Somewhere behind her, the sound of voices rode across the noise of the outside. Leary stepped through the hatch onto a narrow walkway that led forward. The small walkway ran along the edge of the superstructure just below a signal deck opened to the elements. A bulkhead to a compartment provided the starboard side of the walkway. The port side had a couple of chain safety lines running between several stanchions to give the mariner something to hold onto while walking along the narrow walkway. The lines, which dropped in the center between stanchions, weren't meant for a storm such as this. If you fell through these lines, you were either going into the ocean or smashed on the main deck like a bug hitting a windshield.

"Look!" Senior Chief Leary shouted over the sound of the storm. "The bridge." He pointed toward the hatch at the far end of the walkway. Rain ran off his face.

Water soaked their flight suits, turning them a dark green while draining from the fire retardant material onto their flight boots and into their socks.

Their destination jutted out slightly left from the walkway. A bank of windows wormed around the edge of the bridge, giving unfettered views of those inside. The closed hatch at the end of the walkway hid them from those inside the bridge.

"It's daylight," Kelly said in a loud voice, and then pointed left. "And, that looks like Virginia Beach to me."

Early put her opened hand palm-down across the top of her eyes, providing a slight shield from the intense rain pelting them. Through the rising and falling curtains of rain, she made out the coastline. "It's land," she said. "You sure it's Virginia Beach?"

"I don't know. It looked like it for a moment."

"Come on. We'll find out where we're at later." The Senior Chief eased forward, crouched at the waist and holding onto the top safety line while maintaining his grip with his right hand on the AK-47. The AK-47 is not a heavy weapon, weighing slightly less than ten pounds, but any weapon is a burden when you're trying not to be tossed overboard.

The ship rolled right, causing the three of them to fall left into the safety lines. A huge wave bore over the top of the superstructure. Early looked up as it reached its crest. A sheet of seawater sailed over them for a few seconds before breaking apart and slamming down on them.

Early slipped, but her flight boot found the raised edge of the walkway. She twisted her boot sideways and braced against the raised edge.

"Help!" Kelly shouted.

Early looked to the right, where a moment ago the copilot had stood. The curtain of water parted. Kelly was flat on his back. His feet swung into space through the bottom of the safety lines. Both hands gripped the bottom line as he struggled to keep himself from falling overboard. He pulled against the steel chains of the safety lines, trying to pull himself back onto the steel mesh walkway.

Early wanted to reach down to help him, but she would have to let go. If she did, she'd lose her grip and the motion of the ship would do the rest to toss her overboard. They needed the weapons they had if they had any opportunity to survive. For a fraction of a second she debated dropping the AK-47 to help Kelly.

Senior Chief Leary squatted, placed his weapon on the deck, and put his foot on top of it. The ship began to roll right. Leary reached out past the safety lines, grabbed the waist of Kelly's flight suit, and with one heave shoved the thin copilot back onto the walkway. With both hands working furiously, Kelly scrambled backward until his back hit the bulkhead only a couple of feet away.

"Are you okay?" Early asked, shouting over the noise of the storm.

Kelly looked up at her, his eyes wide, his breath coming in quick, short gasps. His face was white. Then his eyes looked past her. "Look out!" he shouted, one hand reaching toward her.

Early rolled forward, coming up against Kelly. The hatch from which they had emerged swung by, crossing the very space where she had been. It slammed against the hatchway. If he hadn't shouted, she would have been crushed between the hatch and the hatchway. She crawled over, reached up, and pulled the lever down, locking the hatch in place, sealing them onto the walkway.

She looked at Kelly and mouthed, "Thanks."

He nodded. "I lost my piece," Kelly said, referring to the AK-47. Rain ran down his face, dripping into his open mouth.

She read his lips more than heard him. "Come on. We've got to keep moving." She looked forward. Senior Chief Leary was at the far hatch that opened into the bridge. Using the starboard roll of the ship to keep his balance, the huge flight engineer leaned out past the safety lines of the walkway to look through the nearest window into the bridge. He jumped back, looked at her and Kelly, and then motioned them forward.

"I counted five with at least three of them with arms." He said when they reached him. "Lieutenant, you lose your gun?"

"It fell overboard when the wave caught him, Senior Chief," Early said. The rain seemed to be slackening. The shoreline was visible again, and she could make out where beach turned to trees. Senior Chief Leary and Lieutenant Kelly must have been looking in the same direction.

"Looks like the old Cape Henry lighthouse," Kelly said. "Been there. It's on Fort Story."

"If that's Fort Story," Early said, "then we're off Virginia Beach like you said, which means whatever is on this ship is probably headed toward the Norfolk Navy base."

The three looked at each other for a moment, the two men deferring to her for a decision. After all, she was the mission commander and the senior Navy officer both on board their aircraft and now on board this ship.

"We're going to take the bridge," she said, feeling her stomach tighten. She was a pilot on a four-engine propeller-driven maritime reconnaissance bird; she wasn't even a fighter pilot, and here she was telling the two of them they were going to attack and take over from armed men the bridge of a terrorist vessel. Armed men probably trained to fight until they were killed. For a brief moment, the idea of jumping overboard and swimming for shore seemed acceptable, but in that same brief moment she realized they'd drown in these seas, sucked beneath by the notorious riptides augmented by the storm surges.

The ship tilted left. Salt water rolled off the top of the open deck above them like a cold shower, again drenching water-saturated flight suits. She wondered for a moment if she looked as bad as they did.

The ship righted itself.

Senior Chief Leary looked at the sky. Clouds passed overhead, heading east with the circular winds. "Looks as if the storm may be headed out to sea, Lieutenant. If it is, then we only have so long before these assholes try to take this ship into the harbor."

Early nodded at the two men, pointed at the Senior Chief, and then nodded toward the door. They weren't going to take the bridge sitting out here.

* * *

CAPTAIN ALRAJOOL BURST THROUGH THE DOOR ON THE starboard side, glancing at the helmsman as he entered the bridge. Across from him, with binoculars dangling from his deck, was his Chief Mate, standing beside the leading seaman of the vessel. An able-bodied seaman entered the bridge with him. Tamursheki was evil—evil to the core—and when the man realized that his hollow cries for martyrdom were going to be answered, it wouldn't surprise Alrajool for this fanatical youth to try to kill him, his crew, and blow the ship up inside the harbor. It was something he himself would do, if he was younger, as stupid, and if roles were reversed.

Abu Alhaul had lied and tricked Tamursheki, but Tamursheki was like other followers of this wanna-be Muhammad. The terrorist leader would never consider that this great charlatan, Abu Alhaul, had intentionally led them to their deaths. Alrajool leaned closer toward the forward windows of the bridge. The faint view of a shoreline blinked in and out through the windshield wipers. About twelve nautical miles away, he figured. Somewhere on that spot of land would be the man Abu Alhaul had vowed to kill—a vow this new leader of radical Islam had taken when he had learned the name of the military person who had led the American Special Forces team responsible for the deaths of his wives and children. The thing about vengeance is it clouds the big picture. What Abu Alhaul failed to understand, but Alrajool did—as did those such as he who retained doubts about their own omnipotence—is that vengeance is a fast tide to failure. He leaned away from the windows. Time to get on with business.

"Chief Mate, call the engine room and tell them to secure their doors. Unless they hear from me personally, they are to obey the orders of the bridge. Keyword is 'Big Apple.' "

The tall, bearded merchant marine officer who was Chief Mate, picked up the handset and passed the instructions to the engineer, who had three sailors with him in the engine room. As he put the handset back in its cradle,

Alrajool envisioned the huge Greek hulk of sinew and muscle who had refused to come out of the engine room since they'd sailed; a Christian distrustful of the terrorists. Alrajool knew the man had had the doors secured before he had been ordered, and now with his instructions relayed, any change to revolutions or directions—forward, reverse—would have to be accompanied by the code word 'Big Apple' otherwise the stubborn Greek would ignore the command.

He pushed the able-bodied seaman standing beside him toward the far hatchway leading from the walkway that ran along the port side of the ship. He didn't expect Tamursheki to come that way, but you never knew what those seeking death are prepared to do. The other able-bodied sailor he positioned near the hatch through which he had entered.

Without saying anything to the two other men manning the bridge, Alrajool turned back to stare across the bow of the freighter. Now came the series of critical moments that would determine whether this mission failed or succeeded. Rain and spray rattled the windows that banked the bridge. He pulled his phone from his pocket and hit the telephone listing buttons a couple of times until the right number appeared. "I'm calling our contact and having them ready the pier, Affendi—my friend," he said to the Chief Mate, who was standing beside him.

He jerked his thumb toward the bulkhead behind him. "Get the weapons out until Tamursheki and his band of assholes are off our ship."

The merchant marine officer nodded. Like Alrajool, he only wanted to finish this dangerous mission and return to sea before the Americans discovered what was happening. Alrajool paced to the starboard side of the bridge while his number-two flipped the locks on the false bulkhead behind the helm. The helmsman stood and slid out of his seat so the officer could open the hidden storage space.

The sound of Alrajool talking mixed with the muffed

noise of the storm as the Chief Mate slid the false wall up and into the overhead. Bolted onto the hidden bulkhead were several pistols along with a couple of older Brazilian Uru 9mm submachine guns. Originally designed in 1974 for the Brazilian Army and police, over the decades these older but still efficient automatic weapons had made their way into hands such as his.

Alrajool closed the cellular telephone and clipped it onto his belt. Now that they were at their target, he needed access to it in the event that those watching and observing had to make last-minute changes. His second in command pulled the weapons away from the mountings and passed them to the bridge crew. A few more American dollars and Alrajool could have bought better and more efficient weapons, but he didn't need a lot. He prided himself on doing his covert missions the way they are supposed to be done—covertly, with stealth. He did not intend to fight an American or a British boarding party. He sure as hell was not foolish enough to fight the French Foreign Legionnaires, who preferred to kill first and ask questions later. He took a deep breath and flipped on the television monitors. He thought of the hidden safe in his stateroom. He possessed enough intelligence to work a deal with the British or the Americans, though most likely it would require him to retire to a life of luxury. He smiled.

A wave washed over the starboard side of the ship, slamming against the windows and the bulkhead of the bridge. The helmsman nearly fell, but the Chief Mate grabbed the helm, holding it steady, while pulling the helmsman upright.

"Keep her steady, Helmsman," Alrajool said, holding on to the overhead safety line that ran the width of the bridge. The makeshift line allowed bridge personnel to move around the confines of the small compartment in the worst of storms as they maneuvered the vessel. On the television monitor showing the second deck, Tamursheki and his men emerged from the medical compartment. For a moment, the terrorist leader looked toward the front of the ship, toward the bridge, as if trying to decide what to do next. Alrajool took a deep breath.

Tamursheki turned away and started down the passageway toward the stern of the ship. Alrajool released his breath when he saw Tamursheki motion the others to follow. The terrorist leader was heading to the rafts. Alrajool shut his eyes for a moment as he said thanks to Allah for getting the fool and his lackeys off his ship. In this rough weather, he'd be surprised if any of them made it ashore, but he didn't care. That wasn't his responsibility. All he cared about right now was having them off his ship. Damn fools.

Alrajool picked up the handset to the radio. "Time to tell the Americans we're coming in. They frown on surprises, so keep them informed and they'll be happy," he said to his Chief Mate.

"Let's see, channel sixteen, harbor common," he said, mumbling to himself as he checked the radio controls. Satisfied, he raised the microphone to his lips.

The hatch from the walkway slammed opened, startling him, causing sweat to break out instantly across his forehead as the thought of Tamursheki crossed his mind. Alrajool caught a glimpse of a huge black monster, screaming at the top of his voice as he rolled through the entrance. He nearly lost bladder control. The roar of the storm drowned out any understanding of the shouts inside the bridge. Water ran from the intruder's face. The man's body looked as if seaweed was stuck tightly against it.

The Chief Mate raised his Brazilian Uru. The automatic weapon in the monster's hand rattled, sending bullets spraying across the bridge, ripping into the Chief Mate. The helmsman was caught in the same burst as he ran toward the far hatch where two others had already dove through and escaped.

The huge figure rose to one knee, cradling the gun and pointing it directly at Alrajool. Behind the attacker, two others entered the bridge.

The sailor near the door fired. The Chief Mate's Uru fired a couple of bursts into the overhead as he fell. Alrajool glanced at the black man and knew he was dead. The three figures opened fire on the able-bodied sailor who was trying to pull a weapon off the bulkhead, sending him reeling backward, jerking like a misused puppet.

The thought burst into his mind that these weren't part of Tamursheki's group. Alrajool dove for the deck, taking the microphone with him, gripping it tightly in his hand, unaware he had the transmit button pushed down.

These were the three prisoners they had had below-decks. What in the hell was Tamursheki thinking, freeing these people? They were Americans. Did he expect them to slink off into some corner, curl into a fetal position and die?

Alrajool released the microphone. The transmit button jumped out, automatically stopping transmissions from the battle. In the storm, gray light cast dark shadows across the deck of the bridge, Alrajool crawled toward the dying sailor near the far door, searching for the pistol the man had dropped. The shooting stopped. He found the pistol, his hand touched it as a cold metal barrel jammed into the small of his neck.

"Try it, asshole," a deep bass voice said. "Just try it."

"Senior Chief!" Early shouted. Kelly lay prone on the deck near the hatchway. A pool of blood grew under the copilot.

Senior Chief Leary never looked up, but pressed the gun barrel deeper into the back of the neck of the man beneath him. "I think I have to kill this one," he said through clinched teeth. "How about it, Lieutenant? We don't need prisoners, do we?"

"Don't kill me!" Alrajool begged, throwing his arms up as far as he could raise them off the deck while laying face down. *Oh, my God,* he thought. "I know stuff. I can be helpful," he offered, his words running together. These were Americans. They would negotiate.

"Yeah, well, I know stuff, too. And, what I know right now is that you're the Captain of this ship where we've been captives for . . . and your men killed good friends of mine."

"Don't, Senior Chief!" Early shouted from where she sat on the deck.

The pressure of the barrel moved away from his neck. He was going to live. *It wouldn't be pleasant for a while, but once they saw his value, life would become good again. Plus, there was that bank account in Liechtenstein. Of course*—Pain surged through his head for a moment, and the thought that the man had shot him accompanied Alrajool into darkness.

The speaker mounted near the merchant radio blared with ships' conversation as various vessels tried to contact harbor control. Early listened to the radio chatter as she and the Senior Chief gently dragged Kelly to the forward bulkhead of the bridge.

"How you feel?" she asked softly. Above her head from the radio came a Coast Guard broadcast about opening the channel in a few hours to traffic into Hampton Roads. Hampton Roads was the generic name for the ports of Norfolk, Little Creek, and Hampton. Communications traffic increased in both volume and garbles as ship after ship demanded priority in entering.

"I feel like shit—but, then, I've been feeling like shit since we've been captured. Only this time, it really hurts." He coughed a couple of times.

Early noticed no blood emerged with the coughs. *That's good news,* she said silently.

"Senior Chief," she said. "What did you do to him?" she asked, nodding toward Alrajool's body.

"I cold cocked him with this here little gun," he said, smiling. "He probably thinks he's dead, and," the man nodded toward Alrajool, "if he makes one move when he wakes up, he's gonna be that way."

She looked at Kelly. "Scott, you picked an awkward time to get yourself shot. You're the only one of us with Surface Warfare experience and who has driven a ship, not counting those little things at Boat U." Boat U was the euphemism for the Navy Academy.

The Senior Chief leaned down and gave Lieutenant Kelly the Uru he had taken from the dead hands of the

Chief Mate. "Here, sir. Lieutenant Early, we need to make contact and drive this big piece of shit," he said, referring to the merchant vessel.

"Anyone can fly an aircraft, Senior Chief," Kelly added. "But—" Coughing broke up the sentence for a few moments before Kelly continued. "It takes a real man to drive a ship."

"If I can help you young'uns drive a P-3, sir, I can drive a ship."

"Remember, Senior Chief, there are more aircraft in the ocean than there are ships in the sky."

"Damn, Lieutenant. Just stay shot. You're a better wounded than a comedian."

Early grabbed the radio handset, turning it over in her hands as she tried to determine how to operate it. "It has a lot of numbers on it," she said aloud, her voice betraying her nervousness.

"Does it say sixteen?" Kelly asked from the deck.

"Yeah."

"Then, you're on harbor common. Everyone's on that, including the Coast Guard and the United States Navy. Broadcast away, Lieutenant, and get the cavalry out here. They—" Kelly broke into coughing. Early could hear liquid behind the cough. That wasn't good.

"Shit, ma'am!" Senior Chief added as he shoved the dead helmsman off the seat, his finger running over the console as he concentrated on the displays. "They can even bring the Air Force as long as we don't have to wait for them to take crews' rest. But push the button and talk to them, please!"

"We've got to move him, Senior Chief. And, we got to do it now." Early jammed the handset back in its holder, bent down, and with both hands under Kelly's armpits, lifted him to a sitting position. "Here, I'm going to slide you against the helm in the center of the bridge," she said.

The coughing stopped. A thin line of blood appeared out of the left corner of his mouth. "That would be nice," he said weakly.

"Got it!" the Senior Chief said, looking over the helm at Early. "Which way you wanna—Here, let me give you a hand." He came around the console and quickly helped Early move the wounded lieutenant the last couple of yards.

They propped Kelly with his back against the console. The ship took a slight roll and the wounded man tilted with the roll. Early grabbed him before he tumbled onto the deck.

Leary touched her on the shoulder. "We got problems, Lieutenant," he said, pointing to the small monitors above the forward bridge windows.

She looked at where the Senior Chief was pointing.

"See the center one?"

Several armed men were scrambling up a ladder. Behind them more poured out of a nearby compartment. A couple of them in the passageway fell and stayed where they fell. Then they split into two groups, with the smaller group of terrorists heading forward while the others, unbeknownst to Early, headed aft, in the direction that Tamursheki and others had taken earlier.

"You think—"

"I don't get paid to think, Lieutenant. That's your job. But since you asked, I would say that in a few seconds we're going to have a lot of company up here on the bridge with us. You really need to get on that radio, ma'am."

Kelly tumbled onto the deck with the return roll, then slowly pushed himself upright. Breathing heavily, he said, "I'm okay."

Early grabbed the handset.

"Don't try to figure it out, Gotta-Be!" Senior Chief shouted. "Just push the button."

She pushed the transmit button just as the hatch to the bridge opened. The ship took a steep roll to port. The roll caught the terrorists off-balance, causing three of them to fall into each other and onto the deck. Guns blazed from behind the three as others fought to enter the bridge. Shots rippled in a line across the overhead.

Early flipped her gun to the right, still holding the handset in her left hand, pulled the trigger, discovering herself surprised that bullets came out of the thing when you did that. Senior Chief Leary fired from the end of the helm console.

The terrorists inside the bridge dove back through the hatch into the passageway. One lay lifeless on the deck. The open hatch moved back and forth to the roll of the ship, bouncing off the head of the dead terrorist blocking the hatchway.

Whoever was following stopped. How were they going to shut the hatch? They should have secured it as soon as they took the bridge. She mentally kicked herself for failing to think of it. Between the starvation and dehydrating diet they'd been on for a week, finding her crew massacred, and fighting for the bridge, it was a wonder they were still alive. Still, she should have been thinking ahead.

She lifted the handset to her lips. "Mayday, mayday, mayday . . ."

CHAPTER 11

THE GRAY OF DAY RODE ACROSS THE SHEETS OF RAIN dancing along the shoreline toward the tower. A hot breakfast had given Tucker his second wind after a restless night. He watched through the window as Pete MacOlson and the First Class continued their work along the piers. A new person was with them. The anchor of a chief petty officer was embroidered on the front of the new one's ball cap.

When Tucker had gone to bed the night before, MacOlson and his men had been setting and resetting the mooring lines on the special operations crafts; when he had risen early at around three in the morning, they had still been out there; and here it was approaching eight o'clock and they were still at it. At least with the SEALs you got a change of scenery every now and again. Granted, a lot of those scenes had bullets in them.

No wonder few remained Surface Warfare officers. Plus, Navy SEALs do get a few hours in a row for a good sleep. Most SWOs were lucky to get four hours in a row, especially when they were at sea. Must drive their wives mad. On the other hand, there could be many happy nights when the sailor came home from the sea.

Footsteps behind him drew Tucker's attention. Commodore West appeared at the head of the stairs, holding papers in his right hand. He waved them at Tucker. "Looks as if we're finally getting some good news," he said, walking toward the Navy SEAL.

"Yes, sir?"

"Our esteemed weather-guessers have met in secret counsel and decided that by noon the malevolent Being driving this storm will be far enough away in its sharp right-hand turn toward the northeast that we should see the rain and seas diminish. The storm is heading toward our brothers and sisters on the British Isles, who, as we all know, are much better qualified to handle weather such as this." He handed the top paper to Tucker. "Personally, I would much rather have it visit the French."

A schematic of the East Coast filled the sheets covered with the myriad of wavy lines that, with the exception of the Cray computers hidden beneath the bowels of NSA, only trained meteorologists could interpret. Little arrows bulging along the lines pointed the directions various fronts were moving, and in the upper right-hand corner, a small block identified the date and time of the data.

West laughed. "I know," he said, taking the paper back and shoving it on the bottom of the stack. "I always feel like a pig looking at a clock when I'm trying to read these printouts, but they surely do get their feelings hurt if I tell them I don't want them." Then, with a humorous, conspiratorial tone, he continued, "But, we must never let the small corps of Navy weathermen figure out we can't read this crap—their spirit of superiority will soar to such heights that we'll never be able to live with them. They're kinda like wives, you know, Commander—can't live with them and can't live without them."

The crackle of the radio at the front of the tower interrupted their conversation as early-morning chatter from the merchant ships riding out the storm off the Virginia Capes focused on the Harbormaster asking permission to enter. Anything was better than riding out a storm this close to shore. This time it was a Japanese roll-on roll-off carrier with a load of new automobiles that had the better volume. Everyday loitering off shore cost money to both operators of ships and the companies whose merchandise lay stagnant on board. This time the Harbormaster gave them a time.

"Looks as if they intend to open the harbor in a few hours," said the Commodore, pursing his lips at the transmission. He sighed and looked at the next paper before handing it to Tucker. "Message from Southern Command," he explained. "They have resumed the search for survivors of Recce Mission 62." West shook his head. "Very doubtful after all this time they'll find anyone alive, but you've got to look. You've got to go through the routine, cross your fingers, and hope that some God out there has reached out and touched the survivors. The Admiral also attached the crew manifest to the message since next-of-kins have all been notified."

Marc St. Cyr, the Frenchman, appeared at the top of the stairs along with Wing Commander Tibbles-Seagraves. St. Cyr had a couple of pastries soaking through some napkins wrapped around them. Tibbles-Seagraves held a hot cup of tea—a string with a small piece of paper fluttered from the lip of the cup—with his thumb and finger.

"Your American weather is great," St. Cyr said. "Reminds me of Chad without the desert and rain."

Tibbles-Seagraves's thick eyebrows bunched. "And, along with my fine French ally, it reminds me of England without the temperature."

"Ally?" St. Cyr said with a smile, placing his hand with spread fingers lightly on his chest. "*Moi*—the French? We are now your allies?"

"Well, for today you're an ally of Britain. Doesn't happen often, about three times last century, I seem to recall. I think two of those times were when we were in France, but I think you French forget sometimes. But, far be it for me to raise that issue. Every now and again, we British believe that allowing the French to associate with us may bring some semblance of civilization and common sense to you." He took a sip of the tea. "But, then again, it hasn't worked so far."

"*C'est vrai,*" St. Cyr said, using the French for "this is true." "But I doubt very much that anyone can bring common sense to any of our countries. Our three militaries are always burdened with the same yoke—politicians."

"*C'est vrai, c'est vrai, c'est vrai,*" Commodore West mumbled in a low but agitated voice to himself.

"Touché," Tibbles-Seagraves replied, slurping from the slightly cooler top layer of tea.

"Glad you've joined us," Commodore West finally said.

Tucker noticed that the friendly voice that had shared conversation with him during the night now seemed more stiff, more formal.

"I just returned from Commander, Special Warfare Group Two, after the morning intelligence brief. Seems with this storm turning northeast and away from us, the search for the rogue freighter continues to be haphazard at best. Admiral Holman has recommended to his French and British counterparts that they reorient their efforts and turn more attention to protecting the most likely target ports such as Rotterdam. Admiral Holman should be back in our area in the next couple of days. The Admiral believes a more layered defense in depth that combines the advantages of a proactive search backed up with a strong second-string defense is the best way to go. Your countries," West said, nodding at St. Cyr and Tibbles-Seagraves, "agree. Britain and France will take the European side of the Atlantic. Admiral Holman will regroup off VACAPES," West continued, using the acronym for the Navy's Virginia Capes, "and start a complete search of the Atlantic behind the departing storm. If the rogue freighter had been heading to Europe or the Mediterranean, they feel it would have been sighted by now. The Spanish and Portuguese military placed an east-west barrier over a thousand miles long running from the coast of Morocco to past the Azores, stopping hundreds of merchant vessels. No joy."

"Have our Navy and our British ally redeployed their ships to protect Rotterdam and the other major ports?" St. Cyr asked, rolling the "r" in Rotterdam.

The radio crackled again. This time multiple calls filled the tower as ships that had been waiting days demanded entry times. The Chief Petty Officer Tucker had seen on the pier with MacOlson a few moments before entered the tower and turned the volume down on the harbor common radio to where it was barely audible.

Commodore West, his eyes narrowed, looked over his bifocals at the Chief, who nodded and turned the volume up slightly. The chatter was still there, but relegated to background noise.

"How about the crew of the missing airplane?" Tibbles-Seagraves asked, setting his cup on the table for a moment. He brushed his hands together.

How do they do it? Tucker asked himself, looking at the blue SAS suit of Tibbles-Seagraves. He glanced down at his and then at St. Cyr's. Theirs were wrinkled and showed the wear of three days, while the Brit's blue outfit still had those knife-sharp creases along the legs and running through the blouse.

West nodded at Tucker. "As I was telling Commander Raleigh, Southern Command has recommenced the search. Expectations are high that if the crew successfully ditched or bailed out, they'll find them."

Several sharp pops interrupted the chatter from the speaker.

"And the other good news—"

St. Cyr held his hand up. "Wait!" He cocked his ear toward the speaker where three ships were arguing about who had arrived first and should be granted first-entry rights.

"What is it?" Tucker asked.

"Turn the volume up, please," St. Cyr asked the Chief Petty Officer while pointing toward the radio.

"Did you hear that?" St. Cyr said to the other officers.

"Hear what?" West asked.

"That! I heard 'm'aider' " St. Cyr insisted, pushing past the Commodore to the harbor radio at the front. He bent down, looking at the controls. "There's nothing here," he said.

"It's an old radio, sir," the Chief Petty Officer offered. "What do you want to do?"

"I want to turn it up. I want to hear what I heard a few seconds ago."

"M'aider?" Commodore West said softly to Raleigh, his right lip curling upward. "What the shit does that mean?"

The Chief reached down and twisted the volume knob. The sound of the chatter rose within the tower.

"Not too loud, Chief," West said. "You get it too loud, you won't be able to hear what they're saying because it'll distort the transmissions."

"Mayday, mayday, mayday. Anyone on this station," shouted a female voice over the speaker.

"See!" St. Cyr said, pointing at the speaker. "M'aider!"

"We need—" The popping sound came again.

"There! You hear that?" St. Cyr looked at Tucker and Tibbles-Seagraves. "Tell me *oui!*"

"Yeah, we heard that." West replied as he moved toward the radio.

"That's gunfire!" Tucker and Tibbles-Seagraves responded in unison.

Tucker hurried over to where St. Cyr stood. Tibbles-Seagraves lifted his cup and walked to where the two men and the Commodore now stood.

"You sure that's gunfire?" the Commodore asked.

"Heard it before. Heard it in Afghanistan. Yemen. And Somalia. Doesn't sound the same when it's—"

"We're on a ship somewhere out here in VACAPES!" the female voice screamed. "We're United States Navy. There are terrorists on board here. We have the bridge—" More pops drowned out the voice. "Mayday, mayday,

mayday! For Christ's sake! Someone's gotta be out there! We need help!"

"You don't think?" Tibbles-Seagraves asked Tucker and St. Cyr, his voice low.

"I don't get paid to think," West interrupted. He rushed over to the red telephone mounted on the far bulkhead and picked it up.

From the top of the stairs, Sam Bradley walked into the main tower. "Well, seems everyone is up and active this morning," she said.

Tucker looked at her. She must have seen something in his look, for the smile left her lips and her eyes widened.

He turned his attention to the radio as they watched the Commodore on the secure telephone. Sam hurried over to Tucker and hugged his arm for a moment. She was dressed in khaki, her hair tugged into a bun. No one spoke.

Sam asked softly, "What's the matter?"

A wave of rain hit the front windows.

Commodore put the telephone down. "I just called NetWars Command. They're turning the local Security Group direction-finding units onto harbor-common to see if they can triangulate the source."

"Could be a hoax," Tucker offered.

"What could be a hoax?" Sam asked, cocking her head to the side. "Something's going on, and I should know about it."

The voice emerged again from the speaker. "We have the bridge, but I don't know how long we can hold it. We have one wounded. The rest of my crew are dead—"

The scrabble of three ships arguing about entry times overrode the faint transmission of the woman. Several minutes passed. The red telephone rang and the Commodore picked it up. He listened for a couple of minutes before hanging it up. Tucker used that time to bring Sam up to date on what they had heard. Unspoken was the thought that the rogue freighter everyone thought was heading toward Europe may be instead off the coast of

Virginia. If so, then who was the American woman calling for help on harbor common and to what "crew" was she referring?

The secure telephone rang from its position on the small desk beneath the red telephone. Commodore West picked it up. He listed for a few minutes, said "sir" into it several times. The "sir" told Tucker and the others that whomever the Commodore was talking with was senior to the older Navy Captain.

The officer hung up, looked down at the handset for a moment before raising his head. "Chief, go get Lieutenant MacOlson and have him and his team report to the briefing room immediately."

"Team?"

"Yes, team," West said, emphasizing the latter word. When the term team was used, it meant special operations. If he had said crew, then he would have been referring to a nautical-maritime function.

"Aye, aye, sir," the Chief said. The man turned and ran across the room, taking the stairs two at a time as he bolted toward the piers.

"What's going on?" Tucker asked.

"We aren't sure, but Naval Security Group is able to hear the woman on harbor common better than we are, and their DF sites working with the Coast Guard coastal units have located the transmission as emanating from a location about eleven miles off the tip of Fort Story near the entrance to the harbor channel."

"One thing they heard that we didn't was her identify herself as Navy Lieutenant Maureen Early." He reached over to the table, shuffled the papers around, found the one he was looking for, and handed it to Tucker.

It was the manifest for the crew of Recce Flight 62. St. Cyr and Tibbles-Seagraves looked at the list with him. The top name on the list of twenty-four trapped his attention, sending a rush of chill bumps up his back and chest. LIEUTENANT MAUREEN EARLY, FLIGHT COMMANDER.

"If what SecGru is saying is correct, Commodore, then how did—"

"—they end up here? I can only guess until you get out there. My gut speculation is that they crashed near the terrorist freighter and they're prisoners. Or were prisoners. They seem to be free for the moment. Regardless of whether it's true or not—whether this is a hoax or not—we can't take a chance. I have sent the Chief to round up the Lieutenant and his teams. Those sailors out there with the patrol boats are not your everyday sailors as you are aware. They're also a mix of SEALs and explosive ordnance experts—EODs. The Chief is going to be your team leader. He has in-country experience in Iraq, Somalia, and Liberia."

"Okay, I'm going to get my medical kit together."

"You're not going," Tucker said, his brow wrinkling.

"Look, buddy," Sam Bradley said, poking him lightly in the chest. "I may have deep feelings for you, but not enough for you to start telling me how to do my job."

Tucker jerked his head back at the unexpected response. Sam winked. "Someone is wounded, and if this isn't a hoax and is the real thing, then the difference between life and death may be this little ol' nurse from DiLorenzo Tricare Health Clinic, Pentagon." She winked again. "Besides, you need me and you just don't want to say it."

"She's right. We don't have time to get a medical team here," Commodore West said, jerking his head at her to get going. "We don't have time to get anything together except what we have right here. This storm has trees and electric lines down across Tidewater. I don't think we could get a full team together for hours. Nope." He shook his head. "Commander Raleigh, you'll go with what we have available, and I am ordering you to succeed."

MacOlson ran up the stairs; rain running off his slick, forming a huge puddle around his feet. He shook his head, water splashing Bradley as she leaned away. Smiling, MacOlson gave a mock salute as he removed his ball cap. "Reporting as ordered, sir."

"Your men downstairs, Lieutenant?"

"Some are, sir. The others are coming. Just had to finish those last couple of lines," he replied, wringing his cap without mangling the brim. Water fell from it to join the puddle around his feet. "And, they're enjoying the dry break from the weather, but we can't stay long, Commodore. High tide is fast going out, and we'll need to readjust the lines again."

"You're going to be casting off lines in a few minutes, Lieutenant. Your job is to transport Commander Raleigh, Captain St. Cyr, Wing Commander Tibbles-Seagraves, and five of your team to . . ." and he spent the next few minutes bringing the Surface Warfare officer up to speed on events and stopping MacOlson's objection to taking a Special Operations Craft out in this sea state.

Unraveling a navigational chart of the waters around the Tidewater area of Virginia Beach, Little Creek, and Norfolk, Virginia, the Commodore laid out a basic plan—a plan that called for Raleigh to lead a makeshift SEAL team that had never worked together along with two officers from allied nations to board a freighter they had very little intelligence about and to fight Jihadist terrorists. If their quick estimate was right, some Americans were still alive and fighting on the bridge. Whether they could get there in time to turn the tide of battle and save the Americans seemed doubtful to him, but the Commodore treated it as if there was no doubt in his seasoned veteran mind that those trapped Americans would survive.

Commodore West paused and looked directly at Tucker. "This is not easy to say. We don't have orders yet, telling us to do this, but I want to get you all in place so when those orders do come we're ahead of the game. The weather is still bad, Commander, and it's playing havoc with communications. So, I am going to give you your orders, and unless you hear differently from me or someone senior to me, you will execute them." He pointed at St. Cyr, Tibbles-Seagraves, and MacOlson. "Your first priority is to stop that ship from coming closer to the coast. At all costs, and that includes your own lives. Lieutenant MacOlson, you're to get this team to that freighter regardless of weather, ship survival, or even the safety of your men and you."

Commodore West turned back to Tucker. "You're to take possession of the vessel and hold it in position. If you reach the decision that it's impossible to do so, then you are to do everything within your power to turn it out to sea." Commodore West paused. "I have just spoken with Commander, Second Fleet. They have been listening and evaluating those radio transmissions also. Oceana Naval Air Station in Virginia Beach is socked in right now, but within the next three hours they expect the weather to clear sufficiently to launch a couple of F-18 Hornets that didn't bingo west when the others did."

"So if we don't succeed then those Hornets are going to take the vessel out?"

"How are we going to find this ship?" St. Cyr asked. "I have heard a lot of different ships on the radio. The anchorages must be crowded.

Commodore West nodded but ignored the question. "What you don't know is that Defense Intelligence Agency believes the van lashed down on the stern of the freighter houses a nuclear device."

"That is our assessment, also," Tibbles-Seagraves volunteered. "In the interest of allies united and information-sharing, if I may?" he asked, nodding toward West. He set his cup on the saucer he was holding in his right hand.

"Of course, go ahead."

"British Intelligence believes the van is a diversion from a more sinister weapon, but we aren't sure what. We think it may be biological in nature."

"We think it could also be chemical," St. Cyr added.

"Even more reason for you to take Lieutenant Commander Bradley with you. Take her on board so she can form a quick analysis of what all of our intelligence weenies are saying."

St. Cyr cleared his throat. "Of course, we would have already shared everything we know with our British and American friends. I believe that the appearance of the ship here is directly tied to Commander Raleigh," he said, respectfully nodding once in Tucker's direction.

West stared at the French Captain for a couple of seconds before looking at Raleigh. "Yes, we initially thought this Abu Alhaul's desire to avenge certain actions attributed to Commander Raleigh might draw him here, but the last report by Recce Flight 62 of the merchant vessel heading north, and the storm off our eastern seaboard, combined to convince seniors the ship was bound for Europe."

Sam Bradley came back up the steps, wearing a long Navy-issued raincoat. "I'm ready. My stuff is at the front door."

"Sir, you know this isn't going to be easy," MacOlson said. "Those boats aren't made for this rough weather. We've got no keel—"

"—and, you've got no rudder or propellers, Lieutenant, which means you should be able to skim over the top of those waves with no problems."

"No problems!"

"Lieutenant, you wouldn't want to let an old Surface Warfare officer down, now would you? Besides, those waves are getting smaller and smaller by the minute. Haven't you been listening to the weather? The storm is curving to the northeast, heading across the Atlantic. By late this afternoon the rain may even stop."

"That is indeed good news, sir," MacOlson said. "That means the rescue helicopters should be able to get to us sooner."

The radio crackled, drawing their attention.

"Lieutenant Early, this is Hampton Roads Coast Guard. We have you fivers, ma'am. Can you tell us your location?"

Static followed the transmission for a couple of seconds, followed by more static as another merchant interrupted the channel asking for permission to enter the navigation channel. He was a tanker out of New Iraq heading for the terminals in Norfolk.

"Get the hell off the circuit," Commodore West mumbled. "Jesus Christ! Don't they know we have an emergency out there?"

As if hearing him, the Coast Guard returned to the circuit. "All stations this circuit. You will remain clear of channel sixteen until we have authorized you to use it. Backup channel eighteen is open for all users with the exception of Lieutenant Early. Do not acknowledge this restriction. Lieutenant Early, maintain contact this channel."

Static followed for a few seconds.

"Coast Guard, this is Early." The popping sound of rapid gunfire garbled her words.

The red telephone rang. Commodore West picked it up. Listening, he turned his back to the others. Tucker moved a couple of steps nearer, trying to hear what was being said. West was issuing a lot of "yes, sirs" and "no, sirs." Must be Second Fleet again.

"I think we're east of Fort Story," the voice on the radio broadcast. "We're pretty sure we saw the old Cape Henry lighthouse, but it was—" Gunfire interrupted the transmission.

Fort Story was a little-known Army base situated on the point of land where the coast curves west to butt against the more famous tourist-ridden beaches of Virginia Beach. The Cape Henry lighthouse was one of the first built in America, and while it was not operational, the Army still maintained it in pristine shape as a historical monument.

Repeated calls by the Coast Guard failed to re-establish contact with the P-3C pilot.

Commodore West hung up the telephone and looked at Tucker.

"It's a go. Lieutenant MacOlson, take them out, bear south toward Cape Henry."

"Sir, we aren't sure exactly where they're located and there must be—"

West nodded. "You're right. We don't. But we have a general area and we know that it's got a huge, dark-colored van anchored down on its stern weather deck.

Yes, there are at least a hundred commercial ships anchored out there, but the ship you're looking for has to be within ten to twenty miles of shore, otherwise they wouldn't be able to see the coastline. That was Second Fleet on the telephone. By the time you hit the channel, Lieutenant, the Coast Guard will have their coastal patrol boat, the USCGC *Albacore* out there. She's just returned from evading the storm." The Commodore put on his raincoat. "The *Albacore* will try to provide a weather break for you to close the ship. Should make the going a little smoother."

MacOlson nodded. "How about the other boats tied up here, sir?"

"Why do you think I'm putting on my raincoat? Headquarters is sending some sailors off one of the amphibs to help me watch the lines. Until then, I think me and the First Class can recall enough about ships to keep them safe until the Boatswain Mates off the amphibs arrive." He looked at the men and the lone woman watching him. "Well? Get going. You can't very well help anyone standing here watching me."

Tucker moved quickly, heading toward the stairs.

"One other thing," Commodore West said.

Everyone stopped and turned toward the Commodore. Tucker noticed a look of sadness cross the man's face. *He knows he is sending us off to die.*

"May God go with you."

Tucker nodded once before turning down the stairs. His two Special Forces allies hurried with him. MacOlson had already disappeared, running to his boat. Behind MacOlson ran the SEAL/EOD sailors who had been in the conference room.

Tucker knew the Surface Warfare officer would already have the team outfitted and in position by the time they hit the deck of the boat.

Commodore West shouted, bringing him up short. St. Cyr and Tibbles-Seagraves stopped alongside him. Bradley was halfway down the stairs and kept on going, not having heard the shout. "Commander, that ship can't be allowed into the harbor. Keep her out to sea. If all else fails, scuttle her, but don't let her enter the harbor or close our shores. Navy Intelligence isn't sure what the weapon is on her stern, but whatever it is, it must be something special if Abu Alhaul has gone through all this trouble."

"Yes, sir," Tucker said. He bit his bottom lip for a second. In for a nickel, in for a dime, he thought. "But, they may have a worse-case scenario, Commodore."

West passed them as he hit the stairs. The three men hurriedly followed. "Yeap, worse case it could be a nuclear weapon—a real one. Then it won't matter whether it explodes at sea or ashore; it's going to create a lot of death and destruction, which is why, when you take control, keep it out there, away from here."

SENIOR CHIEF LEARY STOOD BEHIND THE HELM, HIS AK-47 propped across the top of it. "We're steering two-nine-zero," he said, tapping the compass in front of him.

He turned. At first dismissing the noise that sounded like a bouncing metal ball as his fingers drumming the compass.

Kelly saw it first. "Grenade," he said in a voice moist with the blood trickling in his throat. A string of red flowed down the right side of his lips as he raised his hand and pointed toward the hatch on the starboard side of the bridge.

Without thinking about it, Early dashed from where she had been standing near the forward bulkhead. With one hand, she scooped up the still-rolling grenade, and in one smooth underhand softball-like pitch tossed it back toward the open hatchway just as the ship rolled slowly to the port side. The hatch door swung inward, bouncing off the dead man's head as the grenade sailed through the opening, barely missing the edge of the loose hatch by an inch. The explosion blew out the windows directly in front of the hatchway. The concussion sent her reeling backward, tripping over Kelly's feet. Her head felt like it was blowing up inside her skull, and when she landed against the port bulkhead, she was surprised to see the Senior Chief lying beside her.

He looked at her and said something, but the words were muffled and she didn't understand. She shook her head.

The Senior Chief pushed himself up and hurried across the back of the bridge to the open hatchway, reached down, and jerked the body away. Then, while dust and debris continued to settle, he exposed himself for a moment to reach out and slam the hatch shut. He reached up and shoved the lever down and around. The explosion had buckled a latch, causing the lever to stop halfway around. The top of the hatch sealed against its facings, but the explosion had curled the bottom half of the stout metal door up, leaving an opening about two feet across. Big enough for someone to crawl through; big enough for another grenade to be tossed; and too small for an accurate return pitch.

Early twisted her jaws back and forth, feeling the pop of air as the pressure in her ears equalized. She pulled herself up and to the front, but kept her position to the left side of the bridge.

"We need to turn it away from the coast," Kelly said, his words straining through pain.

Lieutenant Early looked at the wounded man. It had been five minutes since the Coast Guard had announced their imminent arrival, but imminent in the military services was directly related to the readiness of the unit being committed. In this weather, she doubted they had a ship large enough and close enough to be here soon. A fresh spot of blood appeared on Kelly's right leg where a piece of shrapnel had hit him. It didn't look too serious. But then, it wasn't her wound.

Kelly pulled himself back up into a sitting position. Blood ran out of his left ear, dripping onto the shoulder of his wounded side.

Lieutenant Early and Senior Chief Leary hurriedly moved the wounded copilot around to the port side of the helm console, putting the controls of the ship between the copilot and the damaged hatch, which pinged repeatedly as the terrorists renewed firing. Bullets entered the bridge through the buckled bottom half of the hatch. Most went out the broken windows, a few ricocheted inside the bridge, luckily missing them. The three huddled around the console until the firing died.

"Is there some way we can disable the helm? Stop the ship's movement? We need to do something so if they do—" Early stopped in mid sentence. If the terrorists regained control of the bridge, it meant the three of them were dead.

Kelly coughed. "There should be an automatic pilot that can be turned on; but once it's turned off, who ever is at the helm can turn the ship wherever he wants it to go."

Early faced the truth of their situation. They were outnumbered, and it was only a matter of time before they were overrun or killed.

"How about we turn it on—"

A grenade sailed through the opening. Early and Leary saw it at the same time. Both dived behind the console as the grenade exploded. Automatic gunfire from the attackers filled the opening.

Early and Leary stood, their AK-47s pointed toward the hatch, expecting any moment for the terrorists to burst through.

"Looks as if that idea is dead, Lieutenant," Leary said, catching her eye and nodding toward the other end of the console where the smooth metal casing housing the automatic pilot had been replaced by a mangle of aluminum, sparking wires, and smoke.

The radio on the bulkhead rode over the noise of the fight. "Lieutenant Early, this is Commodore West. Help is on the way. Hold out, shipmates. Give us thirty minutes."

"Thirty minutes! Christ! We'll be lucky to hold out another five."

* * *

WEST WAITED FOR NEARLY A MINUTE BEFORE HE MOVED the handset away from his head and clipped it back on his belt.

Sailors rushed along the side of the low-profile dark Mark V Special Operations Craft docked at the end of the inboard pier. They had singled up all lines, and exhaust from the two K50S waterjets that drove this boat like a low-flying aircraft quickly flew away with the winds. Standing outside the covered portion of the small eighty-two-foot craft were Tucker, St. Cyr, and Tibbles-Seagraves. The three stared at the Commodore, who walked to the edge of the pier and shook his head.

"No reply! No answer!" West shouted, unclipping his radio and holding up for a moment. "May be too late."

"Let go all lines!" MacOlson shouted through a bullhorn.

West covered his ears.

Tucker bit his lower lip as he nodded at the four-striper. It meant either Early and those with her in the bridge of this ship—and they weren't even sure what it looked like or where it was . . . *Were they dead or too busy to answer?* All they had to go on was that Early said they could see the Cape Henry lighthouse, which was located on a spit of land inside Fort Story. The fact that it would be a few hours before the weather would allow helicopters to be airborne also narrowed down their options if they got out there and ran into more than the three of them balanced with five enlisted SEAL/EODs could handle. So close to American shores and yet so far from additional support, all thanks to Mother Nature.

Tucker was glad the Commodore had decided to make this an eight-person team instead of the usual four-person. Even so, the eight of them had never worked together. They were going out cold turkey with no idea of the odds against them or what they were facing. Somewhere behind them, a lot of intelligence officers were stuck in traffic after a warm night's sleep.

SEAL Team Four at the Dam Neck, Virginia, training facility was being assembled. The Air Force had some

Special Forces helicopters, commonly referred to as Pave Low, at Langley anxiously waiting for the weather to change so they could pick up SEAL Team Four. Until then, it was this hodgepodge SEAL team that was heading into battle. Tucker would be surprised if they all lived through it. He glanced down into the crew compartment where they would ride. Sam Bradley leaned forward at the end of the seat row and did something inside the black medical kit she had braced between her legs. Nine of them going aboard, since Sam had inserted herself into what could be a one-way mission. Tucker made a mental vow that the next time he was wounded he would have the nurse sign a limited length of authority agreement.

MacOlson's head stuck outside the compartment. "Come on, Commander. Better get inside!"

Tucker, St. Cyr, and Tibbles-Seagraves ducked as they stepped down into the small staging compartment of the Mark V. A row of seats along both sides of the bulkheads provided the small comfort to the SEALs who rode these high-speed boats into harm's way. The Mark V was never meant to be a long-range craft. It wasn't even built to allow those assigned duty to it to sleep on board, though many did. They brought their own sleeping gear and, like sailors, submariners, and aircrewmen through the years, discovered that sleep was hidden in all the strange places of a warship and warplane. All it took was warfighter ingenuity and an ability to ignore fear, discomfort, danger, and the smells and sounds of others in close quarters.

Tucker swung into the seat beside Sam. "You okay?" he asked.

"And why wouldn't I be?" she asked, in a voice loud enough to ride over the mixed sounds of the waterjet engines and the storm.

Tucker pulled his carbine from the rack behind him. He checked the chamber, the magazine, and the safety before clipping it back into its storage area. The boat ceased backing.

The sound of the engines decreased for a moment, then increased steadily in volume until the boat moved forward, slowly at first and then quickly picking up speed. As it gathered speed, the effects of the waves beating into the closed waterway they traveled increased in intensity. The small boat heaved upward for a moment before slamming back down on the ocean. The moment of weightlessness between when the upward movement stopped and the downward fall began caused Tucker's stomach to drag upward each time as they fell the couple of feet to the surface. That was all he needed—to become seasick.

They weren't going to be much use to those airdales on board that rogue freighter if they drowned before they got there. Then, as if reading his mind, the pounding of the water against the Mark V dropped in intensity as if a curtain had fallen across a gripping seat-edge act. What Tucker knew was that the real event was yet to come.

MacOlson crawled down from his seat in the small bridge of the boat and, balancing himself with his hands, worked his way back to where Tucker sat. "Commander," he said over the noise of the waterjets and storm. "Coast Guard Cutter *Albacore* will rendezvous with us in five minutes. They're going to take the seaward track and let us sail in their lee side. This should reduce the wave action on our Mark V."

Tucker acknowledged MacOlson, who grinned, leaned down, and said, "Ain't life grand for a sailor at sea?" Then he turned and worked his way back to the bridge area, where sailors occupied four of the five seats in the small compartment.

The door leading to the bridge area remained open.

"What's he doing?" Sam asked, leaning over to Tucker so he could hear her. She pointed through the door to the petty officer who was sitting in the center of the bridge compartment, each hand on a long rod that seemed to grow from the floor.

As they watched, the sailor moved the rods slightly back and forth.

"That's the helmsman," Tucker said, leaning over so his lips brushed her ear. "Those things he's holding are the things that drive the two waterjets. The Mark V doesn't have a rudder, propellers, or shafts like a normal boat or ship. He pushes and pulls those waterjets to control the direction we're going." Tucker leaned back and looked through the hatch at the bridge, then leaned toward Sam. "I think he also controls the speed of the craft, but I'm not sure how."

MacOlson stuck his head through the open door. "We've got a visual on the Coast Guard cutter. Should be a little smoother ride in a moment. And by the way," he continued. "They've narrowed down the freighter we are after to five that are in the area."

"IF WE ABANDON THE BRIDGE, WE'RE GIVING CONTROL TO them."

"Right, Maureen, but right now, it doesn't look like much of a bridge."

"We've got two problems," the Senior Chief added, the words running together nervously.

If he was nervous, Early figured she had better be also. "We're not only going to have to go back out the way we came in, but we're going to have to carry Lieutenant Kelly also."

His voice was garbled. She couldn't understand what he was saying. Early leaned around the destroyed helm and saw that the Senior Chief was peering around the edge of the hole in the bottom of the hatch. A shadow crossed in front of the light in the passageway. Leary jumped back, stuck the barrel of his automatic weapon through the hole, and fired a burst. A short cry of pain abruptly cut off told her the Senior Chief's fire had been accurate.

"Outside, we're sitting ducks," Early said.

"We've been lucky so far," Kelly mumbled.

"If they throw any more grenades into here, we could be dead meat," the Senior Chief said. He looked down at the copilot. "And, your body can't afford much more luck, Lieutenant."

Movement on the couple of monitors still working above the forward bridge windows caught Early's attention. Four smoldered from the damage caused by the grenades and bullets. The fifth had an erratic white line riding up a dark screen only to reappear at the bottom and start its upward journey again. On the only one working, she saw two men standing at the van on the aft deck, doing something to it.

Then firing came through the damaged door again, causing her to hunker down near Kelly. Seconds later, the gunfire slackened, then suddenly stopped altogether. She used the pause to crawl to the port hatch where they had attacked the bridge. Pushing herself off the deck, keeping her back against the rear bulkhead, Early stood up. She held the AK-47 at an angle so she could fire at whatever she found on the other side. Early reached up and swung the lever down fast, pushing the hatch outward. The heavy metal hatch swung out until it hit the safety lines. The ship rolled slowly to starboard at the same time. The hatch bounced off the safety lines, curving inward to slam off the facings a couple of times before stopping in the closed position. Early reached up and pulled the lever back down.

"Nothing out there."

A burst of gunfire came through the hole. Another round of ricocheting bullets bounced around the bridge.

"They're up to something, ma'am. The firing is slackening. Means either we've killed a lot of them, *which I doubt*. Or, they've decided to do something else, and whatever it is, it won't be good for us. You oughta try that radio again and see where the cavalry is," he suggested, nodding at the forward bulkhead.

Early's eyes narrowed as she surveyed the area around the radio. The speaker was intact. Should still be working. Then she saw the dangling transmission cord that had been connected to the handset before the fight had begun. They could hear, but they couldn't contact anybody. Most of what happened now was out of her hands. She hoped whoever was coming would get there quickly.

"Merchant vessel to my starboard," came a voice from

the speaker. "What are your intentions? You are closing my port side."

Early looked through the windows. The ship was in a starboard turn with the bow of another ship entering into view from the right. Two chains rose from the surface of the ocean into the bow of the vessel.

"I am anchored and unable to maneuver. Request you alter course immediately, merchant vessel!" the voice shouted.

The silhouette of the anchored merchant vessel slid rapidly across the bow of their ship.

"What's going on?" Kelly asked.

Senior Chief Leary slid back from the hold in the starboard hatch and pulled himself up behind the bridge console. "The compass is going around clockwise," he said.

"What are the rudders doing, man?" Kelly asked, then commenced coughing.

"Rudders, rudders, rudders," the Senior Chief muttered as his eyes searched the damaged console. "What do they look like?"

"There should be a gauge or display unit up there that shows the angle of the rudders so you know how much of a turn you are in."

Leary looked a few more seconds. "Dammit! Ain't nothing up here, Lieutenant. Must have been part of this—"

The barrel of a gun poked through the lower half of the damaged hatch, turned toward the Senior Chief, and fired a burst before being jerked back.

One bullet grazed his right shoulder. "Damn—shit—fuck!"

"Okay, Senior Chief. If you can't find it, you can't find it."

"Don't need to find it," Early said, pointing forward. "I think we're going to miss this ship, but if we're in a circle, then we're going to come back this way again, and if that ship is still there, we may hit her."

The familiar metal bouncing sound of another grenade sent the Senior Chief and Early diving for cover on the left side of the helm console, their bodies draped over the wounded Lieutenant. The explosion filled the bridge with fresh dust. Early's ears hurt as she picked herself up.

"Everyone—" she started, then realized the Senior Chief was gone.

Early stood up, her weapon pointing toward the buckled hatch.

She saw him. He was scrambling along the rear bulkhead, over pieces of sharp metal cutting his knees. Leary reached the buckled hatch, threw himself to the deck, stuck the barrel of the AK-47 through the opening, and fired. The automatic gunfire was accompanied by a litany of cursing, parental epithets, and descriptive socially unacceptable metaphors that only a career sailor could learn by actively working on the job. If the bullets didn't kill them, the language surely would wound them.

"Lieutenant Early, this is Coast Guard Cutter *Cyclone*. We believe we have you identified. Five minutes to rendezvous, ma'am. Acknowledge, please."

There was no way she could acknowledge. Five minutes. In battle, five minutes was a lifetime. It didn't sound like much, but time was measured in seconds when bullets were flying, and minutes became like hours. They had little choice. They had to hold the bridge. If the Coast Guard was going to broadcast what they were doing, then Early couldn't afford to allow the terrorists to take the bridge.

Unknown to the three was that only five of the terrorists had remained in the passageway outside the bridge, and Senior Chief Leary had killed two of them.

TAMURSHEKI HAD DETERMINED THAT ONCE HE COULDN'T take the bridge without losing more than the one killed when they'd first assaulted it, they had to follow through with their mission. "Boulas, you and Nafiz harass them. Keep them where they are for ten minutes, then join us at the back of the boat so we can leave." He helped carry the one wounded man with them down the ladder.

Tamursheki stopped at the medical clinic and had the others help the three who could barely stand to the aft portion of the vessel. He glanced at the man wounded on the bridge, ran his hand along the Jihadist's head, and turned, leaving the man bleeding on the medical table.

By the time the Coast Guard transmitted their time line across channel sixteen, Tamursheki and his men had already inflated two Zodiac rafts stored near the huge van anchored to the stern weather deck.

As the men moved the rafts toward the port side of the merchant vessel, Tamursheki and Qasim stood near the small welded-shut door leading into the van. Unseen by the two was the small camera attached to the top bulkhead behind them—a camera that connected to the monitors on the bridge.

"What do you think, Amir?" Qasim asked. "Is Alrajool right and this is all a ruse?" The large Arab reached up and slapped his hand on the side of the huge van.

Tamursheki reached above the sealed hatch and with a key opened a small door, revealing a series of lights and buttons. "Even if for some heretical reason I lacked faith in the righteousness of Abu Alhaul, my common sense tells me that no one would go through this much trouble to fool those who would gladly give their lives for him with only a snap of his fingers."

A steady rain replaced the deluge of only an hour before, and the waves beating against the sides of the ship had settled down to an occasional breaker over the top of the deck. Tamursheki watched the wake of the freighter curve as the ship turned, unaware that damage to the automatic pilot of the bridge had shoved the rudders over, causing the ship to start circling.

Not being a mariner, the shape of the wake meant nothing to him. Tamursheki reached up and touched his forefinger to a small sensor that immediately glowed red. A second later, the biometric reader recognized the terrorist leader, and the glow changed to green. Satisfied, he grinned at Qasim and with a series of quick flicks the five green lights glowed red. A digital readout below the control panel started ticking backward using Arabic numbers.

Tamursheki shut the small door and locked it. He pulled the key out and looked at it for a moment before drawing back and throwing it toward the port edge of the ship. The turn of the ship shifted the wind at that instant while the ship rolled to the right, catching the key and causing it to drop unseen on the edge of the deck.

"It's time, Qasim. The weather is improving, and once the clouds and winds are gone, the Americans will have helicopters and boats all over this area. We can assume our prisoners have already told them where we are. Regardless, we know the Americans will mount an attack soon."

Qasim followed Tamursheki to where the two Zodiac rafts waited. With the exception of the three laying on the floor of the rafts unable to move, moaning through blistered lips, the others waited impatiently. Of the twenty-two who started, nine of them remained healthy enough to make shore. The three lying on the bottom of the raft would do their mission in the hospitals of America. He and the others would continue with their mission. Boulas appeared around the edge of the forecastle. He had been one of the two men assigned to keep the Americans busy on the bridge. Tamursheki and the man's eyes met for a moment before Boulas lowered his eyes. That meant there would be thirteen of them to go ashore and complete their mission. The explosion of the ship would serve to distract the Americans while they sailed these small rafts to the beach.

"Let's go," he said, motioning to the men standing alongside the raft nearest the edge. Tamursheki looked behind the ship. The wake was curving sharply. It dawned on him that the ship was turning, but the effect of a turning ship on launching rafts was lost to him. He looked forward at the bow of an anchored merchant vessel. He recognized it as a tanker. The bow of their freighter continued to turn, passing within a couple hundred yards of the anchored tanker. If Tamursheki had a rocket grenade launcher, he could create a spectacular diversion for their escape.

The ship tilted to port for a moment and then back to starboard. A wash of water pushed the key to the van's control panel across the deck, bringing it to rest against the raised deck of the hold opening. Waves crested higher between the two ships as they passed.

Tamursheki jerked an AK-47 out of the hands of one of his men, aimed it at the bridge of the tanker, and fired. Not just one burst but several, pleased as he watched the paint chips fly from the white bulkheads of the bridge. He ceased firing and held the gun aloft, looking around at his men. *There! That should show them who we are. Let their hearts tremble with fear.*

"JESUS CHRIST!" THE SPEAKER ON THE BRIDGE ERUPTED. "That son of a bitch is shooting at us. Coast Guard, you still out there?"

"This is Coast Guard Cutter *Cyclone*. Who just fired on you? And, what are you doing on this channel? We ordered everyone off this channel and onto either eighteen or fourteen."

"Fine, fine, young lady, write me a ticket. This is Cypriot tanker *Mykonos*. I have you three miles off my port beam. You keep going the direction you're heading and you're going to sail right by us. Look to your left. You see that freighter making a right-hand turn? That's the asshole who just shot up my bridge." The voice paused for a moment and then in a more calm tone continued, "No one injured, but they sure as hell messed up my paint job."

"What is your location, *Mykonos?*"

"We're west of Cape Henry lighthouse, nine miles, at anchor. If this guy keeps circling, he's going to hit us, and there's going to be one awful boom. We're carrying a cargo of natural gas. I am weighing anchor, but that's going to take me a few—"

"*Mykonos,* where did the shots come from?"

"It came from that freighter," the person replied, his voice betraying his irritation. "I've already told you that."

"We know, *Mykonos,* but from what part of that freighter?"

"Aft. There's a group of assholes standing around a van tied down onto the stern deck. Wait one," he said.

HEARING THE EXCHANGE, KELLY LOOKED AT THE OTHER two and asked, "What's going on?"

"Sounds like our captors may have given up on us and are back doing something to that thing on the stern."

"Navy Intelligence said that van may hold an explosive device," Early said.

"If it is, then it's gonna have to be one big explosion from out here if they think it's gonna do anything to—" She stopped as her mind reeled with implications.

The three looked at each other, their eyes revealing that each had the same thought.

"You don't think?" the Senior Chief asked, his voice trailing off. "Damn!" Early met his eyes, then shook her head. "Damn, ma'am. I don't suppose we can just sit here and wait for the cavalry to arrive?"

"Coast Guard Cutter *Cyclone,* this is *Mykonos*. One of my officers tells me he sees inflatable rafts on the stern of that runaway ship with what looks like people already in them. Maybe they're abandoning ship. Christ! That's all I need right now—a runaway, unmanned ship off my port beam. Coast Guard, *Mykonos*. I'm out of here. Out!"

Early and the Senior Chief hunched behind the left side of the destroyed helm console, their bodies over the wounded Kelly. Early looked up at the monitor where the van showed in the center of it with people walking back and forth. Whatever the two men were doing at the van, they had finished. What if they were arming it?

"If it's a nuclear device and explodes at sea, the wind's going to carry radioactive water vapor toward shore and across Virginia Beach," Senior Chief Leary offered.

"They'd better hurry," Kelly said.

"They're not gonna make it in time, Lieutenant."

"Lieutenant Early's right. We're going to have to do something."

Kelly pushed against the deck, straightening himself with his back resting against the helm console. He pulled the old Brazilian 9mm Uru automatic weapon into his lap. Early noticed specks of rust on the gun. She hoped it would work when he used it. There hadn't been any gunfire for a few minutes, but eventually they'd work up the nerve to attack them again.

"Good luck. I'll hold the bridge," Kelly said. He held the gun in his left hand, the barrel resting on the deck, his right hand placed over the wound, pressing down on the handkerchief he must have pulled from one of his flight-suit pockets.

Early started to say something, and Kelly raised his hand. "Don't say it. I'll still be here when you come back. Do what you have to do."

She looked at Leary. "Senior Chief," she said.

He nodded. "Guess if the damn thing explodes, I won't need that vasectomy the missus has been bugging me about."

Early glanced at Kelly, who winked and nodded at her. She wondered if she would ever see him alive again. Then she pulled the hatch shut as she stepped through and onto the mesh platform the three of them had used less than an hour before to take the bridge. Inside, Kelly watched the lever seal the hatch. Kelly was confident that the gunfire from outside was only meant to keep them inside the bridge. The bounce of another grenade caught his attention, and then he heard it roll. He looked right, and out of the corner of his eye, he saw the grenade stop about five feet from him. He threw himself to the left as the grenade exploded, everything going black. He never felt the pain of hitting the deck. The earlier wound started a fresh wave of bleeding, but Kelly was unconscious and unable to stop the flow.

Outside the damaged hatch, Nafiz turned and ran toward the aft portion of the ship to join his fellow Jihadists and to where that coward Boulas waited.

MACOLSON STUCK HIS HEAD INSIDE THE COMPARTMENT. "Commander!" he shouted above the noise of the water-jets and the diminishing storm outside. "We're fixing to break apart. Coast Guard is going to speed up and head to the port side of the freighter." He made a motion with his finger pointing to the right. "I'm going to head to the starboard side and try to bring us close enough to—"

The small boat heaved upward, throwing the Surface Warfare Lieutenant off balance, nearly tossing him off the bridge and into the small compartment where the team waited.

"Okay, Skipper!" Tucker replied, giving the officer a thumbs-up. MacOlson had said enough for him to know what was going to happen. The Mark V Special Operations Craft would use the presence of the Coast Guard cutter as cover as they approached the ship from the right side. The challenge was going to be that the rogue freighter was sailing in a circle, which meant that about fifty percent of the time its starboard side was going to be exposed to the storm hitting it from seaward. MacOlson was a professional—or so Commodore West had told him. Maneuvering the small, unstable craft alongside the freighter was the least of their problems. Getting aboard the freighter without getting themselves crushed, drowned, or shot seemed far greater to him. He turned his head to the right and looked at Sam Bradley, who met his gaze.

She smiled. "Something bothering you, Commander?"

He leaned down so his lips were near her ear. "We're going to have to pull ourselves aboard once Mac brings the boat alongside. That means a dangerous ascent. I think you had better remain here until—"

Sam held up her hand and leaned away from him. "You can stop right there, Commander. I'm the lead medical person on board and I'm going on board with you. We've got a wounded American up there."

"And he or she isn't going to get any treatment if you go and get yourself killed."

"True, but that's the risk we take for the big bucks they pay us for doing things like this," she said, winking.

"Okay, five minutes!" MacOlson shouted from the hatchway, holding up his left hand with fingers spread. "Five minutes until we're alongside starboard aft."

Starboard side aft, Tucker thought, biting his lower lip slightly. The van with the bomb aboard it was tied down on the stern weather deck, which meant that he and his team were going to be coming up right in the middle of the terrorists and this "unknown" weapon. The sound of rain hitting the small porthole behind his head reminded him they also had nature to contend with. Nature could be the worst enemy or best friend of a warrior, depending on whether you were winning or losing. It should work in their favor. The terrorists should be focused on the Coast Guard cutter closing on their port side, which may give them sufficient opportunity to make the deck.

MacOlson dashed out of the small bridge area, down into the compartment, and then out the back. A second later he stuck his head inside. "We're here, Commander. Boats is firing a hook. The ship has wire safety lines. They should hold the lines you and the others are going to climb up.

"Ready?" Tucker asked the teams.

"Bien sur," replied St. Cyr.

"Of course," said Tibbles-Seagraves.

The remainder of the team acknowledged him and stood, everyone slipping one arm through the strap on their M-4 Carbine so the automatic rifles were tucked tightly against their backs. Tucker noticed that sometime between the dock and here, everyone had managed to finish their preparation for the fight. Pant legs wrapped tight inside socks held together by tied shoelaces. With the exception of the two foreign officers, the camouflage utilities were the same. St. Cyr's was nearest to theirs, but his had far more patches of light green and Tibbles-Seagraves was the only one in a utility uniform composed of shades of blue. Tucker realized the Brit's uniform was the only one that would really fade into the colors of the ocean.

A slight bump told them they had hit the side of the freighter. A moment later, the muffled sound of a line being fired reached their ears. Five additional muffled sounds followed, seconds apart. This was the critical part of the mission. The grappling hooks would sail upward and over the safety lines along the deck. Their motion should send them sailing back through the lines, tangling themselves on the half-inch line leading back to the small craft. Hundreds of things could go wrong. The terrorists could see the lines and wait to shoot them as they climbed over. The lines could fail to connect sufficiently to hold the weight of the men climbing them, causing them to fall onto the deck of the craft below and have their backs broken, or into the drink, where they risked drowning or being crushed between the two vessels.

Everyone stood, waiting for Tucker to give the go-ahead. There was also the major concern that had been bothering him since they'd started, and that was that none of them had ever worked together before. No training, no pre-mission brief, no rehearsal—just thrown together because of the exigencies of the moment. He looked up at the towering deck edge of the freighter above them. Everything needed for this mission to go wrong was converging at the top of these lines.

MacOlson stuck his head inside the covered compartment. "Go!" he shouted.

Tucker was first. The bottom of the lines had been draped over the top safety line of the craft and then poked under the bottom one. He noticed they had not been tied off and knew that in the event the craft had to pull away, it didn't want to be tied to a rogue freighter that could take it anywhere it wanted.

Tucker saw Sam out of the corner of his eye follow him toward the number-one line near the front of the craft. A small wave whipped over the bow of the Mark V, soaking him. "Sam, you wait until all of us are up there. Need the teams on board first," he said, holding up one finger.

She nodded and leaned against the bulkhead to allow the others to pass. When she looked back, Tucker was already several feet above her, heading toward the top, hand over hand, hurrying as fast as he could.

St. Cyr grabbed a line and quickly followed. Tibbles-Seagraves was on the third line, his shorter arms working furiously to gain on the other two. Two SEALs moved past her, and at about six-foot intervals they pulled themselves up. The small boat heaved and yawed from side to side as the freighter continued its circle. They only had a few more minutes when the course of the ship would take the calmer lee side away and expose them to the full force of the storm. The storm, though curving away from the mainland, was still throwing a rough punch for a small vessel.

Sam grabbed the same line Tucker used. Looking up, she saw him hook a leg to the deck and roll under the safety line. She pulled herself up, hand over hand. The line rocked back and forth against the side of the ship. One time in her ascent she scraped the side of her hand. When Sam reached the top, she saw the back of the last man disappear forward toward the huge van blocking most of the deck. She pulled herself up and over the edge, breathing hard from the exertion. She was alone and had no idea what to do now. Tucker had failed to tell her what the plan was after they got on board.

Little did she know that Tucker himself had little idea what the plan was, other than to get aboard, find the terrorists, and kill them before they could set off the bomb. She looked across the deck. There, about sixty feet from where she lay, was the black van Navy Intelligence had briefed might hold a nuclear device. The rain abruptly stopped. Looking up, Sam saw a hole in the clouds with a spot of sky blue in the center. Then hell broke loose as gunfire erupted out of sight on the other side of the van. She crawled toward a nearby exhaust vent and took position behind it. "Lord, let them win," she prayed, her thoughts on what would happen to her if the terrorists won.

Sam wished she had a gun. Even a small one would give her comfort. The sound of Arabic and English filled the air. She peeked around the funnel-like vent to see the bow of a giant ship emerge slowly past the edge of the freighter's superstructure. It was so close, Sam knew the two were going to hit.

EARLY AND THE SENIOR CHIEF DOVE FOR THE DECK WHEN they heard gunfire. Early turned her head left and caught movement behind them. Turning further, the bow of a huge tanker emerged. They must have completed one complete circle. She winced. "I think we're going to hit it this time." The waves seemed calmer. She reached up and wiped the rain from her forehead. As she watched the huge tanker slide down the length of the ship, gunfire erupted again. High above them, Early saw bits of paint rocket out as bullets hit near the bridge.

Leary glanced aft. "Seems they've found someone else to piss off."

"Let's go," Early said as she crawled forward along the opened top deck of the amidships superstructure. She had to stop worrying about Kelly on the bridge. They had to stop the terrorists from exploding that bomb. At that specific moment, she realized she could die. And die she would if they didn't stop them. *The bomb would vaporize this ship and everyone on it.* The sound of a ship's horn sounding its one long warning blast drowned out the shooting. *And that tanker would go along with it.*

Senior Chief Leary shifted in front of her, widening the gap between them a few feet as they approached the port edge of the walkway. A couple of quick movements and the man reached the edge, where he leaned forward. His head stuck out around the edge of the forecastle, his body prone on the wet deck.

Early kept watch on the ladder leading from the deck below. She guessed they were three decks above the stern weather deck where the van was tied down.

Leary turned to her and with urgent hand motions urged her to join him. She bit her lower lip, looking at the top of the ladder about six feet from her and then back at the Senior Chief. If she moved up beside him, their backs would be exposed to anyone coming up the ladder.

He must have seen her waiver. "Lieutenant!" he said, his voice soft and urgent, as he motioned her again.

"What the hell," she whispered, and then crawled rapidly over to where Leary watched the stern weather deck below them.

When she bumped against him, he slid a couple of feet away, keeping an opening between them. Below was the van. This close she could see the panel door that the man had blocked from view on the monitor. A rush of water carried the key, unnoticed by the terrorists, back toward the van. That must have been what the man had tried to throw overboard, she thought.

"What do ya think?" the Senior Chief asked.

"I think the thing is armed. I saw it on the monitor on the bridge before we left. And that thing washing about on the deck may be the key needed to disarm it, Senior Chief."

"You see what I see?" he asked.

"What?"

"Look past the stern. What do you see?"

Approaching the ship over the raised stern deck was another ship, bearing the white hull with its distinctive red-angled stripe—a Coast Guard cutter. She squinted and looked to the starboard side of the cutter. A small boat bopped and dropped on the waves as it used the cutter to mitigate the waves stirred by the storm. She didn't know what it was, but whatever it was, it was probably good news for them. This was one time she wouldn't mind seeing some Navy SEALs storm aboard. Her experiences with them in the Officers' Clubs had been less than amiable. Right now a raging herd of male testosterone roaring about killing everything would make her day.

"What are they doing?" the Senior Chief asked, nodding down toward the terrorists.

Four of the terrorists, with their guns strapped across their backs, pushed one of the camouflaged Zodiac rafts toward the port side of the rogue freighter. Two bodies lay in the raft. She thought she saw one of them move but couldn't be sure.

Looking back at the two approaching ships, she estimated their distance at less than two thousand yards—a nautical mile. The cutter was changing course toward the port side of the freighter. She looked behind her. The ship's bow was sliding right, passing the amidships angle of the tanker and turning away. She looked down at the terrorists and at the approaching Coast Guard cutter. The small boat had disappeared.

Four men shoved one of the Zodiac rafts and leaped in it as it fell to the rough seas alongside the ship. They disappeared from view for a couple of minutes. Along the rails, the other terrorists watched.

"Lieutenant, we're here. What do you think we ought to do?"

She licked her dry lips. With this much rain, why did her mouth feel so dry?

Senior Chief Leary nodded. "I feel the same way, Lieutenant. I ain't keen on letting them know we're here." He looked back down. "We could wait here until the second bunch leave and then rush down to the deck and . . ." He stopped.

"That's the question, isn't it, Senior Chief? Even if we reach the van after they leave, what do we do?"

"Can't do anything up here, but watch it explode."

She looked down to where she had seen the key come to rest. It was gone. Probably washed overboard. If not, it could be anywhere down there. "If we can find that key and it opens the panel—that's probably where he armed the bomb."

"It should be somewhere along the left side of it."

He shook his head back and forth. "Your eyes are much better than mine, ma'am."

Leary had his lips pursed together as if making up his mind. "Okay, Senior Chief, let's have it. What are you thinking?"

"I'm thinking that if we let them go first, then we're letting those who know how to turn the damn thing off disappear over the side. What if we find this key we just saw and it doesn't open the panel? And if it does, we don't even know what the controls look like, much less how they operate."

"You think we need to stop this last bunch?"

He nodded reluctantly. "Yeah, unfortunately."

Unnoticed by them, five lines topped with grappling hooks rose above the far safety lines, wrapping around when the momentum stopped.

"Let's roll," Early said.

"Remember the Alamo," the Senior Chief added.

The two slid back from the edge of the deck before standing. Moments later they were working their way down, the Senior Chief leading. They reached the main deck, coming out around the corner, out of sight of the remaining terrorists. Filling their vision was the starboard aft side of the tanker as the freighter turned away from it. It was so close, Early thought she could leap across the gap and touch its side before falling into the water between them.

Shouts came from the terrorists, whose race back to the safety line brought them into her line of sight. Early and the Senior Chief leaned back against the bulkhead, trying to remain motionless and not draw attention. As the tanker and freighter grew parallel to each other, it caused the seas between the two massive ships to grow in its force. The tanker was massive, its hull rising about fifty feet higher than the weather decks of the freighter. Early looked up at the tanker, but the ladder under which they hid blocked her view. She doubted the top deck of the freighter superstructure was even level with the main deck of the tanker, such was the enormous size of the anchored ship.

Waves rushed up between the ships, cascading over the

sides of the weather deck, knocking the terrorists down and sending them reeling away from the safety lines. Another spray hit the sides of the superstructure like a broad hand pushing Early and the Senior Chief against the bulkhead, taking away their breath for a moment.

Opening her eyes, Early saw the Zodiac raft that had been launched minutes earlier climb on the crest of a wave to nearly main-deck level before falling away, leaving the raft floating in the air for a second before it fell back out of sight. The terrorists on board tumbled forward and out of the raft.

"Damn, ma'am. If we survive this, Mother Nature may finish them off."

Two terrorists appeared at the safety line as the ships continued to slide by each other. They turned and ran away as another group of waves washed across the deck. This time the raft was upside down and no one was visible. Early caught a glimpse of an arm sticking out of the wave, its hand clenching and unclenching as if begging someone to grab it. She surprised herself with her joy at seeing these enemies of civilization die. It further surprised her to discover that she wished their deaths had been slower and that she could have helped with them.

Early reached up and wiped the water from her face, realizing as she did that the rain had stopped. The overcast disappeared briefly as clouds parted to allow a sliver of sunlight to pass through the mist of the storm. She wasn't a superstitious person, but as she looked around at nature's spotlight on this area, she prayed this was a good omen.

Gunfire erupted on the weather deck, around the edge of the superstructure, out of sight, and Early quickly brought her attention back to the matter at hand. The Senior Chief rushed forward around the ladder toward the weather deck. As he neared where the superstructure ended and the weather deck began, a huge Arab ran around the corner and slammed into him. The man was huge and bleeding from a wound to his left shoulder. The Senior Chief was knocked backward, falling onto the bottom rungs of the ladder. Early saw the Senior Chief's face grimace in pain. The terrorist jumped up, screaming. The man pulled a long curved knife from somewhere around his belt line and jumped on top of Leary, crushing the Senior Chief's back into the metal rungs. Leary grabbed the hand with the knife, holding it up and away from him. He punched the man with his right hand. The man barely noticed it.

The ship rolled to starboard. The name on the stern of the tanker appeared briefly as the freighter continued its turn, opening up the distance between the ships. The roll caught the giant terrorist off balance long enough for Senior Chief Leary to free his right knee and bring it up between the man's legs, knocking him off and against the safety lines.

Shouts in Arabic and English came from out of sight on the weather deck. The shouts startled Early out of the mesmerizing sight of the two men fighting inches from her face. She pulled her AK-47 up, stepped around the ladder, and pulled the trigger. Nothing. She pulled it again. Still nothing happened. Then pain ripped through her as the Jihadist took the opportunity to backhand her, sending her reeling backward against the bulkhead. Another wave hit, propelling her off from the bulkhead and washing her down the deck away from the fight and toward the safety lines. The water receded over the side of the deck. The blow had burst the skin around her swollen eye. She shook her head. Little white dots danced in front of her vision. Behind her, the gunfight continued. Leary and the terrorist were standing, their chests against each other, and their hands locked together, grunting as they fought.

Early forced herself up, bracing against the nearby bulkhead. She shook her head slightly, trying to clear her vision. The Navy Lieutenant stumbled forward toward the weapon, reaching down to pick it up as another wave washed aboard, taking the lightweight AK-47 a few feet farther beyond her grasp. She turned in time to see the Senior Chief slam his right fist into the ample stomach of the terrorist, sending the man back a few feet. It had little effect as the man rushed Leary again, this time the knife slashing back and forth as a lethal barrier between the two. Leary grabbed the railing of the ladder and swung himself out and onto the deck as the terrorist sliced through the air where he had been a moment before.

Early stepped on the gun to hold it in place. She grabbed it and turned back to the deadly fight working its way down the open passageway toward her. The stern of the tanker passed, lessening the sea state between the two ships and increasing the daylight filtering through the heavy overcast. The oily smell from one of the ship's funnels whiffed down the walkway, causing her eyes to sting slightly. Early blinked rapidly a few times, and then wiped the back of a dirty sleeve across them. When she looked up, the Senior Chief was on his back. The terrorist leaped, his knife drawn back. Leary grabbed the man's arms as he came down, pulling him down as he simultaneously jerked his legs up, planting his feet in the man's midsection. The terrorist went flying over the Senior Chief toward Early. Before she could move, the man slammed into her, knocking her against the bulkhead and sending the AK-47 spinning along the weather deck forward.

She screamed. A horrible pain ripped through her as the pressure of the body lifted. She pushed with all her strength and felt the man fall away, surprised she was able to do it. She looked up and the Senior Chief had the man's neck in the crook of his left elbow, using his right hand to squeeze it tighter. The terrorist's arm reached backward with his knife. The knife had blood on it, rain washing it off and onto the deck. Her eyes followed the blood for a moment and saw a larger pool of blood running from beneath her.

A grunt from the Senior Chief drew her attention. The terrorist's knife was deep within Leary's right side. Leary forced the man's hand back until the knife pulled out. Then he fell to the right, shoving the terrorist backward, sending him rolling across the nonskid decks of the open passageway. The terrorist jumped up, screamed "Allah

Akbar" and ran at the Senior Chief. Gunfire rippled from behind the man, and along the front of the large Iraqi small holes erupted with puffs of blood and meat. Blood flowed from the holes as the man looked down at them, took a couple more steps, and fell forward. His knife clattered on the deck, falling within several inches of Early's hand. She reached for it, sending more pain ripping through her body. Early ran her hand along her side, touching herself, trying to find what was wrong. But the saturation of the rain hid the wound and it was only when she lifted her hand and saw it covered with blood that she knew the terrorist had stabbed her.

A shadow blocked her vision. "Lieutenant, you all right?" the Senior Chief asked. He moved her slightly, drawing a cry from her. "Well, now you've gone and done it, ma'am. You done got yourself stabbed, and you ain't even downtown."

A second shadow joined his. "We'll get you some medical service, Lieutenant," the person said. He had on camouflaged utilities. Early saw the specks of blood along the uniform and across the war paint, as they called it, applied to his forehead.

"Who are you?"

"I'm Commander Tucker Raleigh."

A couple of other shadows joined him. "Get this officer to the weather deck where Lieutenant Commander Bradley can see to her."

Early reached up. "The bomb, Commander. They armed the bomb."

"We're working on it, Lieutenant Early. Do you know how long ago they armed it?"

"Been about ten minutes," the Senior Chief answered. "The Lieutenant here, she saw the key the leader used to lock the panel wash back toward the van."

"Thanks. Let's go," Raleigh said to two armed sailors standing behind him.

Early drifted into unconsciousness, her mind swirling round and round as if following a whirlpool taking her into oblivion.

* * *

WHEN EARLY WOKE, SHE DISCOVERED HERSELF IN THE ship's wardroom lying on top of a mattress someone had placed on the table. She felt the slight rocking of the ship. Sunlight entered the room through the small portholes. A tall woman in khakis had her back to her. The sun gave the woman's dark hair a reddish tinge. Early forced out, "Water."

The woman turned. "Ah, you're awake, Lieutenant." She poured a glass of water and brought it to the table. "Tried to make you as comfortable as possible." The woman had the collar devices of a lieutenant commander and a member of the nurse corps. She lifted Early's head and held it while she drank.

"How long have I been out?" Early asked, figuring an hour or so, since she was still on board the freighter.

"I would say about a day and a half. We have more medical personnel arriving later today, and, thankfully, one of them is a surgeon. He'll be the one to reopen the knife wound and make sure I did everything right. Wouldn't want any secondary infection."

Early's eyebrows arched. "We're still aboard?"

The woman let out a big sigh. "Yes, we're still aboard and will be for some time."

The door opened and Senior Chief Leary entered. The man had on a fresh flight suit with the sleeves rolled up. His weeklong beard was gone. "Lieutenant! Damn! Am I glad to see you back among the living. You had me worried there for a while; though Lieutenant Commander Bradley here, she said not to worry. It didn't look as if that giant did much internal damage to you."

"Senior Chief, I saw him knife you, didn't I?" she said softly, surprised to find her breath short.

"He nicked me, you might say. Our favorite nurse on board said it was only a flesh wound. But, this is a flesh wound about eight inches long. Sure as hell didn't feel like any flesh wound."

Early lifted the sheet slightly and was glad to see that

her soiled flight suit had been replaced by a hospital shift. Anything was better than what she had been wearing for the past week. "Where's Scott Kelly?" she asked, staring up at the Senior Chief.

"He's in another compartment. I believe in the former Captain's Cabin. He'll be fine, though. Lieutenant Commander Bradley here had to operate on him. He swears she didn't use no novocaine or anathes . . . anates . . . Oh, you know. They didn't put him to sleep."

Early turned to the nurse. "Why are we still aboard the ship?"

The woman took the empty glass from Early. Early couldn't even remember drinking the water, but she must have, because the glass was empty.

"We're quarantined for the time being, and that time being could be as much as a month."

"Quarantined? Why?"

"Smallpox. Seems the terrorists on board this vessel were all infected with the smallpox virus. The Navy Intelligence rascal they sent on board believes their intentions were to come ashore with various dispersal orders. What they screwed up was that they were infected too soon. If whoever administered the virus had waited two to three days, then the fight could have been different aboard the ship, and if those infected had gotten off and made their way through America, everywhere they went they would have left an epidemic behind them." The nurse sighed. "Thousands could have died."

The door to the wardroom opened and Commander Tucker Raleigh stepped through. Seeing Early's open eyes, he smiled. "Looks like you're with us again, Lieutenant."

"I've had better days," she said humorously. "Six days ago, if someone had told me that as a P-3C pilot I would be lying wounded on a wardroom table on a terrorist ship, I would have taken bets."

"Lots of us would have." He turned to Sam Bradley. Early saw the change in the man's face. She had seen that look only once in her life, and for a brief second she felt a slight envy of the nurse.

CHAPTER 12

ADMIRAL HOLMAN LOWERED HIS BINOCULARS AND TOOK a deep puff on his cigar before lifting his ball cap to wipe the sweat from his forehead. The two-star Commander of the Atlantic Fleet Amphibious Group Two leaned forward, folding his hands across the top of the starboard wing stanchion. Grunting, he pulled his khaki belt tighter. God, it was good to see a couple of pounds gone this morning. He lifted the binoculars again and scanned the horizon for a moment before lowering them.

"Damn!" he said, slapping the metal railing. "How in the hell did we allow them to slip through our net and make it this far? You tell me, *Leonard Upmann,* how in the hell we allowed this to happen?" He looked up at his Chief of Staff, meeting his stare.

"Well, sir, if I may be so kind," Upmann said, jerking his head to the right sharply. "I would say there is enough blame to go around for everyone. What part would you like me to share?" he asked, his voice level.

Holman smiled slightly as he put the huge cigar back between his lips, shoving it to the left. "I'll tell you, then, my fine Chief of Staff. I'm the one who should shoulder this debacle." He pointed at the anchored freighter and then tapped his collar devices. "Right here is where the buck should stop."

The *chop-chop-chop* of an approaching helicopter caught their attention. A second later a huge CH-53 Sea Stallion flew over the USS *Boxer,* its prop wash rushing down on the two Navy officers standing on the starboard bridge wing, the smell of its exhaust enveloping them. Holman instinctively squinted his eyes shut to keep the fine particles the wind would churn up from blowing into them. Burning ashes from his cigar stung his cheeks. As the prop wash vanished and the propeller noise diminished, he opened his eyes. They watched silently as the battle-green helicopter continued toward the quarantined freighter. The freighter rode lightly on top of the calm seas, the slight west wind spinning it slowly on the single anchor running from its bow. Huge spots of rust rode over the dull red hull of the ship.

"Daily rations," Upmann said. He reached up, removed his ball cap with the scrambled eggs of a senior officer embroidered on its brim, and ran his arm along his brow to remove the sweat.

"What did Mary Davidson say this morning?" Holman asked, referring to the Amphibious Group Two Intelligence Officer.

"She said two died last night."

"Americans?"

"No. Just assholes."

"When do these medical pariahs think we can bring our people home?"

Upmann shook his head. He pulled a small tube of sunscreen from his khaki pants pocket and started rubbing the lotion on his forehead. "They haven't. Right now, we are on the same 'subject to change' time schedule they put out a week ago."

Holman glanced at the man, pointed at the sunscreen, and opened his mouth to speak.

"Don't even think it, Admiral," Upmann said. "It is indeed an urban folk myth that black people don't sunburn. We just camouflage it better than you white folk; kind of like blushing."

Holman's mouth dropped, causing him to nearly lose his cigar. "Captain Upmann, I am truly appalled you would think that such a thing was crossing my thoughts."

"Your apology is accepted, sir," Upmann said with a slight nod. He screwed the top down on the tube and stuck it in his pocket. "Lots of good information this morning at the intelligence briefing, Admiral. You may want to have Mary do a swing-by at your convenience and give you an update."

Holman nodded.

The helicopter tail spun to the east, aligning the fuselage with the stern of the freighter. The dark van was still anchored to the stern deck, but the raised afterdeck where the helicopter hovered remained bar. They had been using this uncluttered area as an ad hoc helicopter deck. Several white-clad figures emerged from the main forecastle, edged their way around a bunch of figures working on the van, and climbed a ladder to the raised afterdeck. Shielding their eyes from the summer sun, they looked up at the helicopter as its side door slid opened. An aircrewman inside the CH-53 leaned out the open door, slung out the metal arm that held the line, and pushed out a load of cargo. A cargo net, wrapped around a jumble of boxes, eased downward to the waiting personnel on the ship.

"Guess life goes on, doesn't it," Holman said, pointing at the replenishing evolutions ongoing with the helicopter. He looked up at the tall, lean Surface Warfare officer who was finishing his second year as his Chief of Staff. The Bureau of Navy Personnel would up and jerk Upmann away from him in the coming year, and Holman would be faced with the prospect of selecting a new COS to replace him. The Navy worked to ensure the leadership triage of command never changed all at once, so the commander, his or her deputy, and the senior enlisted leader were transferred and replaced one per year. Holman had never had a deputy as Commander, Amphibious Group Two, though it was the largest amphibious fleet in the world. Next year, Holman would transfer, and the following year his Command Master Chief would hit the road. Thus, continuity of command was maintained. Everyone got his or her chance to screw up.

"EOD is still working on the van," Upmann said, casually pointing at the freighter. "They cleared the last booby trap inside the door and the probe came back indicating all clear. They've been in about thirty minutes. It's lucky for us that Commander Raleigh had MacOlson's EOD sailors with him. I don't think SEALs would have figured out how to turn off the arming mechanism. If they hadn't disarmed that device we wouldn't need lights tonight—our own glow would suffice."

"Are they certain it's a nuclear device?" Holman asked. He held the cigar over the railing and flicked the ashes off. "I figured the van was maybe a large bomb, but when the nurse—what was her name?"

"Lieutenant Commander Samantha Bradley."

"Yeah. I figured when she identified smallpox on board the freighter that the true weapon was biological and, as we have discovered, terrorists, like criminals, are usually stupid anyway. This time, they infected themselves too early."

Upmann sighed. "Still not sure if the van was a feint. Commodore West's EOD'ers have stated it's not a nuclear weapon in terms of an atomic bomb. But they detected radiation when the door leading into the van was opened. Then there was the rigged grenade discovered that caused them to take two days to make sure there were no other bobby traps. Now whether it means we have a dirty bomb sitting out there or the radiation is a diversion for the human biological attack they mounted we won't know until they finish their work."

Holman nodded. "Saw on CNN that the smallpox outbreak in Summer Haven, Florida, is contained. FEMA is handling it with experts from CDC in Atlanta. Soldiers from Fort Stewart have quarantined the small city for the time being."

"It could have been worse. If those deputies hadn't stumbled on the terrorists when they beached themselves last week, they could have been anywhere in America—Atlanta, New York, Los Angeles, even Washington. They could have split along four different routes and infected hundreds of thousands—millions, even—as everyone they infected passed it on to others. God was definitely looking down on America when those deputies grabbed them."

"They were at the right place at the right time." Holman shuddered. "I hate to think what might have been."

"The Army has sealed the roads leading into and out of the small coastal village, and the FBI is joining the effort by going house to house with FEMA and local authorities to check on everyone, looking for any others who may have been exposed."

Holman glanced through the open hatch to the bridge before returning his gaze back to the freighter. "They'll expand that effort farther and farther out—an expanding circle in the hopes they have stopped it."

"Even so, how do we know some visitor, some tourist, didn't stop by there on his or her way home and is even now carrying the smallpox virus to some other place in America? It would definitely complicate things. Look what happened out there," Upmann said, pointing at the freighter. "Every military man and woman vaccinated against smallpox and we still had five people come down with it. Two of the medical group, two of the EOD'ers who seized the ship, and one of the other EOD people who arrived within minutes of taking the son-of-a-bitch. Every one of those who came down with the disease had been vaccinated, and every one of them now with the disease. Maybe it's a variant—something some mad scientist worked up to defeat the vaccination."

"Hope you're wrong, Leo," Holman answered. "Three of our people who had the vaccination did come down with smallpox, but Doc told me this morning that the other two who got it had never received the vaccination, which, of course, raises the question as to why they were sent out there anyway.

"I didn't know that."

Holman nodded and flicked ashes off the end of his cigar. "One of the SEALs wasn't vaccinated. He had been excused because of some sort of allergy complaint." Holman shook his head in disbelief. "And one of the corpsmen was a Jamaican national—not even an American citizen—and somehow managed to avoid taking his. The other three we don't know why or how they came down with it. They should have been immune. Which is why we have isolated the freighter, and inside that rusting bucket of bolts out there, all five of them have been further isolated. They are doing everything they can to control it. Bethesda Medical is sending down experts to help Portsmouth Naval Hospital, who provided the bulk of the doctors and nurses out there now. They've been working nonstop since the SEALs seized the freighter ten days ago."

"Good thing we didn't bring the freighter in—"

"Good thing Commodore West had the foresight to send a Navy nurse with them. I don't think I would have thought of it."

"We have four wounded out there."

"I understand with the exception of the copilot of the P-3C, the others have minor wounds and will recover. The report I saw this morning from Captain Olensyski, head of the medical team, says even Lieutenant Kelly will recover. The emergency operation they performed within minutes of the medical team arriving on board appears to have succeeded. I like an officer who can make a decision. Some insist on having one hundred percent of the information they need before they'll reluctantly do something. Sometimes you have to do things without knowing everything you'd like to. Eighty percent—give me eighty percent of the information needed and I can make a decision. That surgeon—whoever he or she was—had the copilot under the knife within thirty minutes of them landing. Two things about that decision: one, it probably saved the officer's life, and two, if they had waited to ferry him to Portsmouth Naval Hospital, they could have unknowingly taken the smallpox virus with them."

Approaching helicopters drowned out their conversation as two more Sea Stallions approached the operations area, flying across the bow of the anchored USS *Boxer,* heading toward the freighter. The CH-53 hovering over the stern deck of the freighter had finished its mission. They watched as the helicopter veered away from its position over the freighter, freeing the deck for the two approaching.

"That'll be the mortuary team," Upmann volunteered.

"Throats slit and they videotaped each one," Holman said, venom in every word. "CDC has cleared the bodies for removal and turnover for cremation. Because of the smallpox, Department of Defense won't be turning the bodies over to their next of kin."

"Did you have an opportunity to read the message from the Joint Chiefs of Staff, Admiral?"

"The one saying they intend to maintain the quarantine for forty days?"

"Yes, sir."

"They're basing their decision on the opinion of the Joint Staff J4, who based her decision on the disease. It takes one to five days for smallpox infection to set in; six to seventeen for it to incubate; then comes the critical period when for the next four to five days anyone coming in contact can catch it."

"That only adds up to twenty-something days, Admiral."

"It's what happens afterward. For a period of around twenty to forty days the disease breaks out, and you either live or die, depending on your own health and the ability of your body to fight it. We know some of those—the terrorists—are in the later stage. What the message doesn't say, but we know, is that the quarantine isn't so much for those enshrouded in the throes of smallpox but because of the possibility others may catch it. That forty days is only if no one else comes down with it. Between us, Leo, I suspect we'll have this little bit of God's ocean roped off for more than forty days. Wouldn't surprise me to see the Coast Guard continuing their round-the-clock patrols of this freighter for two to three months. Wouldn't surprise me at all." He flicked the cigar over the rail into the serene sea that belied its turbulent nature of ten days before.

Holman looked at his watch. "The search planes should be landing now at Roosevelt Roads. If the remainder of the P-3 crew made it out of the aircraft as the Flight Engineer believes, then the storm must have gotten them."

"What do you think our government will do now?" Upmann asked.

Holman shrugged. "We're doing everything we can already. We know the freighter was a gift of this Abu Alhaul. He's in West Africa. The French pursued him for a while until he vanished north and presumably left the Ivory Coast. Spain, Greece, Singapore, and Hong Kong have boarded and seized six other commercial vessels at the behest of our State Department. Vessels which, along with this one, our intelligence and law enforcement arms of Homeland Security had under surveillance for over a year."

"Should have seized them a year ago."

Holman shrugged. "Who knows the mind of the intelligence community?"

"*The Shadow do,*" Upmann ad-libbed.

"He'll be back."

"Abu Alhaul?"

"Yes. He only came because of Commander Raleigh. We used him as a honeypot to lure the terrorists to us and then when our best brains decided this freighter had turned toward Europe, we jumped the gun and rushed off, leaving our own shores undefended. That won't happen again."

The Officer of the Deck, a Lieutenant Commander, stepped through the hatchway, catching their attention. He held two hot cups of coffee in his hands. "Admiral, Captain Upmann, thought you might enjoy some fresh coffee the mess decks just sent up."

They took the coffee. "Thanks, Commander," Holman said.

The man disappeared back inside to his duty station on the bridge. A ship at anchor still kept a ready crew on the bridge. Anchors were known to give way or break loose, and ships were known to be pushed into the chains leading to them.

Holman slipped a folded paper from his pocket and handed it to Upmann. "This is top secret, Leo."

Captain Upmann unfolded the paper and read the short paragraph on it. "Doesn't surprise me in the least," he said, handing the paper back to Admiral Holman.

"Me either. My directions are, once the quarantine is lifted, to escort our good friend Captain Marc St. Cyr directly to the airport, where an aircraft will be standing by to return him to France. I understand the State Department will quietly tell *our valued ally* that his presence in the United States is no longer desired."

Upmann leaned forward, folding his arms on the bridge wing railing. "You'd think after the confrontation we had with the French last year off Liberia, they'd jump at the chance to put some salve on the diplomatic scars between our two countries. Instead, in the one combined effort of nations, they send an agent to spy on us."

Holman slipped the paper back in his pocket. "Don't let me forget to return this to Mary Davidson for destruction. I know what you mean. I didn't feel comfortable working with the French, but for the sake of improving our relations, I thought the three combined Special Forces teams divided among our three nations was a step in the right direction." He patted his pocket. "I suspect the FBI will arrest whoever the American was that gave the CD to St. Cyr."

"They find anything else in his belongings?"

Holman shook his head. "Don't know. When they went to gather the clothes of those stuck on the ship, the CD was in a hidden compartment in St. Cyr's suitcase." He shrugged again. "Other than what you read, the only other thing I know is the CD originated from the Missile Defense Agency—MDA—and had a lot of technical mumbo jumbo on our laser-weapons programs. St. Cyr didn't get this by himself. Someone had to have given it to him, and the information on the CD tends to indicate that additional information has already been given."

Holman looked over his shoulder before holding his coffee cup over the railing and pouring the coffee out. "Too strong for the afternoon," he said.

Finished, Holman continued. "The espionage isn't within my mission scope. Escorting him to the first plane out of the country is. Trying to figure out what the terrorists will do next is also something about which I will worry. Whoever the traitor is will be caught, and when they do I hope they hang him."

"They caught him. Heard it on CNN a few minutes ago," Upmann added. "The FBI arrested someone at the Navy Annex in Arlington late yesterday."

"What'd they say?"

"Said the man worked on the Air Force's laser weapons program and was assigned to the Missile Defense Agency. They haven't charged him yet. Ought to send him to a plastic surgeon, make him look like Commander Raleigh, and air-drop him into Africa."

"If we air-dropped him into Africa disguised as Commander Raleigh," Upmann went on with the fantasy. "Be just our luck for this African army we've been reading about to catch him before Abu Alhaul."

"Bet they're working with him. Same sort of convergence we're seeing with other terrorist groups."

Holman shook his head. "No, I don't think so. You recall when I went to the Pentagon to see Admiral James and meet this Commander Raleigh?"

Upmann nodded.

"I was also invited to sit along the wall in the Joint Staff Tank as the Joint Chiefs were briefed about this resurrection of Al Qaeda. Along with that briefing was one about this African army. Seems Moslems aren't their favorite people from some of the atrocities being attributed to them. Lots of unknowns. Who's their leader? Don't know. What's their intention? Not sure, but they believe it's nationalistic. Uprising and fights that are nationalistic are a lot easier to handle than something like terrorism, which is global. A national objective is usually restricted to a specific geographical area."

"That would mean Ivory Coast, Liberia, and that area?"

"I heard one of the briefers offer an opinion that the national aim was much bigger."

"Much bigger?"

"Yes, all of Africa."

The helicopters carrying the military morticians from the air base in Dover, Delaware, completed dropping off their passengers. The fact that neither chopper touched their wheels on the deck wasn't lost on the two men watching. Holman, being a pilot, had a good idea what was going through the minds of those helicopter pilots. Mislaid fears that touching down on the freighter would cause the disease to jump on board. He shrugged his shoulders. As much as he hated to admit it, he sympathized with them and doubted he would have touched down on the ship either. Of course, he flew fighter planes such as the Hornet F/A 18, which was better designed to blow the freighter out of the water than land on it.

For the next several minutes, neither man spoke as they watched the maneuvers of the helicopters shifting positions over the stern deck.

"He'll be back," Upmann said. "Abu Alhaul has turned his religious world conquest into a personal vendetta against our Commander. We know it."

"Let's hope he doesn't know we know, because whether Raleigh likes it or not, he's the key for us taking this asshole down, and we're going to use him. We're going to use him because it's the only way for him to live without having to look over his shoulder whenever he sees a young dark-skinned person who could be one of this man's minions."

Holman should have stuck with the original plan calling for Abu Alhaul to come after Commander Raleigh. If he had, they would have stopped that freighter a long ways before it reached Hampton Roads. He turned to Leo Upmann and told him to keep him updated. He'd call him after his meeting with Commander, U.S. Atlantic Fleet. Holman turned and went below to his flag stateroom. It took him about a half-hour to change into summer whites. This wasn't going to be a pleasant meeting. Both he and Commander U.S. Second Fleet were being called on the carpet to explain why this had happened. One thing you can always expect when something goes wrong—shit rolls downhill, and right now a lot of people were looking for where the huge roll should stop. One thing he could be sure of—it wouldn't be on Capitol Hill.

"YOU'LL BE OKAY, SON," HE SAID.

"I don't feel too good, Mom. My eyes burn."

She leaned over the front seat and put her hand against the boy's forehead. "Well, he doesn't feel okay to me," she said to her husband. She turned back around and tightened her seatbelt. "I think we're going to have to stop somewhere and have a doctor look at him."

"We're only a few hours from home. I think the couple at the rest stop was right. Said it was probably just a cold," he said through tightened lips. He didn't want to stop. He wanted to sleep in his own bed tonight after two weeks of touring Florida and the Gulf Coast. This was definitely the last time he tried this. Next time, they'd pick one spot—like Disney World—fly to it, enjoy it, and fly home. The voice of his wife intruded on his thoughts as he braked for the red light.

"Are you listening to me?" she asked, poking him a couple of times on the shoulder. "Or, have you tuned me out?"

"I'm listening."

"Good! See that sign ahead? The blue one with the word *hospital* on it?"

"Yeah, I see it."

"Momma, Daddy; I really don't feel too good."

"Good! Turn there. We're taking Danny to the emergency room. They'll have doctors there, and one of them can see him. Honey," she said in a softer voice to the young boy sitting on the back seat. "Not much longer. We're going to stop and get you something for this. Just hang in there."

The light changed and he eased forward.

"Do you know how much emergency rooms cost?"

The sound of vomiting came from behind him.

"I don't care," she snapped. "He needs to see a doctor. Look at him! He's throwing up!"

He turned at the sign, and after straightening out, he reached up and adjusted the rearview mirror so he could see the face of their twelve-year-old son. A rash of small bumps covered the boy's face, and he noticed that one eye socket was swollen so much that if it kept swelling, Danny wouldn't be able to see out of it.

"You're right. I think he's having an allergic reaction to the seafood we ate earlier. I remember Uncle Harold having something similar when he ate shrimp years ago. Face swelled up—"

"I don't care about Uncle Harold. What I care about is Danny's having a hard time breathing."

He listened for a couple of seconds to a rasping sound from the rear seat. She's right, he thought. He reached up, put on his emergency blinkers, and sped up. Blowing his horn, he followed the signs leading to the hospital. Several times he glanced in the mirror. His son's head now lolled to the side. His wife's arm was draped over the seat, her hand holding their son's.

"There it is," she said, her voice trembling as she pointed to a sign that read WELCOME TO GRADY HOSPITAL—ATLANTA, GEORGIA.

Captain David E. Meadows, U.S. Navy, was recognized by *Writer's Digest* magazine as one of its twelve "First Success" authors for 2001 and profiled in the *Writer's Digest Guide to Writing Fiction* (Fall 2001) yearbook. Captain Meadows is still on active duty serving at the Pentagon on the Joint Staff of the Joint Chiefs of Staff.